ALDOUS HUXLEY

Aldous Huxley was born on 26 July 1894 near Godalming, Surrey. He began writing poetry and short stories in his early twenties, but it was his first novel, *Crome Yellow* (1921), which established his literary reputation. This was swiftly followed by *Antic Hay* (1923), *Those Barren Leaves* (1925) and *Point Counter Point* (1928) – bright, brilliant satires of contemporary society. For most of the 1920s Huxley lived in Italy but in the 1930s he moved to Sanary, near Toulon.

In the years leading up to the Second World War, Huxley's work took on a more sombre tone in response to the confusion of society which he felt to be spinning dangerously out of control. His great novels of ideas, including his most famous work *Brave New World* (published in 1932 this warned against the dehumanising aspects of scientific and material 'progress') and the pacifist novel *Eyeless in Gaza* (1936) were accompanied by a series of wise and brilliant essays, collected in volume form under titles such as *Music at Night* (1931) and *Ends and Means* (1937).

In 1937, at the height of his fame, Huxley left Europe to live in California, working for a time as a screenwriter in Hollywood. As the West braced itself for war, Huxley came increasingly to believe that the key to solving the world's problems lay in changing the individual through mystical enlightenment. The exploration of the inner life through mysticism and hallucinogenic drugs was to dominate his work for the rest of his life. His beliefs found expression in both fiction (*Time Must Have a Stop*, 1944 and *Island*, 1962) and non-fiction (*The Perennial Philosophy*, 1945, *Grey Eminence*, 1941 and the famous account of his first mescalin experience, *The Doors of Perception*, 1954.)

Huxley died in California on 22 November 1963.

ALDOUS HUXLEY

Time Must Have A Stop

'But thought's the slave of life, and life's time's fool,
And time, that takes survey of all the world,
Must have a stop'

William Shakespeare

VINTAGE

1 3 5 7 9 10 8 6 4 2

Vintage
20 Vauxhall Bridge Road,
London SW1V 2SA

Vintage is part of the Penguin Random House group of companies whose
addresses can be found at global.penguinrandomhouse.com

Copyright © Aldous Huxley 1953

First published in Great Britain by Chatto & Windus in 1953

www.vintage-books.co.uk

A CIP catalogue record for this book is
available from the British Library

ISBN 9781784870348

Printed and bound by CPI Group (UK) Ltd, Croydon CR0 4YY

CHAPTER ONE

SEBASTIAN BARNACK came out of the reading room of the public library and paused in the vestibule to put on his shabby overcoat. Looking at him, Mrs. Ockham felt a sword in her heart. This small and exquisite creature with the seraphic face and the pale curly hair was the living image of her own, her only, her dead and vanished darling.

The boy's lips were moving, she noticed, as he struggled into his coat. Talking to himself—just as her Frankie used to do. He turned and began to walk past the bench on which she was sitting, towards the door.

'It's a raw evening,' she said aloud, acting on a sudden impulse to detain this living phantom, to turn the sharp memory in her wounded heart.

Startled out of his preoccupying thoughts, Sebastian halted, turned and, for a second or two, stared at her uncomprehending. Then he took in the significance of that yearningly maternal smile. His eyes hardened. This sort of thing had happened before. She was treating him as though he were one of those delicious babies one pats the heads of in perambulators. He'd teach the old bitch! But as usual he lacked the necessary courage and presence of mind. In the end he just feebly smiled and said, Yes, it *was* a raw evening.

Mrs. Ockham, meanwhile, had opened her bag and pulled out a white cardboard box.

'Would you like one of these?'

She held out the box. It was French chocolate, Frankie's favourite—her own too, for that matter. Mrs. Ockham had a weakness for sweet things.

Sebastian considered her uncertainly. Her accent was all right, and in their rather shapeless tweedy way the clothes were

A   I

substantial and of good quality. But she was fat and old—at least forty, he guessed. He hesitated, torn between a desire to put this tiresome creature in her place and a no less urgent desire for those delicious *langues de chat*. Like a pug, he said to himself, as he looked at that blunt, soft face of hers. A pink, hairless pug with a bad complexion. After which he felt that he could accept the chocolates without compromising his integrity.

'Thanks,' he said, and gave her one of those enchanting smiles which middle-aged ladies always found completely irresistible.

To be seventeen, to have a mind which one felt to be agelessly adult, and to look like a Della Robbia angel of thirteen—it was an absurd and humiliating fate. But last Christmas he had read Nietzsche, and since then he had known that he must Love his Fate. *Amor Fati*—but tempered with a healthy cynicism. If people were ready to pay one for looking less than one's age, why not give them what they wanted?

'How good!'

He smiled at her again, and the corners of his mouth were brown with chocolate. The sword in Mrs. Ockham's heart gave another agonizing twist.

'Take the whole box,' she said. Her voice trembled, her eyes were bright with tears.

'No, no, I couldn't . . .'

'Take it,' she insisted, 'take it.' And she pressed it into his hand—into Frankie's hand.

'Oh, thank you. . . .' It was just what Sebastian had hoped, even expected. He had had experience of these sentimental old dodoes.

'I had a boy once,' Mrs. Ockham went on brokenly. 'So like you he was. The same hair and eyes . . .' The tears overflowed on to her cheeks. She took off her glasses and wiped them; then, blowing her nose, she got up and hurried into the reading room.

Sebastian stood looking after her until she was out of sight. All at once he felt horribly guilty and mean. He looked at the

2

box in his hand. A boy had died in order that he might have these *langues de chat*: and if his own mother were alive, she would be nearly as old now as that poor creature in the spectacles. And if *he* had died, she'd have been just as unhappy and sentimental. Impulsively, he made a movement to throw the chocolates away; then checked himself. No, that would be just silliness and superstition. He slipped the box into his pocket and walked out into the foggy twilight.

'Millions and millions,' he whispered to himself; and the enormity of the evil seemed to grow with every repetition of the word. All over the world, millions of men and women lying in pain; millions dying, at this very moment; millions more grieving over them, their faces distorted, like that poor old hag's, the tears running down their cheeks. And millions starving, millions frightened, and sick, and anxious. Millions being cursed and kicked and beaten by other brutal millions. And everywhere the stink of garbage and drink and unwashed bodies, everywhere the blight of stupidity and ugliness. The horror was always there, even when one happened to be feeling well and happy— always there, just round the corner and behind almost every door.

As he walked down Haverstock Hill, Sebastian felt himself evercome by a vast impersonal sadness. Nothing else seemed to exist now, or to matter, except death and agony.

And then that phrase of Keats's came back to him—'The giant agony of the world!' The giant agony. He racked his memory to find the other lines. 'None may usurp this height . . .' How did it go?

> *None may usurp this height, returned that shade,*
> *But those to whom the miseries of the world*
> *Are misery, and will not let them rest. . . .*

How exactly right that was! And perhaps Keats had thought of it one cold spring evening, walking down the hill from Hampstead, just as he himself was doing now. Walking down, and stopping sometimes to cough up a morsel of his lungs and think of his own death as well as of other people's. Sebastian began again, whispering articulately to himself.

> *None may usurp this height, returned that shade,*
> *But those . . .*

But, good heavens, how awful it sounded when you spoke it aloud! None may usurp *this* height, returned *that* shade, but *those* . . . How could he have let a thing like that get past him? But, of course, old Keats was pretty careless sometimes. And being a genius didn't preserve him from the most ghastly lapses into bad taste. There were things in *Endymion* that made one shudder. And when one reflected that it was supposed to be *Greek* . . . Sebastian smiled to himself with compassionate irony. One of these days he'd show them what could be done with Greek mythology. Meanwhile, his mind went back to the phrases that had come to him just now in the library, while he was reading Tarn's book on Hellenistic civilization. 'Ignore the dried figs!' that was how it was to begin. 'Ignore the dried figs . . .' But, after all, dried figs can be good figs. For slaves there would never be anything but the spoilage and refuse of the crop. 'Ignore the *stale* figs,' then. Besides, in this particular context of sound, 'stale' carried the proper vowel.

> *Ignore the stale figs, the weevils and the whippings,*
> *The old men terrified of death . . .*

But that was horribly flat. Steam-rolled and macadamized, like bad Wordsworth. What about 'scared of dying'?

> *The old men scared of dying, the women . . .*

He hesitated, wondering how to sum up that dismal life of the Gyneceum. Then, from the mysterious source of light and energy at the back of his skull, out popped the perfect phrase: '. . . the women in cages.'

Sebastian smiled at the image that bobbed up—a whole zoo of ferocious and undomesticable girls, a deafening aviary of dowagers. But these would be for another poem—a poem in which he would take vengeance on the whole female sex. At the moment his business was with Hellas—with the historical squalor that was Greece and the imaginary glory. Imaginary, of course, so far as a whole people was concerned, but surely realizable by an individual, a poet above all. Some day, somehow, somewhere, that glory would be within his grasp; of that Sebastian was convinced. But meanwhile it was important not to make a fool of oneself. The passion of his nostalgia would have to be tempered, in the expression, with a certain irony, the splendour of the longed-for ideal with a spice of the absurd. Forgetting all about the dead boy and the giant agony of the world, he helped himself to a *langue de chat* from the store in his pocket and, his mouth full, resumed the intoxicating labour of composition.

> *Ignore the stale figs, the weevils and the whippings,*
> *The old men scared of dying, the women in cages.*

So much for history. Now for imagination.

> *In a perpetual June . . .*

He shook his head. 'Perpetual' was like the headmaster talking about the climate of Ecuador in those asinine geography lessons of his. 'Chronic' suggested itself as an alternative. The associations with varicose veins and the language of Cockney charwomen delighted him.

> *In a chronic June, what Alcibiadeses*
> *Surround the beard of Plato!*

Vile! This was no place for proper names. 'What musculatures' perhaps? Then, like manna, 'what heavyweights' fell from heaven. Yes, yes; 'what highbrow heavyweights.' He laughed aloud. And substituting 'wisdom' for 'Plato' you got:

> *In a chronic June, what highbrow heavyweights*
> *Surround the beard of wisdom!*

Sebastian repeated the words with relish, two or three times. And now for the other sex.

> Hark, near by,
> The twangling and the flutes!

He walked on, frowning to himself. Those prancing Bacchae, those Praxitelean breasts and buttocks, those dancers on the vases—how hellishly difficult to make any kind of sense of them! Compress and express. Squeeze all the voluptuous images into a lump and, in the act, squeeze out of them a liqueur-glassful of verbal juice, at once astringent and heady, tart and aphrodisiac. It was easier said than done. His lips began to move at last.

'Hark,' he whispered again.

> Hark, near by,
> The twangling and the flutes. Before, behind,
> Gyre after gyre, what orbed resiliences,
> The last veil loosened, uneclipse their moons!

He sighed and shook his head. Not quite right yet; but still, it would have to do for the time being. And meanwhile here was the corner. Should he go straight home, or walk round by Bantry Place, pick up Susan and let her hear the new poem? Sebastian hesitated a moment, then decided on the second course and turned to the right. He felt in the mood for an audience and applause.

> . . . what orbed resiliences,
> The last veil loosened, uneclipse their moons!

But perhaps the whole thing was too short. It might be necessary to slip in three or four more lines between those resiliences and his final, purple explosion of Bengal lights. Something about the Parthenon, for example. Or maybe something about Aeschylus would be more amusing.

> Tragical on stilts, bawling sublimities
> Through a tortured mouth-hole . . .

6

But goodness! here were those Bengal lights, rocketing up irrepressibly and uninvited into his throat.

> *And all the time, dazzling upon a thousand*
> *Islands in the hyacinthine sea,*
> *What fierce desires . . .*

No, no, no. Too vague, too fleshlessly abstract!

> *What bulls, what boys, what frenzy of swans and nipples,*
> *What radiant lusts like a red forge panting up*
> *From fire to brighter fire . . .*

But 'brighter' had no kind of resonance, no meaning beyond itself. What he needed was a word that, while it described the growing intensity of the fire, should also convey the substance of his own passionately cherished faith—the equivalence of all the ecstasies, the poetic, the sexual, even the religious (if you went in for that sort of thing), and their superiority to all the merely humdrum and ordinary states of being.

He went back to the beginning, hoping in this way to gather enough momentum to carry him over the obstacle.

> *And all the while, dazzling upon a thousand*
> *Islands in the hyacinthine sea,*
> *What bulls, what boys, what frenzy of swans and nipples,*
> *What radiant lusts, like a red forge panting up*
> *From fire . . . from fire . . .*

He hesitated; then the words came.

> *From fire to purer fire, to Light Itself—*
> *The incandescent copulation of Gods.*

But here was the turning into Bantry Place, and even through the closed and curtained windows of number five he could hear Susan at her piano lesson, playing that thing of Scarlatti's she had been working on all the winter. The sort of music, it struck him, that would happen if the bubbles in a magnum of champagne were to rush up rhythmically and, as they reached the surface, burst into sounds as dry and tangy as the wine from whose depths they had arisen. The simile pleased him so much that Sebastian failed to remember that he had never tasted champagne; and his last reflection, as he rang the bell, was that the music would be even dryer and tangier if it were the harpsichord that were being played and not old Pfeiffer's luscious Blüthner.

Over the top of the piano, Susan caught sight of him as he entered the music-room—those beautiful parted lips of his, and the soft hair she always longed to stroke and run her fingers through (but he would never let her), tousled by the wind into a delicious frenzy of pale curls. How sweet of him to have come out of his way to call for her! She gave him a quick glad smile, and as she did so, noticed all at once that there were tiny little water-drops in his hair, like the lovely dew on cabbage leaves— only here they were smaller, beaded along silk floss; and if one touched them, they would be as cold as ice. To think of it was enough to get her all tangled up in the fingering of her left hand.

Old Dr. Pfeiffer, who was pacing up and down the room like a caged animal—a small, obese bear in unpressed trousers and with the moustache of a walrus—took the much-chewed cigar stump out of the corner of his mouth and shouted in German:

'*Musik, musik!*'

With an effort, Susan expelled from her mind the thought of dewdrops on silky curls, caught up the faltering sonata and played on. To her chagrin, she felt herself blushing.

Crimson cheeks, and the hair auburn almost to redness. Beetroots and carrots, Sebastian reflected without indulgence; and the way she showed her gums when she smiled—it was positively anatomical.

Susan struck the final chord and dropped her hands into her lap, waiting for the master's verdict. It came with a roar and on a blast of cigar smoke.

'Goot, goot, goot!' And Dr. Pfeiffer clapped her on the shoulder, as though he were encouraging a cart-horse. Then he turned to Sebastian.

8

'Und here's der liddle Ariel! Oder, perhaps, der liddle Puck—not?' He twinkled between his narrowed eyelids with what he felt to be the most playfully subtle, the most exquisite and cultured irony.

Little Ariel, little Puck . . . Twice in an afternoon, and this time without any excuse—just because the old buffoon thought he was being funny.

'Not being a German,' Sebastian retorted tartly, 'I haven't read any Shakespeare—so I really can't say.'

'Der Puck, der Puck!' cried Dr. Pfeiffer, and laughed so whole-heartedly that he stirred up his chronic bronchitis and started to cough.

An expression of anxiety appeared on Susan's face. Goodness only knew where this would end. She jumped up from the piano-stool, and when the explosions and the horribly liquid wheezings of Dr. Pfeiffer's cough had somewhat subsided, she announced that they must leave at once; her mother was particularly anxious for her to get back early today.

Dr. Pfeiffer wiped the tears out of his eyes, bit once again on the much-chewed end of his cigar, treated Susan to two or three more of his resounding, cart-horse endearments, and told her in God's name to remember what he had said about the trills in the right hand. Then, picking up from a table the cedar-lined silver box, which a grateful pupil had given him for his last birthday, he turned to Sebastian, laid one huge square hand on the boy's shoulder, and with the other held the cigars under his nose.

'Take one,' he said cajolingly. 'Take a nize big fat Havana. Free of charge, *und guarantiert* it won't make a vomitus even to a sucking baby.'

'Oh, shut up!' Sebastian shouted in a fury that was on the verge of tears; and suddenly ducking down, he slipped from under his persecutor's arm and ran out of the room. Susan stood for a moment, hesitant, then without a word hurried after him. Dr. Pfeiffer took the cigar out of his mouth and shouted after her:

'Quick! Quick! Our liddle genius is crying.'

The door slammed. In defiance of his bronchitis, Dr. Pfeiffer started to laugh again, enormously. Two months before, the liddle genius had accepted one of his cigars and, while Susan did her best with the 'Moonlight Sonata,' had puffed away at it for nearly five minutes. Then there was a panic dash for the bathroom; but he had failed to get there quite in time. Dr. Pfeiffer's sense of humour was medievally robust; for him, that vomitus on the second-floor landing was almost the funniest thing that had happened since the jokes in *Faust*.

CHAPTER TWO

HE was walking so fast that Susan had to run, and even so she came up with him only under the second lamp-post. She caught his arm and squeezed it affectionately.

'Sebastian!'

'Let go,' he commanded angrily, and shook himself free. He wasn't going to be patronized and condoled with by anyone.

There! She'd done the wrong thing again. But why must he be so horribly touchy? And why on earth did he pay any attention to an old ass like Pfeiffy?

For a while they walked along, side by side, in silence. She spoke at last.

'Did you write any poetry today?'

'No,' Sebastian lied. Those incandescent copulations of gods had been quenched and turned to ashes. The very thought of reciting the lines now, after what had happened, made him feel sick—like the thought of eating the cold scraps left over from yesterday's dinner.

CHAPTER TWO

There was another silence. It was a half-holiday, Susan was thinking, and because it was examination-time, there wasn't any football. Had he spent the afternoon with that awful Esdaile creature? She shot a glance at him under the next lamp; yes, there was no doubt of it, he looked dark under the eyes. The pigs! She was filled with sudden anger—anger born of a jealousy, all the more painful for being unavowable. She had no rights; there had never been any question of their being anything but cousins, almost sister and brother; besides, it was too painfully obvious that he didn't even dream of thinking about her in that other way. And incidentally when he *had* asked her, that time, two years before, to let him see her without any clothes on, she had said no, in an absolute panic. Two days later she told Pamela Groves about what had happened; and Pamela, who went to one of those progressive schools and whose parents were so much younger than Susan's, had merely roared with laughter. What a fuss about nothing at all! Why, she and her brothers and her cousins—they were always seeing one another with no clothes on. Yes, and her brothers' friends too. So why on earth shouldn't poor Sebastian do it, if he wanted to? All this silly Victorian prudery! Susan was made to feel ashamed of her own and her mother's old-fashioned views. Next time Sebastian asked, she'd take off her pyjamas immediately and stand there in front of him in the attitude, she decided after some reflection, of that Roman matron, or whoever she was, in the Alma-Tadema engraving in her father's study, smiling and with her arms up, doing her hair. For several days she rehearsed the scene in front of her looking-glass, until finally she had it all absolutely perfect. But unfortunately Sebastian never renewed his request, and she hadn't the nerve to take the initiative. With the result that here he was, doing the most awful things with that Esdaile bitch, and she didn't have any right or reason even to cry. Much less to slap his face, as she would have liked to do, and call him names, and pull his hair, and . . . and make him kiss her.

'I suppose you spent the afternoon with your precious Mrs. Esdaile,' she said at last, trying to sound contemptuous and superior.

Sebastian, who had been walking with bent head, looked up at her.

'What's that to you?' he said after a pause.

'Nothing at all.' Susan shrugged her shoulders and uttered a little laugh. But inwardly she felt angry with herself and ashamed. How often she had vowed never to show any further curiosity about his beastly affair, never to listen again to those horrifying details, which he recounted so vividly and with so manifest a relish! And yet curiosity always got the better of her, and she listened greedily every time. Listened just because these accounts of his love-making with somebody else were so painful to her. Listened, too, because thus to share in his love-making, even theoretically and in imagination, was obscurely exciting to her, and itself constituted a kind of sensual bond between them, a mental embrace, horribly unsatisfying and exasperating, but none the less an embrace.

Sebastian had looked away; but now suddenly he turned back to her with a strange smile almost of triumph, as though he had just scored off somebody.

'All right, then,' he said. 'You've asked for it. Don't blame me if it shocks your maiden modesty.'

He broke off with a rather harsh little laugh, and walked along in silence, meditatively rubbing the bridge of his nose with the tip of his right forefinger. How well she knew the gesture! It was the infallible sign that he was composing a poem, or thinking of the best way to tell one of his stories.

Those stories, those extraordinary stories! Susan had lived in the fantastic worlds of Sebastian's creation almost as long and quite as intensely as she had lived in the real world. More intensely perhaps; for in the real world she had to depend on her own prosaic self, whereas in the story world she found herself endowed with Sebastian's rich imagination, moved and excited by Sebastian's flow of words.

The first of his stories that Susan clearly remembered was the one Sebastian had told her on the beach at Tenby, that summer (it must have been the summer of 1917) when there were five candles on their joint birthday cake. They had found among the seaweed an old red rubber ball, torn almost in half. Sebastian took it to a little pool and washed out the sand with which it was filled. On the wet inner surface of the ball was a kind of wart-like excrescence. Why? Only the manufacturers could say. For a child of five, it was an inexplicable mystery. Sebastian touched the wart with a probing forefinger. That was the tummy-button, he whispered. They looked around furtively to make sure that they were out of earshot: navels were things that verged upon the unmentionable. Everybody's tummy-button grew inwards like that, Sebastian went on. And when she asked him, 'How do you know?' he launched out into a circumstantial account of what he had seen Dr. Carter doing to a little girl in his consulting-room, the last time Aunt Alice had taken him there about his earache. Cutting her open —that was what Dr. Carter was doing—cutting her open with a big knife and fork, to look at her tummy-button from the inside. And when you were too tough for a knife and fork, they had to use one of those saws that butchers cut bones with. Yes, really and truly, he insisted, when she expressed her horrified incredulity, really and truly. And to prove his point, he began sawing at the ball with the side of his hand. The gashed rubber parted under the pressure; the wound gaped wider and wider as the saw cut more deeply into what, for Susan, was now no longer a ball, but a little girl's tummy—for all practical purposes, her own. H-h-h-h, h-h-h-h, h-h-h-h, Sebastian went, trilling the aspirant far back in the throat. The sound was blood-curdlingly like the noise of a meat saw. And then, he went on, when they'd cut far enough, they opened you. Like this—and he pulled the two halves of the wounded ball apart. They opened you, and they turned your top flap inside out—so; and then they scrubbed the tummy-button with soap and water to get the dirt off. Furiously he scratched the mysterious wart, and his nails on the rubber made a small dry noise that, to Susan, was unspeakably horrifying. She uttered a scream and covered her ears with her hands. For years afterwards she had been terrified of Dr. Carter, had howled whenever he came near her; and even now when she knew it was all nonsense about the tummy-button, the sight of his little black bag, of those cabinets in his consulting-room, full of glass tubes and bottles and nickel-plated gadgets, filled her with a vague apprehension which she found it difficult, in spite of all her efforts at reasonableness, to dispel.

Uncle John Barnack was often away for months at a stretch travelling abroad and writing articles for that left-wing paper which Susan's father wouldn't so much as allow his fire to be lighted with. Sebastian had therefore lived a good part of his life under the care of his Aunt Alice and at closest quarters with the youngest of her children, the little girl between whom and himself there was a difference in age of only a single day. With the growth of that small body of his, that precocious and feverishly imaginative mind, the stories that he told her—or rather that he related to himself in her stimulating presence—became ever more complicated and circumstantial. Sometimes they would last for weeks and months, in an interminable series of instalments, composed as they walked back and forth from school, or ate their supper in front of the gas fire in the nursery, or sat together on the roofs of wintry buses while their elders travelled prosaically inside. For example, there was the epic that ran almost uninterruptedly through the whole of 1923—the epic of the Larnimans. Or rather the La-a-arnimans—for the name was always pronounced in a whisper and with a horribly significant prolongation of the first syllable. Those La-a-arnimans were a family of human ogres, who lived in tunnels that radiated out from a central cavern immediately under the lion house at the Zoo.

'Listen!' Sebastian would whisper to her each time they found themselves in front of the Siberian tiger's cage.

'Listen!' And he would stamp his foot on the pavement.

'It's hollow. Don't you hear?'

And, sure enough, Susan did hear and, hearing, shuddered at the thought of the La-a-arnimans sitting there fifty feet below, at the heart of a whirring complex of machinery, counting the money they had stolen from the vaults of the Bank of England, roasting the children they had kidnapped through trap-doors in basements, breeding cobras, to let loose into the drains so that suddenly, one fine morning, just as one was about to sit down, a hooded head would pop up out of the w.c. and hiss. Not that she believed any of it, of course. But even if you didn't believe in it, it was still frightening. Those horrible La-a-arnimans with their cat's eyes and their patent electric guns and their underground switchbacks—they didn't really live under the lion house (even though the ground *did* sound hollow when you stamped on it). But that didn't mean that they didn't exist. The proof of their existence was the fact that she dreamed about them, that she kept a sharp look-out, each morning, for those cobras.

But the Larnimans were ancient history now. Their place had been taken, first, by a detective; then (after Sebastian had read his father's book about the Russian Revolution) by Trotsky; then by Odysseus, whose adventures, during that summer and autumn of 1926, were wilder than anything that Homer had ever reported. It was with the coming of Odysseus that girls first made their appearance in Sebastian's stories. True, they had figured to some extent in the earlier epics, but only as the victims of doctors, cannibals, cobras and revolutionaries. (Anything to make Susan's flesh creep, to elicit that horrified squeal of protest!) But in the new Odyssey they started to play another kind of part. They were pursued and kissed, they were looked at through keyholes without their clothes on, they were discovered bathing at midnight in a phosphorescent sea, and Odysseus would also go swimming.

Forbidden themes, repulsively fascinating, disgustingly attractive! Sebastian would embark on them with a quiet casualness —*pianissimo*, so to speak, and *senza espressione*, as though he were hurrying over some boring transitional passage, some patch of mere five-finger exercises interpolated into the romantic rhapsody of his Odyssey. *Pianissimo, senza espressione*—and then, bang! like a chord by Scriabin in the middle of a Haydn quartet, out he'd come with some frightful enormity! And in spite of all her efforts to take it casually, matter-of-factly, as Pamela would have taken it, Susan would be startled into an exclamation, a blush, a covering of the ears, a rushing away, as though she didn't mean to listen to another word. But always she did listen; and sometimes, when he broke off his narrative to ask her some direct and horribly indiscreet question, she would even speak herself about the impossible subject, muttering with averted eyes, or else in a voice uncontrolledly loud, and modulating, against her will, into a burst of laughter.

Gradually the new Odyssey had petered out. Susan had her music and her School Certificate, and Sebastian spent all his leisure reading Greek and the English poets, and writing verses of his own. There seemed to be no time for story-telling, and if ever they did find themselves together for a little, he liked to recite his latest poems. When she praised them, as she generally did—for she really did think they were wonderful—Sebastian's face would light up.

'Oh, it's not *too* bad,' he would say deprecatingly; but his smile and the irrepressible brightness of his eyes betrayed what he really thought. Sometimes, however, there were lines she didn't understand, or didn't like; and then, if she ventured to say so, he'd flush with anger and call her a fool and a Philistine; or else sarcastically remark that it was only to be expected, seeing that women had the minds of hens, or seeing it was notorious that musicians had no brains, only fingers and a solar plexus.

Sometimes his words hurt her; but more often they only evoked a smile and made her feel, by comparison with his transparent childishness, delightfully old, wise and, in spite of his dazzling gifts, superior. When he behaved like that, Sebastian proclaimed himself an infant as well as a prodigy, and invited her to love him in yet another way—protectively and maternally.

And then suddenly, a few weeks after the beginning of the current term, the stories had started again—but with a difference; for this time they were not fiction, they were autobiography: he had begun to tell her about Mrs. Esdaile. The child in him was still there, still urgently in need of mothering, of being preserved from the consequences of his own childishness; but the grown boy she secretly worshipped with quite another passion was now the lover of a woman—older than herself and prettier, and a million times more experienced; rich too, and with lovely clothes and manicures and make-up; utterly beyond the possibility of competition and rivalry. Susan had never let him see how much she minded; but her diary had been full of bitterness, and in bed at night she had often cried herself to sleep. And tonight she would again have reason to be miserable.

Frowning, Susan glanced sideways at her companion. Sebastian was still pensively caressing his nose.

'That's it,' she burst out with a sudden uprush of resentment; 'rub your beastly little snout till you've got it all pat!'

Sebastian started and looked round. An expression of disquiet appeared on his face.

'Got what all pat?' he asked defensively.

'All your beautiful speeches and witty repartees,' she answered. 'You think I don't know you, I suppose. Why, I bet you're too shy to say anything, even when you're . . .' She broke off, unable to give utterance to the words that would evoke the odious picture of their love-making.

At another time this taunting reference to his timidity—to the humiliating dumbness and incoherence with which he was afflicted whenever he found himself in strange or impressive company—would have roused him to anger. But on this occasion he was merely amused.

'Mayn't I tell even the tiniest lie?' he said. 'Just for art's sake?'

'You mean for *your* sake—to make yourself look like something out of Noel Coward.'

'Out of Congreve,' he protested.

'Out of anybody you like,' said Susan, happy to have this opportunity of venting her accumulated bitterness without betraying its real nature and cause. 'Any old lie, so long as you don't have to show yourself as you really are. . . .'

'A Don Juan without the courage of his conversation,' he put in. It was a phrase he had invented to console himself for having cut such a lamentable figure at the Boveneys' Christmas party. 'And you're annoyed because I put the conversation where it ought to have been. Don't be so horribly literal.'

He smiled at her so enchantingly that Susan had to capitulate.

'All right,' she grumbled. 'I'll believe you even when I know it's a lie.'

His smile broadened; he was the gayest of Della Robbia angels.

'Even when you *know*,' he repeated, and laughed aloud. It was the most exquisite of jokes. Poor old Susan! She *knew* that the accounts of his conversational prowess were false; but she also *knew* that he had got talking with a beautiful dark-haired young woman on the top of a Finchley Road bus, that this woman had asked him to tea at her flat, had listened to his poetry, had told him how unhappy she was with her husband, had made an excuse to leave the drawing-room and then, five minutes later, had called him, 'Mr. Barnack, Mr. Barnack,'—and he had walked out after her, and across the landing and through a half-opened door into a room that was pitch dark, and suddenly had felt her bare arms round him and her lips on his face. Susan knew all that, and a great deal more besides; and the beauty of it was that Mrs. Esdaile didn't exist, that he had found her name in the telephone book, her pale oval face in a volume of Victorian steel engravings, and all the rest in his imagination. And all that poor Susan objected to was the elegance of his conversation!

'She was wearing black lace underclothes today,' he improvised, carried away by his amusement into an emphatic Beardsleyism that at ordinary times he would have despised.

'She would!' said Susan, bitterly thinking of her own stout white cotton.

With his inward eye Sebastian was contemplating a Callipyge in needle-point, patterned all over with spidery arabesques. Like one of those ornamental china horses, on whose flanks the dapplings are leaves and tendrils. He laughed to himself.

'I told her she was the latest archaeological discovery—the Dappled Aphrodite of Hampstead.'

'Liar!' said Susan emphatically. 'You didn't tell her anything of the kind.'

'I shall write a poem about the Dappled Aphrodite,' Sebastian went on, ignoring her.

A fire-works display of lovely phrases began to blaze and crackle in his mind.

'Stippled with scrolls her withers, her velvet croup tattooed with Brussels roses. And round the barrel,' he murmured, rubbing his nose, 'round the rich barrel, like a net of flowery moles, gardens and trellises of bobbin-work.'

And, by golly, there was a perfectly good rhyme! Scrolls and moles—two stout pegs on which one could hang any amount of lace and goddess-skin.

'Oh, shut up!' said Susan.

But his lips continued to move.

'Inked on those creamy quarters, what artful calligraphy, swelling and shrinking with each alternate movement.'

Suddenly he heard his name being shouted and the sound of running feet from behind them.

'Who the devil . . .?'

They stopped and turned round.

19

'It's Tom Boveney,' said Susan.

So it was! Sebastian smiled.

'I'll bet you five bob he says, "Hullo, Suse, how's the booze?"'

Six and a half feet high, three feet wide, two feet thick, sandy-haired and grinning, Tom came rushing up like the Cornish Riviera Express.

'Basty Boy,' he shouted, 'you're just the man I was looking for. Oh, and there's young Suse.—How's the booze, Suse?'

He laughed, and was delighted when Susan and Sebastian also laughed—laughed with unaccustomed heartiness.

'Well,' he went on, turning back to Sebastian, 'it's all settled.'

'What's settled?'

'The dinner problem. Seeing you're going abroad as soon as term's over, I've arranged to put it off to the end of the hols.'

He grinned and patted Sebastian's shoulder affectionately. He too, Susan said to herself. And she went on to reflect that almost everyone felt that way about Sebastian—and he exploited it. Yes, he exploited it.

'Pleased?' Tom questioned.

Basty was his mascot, his child, and at the same time the exquisite and brilliant object of a love which he was too congenitally heterosexual to avow, or even to understand and give a name to. He'd do anything to please little Basty.

But instead of beaming delightedly, Sebastian looked almost dismayed.

'But, Tom,' he stammered, 'you mustn't . . . I mean, you shouldn't put yourself out for me.'

Tom laughed and gave his shoulder a reassuring squeeze.

'I'm not putting myself out.'

'But the other fellows,' said Sebastian, clutching at every straw.

Tom pointed out that the other fellows didn't care whether his farewell party was at the beginning of the hols or at the end.

'A binge is always a binge,' he was saying philosophically,

when Sebastian cut him short with a vehemence altogether unjustified by considerations of mere politeness.

'No, I wouldn't dream of it,' he cried in a tone of finality.

There was a silence. Tom Boveney looked down at him wonderingly.

'You almost sound as if you didn't want to come,' he began in bewilderment.

Sebastian realized his mistake and made haste to protest that of course there was nothing he'd have liked better. Which was true. Dinner at the Savoy, a show, and a night club to wind up with—it would be an unprecedented experience. But he had to refuse the invitation, and for the most humiliating and childish reason: he had no evening clothes. And now, when he thought that everything had been settled so satisfactorily, here was Tom reopening the question. Damn him, damn him! Sebastian positively hated the great lout for his officious friendliness.

'But if you want to come,' Tom insisted with exasperating common sense, 'what on earth are you saying no for?' He turned to Susan. 'Can *you* throw any light on the mystery?'

Susan hesitated. She knew, of course, all about Uncle John's refusal to get Sebastian a suit of evening clothes. It was mean of him. But after all there wasn't anything for Sebastian to be ashamed of. Why didn't he frankly come out with it?

'Well,' she said slowly, 'I suppose it's because . . .'

'Shut up. Shut up, I tell you.' In his fury, Sebastian gave her arm such a pinch that she cried out in pain.

'Serves you right,' he whispered savagely, and turned again to Tom. Susan was astonished to hear him saying that of course he'd come, and it was really terribly nice of Tom to have taken all that trouble to change the date. Terribly nice—and he actually managed to give Tom one of his angelic smiles.

'You didn't think I'd have a party without you, Basty?' Once more Tom Boveney squeezed the shoulder of his mascot, his only child, his infant prodigy and exquisite beloved.

'Now of all times, when I'm going to Canada—and God

knows when I shall be seeing you again. You or any of the other Haverstock fellows,' he added hastily; and to build up the alibi, he addressed himself jocularly to Susan: 'And if it weren't a stag party, I'd ask you too. Plenty of booze for good old Suse.' He slapped her on the back, and laughed.

'And now I've got to fly. Oughtn't to have stopped to talk to you by rights; but it was such a stroke of luck running into you. So long, Suse. So long, Basty.' He turned and started to run, elegantly in spite of his size and weight, like a professional half-miler, into the darkness out of which he had come. The others resumed their walk.

'What I can't understand,' said Susan, after a long silence, 'is why you don't just tell the truth. It isn't your fault that you don't have a dinner jacket. And it's not as if there was a law against wearing your blue serge suit. They won't turn you out of the restaurant, you know.'

'Oh, for God's sake!' cried Sebastian, driven almost to frenzy by the maddening reasonableness of what she was saying.

'But if you'd only explain to me why you don't tell him,' she persisted.

'I don't wish to explain,' he said with a dignified finality.

Susan glanced at him, thought how ridiculous he looked, and shrugged her shoulders.

'You mean, you can't explain.'

In the silence that ensued, Sebastian chewed on the bitter cud of his abasement. He didn't wish to explain because, as Susan had said, he couldn't explain. And he couldn't explain, not because he lacked reasons, but because the reasons he had were so excruciatingly intimate. First that old cow in the library; even that dead son was no excuse for her slobbering over him as though he were still in diapers. Then Pfeiffer and his stinking cigars. And now this last humiliation. It was not only that he looked like a child, when he knew himself to be a hundred times abler than the oldest of them. It was also that he lacked the outward accoutrement and paraphernalia belonging to his real age. If he'd had decent clothes and enough pocket money, the other humiliations would have been tolerable. By his easy spendings and the cut of his coats he could have refuted the specious evidence of his face and stature. But his father gave him only a shilling a week, made him wear his shoddy reach-me-downs till they were threadbare and short in the sleeves, and absolutely refused to get him a dinner jacket. His garments confirmed the testimony of the body they so shabbily covered; he was a child in child's clothing. And here was that fool, Susan, asking him why he didn't tell Tom Boveney the truth!

'*Amor Fati*,' she quoted. 'Didn't you say that was your motto now?' Sebastian did not deign to make a reply.

Looking at him, as he walked beside her, his face set, his body curiously rigid and constrained, Susan felt her irritation melting away into a maternal tenderness. Poor darling! How miserable he managed to make himself! And for such idiotic reasons! Worrying about a dinner jacket! But she'd be prepared to bet that Tom Boveney didn't have an affair with a beautiful married woman. And, remembering how he had cheered up just now at the mention of Mrs. Esdaile, Susan charitably tried again.

'You didn't finish telling me about those black lace under-clothes,' she said at last, breaking the dismal silence.

But this time there was no response; Sebastian merely shook his head without even looking in her direction.

'Please,' she cajoled.

'I don't want to.' And when Susan tried to insist, 'I tell you, I don't want to,' he repeated more emphatically.

There was nothing funny any longer about Susan's gullibility. Seen soberly, in its proper light, this Esdaile business was just another of his humiliations.

His mind harked back to that hideous evening two months before. Outside the Camden Town tube station, a girl in blue, coarsely pretty, with painted mouth and a lot of yellow hair. He walked up and down two or three times, trying to screw up his courage and feeling rather sick, just as he did before one of those ghastly interviews with the headmaster about his maths. The nausea of the threshold. But finally, when one had knocked and gone in and sat down opposite that large and extraordinarily clean-shaven face, it wasn't really so bad. 'You seem to think, Sebastian, that because you're highly gifted in one direction you're excused from working at anything you don't happen to enjoy.' And it would end up with his being kept in for two or three hours on half-holiday afternoons, or having to do a couple of extra problems every day for a month. Nothing so very bad, after all, nothing to justify that nausea. Taking courage from these reflections, Sebastian walked up to the girl in blue and said, 'Good evening.'

In the beginning she wouldn't even take him seriously. 'A kid like you! I'd be ashamed of myself.' He had to show her the inscription in his copy of the *Oxford Book of Greek Verse*, which he happened to be carrying in his pocket. '*For Sebastian, on his seventeenth birthday, from his uncle, Eustace Barnack.* 1928.' The girl in blue read the words aloud, glanced dubiously into his face, then back at the book. From the fly-leaf she turned to a page chosen at random in the middle of the volume. 'Why, it's Yiddish!' She looked curiously into his face. 'I'd never have guessed it,' she said. Sebastian set her right. 'And you mean to tell me you can read it?' He demonstrated his ability on a chorus from the *Agamemnon*. That convinced her; anybody who could do that must be more than just a kid. But did he have any money? He produced his wallet and showed her the pound-note that still remained to him from Uncle Eustace's Christmas present. 'All right,' said the girl. But she had no place of her own; where did he mean to go?

Aunt Alice and Susan and Uncle Fred had all gone away for the week-end, and there was nobody left in the house except old Ellen—and Ellen always went to bed sharp at nine, and was as deaf as a post anyway. They could go to his place, he suggested; and he hailed a taxi.

Of the nightmare that followed Sebastian could not think

without a shudder. That rubber corset and, when they were in his room, her body, as unresponsive as its carapace. The bored perfunctory kisses, and the breath that stank of beer and caries and onions. His own excitement, so frenzied as to be almost instantly self-stultifying; and then, irremediable, the hideously sober coldness that brought with it a disgust for what lay there beside him, a horror as though for a corpse—and the corpse laughed and offered him its derisive condolences.

On the way down to the front door, the girl asked to look at the drawing-room. Her eyes opened wide as the light revealed its modest splendours. 'Hand painted!' she said admiringly, crossing over to the fireplace and running her fingers over the varnish of the presentation portrait of Sebastian's grandfather. That seemed to settle it for her. She turned to Sebastian and announced that she wanted another quid. But he hadn't got another quid. The girl in blue sat down emphatically on the sofa. Very well, then; she'd stay there until he found one. Sebastian emptied his pockets of small change. Three and elevenpence. No, she insisted, nothing less than a quid; and in a hoarse contralto she started to chant the words, 'A quid, a quid, a quid-o,' to the tune of 'When Irish Eyes . . .'

'Don't do that,' he begged. The chant swelled to full-throated song. 'A quid, a quid, a quid-o, a lovely, lovely quid . . .' Almost in tears, Sebastian interrupted her: there was a servant sleeping upstairs, and even the neighbours might hear. 'Well, let them all come,' said the girl in blue. 'They're welcome.' 'But what would they say?' Sebastian's voice quavered as he spoke, his lips were trembling. The girl looked at him contemptuously, and broke out into her loud, ugly laugh. 'Serve you right, cry-baby: that's what they'd say. Wanting to go with girls, when he ought to be staying at 'ome and letting 'is mother blow 'is nose for him.' She started to beat time. 'Now, one, two, three. All together, boys. "When Irish quids are quidding . . ."'

On the little table by the sofa Sebastian caught sight of that gold-mounted tortoise-shell paper-knife which had been presented to Uncle Fred on the twenty-fifth anniversary of his association with the City and Far Eastern Investment Company. Worth much more than a pound. He picked it up and tried to press it into her hands. 'Take this,' he implored. 'Yes, and 'ave them call the p'lice the moment I try to sell it.' She pushed it aside. In another key and more loudly than ever, she began again. 'When Irish quids . . .' 'Stop,' he cried despairingly, 'stop! I'll get you the money. I swear I will.' The girl in blue broke off and looked at her wrist-watch. 'I'll give you five minutes,' she said. Sebastian hurried out of the room and up the stairs. A minute later he was hammering on one of the doors that gave on to the fourth-floor landing. 'Ellen, Ellen!' There was no answer. Deaf as a post. Damn the woman, *damn* her! He knocked again and shouted. Suddenly, and without any warning, the door opened and there was Ellen in a grey flannelette dressing-gown, with her grey hair done up into two little pigtails tied with tape, and no false teeth, so that her round, apple-like face seemed to have caved in and, when she asked him if the house was on fire, he could hardly understand what she said. Making a great effort, he turned on his most angelic smile—the smile with which he had always managed to get round her, all his life. 'Sorry, Ellen. I wouldn't have done it if it weren't so urgent.' 'So what?' she asked, turning her better ear towards him. 'Do you think you could lend me a pound?' She looked blank, and he had to yell at her. 'A POUND.' 'A pound?' she echoed in amazement. 'I borrowed it from a friend of mine, and he's waiting at the door.' Toothlessly, but still with her north-country intonation, Ellen enquired why he couldn't pay it back tomorrow. 'Because he's going away,' Sebastian explained. 'Going to Liverpool.' 'Oh, to Liverpool,' said Ellen in another tone, as though that cast quite a new light on the matter. 'Is he taking a ship?' she asked. 'Yes, to America,' Sebastian shouted, 'to Philadelphia.' *Off to Philadelphia in the morning.* He glanced at his watch. Only another minute or thereabouts, and she'd be starting that other Irish song again. He gave Ellen a yet more enchanting smile. 'Could you manage it, Ellen?' The old woman smiled back at him, took his hand and laid it for a moment against her cheek, then without a word she turned back into the room to look for her purse.

It was when they came back from that week-end—on the Monday afternoon, to be precise, while he was walking home with her from old Pfeiffer's—that he had first told Susan about Mrs. Esdaile. Exquisite, cultured, wildly voluptuous Esdaile in the arms of her triumphant young lover—the reverse of that medal whose other, real face bore the image of the girl in blue and a nauseated child, abject and blubbering.

At the corner of Glanvil Place they parted company.

'You go straight home,' said Sebastian, breaking the long silence. 'I'm going to see if Father's in.' And without waiting for Susan's comments, he turned and quickly walked away.

Susan stood there looking after him as he hurried down the street, so frail and helpless, but marching with such desperate resolution towards inevitable failure. For, of course, if the poor boy imagined he could get the better of Uncle John, he was just asking to be hurt again.

Under the street lamp at the corner, the pale hair came to life like an aureole of tousled flame; then he turned and was lost to sight. And that was life, Susan reflected as she walked on—a succession of street corners. You met with something—something strange, something beautiful and desirable; and the next moment you were at another corner; it had turned and was gone. And even when it didn't turn, it was in love with Mrs. Esdaile.

She mounted the steps of number eighteen, and rang the bell. Ellen opened the door and, before admitting her, made her wipe her feet again on the mat.

'Can't have you muddying my carpets,' she said in her ordinary tone of grumbling affection.

On her way upstairs, Susan looked in to say good-evening to

her mother. Mrs. Poulshot seemed preoccupied, and her kiss was perfunctory.

'Try not to do anything to annoy your father,' she recommended. 'He's feeling a bit out of sorts this evening.'

Oh God, thought Susan, who had suffered ever since she could remember from those moods of his.

'And change into your pale blue,' Mrs. Poulshot added. 'I want Uncle Eustace to see you at your prettiest.'

A fat lot *she* cared if Uncle Eustace thought her pretty! And anyhow, she went on to reflect, as she climbed the stairs, what hope was there of competing with someone who had been married, who had money, who bought her clothes in Paris and was probably drenched—though oddly enough Sebastian had never mentioned the fact—in the most indecent kind of scent.

She lit the gas fire in her room, undressed and walked down half a flight to the bathroom.

The pleasure of soaking in hot water was unpleasantly tempered by Mr. Poulshot's insistence that none but carbolic soap should ever be used in his household. The result was that one came out of one's bath smelling, not like Mrs. Esdaile, but like a newly washed dog. Susan sniffed at herself as she reached for the towel, and made a wry face of disgust at the stink of her own cleanliness.

Sebastian's room was on the opposite side of the landing to hers, and, knowing him absent, she went boldly in, opened the top drawer of his dressing-table and took out the safety-razor which he had bought two months before to keep down a still hypothetical beard.

Meticulously, as though preparing for an evening in a sleeveless gown and a night of passion, she shaved her armpits; then picked out the tell-tale hairs and replaced the razor in its box.

CHAPTER THREE

SEBASTIAN, meanwhile, had walked down Glanvil Place, frowning to himself and biting his lips. This was probably his last chance of getting those evening clothes in time for Tom Boveney's party. His father, he knew, was not expected to dinner that evening, and the next day he was going to Huddersfield, or somewhere, for a conference; wouldn't be back till Wednesday evening, and on Thursday morning they were to set out together for Florence. It must be now or never.

'Evening clothes were a class symbol, and it was a crime to spend money on useless luxuries when people as good as oneself were starving!' Sebastian knew in advance what his father's arguments would be. But behind the arguments was the man—dominating and righteous, hard on others because even harder on himself. If the man were approached in the right way, perhaps the arguments would not be pressed home to their logical conclusion. The great thing, Sebastian had learnt from long and bitter experience, was never to seem too anxious or insistent. He must ask for the dinner jacket—but in such a way that his father wouldn't think that he really longed for it. That, he knew, would be to invite a refusal—nominally, of course, on the score of economy and socialist ethics, but really, he had come to suspect, because his father took a certain pleasure in thwarting the too explicit manifestations of desire. If he managed to avoid the pitfall of over-eagerness, perhaps he would be able to talk his father out of the other, avowable reasons for refusal. But it would take good acting to bring it off, and a lot of finesse, and above all that presence of mind in which, at moments of crisis, he was always so woefully lacking. But perhaps if he worked out a plan of campaign in advance, a piece of brilliant and inspired strategy . . .

Sebastian had kept his eyes fixed upon the pavement at his feet; but now he raised his head, as though the perfect, the irresistible plan were up there in the murky sky, waiting only to be seen and seized. He raised his head, and suddenly there it was on the other side of the street—not the plan, of course, but the Primitive Methodist Chapel, *his* Chapel, the thing that it was worth walking down Glanvil Terrace of an evening on purpose to see. But today, lost as he was in the labyrinth of his own miseries, he had forgotten all about it. And now here it confronted him, faithfully itself, the lower part of its façade suffused with the greenish gas-light of the street lamp in front of it, and the upper part growing dimmer and dimmer as it mounted from the light, until the last spiky pinnacles of Victorian brickwork hung there, opaquely black against the foggy darkness of the London sky. Bright little details and distinctions fading upwards into undifferentiated mystery; a topless darkness of the London sky. Bright little details and distinctions at its foot. Sebastian stood there, looking; and in spite of the memory of his humiliations and his dread of what might be in store for him at his father's, he felt something of that strange, inexplicable elation which the spectacle always evoked in him.

> *Little squalor! transfigured into Ely,*
> *Into Bourges, into the beauty of holiness;*
> *Burgeoning out of gas-light into Elephanta;*
> *Out of school-treats, out of the Reverend Wilkins,*
> *Flowering into Poetry . . .*

He repeated to himself the opening lines of his poem, then looked again at its subject. Built at the worst period, of the shoddiest materials. Hideous, in the day-time, beyond belief. But an hour later, when the lamps were lit, as lovely and significant as anything he had ever seen. Which was the real chapel— the little monstrosity that received the Reverend Wilkins and his flock on Sunday mornings? Or this unfathomably pregnant mystery before him? Sebastian shook his head, and walked on.

The questions admitted of no answer, the only thing you could do was to re-formulate them in terms of poetry.

> *Little squalor! transfigured into Ely,*
> *Into Bourges, into the beauty of holiness . . .*

Number twenty-three was a tall stucco-fronted house, identical with all the others in the row. Sebastian turned in under the pillared porch, crossed the hall, and with a renewal of his momentarily banished apprehension began to climb the stairs.

One flight, two flights, three flights, yet another, and he was standing at the door of his father's flat. Sebastian raised a hand to the bell button, then let it fall again. He felt sick, and his heart was beating violently. It was the blue tart over again, the head-master, the nausea of the threshold. He looked at his watch. Six forty-seven and a half. At six forty-eight he would ring and go in and just blurt it out, anyhow.

'Father, you really must let me have a dinner jacket. . . .' He lifted his hand again and pressed the ball of his thumb firmly against the button. Inside, the bell buzzed like an angry wasp. He waited half a minute, then rang again. There was no answer. His last chance had vanished. Disappointment was mingled in Sebastian's mind with a profound sense of relief that he had been allowed to postpone the hour of his ordeal. Tom Boveney's party was four weeks away; whereas, if his father had been at home, the dreaded interview would be going on now, at this very moment.

Sebastian had gone down only a single flight when the sound of a familiar voice made him halt.

'Seventy-two stairs,' his father was saying down there in the hall.

'*Dio!*' said another, a foreign voice. 'You live half-way up to paradise.'

'This house is a symbol,' the ringing, upper-class English voice continued. 'A symbol of the decay of capitalism.'

Sebastian recognized the conversational gambit. It was the

one John Barnack usually played upon his visitors the first time he accompanied them up those interminable stairs.

'Once the home of a single prosperous Victorian family.' That was it. 'Now a nest of bachelors and struggling business women, with a childless couple or two thrown in for good measure.'

The voice grew louder and more distinct as its owner approached.

'. . . and it's a product, too, of rising unemployment and a falling birth-rate. In a word, of blighted hopes and Marie Stopes.' And on that there was the startling explosion of John Barnack's loud, metallic laughter.

'Christ!' Sebastian whispered to himself. It was the third time he had heard that joke and the subsequent outburst.

'Stope?' queried the foreign voice through the tail-end of the other's merriment. 'Do I know what it signifies, to stope? *Stopare? Stopper? Stopfen?*' But neither Italian, nor French, nor German seemed to throw any light.

Very elaborately, the Cambridge accent started to explain.

Not wishing it to appear that he had been eavesdropping, Sebastian started once more to run down the stairs, and when the two men came round the corner into sight, he uttered a well-simulated exclamation of astonishment.

Mr. Barnack looked up and saw in that small slender figure poised there, six steps above him, not Sebastian, but Sebastian's mother—Rosie on the evening of the Hilliards' fancy-dress dance, in the character of Lady Caroline Lamb disguised, in a monkey-jacket and tight red velvet breeches, as Byron's page. Three months later had come the war, and two years after that she had left him for that vicious imbecile, Tom Hilliard.

'Oh, it's you,' Mr. Barnack said aloud, without allowing the faintest symptom of surprise, or pleasure, or any other emotion to appear on his brown leathery face.

To Sebastian that was one of the most disquieting things about his father: you never knew from his expression what he was feeling or thinking. He would look at you straight and un-waveringly, his grey eyes brightly blank, as though you were a perfect stranger. The first intimation of his state of mind always came verbally, in that loud, authoritative, barrister's voice of his, in those measured phrases, so carefully chosen, so beautifully articulated. There would be silence, or perhaps talk of matters indifferent; and then suddenly, out of the blue of his impassivity, a pronouncement, as though from Sinai.

Smiling uncertainly, Sebastian came down to meet them.

'This is my youngster,' said Mr. Barnack.

And the stranger turned out to be Professor Cacciaguida—the famous Professor Cacciaguida, Mr. Barnack added. Sebastian smiled deferentially and shook hands; this must be that anti-fascist man he had heard his father talking about. Well, it was a fine head, he thought, as he turned away. Roman of the best period, but with an incongruous mane of grey hair brushed romantically back from the forehead—he shot another sur-reptitious glance—as though the Emperor Augustus had tried to get himself up as Liszt.

But how strangely, Sebastian went on to reflect as they climbed the final flight, how pathologically even, the stranger's body fell away from that commanding head! The emperor-genius declined into the narrow chest and shoulders of a boy, then, incongruously, into the belly and wide hips almost of a middle-aged woman, and finally into a pair of thin little legs and the tiniest of patent-leather button-boots. Like some sort of larva that had started to develop and then got stuck, with only the front end of the organism fully adult and the rest hardly more than a tadpole.

John Barnack opened the door of his flat and turned on the light.

'I'd better go and see about supper,' he said. 'Seeing you've got to get away so early, Professor.'

It was an opportunity to talk about the dinner jacket. But when Sebastian offered to come and give a hand, his father peremptorily ordered him to stay where he was and talk to their distinguished guest.

'Then when I'm ready,' he added, 'you must scuttle. We've got some important things to discuss.'

And having thus tersely put Sebastian in his childish place, Mr. Barnack turned and, with quick, decided steps, like an athlete going into combat, strode out of the room.

Sebastian stood hesitating for a few seconds, then made up his mind to disobey, follow his father into the kitchen and have it out with him, there and then. But at this moment the Professor, who had been looking inquisitively around the room, turned to him with a smile.

'But how it is aseptic!' he exclaimed in that melodious voice of his, and with that charming trace of a foreign accent, those odd and over-literary turns of phrase, which merely served to emphasize the completeness of his command of the language.

In that bare, bleak sitting-room, everything, except the books, was enamelled the colour of skim milk, and the floor was a polished sheet of grey linoleum. Professor Cacciaguida sat down in one of the metal chairs and with tremulous, nicotine-stained fingers, lighted a cigarette.

'One awaits the arrival of the surgeon,' he added, 'at any moment.'

But instead, it was John Barnack who came back into the room, carrying plates and a handful of cutlery. The Professor turned in his direction, but did not speak at once; instead, he put his cigarette to his lips, inhaled, held his breath for a couple of seconds, then voluptuously spouted smoke through his imperial nostrils. After which, his craving momentarily assuaged, he called across the room to his host.

'It's positively prophetic!' He indicated the room with a wave of his hand. 'A fragment of the rational and hygienic future.'

'Thank you,' said John Barnack without looking up. He was laying the table with the same focussed attention, Sebastian

34

noticed, the same exasperatingly meticulous care, as he gave to
all his tasks, from the most important to the humblest—laying it
as though he were manipulating an intricate piece of apparatus
in the laboratory, or (yes, the Professor was quite right) performing the most ticklish of surgical operations.

'All the same,' the other went on with a little laugh, 'where
the arts are concerned, I confess to being sentimental. Give me
yesterday rather than tomorrow. Isabella's apartment at Man-
tova, for example. Much dust, no doubt, in the mouldings.
And all that sculptured wood!' He traced a series of volutes
with the smoke of his burning cigarette. 'Full of archaeological
filth! But what warmth, what wealth!'

'Quite,' said Mr. Barnack. He straightened himself up
and stood there, upright and assertive, looking down at his
guest. 'But whose pockets did the wealth come out of?'
And without waiting for an answer, he marched back to the
kitchen.

But the Professor had only just begun.

'What do *you* think?' he asked, turning to Sebastian. The
words were accompanied by a genial smile; but it became
sufficiently obvious, as he went on, that he took not the smallest
interest in what Sebastian thought. All he wanted was an
audience.

'Perhaps dirt is the necessary condition of beauty,' he continued. 'Perhaps hygiene and art can never be bedfellows.
No Verdi, after all, without spitting into trumpets. No Duse
without a crowd of malodorous bourgeois giving one another
their coryzas. And think of the inexpugnable retreats for
microbes prepared by Michelangelo in the curls of Moses'
beard!'

He paused triumphantly, waiting for applause. Sebastian
gave it in the form of a delighted laugh. The effortless vir-
tuosity of the Professor's talk delighted him; and the Italian
accent, the odd unexpected vocabulary, lent an adventitious
charm to the performance. But as the improvisation prolonged

itself, Sebastian's feelings towards it underwent a change. Five minutes later, he was wishing to God that the old bore would shut up.

It was the smell and sizzling of fried lamb chops which finally produced that much-desired result. The Professor threw back his noble head and sniffed appreciatively.

'Ambrosial!' he cried. 'I see we have a second Baronius among the pots and pans.'

Sebastian, who did not know who the first Baronius was, turned round and looked through the open door into the kitchen. His father was standing with his back to him, his grizzled head and the broad strong shoulders bent forward as he pored over the range.

'Not only a great mind, but a great cook as well,' the Professor was saying.

Yes, that was the trouble, Sebastian reflected. And not only a great cook (though he had the utmost contempt for those who cared about food for its own sake), but also a great desk-tidier, a great mountain-climber, a great account-maker, a great botanizer and bird-watcher, a great letter-answerer, a great socialist, a great four-mile-an-hour walker, teetotaler and non-smoker, a great report-reader and statistics-knower, a great everything, in short, that was tiresome, efficient, meritorious, healthful, social-minded. If only he'd take a rest sometimes! If only his armour had a few chinks in it!

The Professor raised his voice a little, evidently hoping that what he was about to say would be heard even in the kitchen and through the noise of frying.

'And the great mind is associated with an even greater heart and soul,' he pronounced in a tone of vibrant solemnity. He leaned over and laid a small hand, very white except for the yellowed finger-tips, upon Sebastian's knee.

'I hope you're as proud of your father as you ought to be,' he went on.

Sebastian smiled vaguely and made a faint inarticulate noise of assent. But how anyone who knew his father could talk about his great heart, he really couldn't imagine.

'A man who could have aspired to the highest political honours under the old party system—but he had his principles, he refused to play their game. And who knows?' the Professor added parenthetically, with a confidential lowering of the voice. 'Perhaps he'll get his reward very soon. Socialism is much nearer than anyone imagines—and when it comes, when it comes . . .' he raised his hand expressively, as though prophesying Mr. Barnack's apotheosis. 'And when one thinks,' he went on, 'of all those thousands he might have made at the Bar. Thousands and thousands! But he abandons all. Like San Francesco. And what he has, he lavishes with a heroic generosity. Causes, movements, suffering individuals—he gives to all. To all,' he repeated, nodding his noble head emphatically. 'All!'

All but one, Sebastian inwardly amended. There was still money enough for political organizations and, he guessed, for exiled professors; but when it came to sending his own son to a decent school, to getting him a few decent suits and a dinner jacket—nothing doing. Sonorously, the Professor renewed his infuriating eloquence. Almost bursting with suppressed anger, Sebastian was thankful when at last the arrival of the chops cut short the panegyric and set him free.

'Tell Aunt Alice I'll be with her after dinner,' Mr. Barnack called after him as he ran down the stairs. 'And make sure that Uncle Eustace doesn't leave before I get there; I've got to make all sorts of arrangements with him.'

Outside in the street his little squalor of a chapel still darkened up into poetry, into inexplicable significance and beauty; but this time Sebastian felt so bitterly aggrieved that he would not even look at it.

CHAPTER FOUR

SHERRY-GLASS in hand, Eustace Barnack was standing on the hearth-rug, looking up at the portrait of his father over the mantelpiece. From its black background, the square, strong face of that cotton-spinning philanthropist glared out into vacancy like a head-lamp.

Meditatively, Eustace shook his head.

'Hundreds of guineas,' he said. 'That's what the subscribers paid for that object. And you'd be lucky if you could get a fiver for it now. Personally,' he added, turning to where his sister was sitting, slender and very upright, on the sofa, 'personally I'd be very ready to give you ten pounds for the privilege of not possessing it.'

Alice Poulshot said nothing. She was thinking, as she looked at him, how shockingly Eustace had aged since last she saw him. Grosser even than he had been three years ago. And the face was like a loose rubber mask sagging from the bones, flabby and soft and unwholesomely blotched. As for the mouth . . . She remembered the brilliant, laughing boy she had once been so proud of; in him, those parted, childish lips had seemed amusing in their incongruity with the manly stature—amusing and at the same time profoundly touching. You couldn't look at him without feeling that you'd like to mother him. But now —now the sight was enough to make you shudder. The damp, mobile looseness of that mouth, its combination of senility and babyishness, of the infantile with the epicurean! Only in the humorously twinkling eyes could she discover a trace of the Eustace she had loved so much. And now the whites of those eyes were yellow and bloodshot, and under them were pouches of discoloured skin.

With a thick forefinger, Eustace tapped the canvas.

'Wouldn't he be furious if he knew! I remember how bitterly he resented it at the time. All that good money going on a mere picture, when it might have been spent on something really useful, like a drinking-fountain or a public lavatory.'

At the words 'public lavatory,' his nephew, Jim Poulshot, looked up from the *Evening Standard* and uttered a loud guffaw. Eustace turned and regarded him curiously.

'That's right, my boy,' he said with mock heartiness. 'It's English humour that has made the Empire what it is.'

He walked over to the sofa and cautiously lowered his soft bulk into a sitting posture. Mrs. Poulshot moved further into the corner to give him room.

'Poor old father!' he said, continuing the previous conversation.

'What's poor about him?' Alice asked rather sharply. 'I should have thought we were the poor ones. After all, he accomplished something. Where's our achievement, I'd like to know?'

'Where?' Eustace repeated. 'Well, certainly not in the rubbish-heap, which is where *his* is. The mills working half-time because of Indian and Japanese competition. Individual paternalism replaced by State interference, which he regarded as the devil. The Liberal Party dead and buried. And earnest high-minded rationalism transformed into cynical libertinage. If the old man isn't to be pitied, I'd like to know who is?'

'It's not the results that matter,' said Mrs. Poulshot, changing her ground.

She had worshipped her father; and to defend a memory which she still reverenced as something all but divine, she was ready to sacrifice much more than mere logical consistency.

'It's motives, and intentions and hard work—yes, and self-denial,' she added significantly.

Eustace uttered a wheezy chuckle.

'Whereas *I*'m disgustingly self-indulgent,' he said. 'And if I happen to be fat, it's entirely my own vicious fault. Has it ever struck you, my dear, that if Mother had lived, she'd have probably grown to be as big as Uncle Charles?'

'How can you say such things!' cried Mrs. Poulshot indignantly. Uncle Charles had been a monster.

'It was in the family,' he answered; and patting his belly complacently, 'It still is,' he added.

The sound of a door being opened made him turn his head.

'Aha,' he cried, 'here comes my future guest!'

Still brooding on his reasons for being angry and miserable, Sebastian looked up with a start. Uncle Eustace . . . in his preoccupation with his own affairs he had forgotten all about him. He stood there, gaping.

'"In vacant or in pensive mood,"' Eustace continued genially. 'It's all in the great poetical tradition.'

Sebastian advanced and shook the hand extended to him. It was soft, rather damp and surprisingly cold. The realization that he was making a deplorable impression just at the very moment when he ought to have been at his best, increased his shyness to the point of rendering him speechless. But his mind continued to work. In that expanse of flabby face the little eyes, he thought, were like an elephant's. An elegant little elephant in a double-breasted black coat and pale-grey check trousers. Oh, and even a monocle on the end of a string to make him look still more like the elderly dandy on the musical comedy stage!

Eustace turned to his sister.

'He gets more and more like Rosie every year,' he said. 'It's fantastic.'

Mrs. Poulshot nodded without speaking. Sebastian's mother was a subject which it was best, she thought, to avoid.

'Well, Sebastian, I hope you're prepared for a pretty strenuous holiday.' Once again Eustace patted his stomach. 'You see before you the world's champion sight-seer. Author of "Canters through Florence," "The Vatican on Roller Skates," "Round the Louvre in Eighty Minutes." And my speed record for the English cathedrals has never even been challenged.'

40

'Idiot!' said Mrs. Poulshot, laughing.

Jim roared in unison, and in spite of the dinner jacket, Sebastian couldn't help joining in. The idea of this dandified elephant galloping through Canterbury in sponge-bag trousers and a monocle was irresistibly grotesque.

Noiselessly, in the midst of their merriment, the door swung open again. Grey, lugubrious, long-faced like a horse, like his own image in a distorting mirror, Fred Poulshot entered as though on soles of felt. Catching sight of him, Jim and Sebastian checked themselves abruptly. He walked over to the sofa to greet his brother-in-law.

'You're looking well,' said Eustace as they shook hands.

'Well?' Mr. Poulshot repeated in an offended tone. 'Get Alice to tell you about my sinus some time.'

He turned away, and, with the scrupulous care of one who measures out a purgative, poured himself one-third of a glass of sherry.

Eustace looked at him and felt, as he had so often done in the past, profoundly sorry for poor Alice. Thirty years of Fred Poulshot—imagine it! Well, such was family life. He felt very thankful that he was now alone in the world.

Susan's headlong entrance at this moment did nothing to mitigate his thankfulness. True, she possessed the enormous adventitious advantage of being seventeen; but even the perverse and slightly comic charms of adolescence could not disguise the fact that she was a Poulshot and, like all the other Poulshots, unutterably dull. The most that could be said for her was that, up to the present at any rate, she was a cut above Jim. But then, at twenty-five, poor Jim was just an empty pigeon-hole waiting to be occupied by the moderately successful stockbroker he would be in 1949. Well, that was what came of choosing a father like Fred. Whereas Sebastian had had the wit to get himself sired by a Barnack and conceived by the loveliest of irresponsible gipsies.

'Did you tell him about my sinus?' Mr. Poulshot insisted.

But Alice pretended not to have heard him.

'Talking of canters through Florence,' she said rather loudly, 'do you ever see Cousin Mary's son when you're out there?'

'You mean Bruno Rontini?'

Mrs. Poulshot nodded.

'Why on earth she should ever have married that Italian I simply cannot imagine,' she said in a tone of disapproval.

'But even Italians are very nearly human.'

'Don't be silly, Eustace. You know exactly what I mean.'

'But how you'd hate it if I were to tell you!' said Eustace, smiling.

For what she meant, of course, was just plain prejudice and snobbery—an insular dislike of foreigners, a bourgeois conviction that all unsuccessful people must be in some way immoral.

'Father was endlessly kind to the man,' Mrs. Poulshot went on. 'When I think of all the opportunities he gave him!'

'And wise old Carlo made a mess of every one of them!'

'Wise?'

'Well, he got himself paid four pounds a week to keep out of the cotton business and go back to Tuscany. Don't you call that wisdom?'

Eustace drank the rest of his sherry and put down the glass.

'The son still runs his second-hand bookshop,' he went on. 'I'm really very fond of funny old Bruno. In spite of that tiresome religiosity of his. Nothing but the Gaseous Vertebrate!'

Mrs. Poulshot laughed. In the Barnack family, Haeckel's definition of God had been a standing joke for the past forty years.

'The Gaseous Vertebrate,' she repeated. 'But then, think how he was brought up! Cousin Mary used to take him to those Quaker meetings of hers when he was a boy. *Quakers!*' she repeated with a kind of incredulous emphasis.

The parlour-maid appeared and announced that dinner was served. Active and wiry, Alice was on her feet in an instant.

Her brother hoisted himself up more painfully. Followed by the rest of the family, they moved towards the door. Mr. Poulshot walked over to the electric switches and, as the last person crossed the threshold, turned out the lights.

As they went downstairs to the dining-room, Eustace laid a hand on Sebastian's shoulder.

'I had the devil of a time persuading your father to let you come and stay with me,' he said. 'He was afraid you'd learn to live like the idle rich. Luckily, we were able to checkmate him with an appeal to culture—weren't we, Alice?'

Mrs. Poulshot nodded a little stiffly. She didn't like her brother's habit of discussing grown-up affairs in front of the children.

'Florence is part of a liberal education,' she said.

'Exactly. What Every Young Boy Ought to Know.'

Suddenly the staircase lights went out. Even in his blackest moods, Fred never forgot to be economical.

They entered the dining-room—red-papered still, Eustace noticed, and as uncompromisingly hideous as ever—and took their seats.

'Mock turtle,' said Alice as the parlour-maid set down the soup in front of him.

Mock turtle—it would be! Dear Alice had always displayed a positive genius for serving the dreariest kind of English food. On principle. With a smile at once affectionate and faintly ironic, Eustace laid a thick oedematous hand over his sister's bony fingers.

'Well, my dear, it's been a long, long time since last I sat here at your festive board.'

'No fault of mine,' Mrs. Poulshot answered. Her voice took on a note of rather sharp and perky jocularity. 'The Prodigal's place was always laid for him. But I suppose he was too busy filling his belly with the caviar that the swine did eat.'

Eustace laughed with unaffected good-humour. Twenty-three years before, he had given up what everybody said was a most promising career in radical politics to marry a rich widow with a weak heart, and retire to Florence. It was an act which neither his sister nor his brother, though for different reasons, had ever forgiven. With John it was a matter of outraged political principle. But what Alice resented was the insult to her father's memory, the wound inflicted on her family pride. Theirs was the third generation of low-living, high-minded Barnacks; and, with the exception of unmentionable Great-Uncle Luke, Eustace was the first who had ever gone over to the hostile camp of luxury and leisure.

'*Ve-ry* pretty,' he said to her in the phrase and tone of one who applauds a particularly well directed stroke at billiards.

With an income of six thousand a year, he could afford to be magnanimous. Besides, his conscience had never troubled him for what he had done. For the five years of their brief married life he had been as good a husband as poor dear Amy could expect. And why any quick-witted and sensitive person should feel ashamed of having said good-bye to politics, he couldn't imagine. The sordid intrigues behind the scenes! The conscious or unconscious hypocrisy of every form of effective public speaking! The asinine stupidity of that interminable repetition of the same absurd over-simplifications, the same illogical arguments and vulgar personalities, the same bad history and baseless prophecy! And that was supposed to be a man's highest duty. And if he chose instead the life of a civilized human being, he ought to be ashamed of himself.

'*Ve-ry* pretty,' he repeated. 'But what an implacable Puritan you are, my dear! And without the smallest metaphysical justification.'

'Metaphysics!' said Mrs. Poulshot in the contemptuous tone of one who is above and beyond such fooleries.

The soup plates, meanwhile, had been cleared away and the saddle of mutton brought in. In silence and without in any way altering his expression of irremediable suffering, Mr. Poulshot set to work to carve the roast.

Eustace glanced at him, then back at Alice. She, poor thing, was looking at Fred with an expression of apprehensive distress —wishing, no doubt, that the sulky old baby would be on his good behaviour in front of strangers. And perhaps, Eustace went on to reflect, perhaps that was why she had been so sharp towards himself. White-washing her husband by black-washing her brother. Not very logical, no doubt, but all too human.

'I hope it's cooked as you like it, Fred,' she called down the table.

Without answering or even looking up, Mr. Poulshot shrugged his narrow shoulders.

With an effort, Mrs. Poulshot adjusted her expression and turned to Eustace.

'Poor Fred has such a dreadful time with his sinus,' she said, trying to make amends to her husband for what she had done in the drawing-room.

As old Ellen came in with the vegetables, a half-grown kitten slipped into the room and came to rub itself against the leg of Alice's chair. She stooped and picked it up.

'Well, Onyegin,' she said, tickling the little beast behind the ears. 'We call him Onyegin,' she explained brightly to her brother, 'because he's the masterpiece of our late-lamented Puss-kin.'

Eustace smiled politely.

The consolations of philosophy, he reflected, of religion, of art, of love, of politics—none of these for poor dear Alice. No, hers were the consolations of an Edwardian sense of humour and the weekly copy of *Punch*. Still it was better to make bad puns and be whimsical in the style of 1912 than to indulge in self-pity or capitulate to Fred's black moods, as everyone else at the table had done. And, by God, it was pretty difficult not to capitulate. Sitting there behind his bulwark of mutton, Fred Poulshot fairly beamed with negativity. You could positively *feel* it as it beat against you—a steady, penetrating radiation that was the very antithesis of life, the total denial of all human warmth. Eustace decided to attempt a diversion.

'Well, Fred!' he called out in his jolliest tone. 'How's that City of yours? How's the gorgeous East? Business pretty good?'

Mr. Poulshot looked up, pained but, after a moment, forgiving.

'It could hardly be worse,' he pronounced.

Eustace raised his eyebrows in mock alarm.

'Heavens! How's that going to affect my Yangtze and South China Bank dividends?'

'They talk of reducing them this year.'

'Oh dear!'

'From eighty per cent. to seventy-five per cent.,' said Mr. Poulshot gloomily; and turning away to help himself to the vegetables, he relapsed once more into a silence that engulfed the entire table.

How much less awful the man would be, Eustace was thinking, as he ate his mutton and brussels sprouts, if only he sometimes lost his temper, or got drunk, or went to bed with his secretary—though God help the poor secretary if he did! But there had never been anything violent or extreme in Fred's behaviour. Except for being absolutely intolerable, he was the perfect husband. One who loved the routine of marriage and domestic life—carving mutton, begetting children—just as he loved the routine of being (what was it?) Secretary and Treasurer of that City and Far Eastern thingummy-bob. And in all that concerned these routines, he was the soul of probity and regularity. Swear, get angry, deceive poor dear Alice with another woman? Why, he'd as soon embezzle the company's petty cash. No, no, Fred took it out of people in a very different way. He didn't have to *do* anything; it was enough for him just to *be*. They shrivelled and turned black by mere infection.

Suddenly Mr. Poulshot broke the long silence, and in a dead, toneless voice asked for the red-currant jelly.

Startled as though by a summons from the other world, Jim looked wildly round the table.

'Here you are, Jim.' Eustace Barnack pushed the dish across to him.

Jim gave him a grateful look, and passed it on to his father. Mr. Poulshot took it without a word or a smile, helped himself, and then, with the evident intention of involving another victim in this rite of woe, handed it back, not to Jim, but to Susan, who was in the very act of raising her fork from her plate. As he had foreseen and desired, Mr. Poulshot had to wait, dish in hand and with an expression on his face of martyred patience, while Susan hastily poked the mutton into her mouth, put down her knife and fork with a clatter and, blushing crimson, accepted the proffered jelly.

From his front-row seat at the human comedy, Eustace smiled appreciatively. What an exquisite refinement of the will to power, what elegant cruelty! And what an amazing gift for that contagious gloom which damps even the highest spirits and stifles the very possibility of joy. Well, nobody could accuse dear Fred of having buried his talent.

Silence, as though there were a coffin in the room, settled all at once upon the table. Mrs. Poulshot tried desperately to think of something to say—something bright, something defiantly funny—but could find nothing, nothing at all. Fred had broken through her defences and stopped up the source of speech, of life itself, with sand and ashes. She sat there empty, conscious only of the awful fatigue accumulated during thirty years of unremitting defence and counter-attack. And as though it had somehow become aware of her defeat, the kitten sleeping on her knee uncurled itself, stretched and jumped noiselessly to the floor.

'Onyegin!' she cried, and reached out a hand; but the little cat slid away, silky and serpentine, from under her fingers. If she had been less old and sensible, Mrs. Poulshot would have burst into tears.

The silence lengthened out, punctuated by the ticking, now for the first time audible, of the brass clock on the mantelpiece. Eustace, who had begun by thinking that it would be amusing to see how long the intolerable situation could last, found himself suddenly overcome by pity and indignation. Alice needed help, and it would be monstrous if that creature there, that tapeworm, were left to enjoy his triumph. He leaned back in his chair, wiped his mouth and, looking about him, gaily smiled.

'Cheer up, Sebastian,' he called across the table. 'I hope you're not going to be glum like this when you're staying with *me* next week.'

The spell was broken. Alice Poulshot's fatigue dropped away from her, and she found it once more possible to speak.

'You forget,' she broke in waggishly, as the boy tried to mumble something in response to his uncle's challenge, 'our little Sebastian's got the poetic temperament.' And rolling her r's like an old-fashioned reciter, she added, '"Tear-rs from the depth of some divine despair-r."'

Sebastian flushed and bit his lip. He was very fond of Aunt Alice—as fond of her as she herself would ever allow anyone to be. And yet, in spite of his affection, there were times—and this was one of them—when he would have liked to kill her. It wasn't merely himself that she outraged with this sort of remark; it was beauty, poetry, genius, everything above the level of the commonplace and the conventional.

Eustace observed the expression of his nephew's face, and felt sorry for the poor boy. Alice could be curiously hard, he reflected—on principle, just as she preferred bad cooking. Tactfully, he tried to change the subject. Alice had quoted Tennyson; what did the young think of Tennyson nowadays?

But Mrs. Poulshot did not permit the subject to be changed. She had undertaken Sebastian's education, and if she allowed him to indulge his native moodiness, she wouldn't be doing her duty. It was because that silly mother of his had always given in to him that Fred now behaved as he did.

'Or perhaps,' she went on, her tone growing more flippant as her intention became more severely didactic, 'perhaps it's a case of first love. "Deep as first love, and wild with all regret." Unless, of course, it's Epsom Salts that the poor boy needs.'

At this reference to Epsom Salts, young Jim broke into a peal of laughter all the more explosive because of the constraint imposed upon him by his proximity to the source of gloom behind the mutton. Susan glanced with solicitude at Sebastian's reddening face, then frowned angrily at her brother, who didn't even notice it.

'I'll cap your Tennyson with some Dante,' said Eustace, coming once again to Sebastian's relief. 'Do you remember? In the fifth circle of Hell:

> *Tristi fummo*
> *Nell' aer dolce che del sol s'allegra.*

And because they were sad, they were condemned to pass eternity stuck there in the swamp; and their horrid little *Weltschmerz* came bubbling up through the mud, like marsh gas. So you'd better be careful, my lad,' he concluded mock-menacingly, but with a smile which signified that he was entirely on Sebastian's side, and understood his feelings.

'He needn't bother about the next world,' said Mrs. Poulshot with a touch of asperity. She felt strongly about this immortality nonsense—so strongly that she didn't like to hear it talked about, even in joke. 'I'm thinking about what'll happen to him when he's grown up.'

Jim laughed again. Sebastian's youthfulness seemed to him almost as funny as his possible need of a purge.

That second laugh spurred Mr. Poulshot into action. Eustace, of course, was just a hedonist, and even from Alice he could really expect nothing better. She had always (it was her only failing, but how enormous!) proved herself shockingly insensitive to his inner sufferings. But Jim, happily, was different. Unlike Edward and Marjorie, who in this respect were altogether too like their mother, Jim had always shown a decent respect and sympathy. That he should now so far forget himself as to laugh twice, was therefore doubly painful—painful as an outrage to his sensibilities and an interruption to his sad and sacred thoughts; painful, too, because so disappointing, such a blow to one's faith in the boy's better nature. Raising the eyes which he had kept so resolutely fixed upon his plate, Mr. Poulshot looked at his son with an expression of sorrow. Jim flinched away from that reproachful regard and, to cover his confusion, filled his mouth with bread. Almost in a whisper, Mr. Poulshot spoke at last.

'Do you know what day this is?' he asked.

Anticipating the rebuke that was to come, Jim blushed and muttered indistinctly through the bread that he thought it was the twenty-seventh.

'March the twenty-seventh,' Mr. Poulshot repeated. He nodded slowly and emphatically. 'This day, eleven years ago, your poor grandfather was taken from us.' He looked fixedly for a few seconds into Jim's face, observing with satisfaction the symptoms of his discomfiture, then dropped his eyes and lapsed once again into silence, leaving the young man to feel ashamed of himself.

At the other end of the table Alice and Eustace were laughing together over reminiscences of their childhood. Mr. Poulshot did his best to pity them for the frivolity that made them so heartlessly insensitive to the finer feelings of others. 'Forgive them, for they know not what they do,' he said to himself; then, closing his mind against their idle chatter, he addressed himself to the task of reconstructing in detail his negotiations, on the evening of March the twenty-seventh, 1918, with the undertaker.

CHAPTER FIVE

IN the drawing-room, when dinner was over, Jim and Susan settled down to chess, while the others grouped themselves around the fire. Fascinated, Sebastian looked on, while his Uncle Eustace lighted the massive Romeo and Juliet which, knowing Alice's principles and Fred's economical habits, he had prudently brought with him. First the ritual of piercing; then, as he raised the cigar to his mouth, the smile of happy anticipation. Damply, lovingly, the lips closed over the butt; the match was ignited; he pulled at the flame. And suddenly Sebastian was reminded of his cousin Marjorie's baby, nuzzling with blind concupiscence for the nipple, seizing it at last between the soft prehensile flaps of its little mouth and working away, working away in a noiseless frenzy of enjoyment. True, Uncle Eustace had rather better manners; and in this case the nipple was coffee-coloured and six inches long. Images floated up before his mind's eye; words, grotesque and mock-heroic, started to arrange themselves:

Old but an infant, mouthing with lustful lip
The wet brown teat, incarnate where he sucks,
Of some imaginary, largest Queen
Of all the Hottentots . . .

He was interrupted by the sudden opening and then the slam of the door. John Barnack entered the room, and strode over to where Mrs. Poulshot was sitting on the sofa.

'Sorry I couldn't be with you for dinner,' he said, laying his hand on her shoulder. 'But it was my only chance of seeing Cacciaguida. Who tells me, by the way,' he added, turning to his brother, 'that Mussolini has definitely got cancer of the throat.'

Eustace took the tobacco-teat from between his lips and smiled indulgently.

'It's the throat this time, is it? *My* anti-fascists seem to prefer the liver.'

John Barnack was offended, but made an effort not to show it.

'Cacciaguida has very reliable sources of information,' he said a little stiffly.

'Don't I remember somebody saying something about wishes being fathers to thoughts?' Eustace asked with exasperating mildness.

'Of course you do,' said John. 'You remember it because you need an excuse for disparaging a great political cause and belittling its heroes.' He spoke in his usual measured and perfectly articulated style, but in a tone that betrayed his inner feelings by being a trifle louder and more vibrant than usual. 'Cynical realism—it's the intelligent man's best excuse for doing nothing in an intolerable situation.'

Alice Poulshot glanced from one to the other and wished to goodness that her two brothers didn't have to quarrel every time they met. Why couldn't John just accept the fact that Eustace was a bit of an old pig, and have done with it? But, no; he always lost his temper in that awful suppressed way of his, and then pretended it was moral indignation. And on his side Eustace deliberately provoked the explosions by waving political red rags and throwing poisoned darts. They were really incorrigible.

'King Log or King Stork?' Eustace was saying blandly. 'I'm for dear old Log every time. Just keeping out of mischief —it's the greatest of all the virtues.'

Standing there by the fireplace, his arms hanging by his sides, his feet apart, his body very straight and tense, in the posture of an athlete poised on the brink of action, John Barnack looked down at his brother with the calm unwavering regard which, in the law courts, he reserved for hostile witnesses and prevaricating defendants. It was a look which, even when directed on someone else, filled Sebastian with a shrinking terror. But Eustace merely let himself sink more deeply into the upholstery of the sofa. Closing his eyes, he tenderly kissed the end of his cigar and sucked.

'And you imagine, I suppose,' said John Barnack after a long silence, 'that you're one of the great exponents of that virtue?'

Eustace blew out a cloud of aromatic smoke, and answered that he did his best.

'You do your best,' John repeated. 'But I believe you've got a comfortable holding in the Yangtze and South China Bank?'

Eustace nodded.

'And along with the right to fatten on exploitation in China and Japan, a lot of jute shares—isn't that so?'

'Very nice shares too,' said Eustace.

'Very nice indeed. Thirty per cent. even in a bad year. Earned for you by Indians who are getting paid a daily wage that wouldn't buy more than a third of one of your cigars.'

Mr. Poulshot, who had sat in gloomy silence, disregarded by all, startlingly broke into the conversation.

'They were all right until the agitators got to work on them,' he said. 'Organizing unions, stirring up trouble against the owners. They ought to be shot. Yes, they ought to be shot!' he repeated with ferocious emphasis.

John Barnack smiled ironically.

'Don't you worry, Fred. The City of London will see to it.'

'What *are* you talking about?' said Alice irritably. 'The City of London isn't in India.'

'No; but its agents are. And they're the fellows with the machine-guns. Fred's agitators will duly get shot, and Eustace here will go on keeping out of mischief—keeping out of it with all the inimitable grace we've learnt to admire in him.'

There was a silence. Sebastian, who had dearly hoped to see his father discomfited, glanced miserably in the direction of his uncle. But instead of sitting there crushed and dejected, Eustace was heaving with noiseless laughter.

'Admirable!' he cried, when he had recovered breath enough to speak. 'Quite admirable! And now, John, you should drop the sarcasm and give them five minutes of simple pathos and indignation; five heart-warming minutes of straightforward manly sentiment. After which the jury finds me guilty without even leaving the box, and adds a rider recommending that counsel for the plaintiffs be appointed Tribune of the People. Tribune of the People,' he repeated sonorously. 'All in classical fancy dress. And, by the way, what's the technical name for that noble Roman toga that political gentlemen drape over the will-to-power when they want to make it look respectable? You know that, don't you, Sebastian?' And when Sebastian shook his head, 'Goodness,' he exclaimed, 'what *do* they teach you nowadays? Why, its technical name is Idealism. Yes, my dear,' he went on, addressing himself to Susan, who had looked up, startled, from her game of chess, 'that was what I said: Idealism.'

John Barnack yawned ostentatiously behind his hand.

'One gets a bit bored with this kind of cheap seventeenth-century psychology,' he said.

'And now tell us,' said Eustace, 'what do you expect to get when the right people come into power? The Attorney-Generalship, I suppose.'

'Now, Eustace,' said Mrs. Poulshot firmly, 'that's enough.'

'Enough?' Eustace repeated in a tone of mock-outrage. 'You think it's enough—a piddling little Attorney-Generalship? My dear, you underrate your brother. But now, John,' he added, in another tone, 'let's get down to more serious matters. I don't know what *your* plans are; but whatever happens, I've got to leave for Florence tomorrow. I'm expecting my mother-in-law on Tuesday.'

'Old Mrs. Gamble?' Alice looked up from her knitting in surprise. 'Do you mean to say *she* still travels about Europe? At *her* age?'

'Eighty-six,' said Eustace, 'and, except for being pretty well blind with cataract, as fit as a fiddle.'

'Goodness!' exclaimed Mrs. Poulshot. 'I do hope *I* don't

have to hang on as long as that!' She shook her head emphatically, appalled by the thought of thirty-one more years of housekeeping, and Fred's black moods, and the utter pointlessness of everything.

Eustace turned back to his brother.

'And when do you two intend to start?'

'Next Thursday. But we spend a night in Turin. I have to get in touch with some of Cacciaguida's people,' John explained.

'Then you'll deliver Sebastian to me on Saturday?'

'Or rather he'll deliver himself. I'm getting off the train at Genoa.'

'Oh, you don't deign to come yourself?'

John Barnack shook his head. The boat was leaving Genoa that same evening. He'd be in Egypt for three or four weeks. Then his paper wanted him to report on the condition of the natives in Kenya and Tanganyika.

'And while you're about it,' said Eustace, 'do find out why my East African coffee shares aren't doing better.'

'I can tell you here and now,' his brother answered. 'A few years ago there was a lot of money in coffee. Result: millions of acres of new plantations, with all the Gadarene swine of London and Paris and Amsterdam and New York rushing down a steep place into coffee investments. Now there's such a surplus of beans, and the price is so low, that even sweated black labour can't give you a dividend.'

'Too bad!'

'You think so? Wait till your keeping out of mischief has brought on rebellion among the subject peoples and revolution at home!'

'Luckily,' said Eustace, 'we shall all be dead by that time.'

'Don't you be too sure.'

'We may all hang on like poor old Mrs. Gamble,' said Alice, who had been trying to imagine what Fred and she would be like in 1950.

'No need for that,' said John Barnack with manifest satisfaction. 'It's coming a great deal sooner than any of you imagine.' He looked at his watch. 'Well, I've got some work to do,' he announced. 'And tomorrow I must be up at cockcrow. So I'll say good-night, Alice.'

Sebastian's heart started to beat violently, he felt all at once rather sick. The moment had come at last, the absolutely final opportunity. He drew a deep breath, got up and walked over to where his father was standing.

'Good-night, father,' he said; and then, 'Oh, by the way,' he brought out in the most casual tone he could command, 'don't you think I might . . . I mean, don't you think I really ought to have some evening clothes now?'

'Ought?' his father repeated. 'Ought? It's a case of the Categorical Imperative, eh?' And suddenly, alarmingly, he uttered a short explosive bray of laughter.

Overwhelmed, Sebastian mumbled something to the effect that it hadn't been necessary when he asked last time; but now . . . now it was really urgent: he had been asked to a party.

'Oh, you've been asked to a party,' said Mr. Barnack; and he recalled the ecstatic tone in which Rosie used to pronounce that hated word; he remembered the brightening of her eyes as she heard the music and the confused roaring of the crowd, the all but frenzy of her wild gaiety as the evening progressed.

'More and more categorical,' he added sarcastically.

'Your father's had a lot of expense recently,' Mrs. Poulshot interposed in a well-meant effort to cushion poor Sebastian against the impact of her brother's intransigence. After all, it hadn't been Rosie's fault entirely. John had always been hard and exacting, even as a boy. And now, to make things worse, he had to poison people's lives with these ridiculous political principles of his. But meanwhile the hardness and the principles were facts; and so was Sebastian's sensitiveness. Her policy was to try to keep the two sets of facts from colliding. But the attempt, on this occasion, was worse than fruitless.

'My dear Alice,' said John Barnack in the tone of a courteous

56

but absolutely determined debater, 'it isn't a question of whether I can *afford* to buy the boy his fancy dress.' (The words evoked an image of the red velvet breeches of Lady Caroline Lamb as Byron's—as young Tom Hilliard's—page.) 'The point at issue is whether it's *right* to do so.'

Eustace took the teat out of his mouth to protest that this was worse than Savonarola.

John Barnack emphatically shook his head.

'It has nothing in common with Christian asceticism, it's just a question of decency—of not exploiting one's accidental advantages. *Noblesse oblige.*'

'Very nice,' said Eustace. 'But meanwhile, you begin by *oblige*-ing the *noblesse*. It's just plain coercion.'

'Sebastian has absolutely no sense of social responsibility. He's got to learn it.'

'Isn't that exactly what Mussolini says about the Italian people?'

'And anyhow,' Mrs. Poulshot put in, glad of this opportunity of fighting Sebastian's battle with the support of an ally, 'why make all this fuss about a miserable dinner jacket?'

'A paltry *smoking*,' Eustace elaborated in a tone that was meant to shift the whole argument on to the level of mere farce, 'a twopenny-halfpenny Tuxedo. Oh, and that reminds me of my young man of Peoria—you didn't know I was a poet, did you, Sebastian?

> *Who to keep up his sense of euphoria*
> *Would don his Tuxedo*
> *And murmur the Credo,*
> *Along with the Sanctus and Gloria.*

And here you go, John, depriving your poor child of the benefit of the sacraments.'

More loudly than usual, because of his nervousness, Sebastian started to laugh; then, at the sight of his father's grave, unsmiling face and resolutely closed lips, he checked himself abruptly.

Eustace twinkled at him between his puffy eyelids.

'Thank you for the applause,' he said. 'But I'm afraid we are *not* amused.'

Mrs. Poulshot intervened once more, in an attempt to undo the effects of Eustace's false step.

'After all,' she said, trying to bring the discussion back to seriousness, 'what *is* evening dress? Nothing but a silly little convention.'

'Silly, I grant you,' said John in his measured, judicious way. 'But when it involves a class symbol, no convention can be called little.'

'But, Father,' Sebastian broke in, 'all the boys of my age have got evening clothes.' His voice was shrill and unsteady with emotion.

Bent over the chess-board, Susan heard it, recognized the danger signal, and at once raised her eyes. Sebastian's face was darkly flushed, and his lips had started to tremble. More than ever he looked like a little boy. A little boy in distress, a helpless little boy to whom a grown-up is being cruel. Susan was overwhelmed by loving pity. But what a mess he was making of the whole business! she thought, feeling suddenly furious with him, not in despite of her love and pity, but precisely because she cared so much. And why on earth couldn't he use a little self-control, or if that was impossible, just keep his mouth shut?

For a few seconds John Barnack looked in silence at his son—looked intently at the image of the childish wife who had betrayed him, and was now dead. Then he smiled sarcastically.

'*All* the other boys,' he repeated, 'every single one.' And, in the tone he employed in court to discredit the other side's star witness, he added, contemptuously ironic: 'In South Wales the sons of the unemployed miners make a point of wearing tails and white ties. Not to mention gardenias in their buttonholes. And now,' he commanded peremptorily, 'go to bed, and don't ever talk to me about this foolery again.'

Sebastian turned and, speechless, hurried out of the room.

'Your play,' said Jim impatiently.

Susan looked down again, saw the black knight standing immediately in front of her queen and took it.

'Got him!' she said ferociously. The black knight was Uncle John.

Triumphantly, Jim moved a castle across the board and, as he dropped her queen into the box, shouted, 'Check!'

Three-quarters of an hour later, in her pyjamas, Susan was squatting on the floor in front of the gas fire in her bedroom, writing her diary. 'B+ for History, B for Algebra. Which might be worse. Miss C. gave me a bad mark for untidiness, but of course didn't say a word to her beloved Gladys. *Really! ! !* Scarlatti went better, but Pfeiffy tried to be funny with S. about cigars, and then Tom B. met us and asked him to come to his party, and S. was miserable about his wretched dinner jacket. Otherwise I should have hated him because he was with Mrs. E. again today and she was wearing *black lace* next her skin. But I only felt dreadfully sorry for him. And this evening Uncle J. was *horrible* about the dinner jacket; I really hate him sometimes. Uncle E. tried to stick up for S., but it wasn't any good.'

It wasn't any good, and what made it worse was that she had to sit there, waiting till first Uncle John and then Uncle Eustace took leave; and even when she had been free to go to bed, she hadn't dared to go and comfort him, for fear her mother or Jim might hear her and come up and find her in his room, and, if it were Jim, guffaw as though he had seen her in the lavatory, or if her mother, make some little jocular remark that would be worse than death. But now—she looked at the clock on the mantelpiece—now it ought to be safe. She got up, locked the diary into the drawer of her writing-desk and hid the key in its usual place behind the looking-glass. Then she turned out the light, cautiously opened the door, and looked out. The lights on the lower landings had been extinguished; the house was so still that she could hear the heavy beating of her own heart. Three steps brought her to the door on the other side of the landing; the handle turned noiselessly, and noiselessly she slipped in. The room was not entirely dark; for the blinds had not been drawn, and the lamp across the street threw an oblong of greenish twilight across the ceiling. Susan closed the door behind her and stood, listening—listening at first only to her own heart. Then the springs of the bed creaked faintly, and there was the sound of a long sobbing inhalation of breath. He was crying. Impulsively, she moved forward; her outstretched hand touched a brass rail, moved to the blanket beyond, and, from wool, slid over to the smoothness of the turned-back sheet. The white linen was ghostly in the darkness, and against the dimly seen pillow Sebastian's head was a black silhouette. Her fingers touched the nape of his neck.

'It's me, Sebastian.'

'Get away,' he muttered angrily. 'Get away!'

Susan said nothing, but sat down on the edge of the bed. The little bristles left by the barber's clippers were electrical against her finger-tips.

'You mustn't mind, Sebastian darling,' she whispered. 'You mustn't let yourself be hurt.'

She was patronizing him, of course; she was treating him like a child. But he was utterly miserable; and besides, humiliation had gone so far that he no longer had the energy of pride to keep up his resentment. He lay still, permitting himself to enjoy the comforting reassurance of her proximity.

Susan lifted her hand from his neck and held it poised in mid-air, breathlessly hesitant. Did she dare? Would he be furious if she did? Her heart thumped yet more violently against her ribs. Then, swallowing hard, she made up her mind to risk it. Slowly the lifted hand moved forwards and downwards through the darkness, until the fingers were touching his hair—that pale bright hair, curly and wind-ruffled, but now invisible, no more now than a scarcely perceptible unravelling of living silk against her skin. She waited tremulously, expecting every moment to hear his angry command to let him alone. But no sound came, and, emboldened by his silence, she lowered her hand a little further.

Inert, Sebastian abandoned himself to the tenderness which at ordinary times he would never allow her to express, and in the very act of self-abandonment found a certain consolation. Suddenly and irrelevantly, it came into his mind that this was one of the situations he had always looked forward to in his dream of a love-affair with Mary Esdaile—or whatever other name one chose to give the dark-haired mistress of his imagination. He would lie there inert in the darkness, and she would kneel beside the bed, stroking his hair; and sometimes she would bend down and kiss him—or perhaps it wouldn't be her lips on his, but the touch of her naked breast. But, of course, this was only Susan, not Mary Esdaile.

She was running her hand through his hair now, openly, undisguisedly, just as she had always longed to do—the finger-tips passing from the smooth taut skin behind the ears, pushing their way among the roots of his hair, while the thick resilient curls slid along between the fingers as she moved her hand up to the crown of his head. Again, again, indefatigably.

'Sebastian?' she whispered at last; but he did not answer, and his breathing was almost imperceptibly soft.

With eyes that had grown accustomed to the darkness, she looked down at the sleeping face, and the happiness she experienced, the unutterable bliss, was like what she had sometimes felt while she was holding Marjorie's baby, but with all these other things added—this desire and apprehension, this breathless sense of forbiddenness, as she felt the electrical contact of his hair against her finger-tips, this aching pleasure in her breasts. Bending down, she touched his cheek with her lips. Sebastian stirred a little, but did not wake.

'Darling,' she repeated and, sure that he could not hear her, 'my love, my precious love.'

CHAPTER SIX

EUSTACE woke up, that Saturday morning, at a few minutes before nine, after a night of dreamless sleep, induced by nothing stronger in the way of narcotics than a pint of stout taken at midnight, with two or three small anchovy sandwiches.

Waking was painful, of course; but the taste in his mouth was less brassy, and that tired ache in all his limbs decidedly less acute than it ordinarily was at this black hour of the morning. True, he coughed a bit and brought up some phlegm; but the exhausting paroxysm was over more quickly than usual. After his early cup of tea and a hot bath he felt positively young again.

Beyond the circular shaving-mirror and the image of his lathered face lay the city of Florence, framed between the cypresses of his descending terraces. Over Monte Morello hung fat clouds, like the backsides of Correggio's cherubs at Parma; but the rest of the sky was flawlessly blue, and in the flower-beds below the bathroom window the hyacinths were like carved jewels in the sunlight, white jade and lapis-lazuli and pale-pink coral.

'The pearl-grey,' he called out to his valet without looking round, and then paused to wonder which tie would go best with the suit and the gay weather. A black-and-white check? But that would be too much the jaunty stockbroker. No; what the place and time required was something in the style of those tartans on a white ground from the Burlington Arcade. Or better still, that delicious salmon-pink fellow from Sulka's. 'And the pink tie,' he added, 'the new one.'

There were white and yellow roses on the breakfast table. Really quite prettily arranged! Guido was beginning to learn. He pulled out a virginal white bud and stuck it in his buttonhole, then addressed himself to his hot-house grapes. A bowl of porridge followed, then two poached eggs on toast, a kipper and some scones and marmalade.

As he ate, he read his letters.

A note, first of all, from Bruno Rontini. Was he back in Florence? And, if so, why not drop in at the shop one day for a chat and a glance at the books? A catalogue of the new arrivals was enclosed.

Then there were two charity appeals from England—those beastly Orphans again, and a brand-new lot of Incurables, whom he'd have to send a couple of guineas to, because Molly Carraway was on the committee. But to make up for the Incurables was a most cheering note from the manager of his Italian bank. Using the two thousand pounds of liquid capital he'd given them to play with, they'd succeeded in netting him, during the previous month, fourteen thousand lire. Just by buying and selling on the dollar-franc exchange. Fourteen thousand. . . . It was quite a windfall. He'd give the Incurables a fiver and buy himself a little birthday present. A few nice books perhaps; and he unfolded Bruno's catalogue. But, really, who wanted the first edition of Scupoli's *Spiritual Combat*? Or the *Opera Omnia* of St. Bonaventura edited by the Franciscans of Quaracchi? Eustace threw the catalogue aside and settled down to the task of deciphering the long illegible scribble from Mopsa Schottelius, which he had reserved to the last. In pencil and the most disconcerting mixture of German, French and English, Mopsa described for him what she was doing at Monte Carlo. And what that girl wasn't doing could have been set down on the back of a postage-stamp. How appallingly thorough these Germans always managed to be, how emphatic! In sex no less than in war—in scholarship, in science. Diving deeper than anyone else and coming up muddier. He decided to send Mopsa a picture, postcard advising her to read John Morley on 'Compromise.'

It was in accord with these same Morleian principles that he decided, when the meal was over, to smoke one of those small Larranaga *claros* which had pleased him so much when he tried one at his London tobacconist's that he bought a thousand of them on the spot. The doctors were always nagging at him about his cigars, and he had promised to smoke only two a day, after lunch and dinner. But these little fellows were so mild that it would take a dozen of them to produce the same effect as one of his big Romeo and Juliets. So, if he were to smoke one of them now, and another after lunch, and perhaps a third after tea, with only a single big one after dinner, he would still be well on the right side of excess. He lit his cigar and leaned back, savouring the delicate lusciousness of its aroma. Then he got up and, giving orders to the butler to ring up Casa Acciaiuoli and find out if the Contessa could receive him this afternoon, made his way to the library. The four or five books which he was simultaneously reading lay piled on the table that stood beside the chair into which he now cautiously lowered himself: Scawen Blunt's *Journals*, the second volume of *Sodome et Gomorrhe*, an illustrated *History of Embroidery*, the latest novel by Ronald Firbank ... After a moment's hesitation, he decided on the Proust. Ten pages were what he usually managed to read of any book before desiring a change; but this time he lost interest after only six and a half, and turned instead to the section on the *Opus Anglicanum* in the *History of Embroidery*. Then the clock in the drawing-room struck eleven, and it was time for him to go up to the west wing and say good-morning to his mother-in-law.

Brightly painted, and dressed in the most elegant of canary-coloured tailor-mades, old Mrs. Gamble was sitting in state, having her right hand manicured by her French maid, stroking her toy Pomeranian, Foxy VIII, with her left, and listening to Sir Oliver Lodge's *Raymond* read aloud to her by her companion. At Eustace's entrance, Foxy VIII jumped down from her knee, rushed towards him and, retiring backwards as he advanced, furiously barked.

'Foxy!' cried Mrs. Gamble in a tone almost as harshly shrill as the Pomeranian's. 'Foxy!'

'Little hell-hound!' said Eustace genially; and, turning to the reader, who had broken off in the middle of a sentence, he added: 'Please don't let me interrupt you, Mrs. Thwale.'

Veronica Thwale raised her impeccably oval face and looked at him with a calm intentness.

'But it's a pleasure,' she said, 'to get back from all these ghosts to a bit of solid flesh.'

She lingered a little over the final consonant. As 'flesh-sh,' the word took on a meatier significance.

Like an Ingres madonna, Eustace reflected, as he twinkled back at her. Smooth and serene almost to the point of impersonality, and yet with all the sex left in—and perhaps even a little added.

'Too, too solid, I'm afraid.'

Chuckling, he patted the smooth convexity of his pearl-grey waistcoat.

'And how's the Queen Mother this morning?' he added, crossing over to Mrs. Gamble's chair. 'Having her claws sharpened, I see.'

The old lady uttered a thin crackling laugh. She was proud of her reputation for reckless plain speaking and malicious wit.

'You're a rascal, Eustace,' she said, and the thin old voice was still vibrant with those rasping intonations of authority which make so many rich and aristocratic old ladies sound like sublimated sergeant-majors. 'And who's talking of flesh?' she added, turning her unseeing eyes inquisitorially from where she imagined Eustace was to where Mrs. Thwale had seemed to be sitting. 'Are *you* putting on flesh, Eustace?'

'Well, I'm not quite as sylph-like as you are,' he answered, looking down with a smile at the blind little shrunken mummy in the chair beside him.

'Where are you?' Mrs. Gamble asked; and leaving one gnarled hand to the manicurist, she pawed with the other at the air, then found the lapel of his coat and, from that, ran her fingers over the pearl-grey bulge below. 'Heavens!' she exclaimed.

E

'I had no idea! You're gross, Eustace, *gross*!' The thin voice grated again, like a petty officer's. 'Ned was gross too,' she went on, comparing mentally the stomach under her hand with the remembered paunch that had been her husband's. 'That was why he passed on so young. Only sixty-four. No fat man ever lived even to seventy.'

The conversation had taken a turn which Eustace could not help finding a bit distasteful. He decided to laugh his way out into a more congenial subject.

'That was up to the best of your old form,' he said gaily. 'But tell me,' he added, 'what happens to fat people when they die?'

'They don't die,' said Mrs. Gamble. 'They pass on.'

'When they pass on,' Eustace amended, with an intonation that put the words between inverted commas. 'Are they still obese on the other side? I'd like to ask next time you have a séance.'

'You're being frivolous,' said the Queen Mother severely.

Eustace turned to Mrs. Thwale.

'Did you finally succeed in locating a good witch?'

'Unfortunately, most of them speak only Italian,' she answered. 'But now Lady Worplesden's given us the name of an English one, who she says is very satisfactory.'

'I'd have preferred a trumpet medium,' said Mrs. Gamble. 'But when one's travelling, one has to put up with what one can find.'

Noiselessly, the French maid rose, moved her chair over and, taking Mrs. Gamble's other hand from where it lay, clawlike, on Foxy's orange fur, began to file the pointed nails.

'That young nephew of yours is arriving today, isn't he?'

'This evening,' Eustace answered. 'We may be a little late for dinner.'

'I like boys,' the Queen Mother pronounced. 'That is, when they have decent manners, which very few of them have nowadays. And that reminds me, Veronica, of Mr. De Vries.'

'He's coming to tea this afternoon,' said Mrs. Thwale in her calm, level voice.

'De Vries?' Eustace questioned.

'You met him in Paris,' said the Queen Mother. 'At my New Year cocktail party.'

'Did I?' Eustace's tone was vague. He had also met about five thousand other people on the same occasion.

'American,' the Queen Mother went on. 'And he took the greatest fancy to me. Didn't he, Veronica?'

'He certainly did,' said Mrs. Thwale.

'Came to see me constantly all this winter—constantly. And now he's in Florence.'

'Money?'

Mrs. Gamble nodded.

'Breakfast Food,' she said. 'But what he's really interested in is science and all that kind of stuff. However, as I keep telling him, facts are facts, whatever your Mr. Einstein may say.'

'And not only Mr. Einstein,' said Eustace with a smile, 'Mr. Plato, Mr. Buddha, Mr. Francis of Assisi.'

A curious little grunting sound made him turn his head. Almost voicelessly, Mrs. Thwale was laughing.

'Did I say anything so amusing?' he asked.

The pale oval face resumed its customary serenity.

'I was thinking of a little joke my husband and I used to have together.'

'About Mr. Francis of Assisi?'

For a second or two she looked at him without speaking.

'About Brother Ass-ss,' she said at last.

Eustace would have liked to enquire further, but thought it more tactful, seeing that Thwale was so lately dead, to refrain.

'If you're going down into the town this morning,' Mrs. Gamble broke in, 'I wish you'd take Veronica.'

'I'd be enchanted.'

'She's got some shopping to do for me,' the old woman continued.

Eustace turned to Mrs. Thwale.

'Then let's have lunch together at Betti's.'

But it was the Queen Mother who declined the invitation.

'No, Eustace, I want her to come straight back. In a taxi.'

He glanced anxiously at Mrs. Thwale to see how she was taking it. The face of the Ingres madonna was expressionlessly calm.

'In a taxi,' she repeated in her clear, level voice. 'Very well, Mrs. Gamble.'

Half an hour later, in the sober elegance of her black tailor-made, Veronica Thwale walked out into the sunshine. At the foot of the front steps stood the Isotta, large, dark blue, and prodigiously expensive-looking. But Paul De Vries, she reflected as she got in, was probably at least as well off as Mr. Barnack.

'I hope you don't object,' said Eustace, holding up the second of the day's cigars.

She raised her eyelids at him, smiled without parting her lips, and shook her head; then looked back again at the gloved hands lying limply folded in her lap.

Slowly the car rolled down between the cypresses and out into the steep winding road beyond the gates.

'Of all the specimens in my collection,' said Eustace, breaking the long silence, 'I think the Queen Mother is perhaps the most remarkable. A fossil scorpion out of the Carboniferous, almost perfectly preserved.'

Mrs. Thwale smiled at her folded hands.

'I'm not a geologist,' she said. 'And, incidentally, the fossil is my employer.'

'Which is the thing I find most surprising of all.'

She looked up at him enquiringly.

'You mean, that I should be acting as Mrs. Gamble's companion?'

The final word, Eustace noted appreciatively, was faintly emphasized, so that it took on its fullest, Brontëan significance.

'That's it,' he said.

Mrs. Thwale examined him appraisingly, taking in the tilted hat, the beautifully fitting pearl-grey suit, the Sulka tie, the rosebud in his buttonhole.

'*Your* father wasn't a poor clergyman in Islington,' she brought out.

'No, he was a militant anti-clerical in Bolton.'

'Oh, it's not the faith I'm thinking about,' she answered, smiling with delicate irony. 'It's what your mother-in-law calls the Facts.'

'Such as?'

She shrugged her shoulders.

'Chilblains, for example. Living in a cold house. Feeling ashamed because one's clothes are so old and shabby. But poverty wasn't the whole story. *Your* father didn't practise the Christian virtues.'

'On the contrary,' said Eustace, 'he was a professional philanthropist. You know—drinking-fountains, hospitals, boys' clubs.'

'Ah, but he only gave the money and had his name written up over the door. He didn't have to work in his beastly clubs.'

'Whereas *you* did?'

Mrs. Thwale nodded.

'From the time I was thirteen. And after I was sixteen it was four nights a week.'

'Did they force you?'

Mrs. Thwale shrugged her shoulders and did not immediately answer. She was thinking of her father—those bright eyes in the face of a consumptive Phoebus, that long thin body, stooping and hollow-chested. And beside him stood her mother, tiny and fragile, but the protector of his helpless unworldliness, the little bird-like Atlas who sustained the whole weight of his material universe.

'There's such a thing as moral blackmail,' she said at last. 'If the people around you insist on behaving like Early Christians, you've got no choice, have you?'

'Not much, I admit.'

Eustace took the cigar out of the corner of his mouth and exhaled a cloud of smoke.

'That's one of the reasons,' he added with a chuckle, 'why it's so important to eschew the company of the Good.'

'One of the Good was your stepdaughter,' said Mrs. Thwale after a little pause.

'Who, Daisy Ockham?'

She nodded.

'Oh, then your father must be that Canon What's-his-name she's always talking about.'

'Canon Cresswell.'

'That's it—Cresswell.' Eustace beamed at her. 'Well, all I can say is that you ought to hear her on the subject.'

'I have,' said Mrs. Thwale. 'Very often.'

Daisy Ockham, Dotty Freebody, Yvonne Graves—the Holy Women. One fat, two scraggy. She had once drawn a picture of them squatting at the foot of the cross on which her father was being crucified by a troop of Boy Scouts.

Eustace broke the silence with a little laugh at his step-daughter's expense—at Canon Cresswell's too, incidentally. But there didn't seem to be any filial piety to consider in this case.

'All those deplorably good works of hers!' he said. 'But then of course,' he added commiseratingly, 'there wasn't much alternative for the poor thing, after she'd lost her husband and the boy.'

'She used to do them even before,' said Mrs. Thwale.

'So there's really *no* excuse!' he said.

Mrs. Thwale smiled and shook her head. Then, after a pause, she volunteered that it was Daisy Ockham who had originally introduced her to Mrs. Gamble.

'Rare privilege!' said Eustace.

'But it was at her house that I met Henry.'

'Henry?' he questioned.

'That was my husband.'

'Oh, of course.'

There was a silence, while Eustace sucked at his cigar and tried to remember what the Queen Mother had said about Henry Thwale. A partner in the firm of solicitors who managed her affairs. Very pleasant and well-bred, but had passed on of a ruptured appendix at only—what was the age she had mentioned, with her usual ghoulish accuracy about such things? Thirty-eight, he seemed to recall. So that he would have been at least twelve or fourteen years older than his wife.

'How old were you when you married?' he asked.

'Eighteen.'

'Just the right age, according to Aristotle.'

'But not according to my father. He'd have liked me to wait a couple of years.'

'Fathers are never supposed to relish the thought of their young daughters getting married.'

Mrs. Thwale looked down at her folded hands and thought of their honeymoon and summer holiday beside the Mediterranean. The swimming, the deliciously stupefying sun-baths, the long siesta hours in the aquarium twilight of their green-shuttered bedroom.

'I'm not altogether surprised,' she said, without raising her eyes.

At the memory of those extremes of pleasure and shameless-ness and self-abandonment she smiled a little to herself. 'Nature's lay idiot, I taught thee to love.' And to the quotation Henry had added, as his personal testimonial, that she was a model pupil. But then he had been a good master. Which didn't prevent him, unfortunately, from having the most abominable temper and being mean about money.

'Well, I'm glad you managed to make your escape,' said Eustace.

Mrs. Thwale was silent for a little. 'After Henry died,' she said at last, 'it almost looked as if I might have to go back to where I'd come from.'

'To the Poor and the Good?'

'To the Poor and the Good,' she echoed. 'But fortunately Mrs. Gamble needed somebody to read to her.'

'So now you live with the Rich and the Bad, eh?'

'As a parasite,' said Mrs. Thwale calmly. 'As a kind of glorified lady's maid. . . . But it's a question of making one's choice between two evils.'

She opened her handbag, took out a handkerchief and, raising it to her nose, inhaled its perfume of civet and flowers. In her father's house there was chronically the smell of cabbage and steamed puddings, and at the Girls' Club—well, the smell of girls.

'Personally,' she said, as she put away the handkerchief again, 'I'd rather be a hanger-on in a house like yours than on my own with—what would it have been? About fifty shillings a week, I suppose.'

There was a brief silence.

'In your position,' said Eustace at last, 'perhaps I'd have made the same choice.'

'It wouldn't astonish me,' was Mrs. Thwale's comment.

'But I think I'd have drawn a line . . .'

'People don't draw lines unless they can afford it.'

'Not even at fossil scorpions?'

Mrs. Thwale smiled.

'Your mother-in-law would have preferred a trumpet medium. But even she has to be content with what she can find.'

'Even she!' Eustace repeated with a wheezy laugh. 'But I must say, she was pretty lucky to find you, wasn't she?'

'Not so lucky as I was to find her.'

'And if you hadn't found one another, what then?'

Mrs. Thwale shrugged her shoulders.

'Perhaps I could have made a little money illustrating books.'

'Oh, you draw?'

72

She nodded.

'Secretly,' she answered.

'Why secretly?'

'Why?' she repeated. 'Partly from mere force of habit. You see, one's drawings weren't much appreciated at home.'

'On what grounds? Aesthetic or ethical?'

She smiled and shrugged her shoulders. 'Who knows?'

But Mrs. Cresswell had been so dreadfully upset by the discovery of her sketch-book that she had gone to bed for three days with a migraine headache. After that, Veronica had never done any drawing except in the w.c. and on bits of paper that could be thrown away without risk of stopping up the drains.

'Besides,' she went on, 'secrecy's such fun just for its own sake.'

'Is it?'

'Don't tell me you feel like my husband about it! Henry would have been a nudist if he'd been born ten years later.'

'But you wouldn't, even though you *were* born ten years later?'

She shook her head emphatically.

'I wouldn't even write out a laundry list with somebody else in the room. But Henry . . . Why, the door of his study was never shut. Never! It used to make me feel quite ill even to look at him.'

She was silent for a moment.

'There's an awful prayer at the beginning of the Communion Service,' she went on. 'You know the one: "Almighty God, unto whom all hearts are open, all desires known and from whom no secrets are hid." Really awful! I used to make drawings about it. Those were the ones that seemed to upset my mother most of all.'

'I can well believe it,' said Eustace with a chuckle. 'One day,' he added, 'will you show me some of your drawings?'

Mrs. Thwale glanced at him searchingly, then averted her eyes. For a few seconds she did not speak. Then, slowly and

73

in the tone of one who has thought out a problem and come at last to a decision, she gave her answer.

'You're one of the few people I wouldn't mind showing them to.'

'I feel flattered,' said Eustace.

Mrs. Thwale opened her handbag and, from among its perfumed contents, extracted half a sheet of notepaper.

'Here's something I was working on before breakfast this morning.'

He took it and put up his monocle. The drawing was in ink and, in spite of its smallness, extraordinarily detailed and meticulous. Competent, was Eustace's verdict, but unpleasantly niggling. He peered at it closely. The drawing represented a woman, dressed in the severest and most correctly fashionable of tailor-made suits, walking, prayer-book in hand, up the aisle of a church. Behind her, at the end of a string, she trailed a horseshoe magnet—but a horseshoe magnet so curved and rounded as to suggest a pair of thighs tapering down to the knees. On the ground, a little way behind the woman, lay an enormous eyeball, as big as a pumpkin, its pupil staring wildly at the retreating magnet. From the sides of the eye sprouted two wormlike arms, ending in a pair of huge hooked hands that clawed at the floor. So strong had been the attraction and so desperate the futile effort to resist, that the dragging fingers had scored long grooves in the flagstones.

Eustace raised his left eyebrow and allowed the monocle to drop.

'There's only one thing about the parable I don't understand,' he said. 'Why the church?'

'Oh, for any number of reasons,' Mrs. Thwale answered, shrugging her shoulders. 'Respectability always heightens a woman's attractiveness. And blasphemy gives an extra spice to pleasure. And, after all, churches are places people get married in. Besides, who tells you that that isn't the *Decameron* she's carrying, bound in black leather like a prayer-book?'

She took the sheet of paper and put it away again in her bag.

'It's a pity fans have gone out of fashion,' she added in another tone. 'And those big white masks they used to wear in Casanova. Or talking from behind screens, like the ladies in "The Tale of Genji." Wouldn't that be heavenly!'

'Would it?'

She nodded, her face bright with unwonted animation.

'One could do the oddest things while one was chatting with the Vicar about . . . well, let's say the League of Nations. Oh, the *oddest*!'

'Such as?'

A little grunt of voiceless laughter was all the answer she vouchsafed. There was a pause.

'And then,' she added, 'think of the enormities one could bring out without blushing!'

'And you feel you'd like to bring out enormities?'

Mrs. Thwale nodded.

'I'd have been a good scientist,' she said.

'What's that got to do with it?'

'But can't you see?' she said impatiently. 'Can't you see? Cutting bits off frogs and mice, grafting cancer into rabbits, boiling things together in test-tubes—just to see what'll happen, just for the fun of the thing. Wantonly committing enormities —that's all science is.'

'And you'd enjoy it *outside* the laboratory?'

'Not in public, of course.'

'But if you were ambushed behind a screen, where the Good couldn't see you . . .'

'Ambushed behind a screen,' Mrs. Thwale repeated slowly. 'And now,' she went on in another tone, 'I shall have to get out. There's a shop somewhere here on the Lungarno where you can buy rubber rats for dogs. Rats with a chocolate flavour. Foxy's very keen on the chocolate, it seems. Ah, here we are!'

She leaned forward and rapped the glass.

Eustace watched her go. Then, replacing his hat, he ordered the chauffeur to drive to Weyl's in the Via Tornabuoni.

CHAPTER SEVEN

'WEYL FRÈRES, Bruxelles, Paris . . .'

Eustace pushed open the door and walked into the crowded shop. '"Where every prospect pleases,"' he was humming, as he always hummed on these occasions, '"and only man is Weyl Frères, Bruxelles, Paris, Florence, Vienne."'

But this morning it was woman, not man. Mme Weyl was engaged, as he entered, in trying to talk what was obviously an Anglo-Indian colonel into buying a Braque. The performance was so ludicrous and the performer so ravishingly pretty that Eustace simulated an interest in a particularly hideous piece of majolica in order to have an excuse to watch and listen at close quarters.

Pearly, golden, deliciously pink and plump, how had this sumptuous young creature escaped from the Rubens canvas which was so obviously her home? And how, good heavens, did it happen that a figure from Peter Paul's mythology was wearing clothes? But even in her incongruous twentieth-century frills, Weyl's Flemish Venus remained enchanting. Which only heightened the absurdity of the act she was now staging for the colonel. With the earnestness of a little girl who is doing her very best to reproduce, word-perfect, the lesson so laboriously learned by heart, she was conscientiously repeating the nonsense phrases with which her husband adorned his incomparable patter. 'Tactile Values,' 'rhythm,' 'significant forms,' 'repoussoirs,' 'calligraphic outline'—Eustace recognized all the stereotypes of contemporary criticism, and along with them such products of

Weyl's own luxuriant genius as 'four-dimensional volumes,' '*couleur d'éternité*,' and 'plastic polyphony'; the whole uttered with a French accent so strong, so indecently 'cute,' so reminiscent of the naughty-naughty twitterings of a Parisian miss on the English musical comedy stage, that the colonel's ruddy face was fairly beaming with concupiscence.

Suddenly there was a rush of feet and the loud, delighted cry of 'Monsieur Eustache!' Eustace turned his head. Short, broad-shouldered, astonishingly quick and agile, it was Gabriel Weyl himself, darting towards him between the baroque statues and the cinquecento furniture. Seizing Eustace's hand in both of his, he shook it long and ardently, assured him, in a torrent of incorrigibly Belgian English, how happy he was, how proud, how deeply touched and flattered; and then, lowering his voice, whispered dramatically that he had just received something from his brother in Paris, a consignment of treasures which he had said to himself the very first moment he looked at them that he wouldn't show to anyone, not a soul, not to Pierpont Morgan himself, by God, until *ce cher Monsieur Eustache* had plucked the virginity of the portfolio and rifled its choicest sweets. And what sweets! Degas drawings such as nobody had ever seen the like of.

Still boiling over with enthusiasm, he led the way into the back room. On an elaborately carved Venetian table lay a black portfolio.

'There!' he cried, pointing at it with the gesture of one who, in an Old Master, somewhat superfluously calls attention to the Transfiguration or the martyrdom of St. Erasmus.

He was silent for a moment; then, changing his expression to the libidinous leer of a slave-dealer peddling Circassians to an ageing pasha, he started to undo the strings of the portfolio. The hands, Eustace noticed, were deft and powerful, their backs furred with a growth of soft black hair, their short fingers exquisitely manicured. With a flourish M. Weyl threw back the heavy flap of cardboard.

'Look!'

The tone was triumphant and assured. At the sight of those newly budded paps, that incomparable navel, no pasha, however jaded, could possibly resist.

'But look!'

Putting up his monocle, Eustace looked, and saw the charcoal sketch of a naked woman standing in a tin bath like a Roman sarcophagus. One foot, much distorted by the wearing of tight shoes, was planted on the edge of the bath, and the woman was bending down, hair and bosom falling one way, rump bonily jutting another, one knee crooked outward at the most ungraceful of all possible angles, to scrub a heel which one divined, through some unanalysable subtlety of the drawing, as yellow and, in spite of soap, chronically dirty-looking.

'Was *this* the face . . . ?' Eustace murmured.

But really there was nobody quite like Degas, nobody who could render the cosy and domestic squalors of our physiology with so much intensity and in forms so exquisitely beautiful.

'You oughtn't to have sold me that Magnasco,' he said aloud. 'How can I possibly afford one of these?'

The slave-dealer shot a glance at his pasha and saw that the Circassians were beginning to have the desired effect. But they were so cheap, he protested; and the soundest of investments— as good as shares in the Suez Canal Company. And now let Monsieur Eustache look at this one!

He removed the first drawing; and this time the face that launched the thousand ships was seen squarely from the rear, leaning forward over the tin sarcophagus and vigorously towelling the back of its neck.

Gabriel Weyl laid a thick, perfectly manicured forefinger on the buttocks.

'What values!' he breathed ecstatically, 'what volumes, what *calligraphy*!'

Eustace burst out laughing. But, as usual, it was M. Weyl who laughed last. Little by little the jaded pasha began to yield. He

78

might perhaps consider it—that was to say, if the price weren't too exorbitant. . . .

Only eight thousand lire, wheedled the slave-dealer, eight thousand for something that was not only a masterpiece, but also a gilt-edged security.

It was quite a reasonable figure; but Eustace felt bound to protest.

No, no, not a centesimo less than eight thousand. But if Monsieur Eustache would take two of them, and pay cash, he could have them for only fourteen.

Fourteen, fourteen . . . After this morning's letter from the bank one might almost say that one was getting two Degases free gratis and for nothing. His conscience salved, Eustace pulled out his cheque-book.

'I'll take them with me,' he said, indicating the foot-washer and the towel-wielder.

Five minutes later, with the square flat package under his arm, he emerged again into the sunlight of the Via Tornabuoni.

From Weyl's Eustace made his way to Vieusseux's lending library, to see if they had a copy of Lamettrie's *L'Homme Machine*. But of course they hadn't; and after turning over the pages of the latest French and English reviews in the vain hope of finding something one could read, he walked out again into the jostle of the narrow streets.

After a moment of hesitation he decided to pop into the Bargello for a moment and then, on the way to lunch, to look in on Bruno Rontini and ask him to arrange about taking Sebastian round the Villa Galigai.

Ten minutes were enough to whizz through the Donatellos and, his head full of heroic bronze and marble, he strolled up the street in the direction of the bookshop.

Yes, it would have been nice, he was thinking, it would have been very nice indeed if one's life had had the quality of those statues. Nobility without affectation. Serenity combined with passionate energy. Dignity wedded to grace. But, alas, those were not precisely the characteristics that one's life had exhibited. Which was regrettable, no doubt. But of course it had its compensating advantages. Being a Donatello would have been altogether too strenuous for his taste. That sort of thing was much more John's cup of tea—John who had always seen himself as the equivalent of a mixture between Gattamelata and the Baptist. Instead of which, his actual life was . . . what? Eustace cast about for the answer, and finally decided that John's life was best compared to a war picture by one of those deplorable painters who were born to be magazine illustrators but had unfortunately seen the Cubists and taken to High Art. Poor John! He had no taste, no sense of style. . . .

But here was Bruno's corner. He opened the door and walked into the dark little book-lined cavern.

Seated at the counter, a man was reading by the light of a green-shaded lamp that hung from the ceiling. At the sound of the door-bell he put away his book and, with movements that were expressive more of resignation to the interruption than of delight at seeing a customer, got up and advanced to meet the newcomer. He was a young man in the middle twenties, tall, large-boned, with a narrow convex face like that of a rather tense and over-earnest, but still not very intelligent ram.

'*Buon giorno*,' said Eustace genially.

The young man returned his greeting without the trace of an answering smile. Not, Eustace felt sure, from any desire to be discourteous, but just because, to a face of that kind, smiling was all but an impossibility.

He asked where Bruno was, and was told that Bruno would be out for at least another hour.

'Gallivanting about as usual!' Eustace commented with that unnecessary and rather pointless jocularity into which the desire to display his perfect command of the Tuscan idiom so often betrayed him when he spoke Italian.

'If you like to put it that way, Mr. Barnack,' said the young man with quiet gravity.

'Oh, you know who I am?'

The other nodded.

'I came into the shop one day last autumn, when you were talking with Bruno.'

'And when I'd gone, he treated you to a thorough dissection of my character!'

'How can you say that!' the young man cried reproachfully. 'You who've known Bruno for so long.'

Eustace laughed and patted him on the shoulder. The boy was humourless, of course; but in his loyalty to Bruno, in the solemn ovine sincerity of all he said, curiously touching.

'I was only joking,' he said aloud. 'Bruno's the last person to gossip about a man when his back is turned.'

For the first time during the conversation, the young man's face brightened into a smile.

'I'm glad you realize it,' he said.

'Not only realize, but sometimes even regret it,' said Eustace mischievously. 'There's nothing that so effectively ruins conversation as charitableness. After all, nobody can be amusing about other people's virtues. What's your name, by the way?' he added, before the other had time to translate the pained disapproval of his expression into words.

'Malpighi, Carlo Malpighi.'

'No relation of Avvocato Malpighi?'

The other hesitated; an expression of embarrassment appeared on his face.

'He's my father,' he said at last.

Eustace betrayed no surprise; but his curiosity was aroused. Why was the son of a highly successful lawyer selling second-hand books? He set himself to find out.

'I expect Bruno's been very helpful to you,' he began, taking what he divined would be the shortest way to the young man's confidence.

He was not mistaken. In a little while he had young ram-face almost chattering. About his sickly and conventional mother;

F   81

about his father's preference for the two older and cleverer sons; about the impact of *il Darwinismo* and his loss of faith; about his turning to the Religion of Humanity.

'The Religion of Humanity!' Eustace repeated with relish. How deliciously comic that people should still be worshipping Humanity!

From theoretical socialism the step to an active anti-fascism was short and logical—particularly logical in Carlo's case, since both his brothers were party members and climbing rapidly up the hierarchical ladder. Carlo had spent a couple of years distributing forbidden literature; attending clandestine meetings; talking to peasants and workmen in the hope of persuading them to put up some kind of resistance to the all-pervading tyranny. But nothing happened; there were no results to show for all these efforts. In private, people grumbled and exchanged whispered jokes and little obscenities about their masters; in public, they continued to shout '*Duce, Duce!*' And meanwhile, from time to time, one of Carlo's associates would be caught, and either beaten up in the old-fashioned way, or else shipped off to the islands. That was all, that was absolutely all.

'And even if it hadn't been all,' Eustace put in, 'even if you'd persuaded them to do something violent and decisive, what then? There'd have been anarchy for a little while. And then, to cure the anarchy, another dictator, calling himself a communist, no doubt, but otherwise indistinguishable from this one. Quite indistinguishable,' he repeated with the jolliest of chuckles. 'Unless, of course, he happened to be rather worse.'

The other nodded.

'Bruno said something of that kind too.'

'Sensible fellow!'

'But he also said something else . . .'

'Ah, I was afraid of that!'

Carlo ignored the interruption, and his face glowed with sudden ardour.

'. . . That there's only one corner of the universe you can be certain of improving, and that's your own self. Your own self,' he repeated. 'So you have to begin there, not outside, not on other people. That comes afterwards, when you've worked on your own corner. You've got to *be* good before you can *do* good—or at any rate do good without doing harm at the same time. Helping with one hand and hurting with the other— that's what the ordinary reformer does.'

'Whereas the truly wise man,' said Eustace, 'refrains from doing anything with either hand.'

'No, no,' the other protested with unsmiling earnestness. 'The wise man begins by transforming himself, so that he can help other people without running the risk of being corrupted in the process.'

And with the incoherence of passion he began to talk about the French Revolution. The men who made it had the best of intentions; but these good intentions were hopelessly mixed up with vanity and ambition and insensitiveness and cruelty. With the inevitable consequence that what had begun as a movement of liberation degenerated into terrorism and a squabble for power, into tyranny and imperialism and the world-wide re-actions to imperialism. And this sort of thing was bound to happen wherever people tried to do good without being good. Nobody could do a proper job with dirty or misshapen instru-ments. There was no way out except Bruno's way. And, of course, Bruno's way was the way that had been pointed out by . . .

Suddenly he broke off and, taking cognizance of Eustace as a potential customer, looked very sheepish.

'I'm sorry,' he said in a tone of apology. 'I don't know why I'm talking to you like this. I ought to have asked you what you wanted.'

'Exactly what you've given me,' said Eustace with a smile of amused and slightly ironic friendliness. 'And I'll buy any book you recommend, from Aretino to Mrs. Molesworth.'

Carlo Malpighi looked at him for a moment in hesitant silence.

Then, deciding to take him at his word, he stepped over to one of the shelves and came back with a rather battered volume.

'It's only twenty-five lire,' he said.

Eustace put up his monocle, opened the book at random, and read aloud:

'"Grace did not fail thee, but thou wast wanting to grace. God did not deprive thee of the operation of his love, but thou didst deprive his love of thy co-operation. God would never have rejected thee, if thou hadst not rejected him."

Golly!' He turned back to the title page. 'Treatise of the Love of God by St. François de Sales,' he read. 'Pity it isn't de Sade. But then,' he added, as he pulled out his wallet, 'it would have cost a good deal more than twenty-five lire.'

CHAPTER EIGHT

CONFIDENT that, at Betti's, he would find a friend to share his meal, Eustace had made no luncheon engagement. Unwisely, as he now realized on entering the restaurant. For Mario De Lellis was swallowed up in the midst of a large convivial party, and could only wave a distant greeting. And Mopsa's father, solemn old Schottelius, was pontificating about world politics to two other Germans. And as for Tom Pewsey, he was lunching so intimately with such an extraordinarily handsome young Nordic that he failed even to notice the entry of his oldest friend.

Seated at the table assigned to him, Eustace was preparing, rather mournfully, to eat a solitary meal, when he became aware, over the top of his menu, of an intruding presence. Raising his head, he saw a slender young man looking down at him with all the focussed intentness of two very bright brown eyes and the fixedly staring nostrils of a tilted and inquisitive nose.

'I don't suppose you remember me,' said the stranger.

It was a New England voice; and its intonations curiously combined a native eagerness with a studiedly academic flatness, deliberation and monotony.

Eustace shook his head.

'No, I'm afraid I don't,' he admitted.

'I had the pleasure of being introduced to you in Paris last January. At Mrs. Gamble's.'

'Oh, you're Mr. De Jong.'

'De Vries,' the young man emended. 'Paul De Vries.'

'I know all about you,' said Eustace. 'You talk to my mother-in-law about Einstein.'

Very brightly, as though he were deliberately turning on a light, the young man smiled.

'Could any subject be more exciting?'

'None—unless it's the subject of lunch when the clock says half-past one. Will you join me in discussing that?'

The young man had evidently been hoping for just such an invitation.

'Thank you so much,' he said; and, putting down the two thick volumes he was carrying, he seated himself, planted his elbows on the table and leaned forward towards his new companion.

'Everyone ought to know something about Einstein,' he began.

'One moment,' said Eustace. 'Let's start by deciding what we're going to eat.'

'Yes, yes, that's very important,' the other agreed, but with an obvious lack of all conviction. 'The stomach has its reasons, as Pascal would say.' He laughed perfunctorily, and picked up the bill-of-fare. When the waiter had taken the orders, he planted his elbows as before, and began again.

'As I was saying, Mr. Barnack, everyone ought to know something of Einstein.'

'Even those who can't understand what he's talking about?'

'But they *can*,' the other protested. 'It's only the mathematical techniques that are difficult. The principle is simple—and after all, it's the understanding of the principle that affects values and conduct.'

Eustace laughed aloud.

'I can just see my mother-in-law changing her values and conduct to fit the principles of relativity!'

'Well, of course she *is* rather elderly,' the other admitted. 'I was thinking more of people who are young enough to be flexible. For example, that lady who acts as Mrs. Gamble's companion . . .'

Ah, so that was why he had been so assiduous in his attentions to the Queen Mother! But in that case the picture of the magnetized eye was perhaps not only a parable but a piece of history.

'. . . Mathematically speaking, almost illiterate,' the young man was saying. 'But that doesn't prevent her from realizing the scope and significance of the Einsteinian revolution.'

And what a revolution, he went on with mounting enthusiasm. Incomparably more important than anything that had happened in Russia or Italy. For this was the revolution that had changed the whole course of scientific thinking, brought back idealism, integrated mind into the fabric of Nature, put an end for ever to the Victorians' nightmare universe of infinitesimal billiard balls.

'Too bad,' said Eustace in parenthesis. 'I really loved those little billiard balls.'

He addressed himself to the plate of ribbon-like *lasagne verdi* which the waiter had set before him.

'First-rate,' he said appreciatively with his mouth full. 'Almost as good as at the Pappagallo in Bologna. Do you know Bologna?' he added, hoping to divert the conversation to more congenial themes.

But Paul De Vries knew Bologna only too well. Had spent a week there the previous autumn, having talks with all the most interesting people at the university.

'The university?' Eustace repeated incredulously.

The young man nodded and, putting down his fork, explained that, during the last two years, he had been making a tour of all the leading universities of Europe and Asia. Getting in touch with the really significant people working in each. Trying to enlist their co-operation in his great project—the setting up of an international clearing house of ideas, the creation of a general staff of scientific-religious-philosophic synthesis for the entire planet.

'With yourself as the commander-in-chief?' Eustace couldn't resist putting in.

'No, no,' the other protested. 'Only the liaison officer and interpreter. Only the bridge-building engineer.'

That was the full extent of his ambition: to be a humble bridge-builder, a *pontifex*. Not *maximus*, he added with another of his bright deliberate smiles. *Pontifex minimus*. And he had good hopes of succeeding. People had been extraordinarily kind and helpful and interested. And meanwhile he could assure Eustace that Bologna was living up to her ancient reputation. They were doing the most exciting work in crystallography; and in his latest lectures on Aesthetics, Bonomelli was using all the resources of modern psycho-physiology and the mathematics of many dimensions. Nothing quite like Bonomelli's Aesthetics had ever been seen before.

Eustace wiped his mouth and drank some Chianti.

'I wish one could say the same thing of contemporary Italian art,' he remarked, as he refilled his glass from the big-bellied flask in its swinging cradle.

Yes, the other admitted judicially, it was quite true that easel paintings didn't amount to much in modern Italy. But he had seen the most remarkable specimens of socialized and civic art. Classico-functional post offices, giant football stadiums, heroic murals. And after all, that was going to be the art of the future.

'God,' said Eustace, 'I hope I shan't live to see it!'

Paul De Vries signed to the waiter to remove his almost untouched plate of *lasagne*, hungrily lighted a cigarette and continued:

'You're a specimen, if I may say so, of Individualistic Man. But Individualistic Man is rapidly giving place to Social Man.'

'I knew it,' said Eustace. 'Everyone who wants to do good to the human race always ends in universal bullying.'

The young man protested. He wasn't talking about regimentation, but integration. And in a properly integrated society a new kind of cultural field would arise, with new kinds of aesthetic values coming into existence within it.

'Aesthetic values!' Eustace repeated impatiently. 'That's the sort of phrase that fills me with the profoundest mistrust.'

'What makes you say that?'

Eustace answered with another question.

'What's the colour of the wall-paper in your bedroom at the hotel?' he asked.

'The colour of the wall-paper?' the young man echoed in a tone of astonishment. 'I haven't the faintest idea.'

'No, I thought not,' said Eustace. 'And that's why I mistrust aesthetic values so much.'

The waiter brought the creamed breasts of turkey and he lapsed into silence. Paul De Vries crushed out his cigarette and took two or three mouthfuls, chewing with extraordinary rapidity, like a rabbit. Then he wiped his lips, lighted another cigarette and fixed Eustace with his bright eyes and staring nostrils.

'You're right,' he said, 'you're entirely right. My mind is so busy thinking about values that I don't have time to experience them.'

The admission was made with such ingenuous humility that Eustace was touched.

'Let's go round the Uffizi one day,' he said. 'I'll tell you what I think about the paintings and you shall tell me what I ought to know about their metaphysical and historical and social implications.'

The young man nodded delightedly.

'A synthesis!' he cried. 'The organismic viewpoint.'

Organismic . . . The blessed word released him out of cramping actuality into the wide open spaces of the uncontaminated idea. He began to talk about Professor Whitehead, and how there was no such thing as Simple Location, only location within a field. And the more one considered the idea of the organized and organizing field, the more significant it seemed, the more richly exciting. It was one of the great bridge-ideas connecting one universe of discourse with another. You had the electro-magnetic field in physics, the individuation field in embryology and general biology, the social field among insects and human beings. . . .

'And don't forget the sexual field.'

Paul De Vries looked questioningly at the interrupter.

'It's something that even you must have noticed,' Eustace continued. 'When you come into the neighbourhood of certain young ladies. Like Faraday's tubes of force. And you don't need a galvanometer to detect it,' he concluded with a chuckle.

'Tubes of force,' the young man repeated slowly. 'Tubes of force.'

The words seemed to have made a deep impression on him. He frowned to himself.

'And yet of course,' he went on after a little pause, 'sex has its values—though I know you dislike the word.'

'But not the thing,' said Eustace jovially.

'It can be refined and sublimated; it can be given wider reference.'

He made a gesture with his cigarette to indicate the wideness. Eustace shook his head.

'Personally,' he said, 'I prefer it raw and narrow.'

There was a silence. Then Eustace opened his mouth to remark that little Mrs. Thwale had a pretty powerful field around her; but before the words were out he had shut it again. No point in making trouble for oneself or other people. Besides, the oblique attack was generally the more effective; and since the Queen Mother had come to stay for a month, he would have all the time in the world to satisfy his curiosity.

Pensively, Paul De Vries began to talk about celibacy. People had come to mistrust the idea of vows and orders; but after all, they provided a simple and effective mechanism for delivering the dedicated intellectual from emotional entanglements and the distracting responsibilities of family life. Though of course, he added, certain values had to be sacrificed. . . .

'Not if the vows are judiciously tempered with a little fornication.'

Eustace beamed at him over the top of his wine-glass. But the young man's expression remained obstinately serious.

'Perhaps,' he said, 'there might be a modified form of celibacy. Not excluding romantic love and the higher forms of sex, but only barring marriage.'

Eustace burst out laughing.

'But after all,' the other protested, 'it's not love that's incompatible with the life of a dedicated intellectual; it's the whole-time job of a wife and family.'

'And you expect the ladies to share your views?'

'Why not—if they were dedicated to the same kind of life?'

'You mean, the intellectuals would only sleep with female mathematicians?'

'Why only mathematicians? Poetesses, women scientists and musicians and painters.'

'In a word, every girl who can pass an examination or strum the piano. Or even turn out a drawing,' he added as an afterthought. 'You modified celibates ought to have some fun!'

But what an ass! Eustace thought, as he went on eating. And how pathetically transparent! Caught between his ideals and his desires, and trying to rationalize his way out of that absurdly commonplace situation by talking nonsense about values and dedicated intellectuals and modified celibacy. It was really pathetic.

'Well, now that we've dealt with the sexual field,' he said aloud, 'let's get on to the others.'

Paul De Vries looked at him for a moment without speaking, then turned on one of his bright smiles and nodded his head.

'Let's get on to the others,' he repeated.

Pushing aside his half-eaten turkey, he planted his elbows on the table and in a moment was off once more into the open.

Take the case, for example, of psychic fields, and even spiritual fields. For if one looked into the matter open-mindedly and without preconceived ideas, one simply had to accept such things as facts—didn't one?

Did one? Eustace shrugged his shoulders.

But the evidence was overwhelmingly strong. If you read the Proceedings of the Society for Psychical Research, you couldn't fail to be convinced. Which was why most philosophers so scrupulously refrained from reading them. That was what came of having to do your work within the old-fashioned academic field. You couldn't think honestly about certain things, even if you wanted to. And, of course, if the field was a strong one, you wouldn't want to.

'You should talk to my mother-in-law about ghosts,' said Eustace.

The advice was unnecessary. Paul De Vries had already sat in at a number of the old lady's séances. Bridging the gap between the phenomena of spiritualism and the phenomena of psychology and physics was one of his jobs as *pontifex minimus*. An uncommonly difficult job, incidentally, since nobody had yet formulated a hypothesis in terms of which you could think coherently of the two sets of facts. For the present, the best one could do was just to skip from one world to the other—hoping, meanwhile, that some day one might get a hunch, an illuminating intuition of the greater synthesis. For a synthesis there undoubtedly must be, a thought-bridge that would permit the mind to march discursively and logically from telepathy to the four-dimensional continuum, from poltergeists and departed spirits to the physiology of the nervous system. And beyond the happenings of the séance room there were the events of the oratory and the meditation hall. There was the ultimate all-embracing field—the Brahma of Sankara, the One of Plotinus, the Ground of Eckhart and Boehme, the . . .

'The Gaseous Vertebrate of Haeckel,' Eustace interjected.

And within that ultimate field, the young man hurried on, determined not to be interrupted, there were subordinate fields—such as that which the Christians called the Communion of Saints and the Buddhists . . .

But Eustace would not leave him in peace.

'Why stop there?' he broke in sarcastically, as he selected a cigar and prepared to light it. 'Why not the Immaculate Conception and the Infallibility of the Pope?'

He sucked at the burning match, and the smoke gushed from his nostrils.

'You remind me,' he said, 'of the Young Man of Cape Cod, who applied Quantum Theory to God . . .'

And nipping in the bud the other's effort to start again, he went on to recite a selection from what he called his New World Suite—the Young Girl of Spokane, the Young Man of Peoria, the Two Young Girls of Cheyenne. Paul De Vries's laughter, he noticed, was a bit forced and perfunctory; but he went on all the same—on principle; for one really couldn't allow the fellow to get away with his pretensions. Implicitly claiming to be religious just because he could talk a lot of high-class boloney about religion. A little honest dirt would clear the air of philosophic cant and bring the philosopher down to the good old human barnyard, where he still belonged. That ram-faced boy at Bruno's might be absurd, and Bruno himself an amiable but misguided imbecile; but at least they weren't pretentious; they practised what they preached and, what was almost more remarkable, refrained from preaching what they practised. Whereas young *pontifex minimus* here . . .

Eustace took the cigar from between his lips, blew out a cloud of smoke and, lowering his voice a little, recited his limerick about the Bishop of Wichita Falls.

CHAPTER NINE

FROM Betti's, when lunch was finished, he strolled over to his bank. Catching sight of him, as he stood waiting for the cashier to give him his money, the manager came running out to tell him enthusiastically that, next month, they hoped to do even better on the exchanges. The bank had a new correspondent in Berne, a certain Dr. Otto Loewe, who had a truly wonderful gift for this branch of speculation—a real genius, one might say, like Michelangelo or Marconi. . . .

Still carrying his Degas drawings and his *Treatise of the Love of God*, Eustace made his way to the Piazza and, hailing a taxi, gave the driver Laurina Acciaiuoli's address. The cab started; he leaned back in his corner and sighed with a weary resignation. Laurina was one of his crosses. It was bad enough that she should be sick and importunate and embittered. But that was only the beginning. This haggard, arthritic cripple had once been the woman he had loved with an intensity of passion such as he had never experienced before or since. Another woman would have resigned herself to forget the fact. Not so Laurina. Twisting the dagger in her wound, she would spend whole afternoons talking to him about past beauty and present hideousness, past loves and present neglect, present loneliness and misery. And when she had worked herself up sufficiently, she would turn against her visitor, pointing accusingly with her swollen fingers and, in that low voice (once so enchantingly husky, now hoarse with sickness and over-smoking and sheer hatred), telling him that he had only come to see her out of a sense of duty—worse, out of mere weakness; that he had cared for her only when her body was young and straight, and that now she was old and crippled and unhappy he could hardly bring himself even to feel pity. Challenged to deny these all too painfully obvious truths, Eustace would find himself floundering in a quagmire of hypocritical platitudes; and what he said was generally so very unconvincing that Laurina would end by laughing outright—laughing with a ferocity of sarcasm much more wounding to herself, of course, than to him; for, after all, he was not the one who had the arthritis. But even so, it was painful enough. Apprehensively, he wondered what the present afternoon would bring. Another of those unutterably boring threats of suicide, perhaps. Or else . . .

'*Bebino!*' a piercing voice shouted almost in his ear. '*Bebino!*'

He turned with a start. Through the narrow, crowded street the cab was making its way at a foot pace, and trotting along beside it, her hand on the frame of the open window, was the inventor (for reasons which she and she alone could understand) of that grotesquely infantile nickname.

'Mimi!' he exclaimed, and hoped to God there was nobody of his acquaintance within sight or earshot.

In that extraordinary purple outfit she looked not merely like the pretty little tart she was, but like the caricature of a pretty little tart in a comic paper. Which was what he liked about her, of course. The simple and unaffected vulgarity of her style was absolutely consummate.

Leaning forward, he called to the driver; and when the cab had stopped, opened the door for her. Mimi would look less conspicuous inside than out.

'*Bebino mio!*' She snuggled up against him on the seat, and he found himself enveloped by the reek of cheap perfume. 'Why haven't you been to see me, *Bebino?*'

As the cab drove on, he began to explain that he had been in Paris for a couple of months, and after that in England. But instead of listening, she continued to overwhelm him with reproaches and questions. Such a long, long time! But that was what men were like—*porchi*, real *porchi*. Didn't he love her any more? Was he making her horns with someone else?

'I tell you, I was in Paris for a couple of months,' he repeated.

'*Sola, sola,*' she broke in on a note of heart-felt grief.

'. . . And then a few weeks in London,' he went on, raising his voice in an effort to get himself heard.

'And I who did everything you ever asked!' There were actually tears in her brown eyes. 'Everything,' she insisted plaintively.

'But I tell you I was away!' Eustace shouted impatiently.

Abruptly changing her expression, the girl gave him a look and smile of the frankest lasciviousness and, catching up his hand, pressed it against her plump young bosom.

'Why don't you come with me now, *Bebino*?' she cajoled. 'I'll make you so happy.' And leaning towards him she whispered in baby language, 'Hair-brush—naughty little *Bebino* needs the hair-brush.'

Eustace looked at her for a moment in silence, then consulted his watch. No, there wouldn't be time, before the train arrived, to fit in both. It would have to be one or the other. The past or the present; commiseration or enjoyment. He made his choice.

'Gather ye peaches while ye may,' he said in English, and tapping the glass he told the driver that he had changed his mind: he wanted to be taken somewhere else, and he gave the address of Mimi's apartment near Santa Croce. The man nodded and gave him an understanding wink.

'I have to telephone,' said Eustace when they arrived.

And while Mimi was changing her clothes, he rang up his house and left orders that the car was to be waiting at the main entrance of Santa Croce at a quarter to six. Then it was Laurina's turn. Could he speak to the Contessa? Waiting for the connection, he elaborated his little fiction.

'Eustace?' came the low husky voice that had once had power to command him anything.

'*Chère*,' he began volubly, '*je suis horriblement ennuyé . . .*' Polite insincerity seemed to come more easily in French than in English or Italian.

He broke it to her gradually, in a spate of foreign words— the bad, bad news that he had broken the little contraption which had to take the place of his vanished teeth. Not yet a full-scale *râtelier*, thank goodness—*plutôt un de ces bridges—ces petits ponts qui sont les Ponts des Soupirs qu'on traverse pour aller du palais de la jeunesse aux prisons lugubres de la sénilité.* He chuckled appreciatively at his own elegant joke. Well, the long and the short of it was that he'd been compelled to go *en hâte* to the dentist's, and would have to stay there until his bridge was repaired. And that, *hélas*, would prevent him from coming to tea.

Laurina took it a great deal better than he had dared to hope. Dr. Rossi, she told him, had imported a new kind of lamp from Vienna, a marvellous new drug from Amsterdam. For days at a time now she was almost free from pain. But that wasn't the whole story. Passing on from the subject of her health, she remarked with a casualness of tone that was meant to mask, but actually betrayed, her sense of triumph, that D'Annunzio had recently come to see her—several times, and had talked so poetically about the past. And dear old Van Arpels had sent her his new book of poems, and with it the most charming of letters. And, talking of letters, she'd been going through her collection— and he had no idea what a lot there were, and how interesting.

'They must be,' said Eustace. And he thought of the almost insane intensities of feeling she had evoked in the days of her fascination, the agonies of craving and jealousy. And in such a variety of men—from pure mathematicians to company promoters, from Hungarian poets to English baronets and Estonian tennis champions. And now . . . He called up the image of Laurina as she was today, twenty years after: the gaunt cripple in her invalid-chair, and those brassy yellow curls above a face that might have been Dante's death-mask. . . .

'I'd got out some of your letters to read to you,' said the voice in the microphone at his ear.

'They must sound pretty silly now.'

'No, no, they're charming,' she insisted. 'So witty; *et en même temps si tendres—così vibranti!*'

'*Vibranti?*' he repeated. 'Don't tell me I was ever vibrant!'

A sound made him turn his head. In the open doorway stood Mimi. She smiled at him and blew him a kiss; her claret-coloured kimono fell open.

At the other end of the wire paper sharply rustled.

'Listen to this,' said Laurina's husky voice. '"You have the power of arousing desires that are infinite and, being infinite, can never be assuaged by the possession of a merely finite body and personal mind."'

'Golly!' said Eustace. 'Did I write that? It sounds like Alfred de Musset.'

Mimi was standing beside him now. With his free hand he gave her a couple of friendly pats on the buttocks. Gather ye peaches . . .

The husky voice went on reading. '"So it looks, Laurina, as though the only cure for being in love with you were to become a Sufi or a John of the Cross. God alone is commensurate with the cravings you inspire . . ."'

'*Il faudrait d'abord l'inventer,*' Eustace interjected with a little chuckle. But at the time, he remembered, it had seemed quite sensible to say that sort of thing. Which just showed to what a condition this damned love could reduce a reasonable being! Well, thank goodness, now he was finished with *that* sort of thing! He administered another gentle smack and looked up at Mimi with a smile.

'*Spicciati, Bebino,*' she whispered.

'And here's another adorable thing you wrote,' said Laurina's voice in the same instant: '"Loving you as I do . . ."'

Mimi tweaked his ear impatiently—

'". . . As though one had been born again into another and intenser kind of life,"' the voice at the telephone read on.

'Sorry to have to interrupt my own raptures,' said Eustace, speaking into the receiver. 'But I've got to ring off. . . . No, no, not a moment more, my dear. Here's the dentist. *Ecco il dentista,*' he repeated for Mimi's benefit, accompanying the words with a playful little pinch. '*Adesso commincia la tortura.*'

He hung up, turned and, pulling the girl down on to his knee, began with thick stubby fingers to tickle her well-covered ribs.

'*No, no, Bebino . . . no!*'

'*Adesso commincia la tortura,*' he said again through the peals of her hysterical laughter.

CHAPTER TEN

SEATED at the counter of his cavernous little shop, Bruno Rontini was engaged in pricing a newly purchased batch of books. Fifteen lire, twelve, twenty-five, forty . . . His pencil moved from fly-leaf to fly-leaf. The light that fell almost vertically downwards from the hanging lamp above his head brought out black shadows within the deeply sunken sockets of the eyes and under the cheek-bones and the prominent nose. It was a beaked skull that bent over the books; but when he looked up, the eyes were blue and bright, the whole face wore an expression almost of gaiety.

Carlo had gone home, and he was alone—all alone with that which made his solitudes so pregnant with an inexpressible happiness. The noises of the street were loud beyond the window; but inside the little shop there was a core, as it were, of quintessential silence, to which every noise was an irrelevance, and which persisted through any interruption. Seated at the heart of that silence, Bruno was thinking that the crossed L which he was tracing out before the numerals on every fly-leaf stood not only for Lire, but also for Love, also for Liberation.

The door-bell rang, and a customer entered the shop. Bruno raised his head and saw a young, almost childish face. But how oddly skimped! As though Nature, suddenly parsimonious, had refused to provide a sufficiency of material for full-sized and significant features. Only the uneven and projecting teeth were large—those and the concave spectacles, through which, with a shy, sharp furtiveness, there beamed an intelligence that was obviously being used as an instrument, not for the discovery of truth, but for self-defence and, above all, for self-reassurance in humiliation.

The stranger coughed nervously and said that he wanted a good book on comparative religion. Bruno produced what he had in stock—a standard Italian text-book, a popular work in French, a translation, in two volumes, from the German.

'I recommend the Frenchman,' he said in his soft voice. 'Only two hundred and seventy pages. You'll hardly waste more than a couple of hours on him.'

He received a contemptuous smile.

'I'm looking for something a little more solid.'

There was a little silence while the stranger turned over the pages of the other two books.

'You're going into teaching, I take it?' said Bruno.

The other glanced at him suspiciously; then, finding no trace of irony or impertinence in the bookseller's expression, he nodded.

Yes, he was going into teaching. And meanwhile he'd take the translation from the German.

'*Peccato*,' said Bruno, as he picked up the two thick volumes.

'And when you finally get to be a university professor,' he added, 'what then?'

The young man held up the Italian text-book.

'I shall write,' he answered.

Yes, he'd write, Bruno said to himself, rather sadly. And either in despair, or out of an ingenuous respect for professors as such, some woman would have married him. And, of course, it is better to marry than to burn; but this one, it was all too obvious, would go on burning even after he was married— furtively, but with the inextinguishable violence characteristic of such frail and nervous temperaments. And under the crust of respectability and even eminence, the life of God-eclipsing phantasy, the secret addiction to self-inflicted pleasure, would persist almost into old age. But of course, he quickly reminded himself, nothing could ever be certainly prognosticated of any human being. There was always free will, there was always a sufficiency of grace if one wished to co-operate with it.

'I shall write with authority,' the young man went on almost aggressively.

'And not as the scribes and Pharisees,' Bruno murmured with a little smile. 'But what then?'

'"What then?"' the other repeated. 'What do you mean by "what then?" I shall go on writing.'

No, there was no chink yet in that protective carapace. Bruno turned away and began to tie up the books in brown paper. Shrinking from the vulgar transference of coin from hand to hand, the young man laid out the money along the edge of the counter. For him, no physical contacts with other human beings except the sexual. And even those, thought Bruno, even those would always prove disappointing, even a bit repulsive. He tied the final knot and handed over the parcel.

'Many thanks,' he said. 'And if ever you should get tired of this kind of . . .' He hesitated; in their deep sockets the blue eyes twinkled with an almost mischievous light. '. . . This kind of learned frivolity,' he went on, laying his finger on the parcel, 'remember, I've got quite a considerable stock of really serious books on the subject.' He pointed to a section of the shelves on the opposite wall. 'Scupoli, the Bhagavata, the Tao Teh King, the Theologia Germanica, the Graces of Interior Prayer . . .'

For a few seconds the young man listened—listened with the uneasy expression of one who finds himself closeted with a potentially dangerous lunatic; then, looking at his wrist-watch, he muttered something about its being very late, and hurried out of the shop.

Bruno Rontini sighed, and went back to the pricing of his books. L for Lire, L for Liberation. Out of ten thousand only one would ever break out of his carapace completely. Not a high proportion. But out of all those galaxies of eggs, how many herrings ever came to be full-sized fish? And herrings, it was to be remembered, suffered only from external interruptions to their hatching and growth. Whereas, in this process of spiritual maturation, every human being was always his own worst enemy. The attacks came from both sides, and from within even more violently and persistently and purposefully than from without. So that, after all, the record of one growing-up in ten thousand trials was really pretty creditable. Something to be admired rather than deplored. Something in regard to which one should not, as one was so often tempted, rail against God for his injustice, but rather give thanks for that divine generosity which granted to so many a reward so incommensurably vast.

L for Liberation, L for Love. . . . In spite of the impatient hooting, in spite of the clang and rumble of the traffic, the silence, for Bruno Rontini, was like a living crystal. Then the door-bell rang again, and looking up, he saw, under its tilted Homburg, the broad sagging face, with its pouchy eyes and its loosely smiling, unweaned lips, of Eustace Barnack. And through the medium of that living crystal he perceived the man as entombed, as coffined away from the light, as immured in an impenetrable privation of beatitude. And the walls of that sepulchre were built of the same sloths and sensualities as he had known within himself, and still knew, still had to beg God to forgive him. Filled with an enormous compassion, Bruno rose and went to greet him.

'Found at last!' Eustace cried. He spoke in Italian, because it was easier, when one was thus consummately acting the part of a jovial Florentine bourgeois, to preserve oneself from the danger of having to talk too seriously—and with Bruno it was particularly important that one should never be serious. 'I've been looking for you all day.'

'Yes, I heard you'd been in this morning,' Bruno answered in English.

'And was received,' said Eustace, still playing his Tuscan comedy, 'by the most ardent young disciple of yours! He even managed to sell me some edifying literature—*qualche trattatino sull' amor del* Gaseous Vertebrate,' he concluded airily.

And now the volume had taken its place between one of Pittigrilli's novels and a dog-eared Dream Book on Mimi's bed-table.

'Eustace, are you well?' Bruno asked with an earnestness that was entirely out of key with the other's jocularity.

Eustace was startled into his native language.

'Never felt better,' he answered. And then, as Bruno continued to look at him with the same intent, distressed expression, a note of irritation and suspicion came into his voice. 'What is it?' he questioned sharply.

Could the fellow see something that permitted him to guess about Mimi? Not that Mimi was anything one had to be ashamed of. No, the intolerable thing was the intrusion on one's privacy. And Bruno, he remembered, had always had this odd, exasperating gift of knowing things without being told about them. And of course, if it wasn't clairvoyance, it might easily be smears of lipstick.

'Why do you stare at me?'

Bruno smiled apologetically.

'I'm sorry,' he said. 'I just thought you looked . . . well, I don't know. Like people look when they're going to have a touch of flu.'

It was the face of a man entombed, and now all of a sudden menaced in his tomb. Menaced by what?

Relieved that it wasn't Mimi who had been detected, Eustace relaxed into a smile.

'Well, if I get the flu,' he said, 'I shall know who wished it on me. And now don't imagine,' he went on genially, 'that I've come here just to feast my eyes on that seraphic mug of yours. I want you to get permission for me to take my young nephew to see the maze in the Galigai gardens. He's arriving this evening.'

'Which nephew?' Bruno asked. 'One of Alice's sons?'

'Those louts?' said Eustace. 'God forbid! No, no; this is John's boy. Quite a remarkable little creature. Seventeen, and childish at that; but writes the most surprising verses—full of talent.'

'John must be a pretty difficult father,' said Bruno after a little pause.

'Difficult? He's nothing but a bullying fool. And of course the boy dislikes him and loathes everything he stands for.'

Eustace smiled. It gave him real pleasure to think of his brother's shortcomings.

'Yes, if only people would realize that moral principles are like measles . . .'

The soft voice tailed away into silence and a sigh.

'Like measles?'

'They have to be caught. And only the people who've got them can pass on the contagion.'

'Fortunately,' said Eustace, 'they don't always succeed in passing it on.'

He was thinking of that little Thwale woman. Any amount of contagion from the Canon and his wife; but no sign of any moral or pietistic rash on the daughter's white, voluptuous skin.

'You're right,' Bruno agreed. 'One doesn't have to catch the infection of goodness if one doesn't want to. The will is always free.'

Always free. People had been able to say no even to Filippo Neri and François de Sales, even to the Christ and the Buddha. As he named them to himself, the little flame in his heart seemed to expand, as it were, and aspire, until it touched that other light beyond it and within; and for a moment it was still in the timeless intensity of a yearning that was also consummation. The sound of his cousin's voice brought his attention back again to what was happening in the shop.

'There's nothing I enjoy more,' Eustace was remarking with relish, 'than the spectacle of the Good trying to propagate their notions and producing results exactly contrary to what they intended. It's the highest form of comedy.'

He chuckled wheezily.

Listening to that laughter coming up from the depths and darkness of a sepulchre, Bruno was moved almost to despair.

'If only you could forgive the Good!' The quiet voice was raised almost to vehemence. 'Then you might allow yourself to be forgiven.'

'For what?' Eustace enquired.

'For being what you are. For being a human being. Yes, God can forgive you even that, if you really want it. Can forgive your separateness so completely that you can be made one with him.'

'The solid vertebrate united with the Gaseous.'

Bruno looked at him for a moment in silence. In their setting of tired soft flesh the eyes were gaily twinkling; the babyish lips were curved into a smile of irony.

'What about the comedy of the Clever?' he said at last. 'Achieving self-destruction in the name of self-interest, and delusion in the name of realism. I sometimes think it's even higher than the comedy of the Good.'

He went behind the counter, and came back with a very old Gladstone bag.

'If you're going to meet that young nephew of yours,' he said, 'I'll go with you to the station.'

He was taking the seven-thirty train to Arezzo, he explained. There was an old retired professor there, who wanted to sell his library. And Monday was the opening day of a very important auction at Perugia. Dealers would be attending from all over the country. He hoped to pick up some of the unconsidered trifles.

Bruno turned out the lights, and they went out into a twilight that was fast deepening into night. Eustace's car was waiting in a side street. The two men got in, and were driven slowly towards the station.

'Do you remember the last time we drove to the station together?' Bruno suddenly asked after a period of silence.

'The last time we drove together to the station,' Eustace repeated doubtfully.

And then, all at once, it came back to him. He and Bruno in the old Panhard. And it was just after Amy's funeral, and he was going back to the Riviera—back to Laurina. No, it hadn't been too creditable, that episode of his life. Definitely on the squalid side. He made a little grimace, as though he had caught a whiff of rotten cabbage. Then, imperceptibly, he shrugged his shoulders. After all, what *did* it matter? It would all be the same a hundred years hence; it would all be the same.

'Yes, I remember,' he said. 'You talked to me about the Gaseous Vertebrate.'

Bruno smiled. 'Oh no, I wouldn't have dared to break the taboo,' he said. 'You began it.'

'Perhaps I did,' Eustace admitted.

Death and that insane passion and his own discreditable behaviour had conspired to make him do a lot of funny things at that time. He felt, all at once, extremely depressed.

'Poor Amy!' he said aloud, speaking under a kind of obscure

compulsion that was stronger than all his resolutions to refrain, in Bruno's presence, from being serious. 'Poor Amy!'

'I don't think she was to be pitied,' said Bruno. 'Amy had reconciled herself to what was happening to her. You don't have to feel sorry for people who are prepared for death.'

'Prepared? But what difference does that make?' Eustace's tone was almost truculent. 'Dying is always dying,' he concluded, happy to be able thus to escape from seriousness into controversy.

'Physiologically, perhaps,' Bruno agreed. 'But psychologically, spiritually . . .'

The car came to a halt before a policeman's outstretched arm.

'Now, now,' Eustace broke in. 'No nonsense about immortality! None of your wishful thinking!'

'And yet,' said Bruno softly, 'annihilation would be pretty convenient, wouldn't it? What about the wish to believe in that?'

From the sepulchre of his privation Eustace made confident answer.

'One doesn't *wish* to believe in annihilation,' he said. 'One just accepts the facts.'

'You mean, one accepts the inferences drawn from one particular set of facts, and ignores the other facts from which different inferences might be drawn. Ignores them because one really wants life to be a tale told by an idiot. Just one damned thing after another, until at last there's a final damned thing, after which there isn't anything.'

There was a blast of the policeman's whistle; and as the car moved on again, the light from a shop window passed slowly across Eustace's face, showing up every pouch and line and blotch in the loose skin. Then the darkness closed down once more, like the lid of a sarcophagus. Closed down irrevocably, it seemed to Bruno, closed down for ever. Impulsively, he laid his hand on the other's arm.

'Eustace,' he said, 'I implore you . . .'

Eustace started. Something strange was happening. It was as though the slats of a Venetian blind had suddenly been turned so as to admit the sunlight and the expanse of the summer sky. Unobstructed, an enormous and blissful brightness streamed into him. But with the brightness came the memory of what Bruno had said in the shop: 'To be forgiven . . . forgiven for being what you are.' With a mixture of anger and fear, he jerked his arm away.

'What *are* you doing?' he asked sharply. 'Trying to hypnotize me?'

Bruno did not answer. He had made his final desperate effort to raise the lid; but from within the sarcophagus it had been pulled down again. And of course, he reflected, resurrection is optional. We are under no compulsion except to persist—to persist as we are, growing always a little worse and a little worse; indefinitely, until we wish to rise again as something other than ourselves; inexorably, unless we permit ourselves to be raised.

CHAPTER ELEVEN

THE train was unexpectedly punctual and, when they reached the station, the passengers were already elbowing their way through the gates.

'If you see a small cherub in grey flannel trousers,' said Eustace, as he stood on tiptoes to peer over the heads of the crowd, 'that's our man.'

Bruno pointed a bony finger.

'Does *that* answer your description?'

'Which one?'

'That little *non Anglus sed angelus* behind the pillar there.'

Eustace caught sight of a familiar head of pale and curly hair and, waving his hand, pushed his way closer to the gate.

'And this is your long-lost second-cousin once removed,' he said, as he returned a minute later with the boy. 'Bruno Rontini—who sells second-hand books and would like everybody to believe in the Gaseous Vertebrate.' And as they shook hands, 'Let me warn you,' he continued in a mock-solemn tone, 'he'll probably try to convert you.'

Sebastian looked again at Bruno and, under the influence of his uncle's introduction, saw only foolishness in the bright eyes, only bigotry in that thin bony face, with its hollows under the cheek-bones, its beaky protrusion of a nose. Then he turned to Eustace and smiled.

'So this is Sebastian,' said Bruno slowly. Ominously significant, it was the name of fate's predestined target.

'Somehow, I can't help thinking of all those arrows,' he went on. 'The arrows of the lusts which this beauty would evoke and would permit its owner to satisfy; the arrows of vanity and self-satisfaction and . . .'

'But arrows go both ways,' said Eustace. 'This martyr will give as good as he gets—won't he, Sebastian?' He smiled knowingly, as from man to man.

Flattered by this display of confidence in his prowess, Sebastian laughed and nodded.

With an affectionate, almost a possessive gesture, Eustace laid a hand on the boy's shoulder.

'*Andiamo!*' he cried.

There was a note of something like triumph in his tone. Not only had he got even with Bruno for what had happened in the car; he had also cut him off from any chance of exerting an influence on Sebastian.

'*Andiamo!*' Bruno repeated. 'I'll take you to the car and get my bag.' Picking up Sebastian's suitcase, he started towards the exit. The others followed.

Hooting in a melodious baritone, the Isotta slowly nosed its way along the crowded street. Sebastian pulled the fur rug a little higher over his knees and thought how wonderful it was to be rich. And to think that, if it weren't for his father's idiotic ideas . . .

'Funny old Bruno!' his uncle remarked in a tone of amused condescension. 'For some reason he always reminds me of those preposterous Anglo-Saxon saints. St. Willibald and St. Wunnibald, St. Winna and St. Frideswide . . .'

He made the names sound so ludicrous that Sebastian burst out laughing.

'But a thoroughly kind, gentle creature,' Eustace went on. 'And considering he's one of the Good, not too much of a bore.'

Interrupting himself, he touched Sebastian's arm and pointed through the left-hand window.

'The Medici tombs are up there,' he said. 'Talk about the Sublime! I can't look at them now. Donatello's my limit these days. But of course it's quite true: the damned things *are* the greatest sculptures in the world. And that's Rossi's, the tailor,' he went on without transition, pointing again. 'Order decent English cloth, and the man will make you as good a suit as you can get in Savile Row, and at half the price. We'll take time off from our sight-seeing to get you measured for those evening clothes.'

Scarcely daring to believe his ears, Sebastian looked at him questioningly.

'You mean . . .? Oh, thank you, Uncle Eustace,' he cried, as the other smiled and nodded.

Eustace looked at the boy and saw, by the transient light of a street lamp, that his face had reddened and his eyes were bright. Touched, he patted him on the knee.

'No need for gratitude,' he said. 'If I were in *Who's Who*, which I'm not, you'd see that my chief recreation was "Annoying my brother."'

They laughed together, conspirators in mischief.

'And now,' cried Eustace, 'bend down and take a squint up through this window at the second-largest egg ever laid.'

Sebastian did as he was told, and saw great cliffs of marble and, above the cliffs, an enormous dome floating up into the sky and darkening, as it rose, from the faint lamplight that still lingered about its base into a mystery more impenetrable than the night itself. It was the transfiguration, not of a little squalor this time, but of a vast harmonious magnificence.

'Light first,' said Eustace, pointing a bloated finger that travelled upwards as he spoke, 'then darkness.'

Sebastian looked at him in astonishment. He too . . . ?

'It's like a looking-glass equation,' the other went on. 'You start with the values of x and y, and you end with an unknown quantity. The most romantic kind of lighting.'

'I didn't know anyone else had noticed it,' said Sebastian.

'Optimist!' Eustace smiled indulgently. What fun to be young, to be convinced, each time one lost a virginity, that this sort of thing had never happened before! 'The Victorian etchers and engravers hardly noticed anything else. All their romantic Matterhorns and ruined castles are darker on top than at the bottom. Which doesn't make the looking-glass equation less amusing.'

There was a little silence. The car turned out of the cathedral square into a street even narrower and more crowded than the one by which they had come from the station.

'I wrote a poem about it,' Sebastian confided at last.

'Not one of those you sent me for Christmas?'

The boy shook his head.

'I didn't think you'd like it. It's a bit . . . well, I don't know . . . a bit religious; that is, if it was about religion, which it isn't. But seeing you've noticed it too . . . I mean, the way things are lighted from the bottom . . .'

'Can you recite it?'

Torn between shyness and a desire to show off, Sebastian hummed and hawed, then finally said yes.

Little squalor! transfigured into Ely,
Into Bourges, into the beauty of holiness . . .

Leaning back in his corner, Eustace listened to the still almost childish voice and, as the lights came and went, scanned the averted face as it gazed with angelic gravity, wide-eyed, into the darkness. Yes, there was talent there all right. But what touched him so profoundly, what moved him almost to tears, was the whole-heartedness, the guileless good faith, the essential purity. Purity, he insisted—even though one couldn't really say what the word meant, or even justify its use. For obviously the boy was obsessed with sex—certainly masturbated—probably had affairs, homosexual or otherwise. And yet there was a purity there, a real purity.

The recitation came to an end, there was a long silence—so long, indeed, that Sebastian began to wonder uneasily if his little squalor were really as good as he believed. Uncle Eustace had taste; and if *he* thought it was no good, then . . . But the other spoke at last.

'That was very beautiful,' he said quietly. The words referred less to the poem than to what he himself had felt while listening to it—this unexpected uprush of high emotion and protective tenderness. 'Very beautiful.' He laid his hand affectionately on Sebastian's knee. Then, after a pause, he added, smiling, 'I used to write verses when I was a few years older than you are now.'

'You did?'

'Dowson and water,' said Eustace, shaking his head. 'With occasional flashes of Wilde and cat-piss.' He laughed. Enough of sentimentality. 'I don't rise above limericks nowadays,' he went on. 'But as Wordsworth so justly remarked,

Scorn not the Limerick, Critic, you have frowned,
Mindless of its just honours; with this key
Shakespeare unlocked his pants; th' obscenity
Of this small lute gave ease to Petrarch's wound . . .

And so on—until, of course, in Milton's hand

> *The Thing became a strumpet; whence he blew*
> *Soul-animating strains—alas, too few!*

After which I really must tell you about the "Young Girl of Spokane."'

He did. The car, meanwhile, had emerged into a larger darkness. Lights gleamed on water; a bridge was crossed, and with gathering speed they rolled for a minute or two along a wide embankment. Then their road swung to the right, grew tortuous, began to climb. Through his window, Sebastian looked on fascinated, as the head-lamps created out of nothingness a confluent series of narrow universes. A gaunt grey goat standing up on its hind legs to munch the wistaria buds that hung across an expanse of peeling stucco; a priest in black skirts pushing a lady's bicycle up the steep hill; a great ilex tree, writhing like a wooden octopus; and at the foot of a flight of steps two startled lovers, breaking apart from their embrace and turning with a flash of eyes and laughing teeth towards the light which had evoked and now, passing, abolished them.

A moment later, the car drew up before tall iron gates. Musically, but imperiously, it hooted for admittance, and a little old man came running out of the shadows to undo the bolts.

The drive wound its way under tall cypresses; a bed of blue hyacinths appeared and vanished, then a little fountain in a shell-shaped niche. As the Isotta made its final turn, the head-lights called into existence half a dozen weathered nymphs, naked on pedestals, then came to rest, as though this were the final, the all-explaining revelation, on an orange tree growing in a very large earthenware pot.

'Here we are,' said Eustace; and at the same moment a butler in a white jacket opened the door and deferentially inclined his head.

They entered a high square vestibule, pillared and barrel-vaulted like a church. The butler took their things, and Eustace led the way up the stone staircase.

'Here's your room,' he said, throwing open a door. 'Don't be alarmed by *that*,' he added, pointing at the enormous canopied bed. 'It's only the carving that's antique. The mattress is contemporary. And your bathroom is in there.' He waved his hand towards another door. 'Do you think you can get yourself washed and brushed in five minutes?'

Sebastian was sure he could; and five minutes later he was downstairs again in the hall. A half-opened door invited; he entered and found himself in the drawing-room. A faint spicy perfume of potpourri haunted the air, and the lamps that hung from the coffered ceiling were reflected, in innumerable curving high-lights, from surfaces of porcelain and silver, turned wood and sculptured bronze and ivory. Mountains of glazed chintz, enormous armchairs and sofas alternated with the elaborately carved and gaily painted discomfort of eighteenth-century Venetian furniture. Underfoot, a yellow Chinese carpet lay like an expanse of soft and ancient sunshine. On the walls, the picture-frames were doorways leading into other worlds. The first he looked into was a strange, bright universe, intensely alive and yet static, definitive and serene—a world in which everything was made of innumerable dots of pure colour, and the men wore stove-pipe hats and the women's bustles were monumental like Egyptian granite. And next to it was the opening into another, a Venetian world, where a party of ladies in a gondola trailed their pink satins against the complementary jade of the Grand Canal. And here, over the mantelpiece, in a maniac's universe of candlelight and brown bituminous shadows, a company of elongated monks sat feasting under the vaults of a cathedral . . .

His uncle's voice brought him back to reality.

'Ah, you've discovered my little Magnasco.'

Eustace came and took his arm.

'Amusing, isn't it?'

But before the boy could answer, he began to speak again.

'And now you must come and look at what I did yesterday,' he went on, drawing him away. 'There!'

He pointed. In an arched recess stood a black *papier-maché* table, painted with scrolls of gilding and inlaid with mother-of-pearl. Upon it stood a bouquet of wax flowers under a glass bell and a tall cylindrical case of stuffed humming-birds. On the wall, between and a little above these two objects, hung a small fourteenth-century painting of young men with bobbed hair and cod-pieces, shooting arrows at a St. Sebastian attached to a flowering apple tree.

'Your namesake,' Eustace said. 'But the real point is that at last one's discovered a way of using minor primitives. Obviously, it's ridiculous to treat this sort of rubbish as though it were serious art. But on the other hand, it's charming rubbish; one doesn't want to waste it. Well, here's the way out of the dilemma. Mix with Mid-Victorian! It makes the most delicious salad. And now, my dear, let's go and eat. The dining-room's over here, through the library.'

They moved away. From behind the door at the other end of the long tunnel of books came the sound of a harsh cracked voice and the clinking of silver and porcelain.

'Well, here we are at last!' Eustace cried gaily as he opened.

Dressed in a steel-blue evening gown, with seven rows of pearls about her mummied neck, the Queen Mother turned sightlessly in their direction.

'You know my habits, Eustace,' she said in her ghost of a sergeant-major's voice. 'Never wait dinner for anyone after seven forty-five. Not for anyone,' she repeated emphatically. 'We've almost finished.'

'Some more fruit?' said Mrs. Thwale softly, putting into the old woman's hand a fork, on which was impaled a quarter of a pear. Mrs. Gamble took a bite.

'Where's the boy?' she asked with her mouth full.

'Here.'

CHAPTER ELEVEN

Sebastian was pushed forward, and gingerly shook the jewelled claw which was held out for him to take.

'I knew your mother,' Mrs. Gamble rasped. 'Pretty, very pretty. But badly brought up. I hope you've been brought up better.' She finished off the rest of the pear and put down the fork.

Sebastian blushed crimson, and made a deprecating, inarticulate noise to the effect that he hoped so.

'Speak up,' said Mrs. Gamble sharply. 'If there's one thing I can't tolerate, it's mumbling. All young people mumble nowadays. Veronica?'

'Yes, Mrs. Gamble?'

'Oh, by the way, boy, this is Mrs. Thwale.'

Sebastian advanced into an aura of perfume and, raising abashed eyes from the folds of a dove-grey dress, almost cried out in amazement at what he saw. That oval face in its setting of smooth dark hair—it was Mary Esdaile's.

'How do you do, Sebastian?'

Oddly enough, he had never, with his inward ear, clearly heard the sound of Mary's voice. But it was obvious, now, that these were its very tones—rather low, but clear and exquisitely distinct.

'How do you do?'

They shook hands.

It was only in the eyes that he found a difference between his fancy and its incarnation. The Mary Esdaile of his day-dreams had always dropped her eyes when he looked at her. And how unwaveringly he was able to look in his dreams, how firmly and commandingly! Like his father. But this was not dream, but reality. And in reality he was still as shy as ever, and those dark eyes were now fixed upon him with a steady and slightly ironic scrutiny, which he found intensely embarrassing. His glance faltered, and at last flinched away.

'*You* know how to speak the king's English, Veronica,' Mrs. Gamble creaked on. 'Give him a few lessons while he's here.'

'Nothing would give me greater pleasure,' said Veronica

Thwale, as though she were reading from a book of Victorian etiquette. She raised her eyes once again to Sebastian's face, the corners of her beautifully sculptured mouth quivered into a tiny smile. Then, turning away, she busied herself with peeling the rest of Mrs. Gamble's pear.

'Let the poor boy come and eat,' called Eustace, who had sat down and was already half-way through his soup. Thankfully, Sebastian moved away to the place assigned to him.

'I ought to have warned you about our Queen Mother,' Eustace went on jocularly. 'Her bite is worse even than her bark.'

'Eustace! I never heard such impertinence!'

'That's because you've never listened to yourself,' he answered.

The old lady cackled appreciatively, and sank her false teeth into another piece of pear. The juice ran down her chin and dropped into the bunch of cattleyas pinned to her corsage.

'As for Mrs. Veronica Thwale,' Eustace went on, 'I know the young lady too little to be able to offer you advice about her. You'll have to find out for yourself when she gives you your mumbling lessons. Do you like giving lessons, Mrs. Thwale?'

'It depends on the intelligence of the pupil,' she answered gravely.

'And do you think that this one looks intelligent?'

Once more Sebastian found himself compelled to flinch away from the steady scrutiny of those dark eyes. But she was beautiful in that grey dress, and the neck was smooth like a white pillar; and the breasts were rather small.

'Very,' said Mrs. Thwale at last. 'But of course,' she added, 'where mumbling is concerned, you can never be quite certain. Mumbling is rather special, don't you think?'

And before Eustace could answer, she uttered her odd little snorting stertorous laugh. For a second only; then the face resumed its grave marble serenity. Delicately, she began to peel a tangerine.

Mrs. Gamble turned in the direction of her son-in-law.

'Mr. De Vries came to see me this afternoon. So I know where you had lunch.'

'"And from whom no secrets are hid,"' said Eustace.

Mrs. Thwale raised her eyelids to give him a quick glance of complicity, then looked down again at her plate.

'A most instructive young man,' he continued.

'I like him,' the Queen Mother pronounced emphatically.

'And he simply adores you,' said Eustace with hardly veiled irony. 'And meanwhile, how are *you* getting on with your Einstein, Mrs. Thwale?'

'I do my best,' she answered without lifting her eyes.

'I bet you do,' said Eustace in a tone of genial mischief.

Mrs. Thwale looked up; but this time there was no complicity in her glance, no hint of answering amusement—only stony coldness. Tactfully, Eustace changed the subject.

'I had a long talk with Laurina Acciaiuoli this afternoon,' he said, turning back to Mrs. Gamble.

'What, hasn't she passed on yet?' The Queen Mother seemed disappointed, almost aggrieved. 'I thought the woman was so desperately ill,' she added.

'Evidently not quite ill enough,' said Eustace.

'Sometimes they drag on for years,' rasped Mrs. Gamble. 'Your mother passed on some time ago, didn't she, Sebastian?'

'In 1921.'

'What?' she cried. 'What? You're mumbling again.'

'In 1921,' he repeated more loudly.

'Don't yell like that,' barked back the ghostly sergeant-major. 'I'm not deaf. Have you had any communications with her since then?'

'Communications?' he repeated in bewilderment.

'Through a medium,' Eustace explained.

'Oh, I *see*. No; no, I haven't.'

'Not because of religious objections, I hope?'

Eustace laughed aloud.

117

'What a preposterous question!'

'Not preposterous at all,' the Queen Mother snapped back. 'Seeing that my own granddaughter has religious objections. Mainly due to your father, Veronica,' she added.

Mrs. Thwale apologized for the Canon.

'No fault of yours,' said the Queen Mother generously. 'But Daisy's an idiot to listen to him. There she sits with a husband and a child on the other side, and does nothing whatever about it. It makes me sick.'

She pushed back her chair and stood up.

'We're going upstairs now,' she said. 'Good-night, Eustace.'

Since she couldn't see him, Eustace didn't bother to stand up.

'Good-night, Queen Mother,' he called back to her.

'And you, boy, you're to have a mumbling lesson tomorrow, do you understand? Now, Veronica.'

CHAPTER TWELVE

MRS. THWALE took the old woman's arm and steered her through the door which Sebastian had opened for them. Her perfume, as she passed him, was sweet in his nostrils—sweet, but at the same time obscurely animal, as though a whiff of sweat had been perversely mingled with the gardenias and the sandalwood. He closed the door and returned to his place.

'A good joke, our Queen Mother,' said Eustace. 'But one's always rather grateful when it's over. Most people never ought to be there for more than five minutes at a time. But that little Thwale, on the contrary . . . Quite a museum piece.'

He broke off to protest against the inadequacy of the portion of filleted sole to which Sebastian had helped himself. A recipe from the Trois Faisans at Poitiers. He had had to bribe the chef to get it. Obediently Sebastian took some more. The butler moved on to the head of the table.

'Quite a museum piece,' he repeated. 'If I were twenty years younger, or you were five years older . . . Except, of course, that you don't have to be any older, do you?'

He beamed with a kind of arch significance. Sebastian did his best to return the right sort of smile.

'*Verb. sap.*,' Eustace continued. 'And never put off till tomorrow the pleasure you can enjoy today.'

Sebastian said nothing. *His* pleasures, he was thinking bitterly, were only those of phantasy. When reality presented itself, he was merely terrified. Couldn't he at least have looked her in the eyes?

Wiping the sauce from his large loose lips, Eustace drank some of the champagne which had been poured into his glass.

'Roederer 1916,' he said. 'I'm really very pleased with it.'

Acting the part of a relishing connoisseur, Sebastian took an appreciative sip or two, then gulped down half a glassful. It had the taste, he thought, of an apple peeled with a steel knife.

'It's awfully good,' he said aloud. Then, remembering Susan's latest piece, 'It's . . . it's like Scarlatti's harpsichord music,' he forced himself to bring out, and blushed because it sounded so unnatural.

But Eustace was delighted by the comparison.

'And I'm so glad,' he added, 'that you don't take after your father. That indifference to all the refinements of life—it's really shocking. Just Calvinism, that's all. Calvinism without the excuse of Calvin's theology.'

He swallowed the last mouthful of his second helping of fish and, leaning back in his chair, looked round with pleasure at the beautifully appointed table, at the Empire furniture, at the Domenichino landscape over the mantelpiece, the life-sized goats by Rosa di Tivoli above the sideboard, at the two men-servants working with the noiseless precision of conjurers.

'No Calvin for me,' he said. 'Give me Catholicism every time. Father Cheeryble with his thurible; Father Chatterjee with his liturgy. What fun they have with all their charades and conundrums! If it weren't for the Christianity they insist on mixing in with it, I'd be converted tomorrow.'

He leaned forward and, with a surprising deftness and delicacy of touch, rearranged the fruits in the silver bowl between the candlesticks.

'"The beauty of holiness,"' he said, '"the beauty of holiness." I'm delighted you used that phrase in your poem. And, remember, it doesn't apply only to churches. There, that's better.' He made a final adjustment on the hot-house grapes, and leaned back again in his chair. 'I used to have a darling old butler once —never hope to find his equal.' He sighed and shook his head. 'That man could make a dinner-party go off with the solemn perfection of High Mass at the Madeleine.'

Creamed chicken succeeded the fish. Eustace made a brief digression on the subject of truffles, then returned to the beauty of holiness, and from that proceeded to life as a fine art.

'But an unrecognized fine art,' he complained. 'Its masters aren't admired; they're regarded as idlers and wasters. The moral codes have always been framed by people like your father —or, at the very best, people like Bruno. People like me have hardly been able to get a word in edgeways. And when we do get our word in—as we did once or twice during the eighteenth century—nobody listens to us seriously. And yet we demonstrably do much less mischief than the other fellows. We don't start any wars, or Albigensian crusades, or communist revolutions. "Live and let live"—that's our motto. Whereas *their* idea of goodness is "die and make to die"—get yourself killed for your idiotic cause, and kill everybody who doesn't happen to agree with you. Hell isn't merely paved with good intentions; it's walled and roofed with them. Yes, and furnished too.'

To Sebastian, after his second glass of champagne, this remark seemed, for some reason, extremely funny, and he broke into a giggle that ended embarrassingly in a belch. This stuff was as bad as ginger beer.

'You're familiar, of course, with the Old Man of Moldavia?'

'You mean the one who wouldn't believe in Our Saviour?'

Eustace nodded.

'"So he founded instead,"' he quoted, '"with himself as the head,"—though that's out of character, mark you; he wouldn't *want* to be the head; he'd just want to enjoy himself quietly and have good manners—"the cult of Decorous Behaviour." Or, in other words, Confucianism. But, unfortunately, China was also full of Buddhists and Taoists and miscellaneous war-lords. People with bullying temperaments, and people with inhibited, scrupulous temperaments. Horrible people like Napoleon, and other horrible people like Pascal. There was an Old Man of Corsica who would not believe in anything but power. And an Old Man of Port Royal who tortured himself by believing in the God of Abraham and Isaac, not of the philosophers. Between them, they don't give the poor Old Man of Moldavia a dog's chance. Not in China or anywhere else.'

He paused to help himself to the chocolate soufflé.

'If I had the knowledge,' he went on, 'or the energy, I'd write an outline of world history. Not in terms of geography, or climate, or economics, or politics. None of these is fundamental. In terms of temperament. In terms of the eternal three-cornered struggle between the Old Man of Moldavia, the Old Man of Corsica, and the Old Man of Port Royal.'

Eustace broke off to ask for some more cream; then continued. Christ, of course, had been an Old Man of Port Royal. So were Buddha and most of the other Hindus. So was Lao-Tsu. But Mahomet had had a lot of the Old Man of Corsica in him. And the same, of course, was true of any number of the Christian saints and doctors. So you got violence and rapine, practised by proselytizing bullies and justified in terms of a theology devised by introverts. And meanwhile the poor Old Men of Moldavia got kicked and abused by everybody. Except perhaps among the Pueblo Indians, there had never been a predominantly Moldavian society—a society where it was bad form to nourish ambitions, heretical to have a personal religion, criminal to be a leader of men, and virtuous to have a good time in peace and quietness. Outside of Zuñi and Taos, the Old Men of Moldavia had had to be content with registering a protest, with applying the brakes, with sitting down on their broad bottoms and refusing to move unless dragged. Confucius had had the best success in moderating the furies of the Corsicans and Port Royalists; whereas, in the West, Epicurus had become a by-word; Boccaccio and Rabelais and Fielding were disregarded as mere men of letters; and nobody bothered to read Bentham any more, or even John Stuart Mill. And recently the Old Men of Port Royal had begun to be treated as badly as those of Moldavia. Nobody read Bentham any more; but equally nobody now read À-Kempis. Traditional Christianity was in process of becoming almost as discreditable as Epicureanism. The philosophy of action for action, power for the sake of power, had become an established orthodoxy. 'Thou hast conquered, O go-getting Babbitt.'

'And now,' he concluded, 'let's go and have our coffee where we can be a bit more comfortable.'

Moving delicately and deliberately within his fragile world of incipient tipsiness, Sebastian followed his uncle into the drawing-room.

'No, thank you,' he said politely to the offer of a cigar even larger and darker than Dr. Pfeiffer's.

'Then take a cigarette,' said Eustace, as he helped himself to a Romeo and Juliet. Damply, lovingly the unweaned lips closed on the object of their desire. He sucked at the flame of the little silver lamp, and a moment later the teat was yielding its aromatic milk, his mouth was full of smoke. Eustace breathed a sigh of contentment. The taste of the tobacco was as new, as exquisitely a revelation as it had seemed when he was a young man; it was as though his palate were virgin and this were its first astounding introduction to pleasure. 'You should hurry up,' he said, 'and acquire the cigar habit. It's one of the major happinesses. And so much more lasting than love, so much less costly in emotional wear and tear. Though of course,' he added, remembering Mimi, 'even love can be considerably simplified. Very considerably.' He took Sebastian's arm affectionately. 'You haven't seen the prize exhibit yet.' And leading him across the room, he turned a switch. Under the light a lovely fragment of mythology sprang into existence. In a green glade, with the Mediterranean in the distance, and a couple of Capris off-shore, Adonis lay asleep among his sleeping dogs. Bending over him a blonde and amorous Venus was in the act of drawing aside the veil of gold-embroidered gauze which was his only covering, while a Cupid in the foreground playfully menaced her left pap with an arrow from the young hunter's quiver.

'The incandescent copulations of gods,' Sebastian said to himself as he gazed enchanted at the picture. Other phrases began to come to him. 'Bright with divine lust.' 'The pure lascivious innocence of heaven.' But what made this particular incandescence so delightful was the fact that it was rendered with a touch of irony, a hint (subtly conveyed by the two white rabbits in the left-foreground, the bullfinch among the oak-leaves overhead, the three pelicans and the centaur on the distant beach) that it was all a tiny bit absurd.

'Real love-making,' Eustace remarked, 'is seldom quite so pretty as Piero di Cosimo's idea of it.' He turned away and began to unwrap the drawings he had bought that morning at Weyl's. 'It's a good deal more like Degas.' He handed Sebastian the sketch of the woman drying the back of her neck.

'When you're seduced,' he said, 'it'll probably be by someone like *this* rather than like *that*.' He jerked his head in the direction of Piero's Venus.

From within his private universe of champagne Sebastian answered with a giggle.

'Or perhaps you have been seduced already?' Eustace's tone

was jocular. 'But of course it's none of my business,' he added, as Sebastian giggled again and blushed. 'Three words of advice, however. Remember that your talent is more important than your amusement. Also that a woman's amusement may sometimes be incompatible not only with your talent, but even with your fun. Also that, if this should happen, flight is your only strategy.'

He poured out some brandy into the two enormous glasses that had been brought in, sugared one of the cups of coffee, and, settling heavily into the sofa, beckoned to the boy to sit down beside him.

Professionally, Sebastian twirled the liquor in his glass and sipped. It tasted like the smell of methylated spirits. He dipped a piece of sugar in his coffee and nibbled at it, as he would have done after a dose of ammoniated quinine. Then he looked again at the drawing.

'What's its equivalent in poetry?' he said reflectively. 'Villon?' He shook his head. 'No. This isn't tragic. Donne's a little more like it—except that he's a satirist, and this man isn't.'

'And Swift,' put in Eustace, 'doesn't know how to convey the beauty of his victims. The fascinating contours of the dowager's hind-quarters, the delicious greens and magentas in a schoolgirl's complexion—he doesn't even see these things, much less make *us* see them.'

They laughed together. Then Eustace gulped down what remained of his brandy and helped himself to some more.

'What about Chaucer?' said Sebastian, looking up from another examination of the drawing.

'You're right!' Eustace cried delightedly. 'You're absolutely right. He and Degas—they knew the same secret: the beauty of ugliness, the comedy of holiness. Now, suppose you were given the choice,' he went on. '*The Divine Comedy* or *The Canterbury Tales*—which would you rather have written?' And without leaving Sebastian time to answer, 'I'd choose *The*

Canterbury Tales,' he said. 'Oh, without hesitation! And as a man—how infinitely one would prefer to be Chaucer! Living through the forty disastrous years after the Black Death with only one reference to the troubles in the whole of his writings—and that a comic reference! Being an administrator and a diplomat, and not regarding the fact as having sufficient importance to require even a single mention! Whereas Dante has to rush into party politics; and, when he backs the wrong horse, he spends the rest of his life in rage and self-pity. Revenging himself on his political opponents by putting them into hell, and rewarding his friends by promoting them to purgatory and paradise. What could be sillier or more squalid? And of course, if he didn't happen to be the second greatest virtuoso of language that ever lived, there'd be nobody to say a good word for him.'

Sebastian laughed and nodded his agreement. The alcohol and the fact that his uncle was taking him seriously, was listening to his opinions with respect, made him feel very happy. He drank some more brandy, and as he munched on the sugar with which he took the taste of it away, he looked again at the drawing of the woman with the towel. Elation quickened his faculties, and almost in a flash he had a quatrain. Pulling out his pencil and his scribbling pad, he started to write.

'What are you up to?'

Sebastian made no answer in words, but tore off the page and handed it to his uncle. Eustace put up his monocle and read aloud:

> *To make a picture, others need*
> *All Ovid and the Nicene Creed;*
> *Degas succeeds with one tin tub,*
> *Two buttocks and a pendulous bub.*

He clapped Sebastian on the knee.

'Bravo,' he cried, 'bravo!'

He repeated the last line, and laughed until he coughed.

'We'll make an exchange,' he said, when the fit was over and he had drunk another cup of coffee and some more brandy. 'I'll keep the poem, and you shall have the drawing.'

'Me?'

Eustace nodded. It was really a pleasure to do things for somebody who responded with such whole-hearted and un-feigned delight.

'You shall have it when you go up to Oxford. A drawing by Degas over the mantelpiece—it'll give you almost as much prestige as rowing in your college eight. Besides,' he added, 'I know you'll love the thing for its own sake.'

Which was a great deal more, it suddenly struck him, than could be said of his stepdaughter. He himself had only a life-interest; after his death, everything would go to Daisy Ockham. Not merely the stocks and shares, but this house and all that was in it, the furniture, the carpets, the china—yes, even the pictures. His absurd little St. Sebastian, his two delicious Guardis, his Magnasco, his Seurat, his Venus and Adonis—which Daisy would certainly consider too indecent to hang up in her drawing-room, in case her Girl Guides, or whatever they were, should see it and get ideas into their heads. And perhaps she'd bring the creatures out here, to the villa. Swarms of female puberties, pasty-faced and pimpled, wandering through his house and giggling in barbarous incomprehension at everything they saw. The very thought of it was sickening. But, after all, Eustace reminded himself, he wouldn't be there to care. And being sickened in advance, with no immediate reason for one's feelings, were merely silly. No less silly was thinking about death. So long as one was alive, death didn't exist, except for other people. And when one was dead, nothing existed, not even death. So why bother? Particularly as he was taking very good care to postpone the event. Smoking only one of these heavenly Romeo and Juliets, drinking only one glass of brandy after dinner . . . But no; he'd already drunk two. This one that he was just raising to his lips was the third. Well, never mind; he'd see that it didn't happen again. Tonight he was celebrating Sebastian's arrival. It wasn't every day that one welcomed an infant prodigy. He took a sip, and rolled the spirit round his mouth; on tongue and palate it consummated the happiest of marriages with the clinging aroma of his cigar.

He turned to Sebastian.

'A penny for your thoughts.'

The other laughed with a touch of embarrassment and answered that they weren't worth it. But Eustace insisted.

'Well, to begin with,' said Sebastian, 'I was thinking . . . well, I was thinking how extraordinarily decent you'd been to me.' It wasn't quite true; for his fancy had been busy with the gifts, not with the giver. 'And then,' he continued rather hurriedly; for he realized, too late as usual, that this perfunctory tribute didn't sound very convincing, 'I was thinking of the things I'd do when I had some evening clothes.'

'Such as taking the entire Gaiety chorus out to supper at Ciro's?'

Caught in the discreditable act of day-dreaming, Sebastian blushed. He had been imagining himself at the Savoy, not indeed with the whole Gaiety chorus, but very definitely with the two girls who were going to be at Tom Boveney's party. And then one of the girls had turned into Mrs. Thwale.

'Am I right?'

'Well . . . not exactly,' Sebastian answered.

'Not *exactly*,' Eustace repeated with benevolent irony. 'Of course, you realize,' he added, 'that you'll always be disappointed?'

'With what?'

'With girls, with parties, with experience in general. Nobody who has any kind of creative imagination can possibly be anything but disappointed with real life. When I was young, I used to be miserable because I hadn't any talents—nothing but a little taste and cleverness. But now I'm not sure one isn't happier that way. People like you aren't really commensurable with the world they live in. Whereas people like me are completely adapted to it.' He removed the teat from between his large damp lips to take another sip of brandy.

'Your business isn't doing things,' he resumed. 'It isn't even living. It's writing poetry. *Vox et praeterea nihil*, that's what you are and what you ought to be. Or rather *voces*, not *vox*. All the voices in the world. Like Chaucer. Like Shakespeare. The Miller's voice and the Parson's voice, Desdemona's and Caliban's and Kent's and Polonius's. All of them, impartially.'

'Impartially,' Sebastian repeated, slowly.

Yes, that was good; that was exactly what he'd been trying to think about himself, but had never quite succeeded, because such thoughts didn't fit into the ethical and philosophical patterns which he had been brought up to regard as axiomatic. Voices, all the voices impartially. He was delighted by the thought.

'Of course,' Eustace was saying, 'you could always argue that you live more intensely in your mental world-substitute than we who only wallow in the real thing. And I'd be inclined to admit it. But the trouble is that you can't be content to stick to your beautiful *ersatz*. You have to descend into evening clothes and Ciro's and chorus girls—and perhaps even politics and committee meetings, God help us! With lamentable results. Because you're not at home with these lumpy bits of matter. They depress you, they bewilder you, they shock you and sicken you and make a fool of you. And yet they still tempt you; and they'll go on tempting you, all your life. Tempting you to embark on actions which you know in advance can only make you miserable and distract you from the one thing you can do properly, the one thing that people value you for.'

It was interesting to be talked about in this way; but the stimulative effects of the alcohol had worn off, and Sebastian felt himself almost suddenly invaded by a kind of stupor that obliterated all thoughts of poetry, voices, evening clothes. Surreptitiously he yawned. His uncle's words came to him through a kind of fog that thickened and then thinned again, permitting the significance to shine through for a little, then rolled in once more, obscuring everything.

'... *Fascinatio nugacitatis*,' Eustace was saying. 'It's translated quite differently in the English version of the Apocrypha. But how wonderful in the Vulgate! The magic of triviality—the being spellbound by mere footling. How well I know the fascination! And how frightfully intense it is! Trifles for trifles' sake. And yet, what's the alternative? Behaving like the Old Man of Corsica, or some kind of horrible religious fanatic. ...'

Once again darkness invaded Sebastian's mind, a stupor diversified only by quivering streaks of dizziness and a faint nausea. He yearned to be in bed. Very distinct and silvery, a clock struck the half-hour.

'Half-past ten,' Eustace proclaimed. '"Time, time and half a time. The innocent and the beautiful have no enemy but time."' He gave vent to a belch. 'That's what I like about champagne—it makes one so poetical. All the lovely refuse of fifty years of indiscriminate reading comes floating to the surface. *O lente, lente currite, noctis equi!*'

O lente, lente ... Funereally slow black horses moved through the fog. And suddenly Sebastian realized that his chin had dropped involuntarily on to his chest. He woke up with a start.

'Faith,' his uncle was saying, 'they can never do without a faith. Always the need of some nonsensical ideal that blinds them to reality and makes them behave like lunatics. And look at the results in our history!' He took another swig of brandy, then sucked voluptuously at his cigar. 'First it's God they believe in—noτ three Gaseous Vertebrates, but one Gaseous Vertebrate. And what happens? They get the Pope, they get the Holy Office, they get Calvin and John Knox and the wars of religion. Then they grow bored with God, and it's war and massacre in the name of Humanity. Humanity and Progress, Progress and Humanity. Have you ever read *Bouvard et Pécuchet*, by the way?'

Rather belatedly, Sebastian started out of his coma and said no. 'What a book!' the other exclaimed. 'Incomparably the finest thing Flaubert ever did. It's one of the great philosophical poems of the world—and probably the last that will ever be written. For, of course, after *Bouvard et Pécuchet* there just isn't anything more to say. Dante and Milton merely justify the ways of God. But Flaubert really goes down to the root of things. He justifies the ways of Fact. The ways of Fact as they affect, not only man, but God as well—and not only the Gaseous Vertebrate, but all the other fantastic products of human imbecility, including, of course, our dear old friend, Inevitable Progress. Inevitable Progress!' he repeated. 'Only one more indispensable massacre of Capitalists or Communists or Fascists or Christians or Heretics, and there we are—there we are in the Golden Future. But needless to say, in the very nature of things, the future *can't* be golden. For the simple reason that nobody ever gets anything for nothing. Massacre always has to be paid for, and its price is a state of things that absolutely guarantees you against achieving the good which the massacre was intended to achieve. And the same is true even of bloodless revolutions. Every notable advance in technique or organization has to be paid for, and in most cases the debit is more or less equivalent to the credit. Except of course when it's more than equivalent, as it has been with universal education, for example, or wireless, or these damned aeroplanes. In which case, of course, your progress is a step backwards and downwards. Backwards and downwards,' he repeated; and, taking the cigar out of his mouth, he threw back his head and gave vent to a long peal of wheezy laughter. Then, all at once, he broke off, and his large face screwed itself up into a grimace of pain. He raised a hand to his chest.

'Heartburn,' he said, shaking his head. 'That's the trouble with white wine. I've had to give up Hock and Riesling completely; and sometimes even champagne. . . .'

Eustace made another grimace, and bit his lip. The pain

subsided a little. With some difficulty he heaved himself up out of his deep seat.

'Luckily,' he added, with a smile, 'there's almost nothing that a little bicarbonate of soda won't set right.'

He reinserted the teat and walked out of the drawing-room, across the hall and along the little passage that led to the downstairs lavatory.

Left to himself, Sebastian rose, uncorked the brandy and poured what remained in his glass back into the bottle. Then he drank some soda-water and felt distinctly better. Going to one of the windows, he pushed aside the curtain and looked out. A moon was shining. Against the sky, the cypresses were obelisks of solid darkness. At their feet stood the pale gesticulating statues, and behind and below, far off, were the lights of Florence. And doubtless there were slums down there, like the slums of Camden Town, and tarts in blue at the street corners, and all the stink and the stupidity, all the miseries and humiliations. But here was only order and intention, significance and beauty. Here was a fragment of the world in which human beings *ought* to be living.

Suddenly, in an act of pure intellectual apprehension, he was aware of the poem he was going to write about this garden. Not of its accidents—the metrical arrangements, the words and sentences—but of its essential form and animating spirit. The form and spirit of a long pensive lyric; of a poetical reflection intensified to the point of cry and song, and sustained in its intensity by a kind of enduring miracle. For a moment he knew it perfectly, his unwritten poem—and the knowledge filled him with an extraordinary happiness. Then it was gone.

He let the curtain drop, walked back to his chair and sat down to wrestle with the problems of composition. Two minutes later he was fast asleep.

There was an onyx ashtray on the lavatory window-sill. Very carefully, so as not to disturb its faultless combustion,

Eustace put down his cigar, then turned and opened the door of the little medicine cupboard above the wash-basin. It was always kept well stocked, so that, if ever during the day he had any need of internal or external first aid, it would be unnecessary for him to go upstairs to his bathroom. In ten years, he liked to say, he had spared himself as much climbing as would have taken him to the top of Mount Everest.

From the row of medicaments on the upper shelf he selected the bicarbonate of soda, unscrewed the stopper and shook out into his left palm four of the white tablets. He was in the act of replacing the bottle, when another spasm of this strangely violent heartburn made him decide to double the dose. He filled a glass, and began to swallow the tablets one by one, with a sip of water after each. Two, three, four, five, six . . . And then suddenly the pain was like a red-hot poker boring through his chest. He felt dizzy, and a whirling blackness obscured the outside world. Groping blindly, his hands slid across the wall and found the smooth enamelled cistern of the toilet. He lowered himself unsteadily on to the seat and almost immediately felt a good deal better. 'It must have been that bloody fish,' he said to himself. The recipe called for a lot of cream, and he had taken two helpings. He swallowed the last two tablets, drank the rest of the water and, reaching out, set down the glass on the window-sill. Just as his arm was at full stretch the pain returned—but in a new form; for it had now become, in some indescribable way, obscene as well as agonizing. And all at once he found himself panting for breath and in the clutch of a terror more intense than any fear he had ever experienced before. It was terror, for a few seconds, absolutely pure and unmotivated. Then all at once the pain shot down his left arm—nauseating, disgusting, like being hit in the wind, like getting a blow in the genitals—and in a flash the causeless fear crystallized into a fear of heart failure, of death.

Death, death, death. He remembered what Dr. Burgess had told him last time he went for a consultation. 'The old pump can't put up with indefinite abuse.' And his wife—she too . . . But with her it hadn't come suddenly. There had been years and years of sofas and nurses and strophanthine drops. Quite an agreeable existence, really. He wouldn't mind that at all; he'd even give up smoking altogether.

More excruciating than ever, the pain returned. The pain and the awful fear of death.

'Help!' he tried to call. But all the sound he could produce was a faint hoarse bark. 'Help!' Why didn't they come? Bloody servants! And that damned boy there, just across the hall in the drawing-room.

'Sebastian!' The shout produced no more than a whisper. 'Don't let me die. Don't let me . . .' Suddenly he was gasping with a strange crowing noise. There was no air, no air. And suddenly he remembered that beastly glacier where they had taken him climbing when he was a boy of twelve. Whooping and gasping in the snow, and vomiting his breakfast, while his father stood there with John and the Swiss guide, smiling in a superior sort of way and telling him it was only a touch of mountain sickness. The memory vanished; and nothing remained but this crowing for breath, this pressure on the darkened eyes, this precipitated thudding of blood in the ears, and the pain increasing and increasing, as though some pitiless hand were gradually tightening a screw, until at last—ah, Christ! Christ! but it was impossible to scream—something seemed to crack and give way; and suddenly there was a kind of tearing. The stab of that redoubled anguish brought him to his feet. He took three steps towards the door and turned the key backwards in the lock; but before he could open, his knees gave way and he fell. Face downwards on the tiled floor, he continued to gasp for a little, more and more stertorously. But there was no air; only a smell of cigar smoke.

With a sudden start Sebastian woke into a consciousness of pins and needles in his left leg. He looked around him and, for a second or two, was unable to remember where he was. Then everything fell into place—the journey, and Uncle Eustace, and the strange disquieting incarnation of Mary Esdaile. His eye fell on the drawing, which was lying where his uncle had left it, on the sofa. He leaned over and picked it up. 'Two buttocks and a pendulous bub.' A genuine Degas, and Uncle Eustace was going to give it to him. And the evening clothes too! He would have to wear them secretly, hide them in the intervals. Otherwise his father would be quite capable of taking them away from him. Susan would let him keep them in her room. Or Aunt Alice, for that matter; for in this case Aunt Alice was as much on his side as Susan herself. And luckily his father would still be abroad when Tom Boveney gave his party.

Musically the clock on the mantelpiece went ding-dong, and then repeated itself, ding-dong, ding-dong. Sebastian looked up and was amazed to see that the time was a quarter to twelve. And it had been only a little after half-past ten when Uncle Eustace left the room.

He jumped up, walked to the door and looked out. The hall was empty, all the house was silent.

Softly, for fear of waking anybody, he ventured a discreet call. 'Uncle Eustace!'

There was no answer.

Did he go upstairs and never come down again? Or perhaps, Sebastian speculated uneasily, perhaps he had come back, found him asleep and left him there—as a joke. Yes, that was probably what had happened. And tomorrow he'd never hear the end of it. Curled up in the armchair like a tired child! Sebastian felt furious with himself for having succumbed so easily to a couple of glasses of champagne. The only consolation was that Uncle Eustace wouldn't be unpleasantly sarcastic. Just a bit playful, that was all. But the danger was that he might be playful in front of the others—in front of that horrible old she-devil, in front of Mrs. Thwale; and the prospect of being treated as a baby in front of Mrs. Thwale was particularly distasteful and humiliating.

Frowning to himself, he rubbed his nose in perplexed uncertainty. Then, since it was obvious that Uncle Eustace had no intention of coming down again at this hour, he decided to go to bed.

Turning out the lights in the drawing-room, he made his way upstairs. Someone, he found, had unpacked for him while he was at dinner. A pair of faded pink pyjamas had been neatly laid out on the majestic bed; the celluloid comb with the three broken teeth and the wood-backed hair-brushes had taken their place incongruously among the crystal and silver fittings of the dressing-table. At the sight he winced. What must the servants think? As he undressed, he wondered how much he would have to tip them when he went away.

It was late; but the luxurious opportunity of taking a midnight bath was not to be missed. Carrying his pyjamas over his arm, Sebastian entered the bathroom, and having, by unthinking force of habit, carefully locked the door behind him, turned on the water. Lying there in the deliciously enveloping warmth, he thought about that garden in the moonlight and the poem he intended to write. It would be something like 'Tintern Abbey,' like Shelley's thing on Mont Blanc—but of course quite different and contemporary. For he would use all the resources of non-poetic as well as of poetic diction; would intensify lyricism with irony, the beautiful with the grotesque. 'A sense of something far more deeply interfused'—that might have been all right in 1800, but not now. It was too easy now, too complacent. Today the something interfused would have to be presented in conjunction with the horrors it was interfused with. And that, of course, meant an entirely different kind of versification. Changeable and uneven to fit a subject matter that would modulate from God Flat Minor to Sex Major and Squalor Natural. He chuckled over his little invention and conjured up the picture of Mary Esdaile in that moonlit garden. Mary Esdaile among the statues, as pale as they, and, between the meshes of her black lace, much nakeder.

But why Mary Esdaile? Why not her incarnation, her real presence? Real to the point of being disquieting, but beautiful, terribly desirable. And perhaps Mrs. Thwale was as passionate as her imaginary counterpart, as unashamedly voluptuous as the Venus in Uncle Eustace's picture. Three comic pelicans and a centaur—and in the foreground the pure lascivious innocence of heaven, the incandescent copulation of a goddess, who certainly knew what she wanted, with her mortal lover. What self-abandonment, what laughter and light-heartedness! Voluptuously he imagined himself a consenting Adonis.

CHAPTER THIRTEEN

THERE was no pain any longer, no more need to gasp for breath, and the tiled floor of the lavatory had ceased to be cold and hard.

All sound had died away, and it was quite dark. But in the void and the silence there was still a kind of knowledge, a faint awareness.

Awareness not of a name or person, not of things present, not of memories of the past, not even of here or there—for there was no place, only an existence whose single dimension was this knowledge of being ownerless and without possessions and alone.

The awareness knew only itself, and itself only as the absence of something else.

Knowledge reached out into the absence that was its object. Reached out into the darkness, further and further. Reached out into the silence. Illimitably. There were no bounds.

The knowledge knew itself as a boundless absence within another boundless absence, which was not even aware.

It was the knowledge of an absence ever more total, more

excruciatingly a privation. And it was aware with a kind of growing hunger, but a hunger for something that did not exist; for the knowledge was only of absence, of pure and absolute absence.

Absence endured through ever-lengthening durations. Durations of restlessness. Durations of hunger. Durations that expanded and expanded as the frenzy of insatiability became more and more intense, that lengthened out into eternities of despair.

Eternities of the insatiable, despairing knowledge of absence within absence, everywhere, always, in an existence of only one dimension. . . .

And then abruptly there was another dimension, and the everlasting ceased to be the everlasting.

That within which the awareness of absence knew itself, that by which it was included and interpenetrated, was no longer an absence, but had become the presence of another awareness. The awareness of absence knew itself known.

In the dark silence, in the void of all sensation, something began to know it. Very dimly at first, from immeasurably far away. But gradually the presence approached. The dimness of that other knowledge grew brighter. And suddenly the awareness had become an awareness of light. The light of the knowledge by which it was known.

In the awareness that there was something other than absence the anxiety found appeasement, the hunger found satisfaction.

Instead of privation there was this light. There was this knowledge of being known. And this knowledge of being known was a satisfied, even a joyful knowledge.

Yes, there was joy in being known, in being thus included within a shining presence, in thus being interpenetrated by a shining presence.

And because the awareness was included by it, interpenetrated by it, there was an identification with it. The awareness was not only known by it but knew with its knowledge.

Knew, not absence, but the luminous denial of absence, not privation, but bliss.

There was hunger still. Hunger for yet more knowledge of a yet more total denial of an absence.

Hunger, but also the satisfaction of hunger, also bliss. And then as the light increased, hunger again for profounder satisfactions, for a bliss more intense.

Bliss and hunger, hunger and bliss. And through ever-lengthening durations the light kept brightening from beauty into beauty. And the joy of knowing, the joy of being known, increased with every increment of that embracing and interpenetrating beauty.

Brighter, brighter, through succeeding durations, that expanded at last into an eternity of joy.

An eternity of radiant knowledge, of bliss unchanging in its ultimate intensity. For ever, for ever.

But gradually the unchanging began to change.

The light increased its brightness. The presence became more urgent. The knowledge more exhaustive and complete.

Under the impact of that intensification, the joyful awareness of being known, the joyful participation in that knowledge, was pinned against the limits of its bliss. Pinned with an increasing pressure until at last the limits began to give way and the awareness found itself beyond them, in another existence. An existence where the knowledge of being included within a shining presence had become a knowledge of being oppressed by an excess of light. Where that transfiguring interpenetration was apprehended as a force disruptive from within. Where the knowledge was so penetratingly luminous that the participation in it was beyond the capacity of that which participated.

The presence approached, the light grew brighter.

Where there had been eternal bliss there was an immensely prolonged uneasiness, an immensely prolonged duration of pain and, longer and yet longer, as the pain increased, durations of intolerable anguish. The anguish of being forced, by participation, to know more than it was possible for the participant to know. The anguish of being crushed by the pressure of that too much light—crushed into ever-increasing density and opacity. The anguish, simultaneously, of being broken and pulverized by the thrust of that interpenetrating knowledge from within. Disintegrated into smaller and smaller fragments, into mere dust, into atoms of mere nonentity.

And this dust and the ever-increasing denseness of that opacity were apprehended by the knowledge in which there was participation as being hideous. Were judged and found repulsive, a privation of all beauty and reality.

Inexorably, the presence approached, the light grew brighter.

And with every increase of urgency, every intensification of that invading knowledge from without, that disruptive brightness thrusting from within, the agony increased, the dust and the compacted darkness became more shameful, were known, by participation, as the most hideous of absences.

Shameful everlastingly in an eternity of shame and pain.

But the light grew brighter, agonizingly brighter.

The whole of existence was brightness—everything except this one small clot of untransparent absence, except these dispersed atoms of a nothingness that, by direct awareness, knew itself as opaque and separate, and at the same time, by an excruciating participation in the light, knew itself as the most hideous and shameful of privations.

Brightness beyond the limits of the possible, and then a yet intenser, nearer incandescence, pressing from without, disintegrating from within. And at the same time there was this other knowledge, ever more penetrating and complete, as the light grew brighter, of a clotting and a disintegration that seemed progressively more shameful as the durations lengthened out interminably.

There was no escape, an eternity of no escape. And through ever-longer, through ever-decelerating durations, from impossible to impossible, the brightness increased, came more urgently and agonizingly close.

Suddenly there was a new contingent knowledge, a conditional awareness that, if there were no participation in the brightness, half the agony would disappear. There would be no perception of the ugliness of this clotted or disintegrated privation. There would only be an untransparent separateness, self-known as other than the invading light.

An unhappy dust of nothingness, a poor little harmless clot of mere privation, crushed from without, scattered from within, but still resisting, still refusing, in spite of the anguish, to give up its right to a separate existence.

Abruptly, there was a new and overwhelming flash of participation in the light, in the agonizing knowledge that there was no such right as a right to separate existence, that this clotted and disintegrated absence was shameful and must be denied, must be annihilated—held up unflinchingly to the radiance of that invading knowledge and utterly annihilated, dissolved in the beauty of that impossible incandescence.

For an immense duration the two awarenesses hung as though balanced—the knowledge that knew itself separate, knew its own right to separateness, and the knowledge that knew the shamefulness of absence and the necessity for its agonizing annihilation in the light.

As though balanced, as though on a knife-edge between an impossible intensity of beauty and an impossible intensity of pain and shame, between a hunger for opacity and separateness and absence and a hunger for a yet more total participation in the brightness.

And then, after an eternity, there was a renewal of that contingent and conditional knowledge: 'If there were no participation in the brightness, if there were no participation . . .'

And all at once there was no longer any participation. There was a self-knowledge of the clot and the disintegrated dust; and the light that knew these things was another knowledge. There was still the agonizing invasion from within and without, but no shame any more, only a resistance to attack, a defence of rights.

By degrees the brightness began to lose some of its intensity, to recede, as it were, to grow less urgent. And suddenly there was a kind of eclipse. Between the insufferable light and the suffering awareness of the light as a presence alien to this clotted and disintegrated privation, something abruptly intervened. Something in the nature of an image, something partaking of a memory.

An image of things, a memory of things. Things related to things in some blessedly familiar way that could not yet be clearly apprehended.

Almost completely eclipsed, the light lingered faintly and insignificantly on the fringes of awareness. At the centre were only things.

Things still unrecognized, not fully imagined or remembered, without name or even form, but definitely there, definitely opaque.

And now that the light had gone into eclipse and there was no participation, opacity was no more shameful. Density was happily aware of density, nothingness of untransparent nothingness. The knowledge was without bliss, but profoundly reassuring.

And gradually the knowledge became clearer, and the things known more definite and familiar. More and more familiar, until awareness hovered on the verge of recognition.

A clotted thing here, a disintegrated thing there. But what things? And what were these corresponding opacities by which they were being known?

There was a vast duration of uncertainty, a long, long groping in a chaos of unmanifested possibilities.

Then abruptly it was Eustace Barnack who was aware. Yes, this opacity was Eustace Barnack, this dance of agitated dust was Eustace Barnack. And the clot outside himself, this other opacity of which he had the image, was his cigar. He was remembering his Romeo and Juliet as it had slowly disintegrated into blue nothingness between his fingers. And with the memory of the cigar came the memory of a phrase: 'Backwards and downwards.' And then the memory of laughter.

Words in what context? Laughter at whose expense? There was no answer. Just 'backwards and downwards' and that stump of disintegrating opacity. 'Backwards and downwards,' and then the cachinnation, and the sudden glory.

Far off, beyond the image of that brown slobbered cylinder of tobacco, beyond the repetition of those three words and the accompanying laughter, the brightness lingered, like a menace. But in his joy at having found again this memory of things, this knowledge of an identity remembering, Eustace Barnack had all but ceased to be aware of its existence.

CHAPTER FOURTEEN

SEBASTIAN had drawn back the curtains when he went to bed, and a little after half-past seven an entering shaft of sunlight touched his face and awoke him. Outside the window there was a sound of birds and church bells, and between the little grey and white clouds the sky was so brilliantly blue that he decided, in spite of the deliciousness of his enormous bed, to go and do a little exploring before anyone else was about.

He got up, took a bath, examined his chin and cheeks to see if there was any need to use his razor, and deciding that there was no need, dressed himself with care in a clean shirt, the newer of his grey flannel trousers and the less shabby of the two outgrown tweed jackets which his father had said must last till June. Then, after giving his rebellious hair a final brushing, he went downstairs and out through the front door.

Hardly less romantic than it had seemed under the moon, the garden revealed itself in all the details of its architectural design, with all the colours of its foliage and April flowers. Six goddesses stood sentinel on the terrace, and between the central pair a great flight of steps went down from landing to paved and parapeted landing, down, between colonnades of cypresses, to a green lawn bounded by a low semicircular wall, beyond which the eye travelled down and on to a distant chaos of brown and rosy roofs, and, floating high above them, in the very centre of the vista, the dome of the cathedral. Sebastian walked down to the bottom of the steps and looked over the retaining wall. Below it stretched a sloping field of vines, still leafless, like an acre of dead men's arms reaching up frantically towards the light. And here, beyond the cypresses, grew an ancient fig tree, all knees and knuckles, with elbowed branches pale as bones against the sky. What intricacies of blue and white when one looked up into it! 'Snatches of heaven,' he whispered to himself, 'seen through an ossuary. A pendent ossuary of arthropods.' And there were those church bells again, and a smell of wood smoke and hyacinths, and the first yellow butterfly. And when one walked back to the foot of the steps and looked up, it was like being inside something by Milton. Like walking about in *Lycidas*, through one of the similes in *Paradise Lost*. Majestic symmetries! And at the top, on their high pedestals, Artemis and Aphrodite stood pale against the foreshortened façade of the house. Beautiful, and at the same time slightly absurd. The appropriate phrases began to come to him.

> *Dian with dog, and Venus modestly*
> *Screening her pubic lichen and the green*
> *Moss on her limestone paps . . .*

And then suddenly he perceived that, without intending it, he had discovered the Open Sesame to his entire poem. 'Limestone'—it had come out casually, as a simple descriptive epithet. But in fact it was the password to his unwritten masterpiece, the key and guiding clue. And, of all people, old walrus-whiskered Macdonald, the science master, was his Ariadne. He remembered the words which had roused him for a moment from the coma into which he habitually sank during his physics and chemistry lessons. 'The difference between a piece of stone and an atom is that an atom is highly organized, whereas the stone is not. The atom is a pattern, and the molecule is a pattern, and the crystal is a pattern; but the stone, although it is made up of these patterns, is just a mere confusion. It's only when life appears that you begin to get organization on a larger scale. Life takes the atoms and molecules and crystals; but, instead of making a mess of them like the stone, it combines them into new and more elaborate patterns of its own.'

The others had only heard the oddities of old Mac's Dundee accent. For weeks, 'the putterrns of uttoms' had been a standing joke. But for Sebastian the joke had made some kind of obscure unrecognized sense. And now suddenly here the sense was, clear and comprehensible.

The primal pattern. And then the chaos made of patterns. And then the living patterns built up out of fragments of the chaos. And then what next? Living patterns of living patterns? But man's world was chaotically ugly and unjust and stupid. More hopelessly refractory than even the lump of stone. For that suffered itself to be carved into breasts and faces. Whereas five thousand laborious years of civilization had resulted only in slums and factories and offices. He reached the top of the stairs and sat down on the smooth flagstones at the foot of Venus's pedestal.

'And human individuals,' he was thinking. As living patterns in space, how incredibly subtle, rich and complex! But the trace they left in time, the pattern of their private lives—God, what a horror of routine! Like the repeats on a length of linoleum, like the succession of identical ornamental tiles along the wall of a public lavatory. Or if they did try to launch out into something original, the resulting scrolls and curlicues were generally atrocious. And anyhow most of them quickly ended in a smudge of frustration—and then it was linoleum and lavatory tiles, lavatory tiles and linoleum, to the bitter end.

He looked up at the house and wondered which of all the shuttered windows was Mrs. Thwale's. If that horrible old hag really wanted him to take lessons in speaking, it would give him an opportunity of talking to her. Would he have the nerve to tell her about Mary Esdaile? It would obviously be a wonderful opening. He imagined a conversation beginning with a witty and ironical confession of his own adolescent phantasies and ending—well, ending practically anywhere.

He sighed, looked down between the cypresses at the distant cupola, then up at the statue above him. What a curious worm's-eye view of a goddess! A green iridescent rose beetle was crawling slowly across her left knee. Or so it seemed to him. But what would the beetle say it was doing? Feeling the sixfold rhythm of its legs, the pull of gravity on its right side, the fascination of strong light on its left eye, the warmth and hardness of a surface diversified with pits and jagged stalagmites and vegetable growths, rank, but uninteresting, since the smell was not one that made it, willy-nilly, cut round holes in leaves or burrow between the petals of flowers. And what, Sebastian wondered, was he himself doing at this moment? Crawling over what enormous knee? Towards what future event, what premeditated flick of a giant's finger-nail?

He got up, dusted the seat of his trousers; then, reaching up, gave the beetle a little fillip. It fell on to the pedestal and lay there on its back, its legs waving. Sebastian bent down to look at it, and saw that its plated belly was covered with minute crawling ticks. Disgustedly, he turned the creature over on to its feet and walked away towards the house. The sun, which had passed for a moment behind a cloud, came out again, and all the garden glowed, as though every leaf and flower had been illumined from within. Sebastian smiled with pleasure, and

K   145

started to whistle the tune of the first movement of Susan's Scarlatti sonata.

As he opened the front door, he was surprised to hear a confused noise of talk, and, stepping across the threshold, he found the hall full of people—half a dozen servants, two old peasant women with shawls over their heads, and a dark-eyed little girl of ten or twelve, carrying a baby in one arm and, with the other hand, holding by the feet, head downwards and inert, a large speckled hen.

Suddenly they all fell silent. From a dark vaulted passage on the right came a sound of laboured shuffling; and a moment later, walking backwards with a pair of grey-trousered legs under his arm, emerged the butler, and then, stooping under the weight of the body, the footman and the chauffeur. One thick yellowish hand trailed palm upwards on the floor, and as the men turned to take their burden up the stairs, Sebastian caught sight of the black gape of an open mouth and two lustreless and discoloured eyes, fixed and mindlessly staring. Then step by step the body was heaved up, out of sight. Dangling from the child's hand, the speckled hen uttered a feeble squawk and tried to flap its wings. The baby broke into crowing laughter.

Sebastian turned and hurried away into the drawing-room. The first animal reaction of surprise and horror had left his stomach turned, his heart violently beating. He sat down and covered his face with his hands. It was as bad as that ghastly time at school when old Mac had made them dissect the dog-fish and he had been sick in one of the laboratory sinks. And this was poor Uncle Eustace. Suddenly snuffed out, reduced to the likeness of that awful Thing they had hauled up the stairs. Like men moving a piano. And it must have happened while he himself was sleeping, here, in this very chair. Perhaps Uncle Eustace had called for him; and perhaps, if he had heard, he could have done something to save his life. But he hadn't heard; he'd just gone on sleeping. Sleeping like a hog, while this man who was his friend, this man who had been more decent to him than almost anyone he could think of, who had treated him with such extraordinary generosity . . .

Suddenly, like a thunderbolt, the thought came to him that now he wouldn't have his evening clothes. Yesterday Uncle Eustace had promised; but today there was nobody to keep the promise. It was good-bye to Tom Boveney's party; good-bye to those girls before he had even known them. The whole structure of that particular set of day-dreams—so rational and substantial since Uncle Eustace had pointed out the tailor's shop on the way from the station—disintegrated into less than nothing. The pang of his disappointment and self-pity brought tears to Sebastian's eyes. Had anyone ever had such bad luck?

Then he remembered Uncle Eustace—remembered him, not as the dispenser of dinner jackets, but as that kindly, lively person who last night had been his friend and now was only a revolting thing—remembered, and was overcome by shame at his own monstrous selfishness.

'God, I'm awful,' he said to himself; and to keep his mind on the real tragedy, he whispered the word, 'Dead, dead,' over and over again.

And then suddenly he caught himself wondering what excuse he could invent for Tom Boveney. That he was ill? That he was in mourning for his uncle?

A bell rang, and through the open door Sebastian saw the footman crossing the hall to the front entrance. A few Italian phrases were exchanged, and then a tall thin man, elegantly dressed and carrying a little black bag, was ushered up the stairs. Evidently the doctor, called in to write the death-certificate. But if he had been called last night, Uncle Eustace might have been saved. And the reason why the doctor wasn't called, Sebastian reminded himself, was that he had been asleep.

The servant came down again and vanished into the kitchen regions. Time passed. Then the clock on the mantelpiece gave vent to four ding-dongs, and struck nine. A moment later, the footman entered through the library door, came to a halt in front of the chair on which Sebastian was sitting, and said something which, because of the distant aroma of coffee and fried bacon, the latter interpreted as an announcement of breakfast. He said 'thank you,' got up and walked into the dining-room. The nausea of surprise and horror had worn off, and he was feeling hungry again. He sat down to eat. The scrambled eggs were absolutely delicious; the bacon, crisp between the teeth and exquisitely pungent; the coffee, a dream.

He had just helped himself for the second time to marmalade when a luminous idea occurred to him. That Degas drawing, which Uncle Eustace had given him . . . What on earth could he do with it for the next few years? Hang it up in his bedroom and have old Ellen complain that it was 'rude'? Put it away until he went to Oxford? But wouldn't it really be much more sensible to sell the thing and use the money to get a suit of evening clothes?

The opening of the door made him look up. Dressed in black, with white ruffles at the neck and wrists, Mrs. Thwale had quietly entered. Sebastian jumped to his feet and, hastily wiping his mouth, said good-morning. With the sheet of notepaper she held in her hand Mrs. Thwale waved him back into his chair, and herself sat down beside him.

'You know what's happened, of course?'

Sebastian nodded, guiltily.

'One feels . . . well, one feels almost ashamed of oneself.'

He was trying to atone for not having given a thought to poor Uncle Eustace during the whole of breakfast.

'You know,' he went on, 'ashamed of being alive.'

Mrs. Thwale looked at him for a moment in silence, then shrugged her shoulders.

'But that's what living happens to be,' she said. 'The physiological denial of reverence and good manners and Christianity. And you're not even a Christian, are you?'

He shook his head. Mrs. Thwale continued with an apparently irrelevant question.

'How old are you?'

'Seventeen.'

'Seventeen?'

Once more she looked at him; looked at him so intently, with an expression of such disquietingly impersonal amusement, that he started to blush, and dropped his eyes.

'In that case,' she went on, 'it's doubly silly of you to feel ashamed of living. At your age one's quite old enough to know what the essence of life really is. Shamelessness, that's all; pure shamelessness.'

Her beautiful steel-engraving face puckered itself into a comic mask, and she uttered the delicate little grunt of her laughter. Then, suddenly serene again, she opened her handbag and took out a pencil.

'There's a whole sheaf of telegrams to be sent,' she went on in a calm, business-like voice. 'You can help me with some of the addresses.'

A few minutes later the butler came in and announced that he had been able to reach Mr. Pewsey on the telephone, and that Mr. Pewsey had offered to make all the necessary arrangements for the funeral.

'Thank you, Guido.'

The butler inclined his head almost imperceptibly, turned and silently went out again. The ritual of his service remained flawless; but Sebastian could see that he had been crying.

'Well, that's a great relief,' said Mrs. Thwale.

Sebastian nodded.

'All that rigmarole of funerals,' he said. 'It's too awful.'

'But evidently less awful than the realization that dying is even more shameless than living.'

'More shameless?'

'Well, at least you don't putrefy when you make love, or eat, or excrete. Whereas when you die . . .' She made a little grimace. 'That's why people are ready to spend such fortunes on last sacraments and embalmers and lead coffins. But what about these telegrams?' She looked back at her list of names. 'Mrs. Poulshot,' she read out. 'Where can she be reached?'

Sebastian was uncertain. Aunt Alice and Uncle Fred were on a motor tour in Wales. Better send the wire to London and hope for the best.

Mrs. Thwale took down the address at his dictation.

'Talking of shamelessness,' she said, as she reached for another telegraph form, 'I knew a girl once who lost her virginity on the night of Good Friday, at Jerusalem—just above the Church of the Holy Sepulchre. Now, what about your father?'

'He left for Egypt yesterday evening,' Sebastian began.

Suddenly through the open door there came a harsh imperious call of 'Veronica, Veronica!'

Without answering or making any remark, Mrs. Thwale rose and, followed by Sebastian, walked into the drawing-room. A storm of shrill barking greeted them. Retreating step by step as they advanced, Foxy VIII almost screamed his defiance. Sebastian glanced from the dog to its mistress. Her rouged face seeming more fantastically gaudy by contrast with the black of her dress and hat, the Queen Mother was standing, small and shrivelled, beside the stolid figure of her maid.

'Quiet!' she called blindly in the direction of the noise. 'Pick him up, Hortense.'

In Hortense's arms Foxy contented himself with an occasional growl.

'Is the boy there too?' Mrs. Gamble enquired, and when Sebastian came forward, 'Well, boy,' she said almost triumphantly, 'what do you think of all this?'

Sebastian murmured that he thought it was terrible.

'I told him only yesterday,' the Queen Mother went on in the same tone. 'No fat man has ever lived even to seventy. Much less to any reasonable age. You've sent a wire to Daisy, have you?'

'It's going off with the others in a few minutes,' said Mrs. Thwale.

'And to think that that goose is inheriting everything!' exclaimed the Queen Mother. 'What can *she* do with it, I'd like to know? All Eustace's pictures and furniture. I always told Amy not to let her have everything.'

Suddenly she turned on the maid.

'What on earth are you standing here for, Hortense? Go away and do something useful. Can't you see I don't need you?'

Silently the woman started to go.

'Where's Foxy?' shouted the Queen Mother in the direction of the retreating footsteps. 'Give him to me.'

She held out a pair of jewelled claws. The dog was handed over.

'Little Foxy-woxy,' Mrs. Gamble rasped affectionately, bending down to rub her cheek against the animal's fur. Foxy responded with a lick. The Queen Mother cackled shrilly and wiped her face with her fingers, smudging the rouge across her sharp and rather hairy chin. 'Only fifty-three,' she went on, turning back to the others. 'It's ridiculous. But what else could you expect with a stomach like that? Boy!' she rapped out sharply. 'Give me your arm.'

Sebastian did as he was bidden.

'I want you to show me the place where he actually passed on.'

'You mean . . .?' he began.

'Yes, I do,' barked the Queen Mother. 'You can stay here, Veronica.'

Slowly and cautiously Sebastian set off towards the door.

'Why don't you talk?' Mrs. Gamble demanded after they had walked a few yards in silence. 'I know a great deal about football, if that's what interests you.'

'Well, not really . . . I'm more interested in . . . well, in poetry and things like that.'

'Poetry?' she repeated. 'Do you write poetry?'

'A little.'

'Very peculiar,' said the Queen Mother. Then after a pause,

'I remember one time,' she went on, 'I was staying at a house where Mr. Browning was one of the guests. I never saw anyone eat so much for breakfast. Never. Except perhaps King Edward.'

They passed out of the hall into the dark little passage. The door at the end was still ajar. Sebastian pushed it open.

'This is the place,' he said.

Mrs. Gamble let go of his arm and, still holding the dog, groped her way forward. Her hand made contact with the wash-basin; she turned on a tap and turned it off again; then groped on, touched and flushed the toilet. Foxy began to bark.

'Which was that Roman emperor?' she asked through the yapping and the noise of the rushing water. 'The one who passed on in the w.c. Was it Marcus Aurelius or Julius Caesar?'

'I think it was Vespasian,' Sebastian ventured.

'Vespasian? I never heard of him,' said the Queen Mother emphatically. 'It smells of cigar smoke here,' she added. 'I always told him he smoked too many cigars. Give me your arm again.'

They walked back through the hall and into the drawing-room.

'Veronica,' said the Queen Mother, speaking at random into the darkness that constituted her world, 'did you ring up that tiresome woman again?'

'Not yet, Mrs. Gamble.'

'I wonder why she didn't answer.' The old lady's tone was fretful and aggrieved.

'She was out,' said Mrs. Thwale quietly. 'Giving a séance perhaps.'

'Nobody has séances at nine in the morning. And anyhow, she ought to have left somebody to take her calls.'

'She probably can't afford a servant.'

'Nonsense!' barked the Queen Mother. 'I've never known a good medium who couldn't afford a servant. Particularly in Florence, where they're dirt-cheap. Ring her up again,

Veronica. Ring her up every hour until you get her. And now, boy, I want to walk up and down the terrace for a little, and you shall talk to me about poetry. How do you start writing a poem?'

'Well,' Sebastian began, 'I usually . . .'

He broke off.

'But it's really too difficult to explain.'

He turned and gave her one of his irresistible, his angelic smiles.

'What a stupid answer!' exclaimed the Queen Mother. 'It may be difficult, but it certainly isn't impossible.'

Remembering too late that she couldn't see his smile, and feeling very foolish indeed, Sebastian relaxed his facial muscles into seriousness.

'Go on!' commanded the old lady.

Stammering, he did his best.

'Well, it's as if you . . . I mean, it's like suddenly *hearing* something. And then it seems to grow by itself—you know, like a crystal in a super-saturated solution.'

'In a what?'

'A super-saturated solution.'

'What's that?'

'Oh, well, it's . . . it's the thing that crystals grow in. But as a matter of fact,' he hastily added, 'that isn't quite the right metaphor. It's more like flowers coming up from seed. Or even like sculpture—you know: adding on little bits of clay and at last it's a statue. Or, still better, you might compare it to . . .'

The Queen Mother cut him short.

'I don't understand a word you're saying,' she rasped. 'And you mumble worse than ever.'

'I'm awfully sorry,' he muttered, yet more inaudibly.

'I shall tell Veronica to give you a lesson in talking the king's English every afternoon, while I'm having my rest. And now start again about your poetry.'

CHAPTER FIFTEEN

'BACKWARDS and downwards,' the laughter and the cigar. For long durations there was nothing else. This was all of himself that he possessed, all of himself that he had been able to find. Nothing but the memory of three words, of a sudden glory and a slobbered cylinder of tobacco. But it sufficed. The knowledge was delightful and reassuring.

Meanwhile, on the fringes of awareness, the light still lingered; and suddenly, between two rememberings, he perceived that it had somehow changed.

In the beginning the brightness had been everywhere, and everywhere the same, a shining silence, boundless and uniform. And essentially it was still without flaw, still indeterminate. And yet, while it remained what it had always been, it was as though that calm boundlessness of bliss and knowledge had been limited by the interpenetration of an activity. An activity that was at the same time a pattern, a kind of living lattice; ubiquitous, infinitely complex, exquisitely delicate. A vast ubiquitous web of beknottednesses and divergences, of parallels and spirals, of intricate figures and their curiously distorted projections—all shining and active and alive.

Once more his single fragment of selfhood came back to him —the same as ever, but in some way associated, this time, with a particular figure in that bright lattice of intricate relationships, located, as it were, on one of its innumerable nodes of intersecting movement.

'Backwards and downwards,' and then the sudden glory of laughter.

But this pattern of intersections was projected from another pattern, and within that other pattern he suddenly found another, larger fragment of himself—found the remembered image of a small boy, scrambling up out of the water of a ditch, wet and muddy to above the knees. And 'Sucks, John, sucks!' he remembered himself shouting; and when the boy said, 'Jump, you coward,' he only shouted 'Sucks!' again, and howled with laughter.

And the laughter brought back the cigar, all slobbered, and along with the cigar, somewhere else in the heart of that ubiquitous lattice, the memory of the feeling of a thumb between the lips, the memory of the pleasure of sitting interminably in the w.c., reading the *Boy's Own Paper* and sucking on a stringy length of liquorice.

And here, going back from projection to projector, was the image of an enormous, firm-fleshed presence, smelling of disinfectant soap. And when he failed to do *Töpfchen*, Fräulein Anna laid him deliberately across her knees, gave him two smacks, and left him lying face downwards on the cot, while she went to fetch the *Spritze*. Yes, the *Spritze*, the *Spritze*. . . . And there were other names for it, English names; for sometimes it was his mother who inflicted the pleasure-anguish of the enema. And when that happened the looming presence smelt, not of disinfectant, but of orris root. And though, of course, he could have done *Töpfchen* if he had wanted to, he wouldn't—just for the sake of that agonizing pleasure.

The lines of living light fanned out, then came together in another knot; and this was no longer Fräulein Anna or his mother; this was Mimi. *Spicciati, Bebino!* And with an uprush of elation he remembered the claret-coloured dressing-gown, the warmth and resilience of flesh beneath the silk.

Through the interstices of the lattice he was aware of the other aspect of the light—of the vast undifferentiated silence, of the beauty austerely pure, but fascinating, desirable, irresistibly attractive.

The brightness approached, grew more intense. He became part of the bliss, became identical with the silence and the beauty. For ever, for ever.

But with participation in the beauty there went participation in the knowledge. And suddenly he knew these recovered fragments of himself for what they so shamefully were; knew them for mere clots and disintegrations, for mere absences of light, mere untransparent privations, nothingnesses that had to be annihilated, had to be held up into the incandescence, considered in all their hideousness by the light of that shining silence, considered and understood and then repudiated, annihilated to make place for the beauty, the knowledge, the bliss.

The claret-coloured dressing-gown fell apart, and he discovered another fragment of his being—a memory of round breasts, wax-white, tipped with a pair of blind brown eyes. And in the thick flesh, deeply embedded, the navel, he recalled, had the absurd primness of a Victorian mouth. Prunes and prisms. *Adesso commincia la tortura.*

Abruptly, almost violently, the beauty of the light and the anguish of participating in its knowledge were intensified beyond the limits of possibility. But in the same instant he realized that it was in his power to avert his attention, to refuse to participate. Deliberately, he limited his awareness to the claret-coloured dressing-gown. The light died down again into insignificance. He was left in peace with his little property of memories and images. To treasure and enjoy them interminably—to enjoy them to the point of identification, to the point of being transubstantiated into them. Again and again, through comfortable durations of cigars and dressing-gowns and laughter and Fräulein Anna, and then cigars again and dressing-gowns. . . .

Then suddenly, within the framework of the lattice, there was an abrupt displacement of awareness, and he was discovering another fragment of himself. . . . They were sitting in that church at Nice, and the choir was singing Mozart's *Ave Verum Corpus*—the men's voices filling all the hollow darkness with a passion of grief and yearning, and the boyish trebles passing back and forth between them, harmonious but beautifully irrelevant with the virginal otherness of things before the Fall, before the discovery of good and evil. Effortlessly, the music moved on from loveliness to loveliness. There was the knowledge of perfection, ecstatically blissful and at the same time sad, sad to the point of despair. *Ave Verum, Verum Corpus.* Before the motet was half over, the tears were streaming down his cheeks. And when he and Laurina left the church, the sun had set and above the dark house-tops the sky was luminous and serene. They found the car and drove back to Monte Carlo along the Corniche. At a bend of the road, between two tall cypresses, he saw the evening star. 'Look!' he said. 'Like the boys singing!' But twenty minutes later they were in the Casino. It was the evening Laurina had her extraordinary run of luck. Twenty-two thousand francs. And in her room, at midnight, she had spread the money all over the carpet—hundreds of gold pieces, dozens and dozens of hundred-franc notes. He sat down beside her on the floor, put an arm round her shoulders and drew her close. '*Ave Verum Corpus,*' he said, laughing. This was the true body.

And now he was at another but an almost identical intersection of the lattice, remembering himself lying in the long grass beside the cricket field at school. Looking up sleepily, through half-closed eyelids, at the hazy, almost tangible blueness of an English summer afternoon. And as he looked, something extraordinary happened. Nothing moved, but it was as though there had been an enormous circular gesture, as though something like a curtain had been drawn back. To all outward seeming that blue nostalgic canopy just above the tree-tops remained unruffled. And yet everything was suddenly different, everything had fallen to bits. The half-holiday afternoon, the routine of the game, the friendliness of familiar things and happenings—all were in bits. Shattered, for all that they were physically intact, by an inward and invisible earthquake. Something had broken through the crust of customary appearance. A lava gush from some other, more real order of existence. Nothing had changed; but he perceived everything as totally different, perceived himself as capable of acting and thinking in totally new ways appropriate to that revolutionary difference in the world.

'What about going down town when the game's over?'

He looked up. It was Timmy Williams—but even Timmy Williams, he suddenly perceived, was something other, better, more significant than the ferret-faced creature he enjoyed talking literature and smut with.

'Something rather queer happened to me this afternoon,' he was confiding, half an hour later, as they sat at the confectioner's, eating strawberries and cream.

But when the story was told Timmy merely laughed and said that everybody had spots in front of their eyes sometimes. It was probably constipation.

It wasn't true, of course. But now that the shattered world had come together again, now that the curtain had fallen into place and the lava gush had flowed back to where it had come from, how nice and comfortable everything was! Better to leave well enough alone. Better to go on behaving as one had always behaved, not risk having to do anything strange or uncomfortable. After a moment's hesitation, he joined in the laughter.

Probably constipation. Yes, probably constipation. And, as though endowed with a life of its own, the refrain began to chant itself to the tune of 'Under the Bamboo Tree.'

> *Probably constip,*
> *Probably constip,*
> *Probably constipaysh;*
> *Probably const,*
> *Probably const,*
> *Probably constipay, pay, pay.*

And *da capo, da capo*—like that barrel organ which was playing the tune outside the Kensington Registry Office the morning he and Amy were married.

> *Under the bamboo,*
> *Under the bamboo,*
> *Probably constipaysh . . .*

CHAPTER SIXTEEN

'WELL,' said Mrs. Thwale, as Foxy's barking and the thin croak of the Queen Mother's endearments died away into the distance, 'now you're my pupil. Perhaps I ought to have provided myself with a birch. Do you get birched at school?'

Sebastian shook his head.

'No? What a pity! I've always thought that birching had considerable charm.'

She looked at him with a faint smile; then turned away to sip her coffee. There was a long silence.

Sebastian raised his eyes and surreptitiously studied her averted face—the face of Mary Esdaile come to life, the face of the woman with whom, in imagination, he had explored what he believed to be the uttermost reaches of sensuality. And here she sat, decorously in black among all the coloured richness of the room, utterly unaware of the part she had played in his private universe, the things she had done and submitted to. Messalina inside his skull, Lucretia inside hers. But of course she wasn't Lucretia, not with those eyes of hers, not with that way of silently impregnating the space around her with her physically feminine presence.

Mrs. Thwale looked up.

'Obviously,' she said, 'the first thing is to discover why you mumble, when it's just as easy to speak clearly and coherently. Why do you?'

'Well, if one feels shy . . .'

'If one feels shy,' said Mrs. Thwale, 'the best thing to do, I've always found, is to imagine how the person you're shy of would look if he or she were squatting in a hip bath.'

Sebastian giggled.

'It's almost infallible,' she continued. 'The old and ugly ones look so grotesque that you can hardly keep a straight face. Whereas the young, good-looking ones look so attractive that you lose all alarm and even all respect. Now, shut your eyes and try it.'

Sebastian glanced at her, and the blood rushed up into his face.

'You mean . . . ?'

He found himself unable to finish the question.

'*I* have no objection,' said Mrs. Thwale composedly.

He shut his eyes; and there was Mary Esdaile in black lace, Mary Esdaile on a pink divan in the attitude of Boucher's *Petite Morphil*.

'Well, do you feel less shy now?' she asked when he had reopened his eyes.

Sebastian looked at her for a moment; then, overwhelmed by embarrassment at the thought that she now knew something of what was happening in the world of his phantasy, emphatically shook his head.

'You don't?' said Mrs. Thwale, and the low voice modulated upwards on a rising coo. 'That's bad. It almost looks as if yours were a case for surgery. S-surgery,' she repeated, and took another sip of coffee, looking at him all the time with bright ironic eyes over the top of her cup.

'However,' she added, as she wiped her mouth, 'it may still be possible to achieve a cure by psychological methods. There's the technique of outrage, for example.'

Sebastian repeated the words on a tone of enquiry.

'Well, you know what an outrage is,' she said. 'A *non sequitur* in action. For example, rewarding a child for being good by giving it a sound whipping and sending it to bed. Or better still, whipping it and sending it to bed for no reason at all. That's the perfect outrage—completely disinterested, absolutely platonic.'

She smiled to herself. Those last words were the ones her father liked to use when he talked about Christian charity.

That damned charity, with which he had poisoned all her childhood and adolescence. Surrounding himself, in its name, with a rabble of the unfortunate and the worthy. Turning what should have been their home into a mere waiting-room and public corridor. Bringing her up among the squalors and uglinesses of poverty. Blackmailing her into a service she didn't want to give. Forcing her to spend her leisure with dull and ignorant strangers, when all she desired was to be alone. And as though to add insult to injury, he made her recite 1 Corinthians xiii every Sunday evening.

'Absolutely platonic,' Mrs. Thwale repeated, looking up again at Sebastian. 'Like Dante and Beatrice.' And after a second or two she added pensively: 'One day that pretty face of yours is going to get you into trouble.'

Sebastian laughed uncomfortably, and tried to change the subject.

'But where does shyness come in?' he asked.

'It doesn't,' she answered. 'It goes out. The outrage drives it out.'

'What outrage?'

'Why, the outrage you commit when you simply don't know what else to do or say.'

'But how can you? I mean, if you're shy . . .'

'You've got to do violence to yourself. As if you were committing suicide. Put the revolver to your temple. Five more seconds, and the world will come to an end. Meanwhile, nothing matters.'

'But it does matter,' Sebastian objected. 'And the world doesn't really come to an end.'

'No; but it's really transformed. The outrage creates an entirely novel situation.'

'An unpleasant situation.'

'So unpleasant,' Mrs. Thwale agreed, 'that you can't think of being shy any more.'

Sebastian looked doubtful.

'You don't believe me?' she said. 'Well, we'll stage a rehearsal. I'm Mrs. Gamble asking you to tell me how you write a poem.'

'God, wasn't that ghastly!' cried Sebastian.

'And why was it ghastly? Because you didn't have the sense to see that it was the sort of question that couldn't be answered except by an outrage. It made me laugh to hear you humming and hawing over psychological subtleties which the old lady couldn't possibly have understood even if she had wanted to. Which, of course, she didn't.'

'But what else could I have done? Seeing that she wanted to know how I wrote.'

'I'll tell you,' said Mrs. Thwale. 'You shouldn't have spoken for at least five seconds; then very slowly and distinctly you should have said: "Madame, I do it with an indelible pencil on a roll of toilet paper." Now, say it.'

'No, I can't . . . really . . .'

He gave her one of his appealing, irresistible smiles. But, instead of melting, Mrs. Thwale contemptuously shook her head.

'No, no,' she said, 'I'm not a bit fond of children. And as for you, you ought to be ashamed of playing those tricks. At seventeen a man ought to be begetting babies, not trying to imitate them.'

Sebastian blushed and uttered a nervous laugh. Her frankness had been horribly painful; and yet with a part of his being he was glad that she should have spoken as she did, glad that she didn't want, like all the rest, to treat him as a child.

'And now,' Mrs. Thwale went on, 'this time you'll say it— do you understand?'

The tone was so coolly imperious that Sebastian obeyed without further protest or demur.

'Madame, I do it with an indelible pencil,' he began.

'That's not an outrage,' said Mrs. Thwale. 'That's a bleat.'

'I do it with an indelible pencil,' he repeated more loudly.

'*Fortissimo!*'

'. . . With an indelible pencil on a roll of toilet paper. . . .'

Mrs. Thwale clapped her hands.

'Excellent!'

She uttered a delicate grunt of laughter. More boisterously, Sebastian joined in.

'And now,' she went on, 'I ought to box your ears. Hard, so that it hurts. And you'll be so startled and angry that you'll shout, "You bloody old bitch," or words to that effect. And then the fun will begin. I'll start screeching like a macaw, and you'll start . . .'

The door of the drawing-room was thrown open.

'*Il Signor De Vries*,' announced the footman.

Mrs. Thwale broke off in the middle of her sentence and instantaneously readjusted her expression. It was a grave madonna who faced the new arrival as he hurried across the room towards her.

'I was out all morning,' said Paul De Vries, as he took her extended hand. 'Didn't get your phone message till I came back to the hotel after lunch. What a shocking piece of news!'

'Shocking,' Mrs. Thwale repeated, nodding her head. 'By the way,' she added, 'this is poor Mr. Barnack's nephew, Sebastian.'

'This must be a dreadful blow to you,' said De Vries as they shook hands.

Sebastian nodded and, feeling rather hypocritical, mumbled that it was.

'Dreadful, dreadful,' the other repeated. 'But of course one must never forget that even death has its values.'

He turned back to Mrs. Thwale.

'I came up here to see if there was anything I could do to help you.'

'That was very kind of you, Paul.'

She lifted her eyelids and gave him an intent, significant look; the unparted lips trembled into a faint smile. Then she looked down again at the white hands lying folded in her lap.

Paul De Vries's face lit up with pleasure; and suddenly, in

a flash of insight, Sebastian perceived that the fellow was in love with her, and that she knew it and permitted it.

He was overcome with a fury of jealousy, jealousy all the more painful for knowing itself futile, all the more violent because he was too young to be able to avow it without making a fool of himself. If he told her what he felt, she would simply laugh at him. It would be another of his humiliations.

'I think I ought to go,' he muttered, and began to move towards the door.

'You're not running away, are you?' said Mrs. Thwale.

Sebastian halted and looked round. Her eyes were fixed upon him. He flinched away from their dark enigmatic regard.

'I've got to . . . to write some letters,' he invented; and turning, he hurried out of the room.

'Do you see that?' said Mrs. Thwale as the door closed. 'The poor boy's jealous of you.'

'Jealous?' the young man repeated in a tone of incredulous astonishment.

He hadn't noticed anything. But then, of course, he seldom did notice things. It was a fact about himself which he knew and was even rather proud of. When one's mind is busy with really important, exciting ideas, one can't be bothered with the trivial little events of daily life.

'Well, I suppose you're right,' he said with a smile. '"The desire of the moth for the star." It's probably very good for the boy,' he added in the tone of a wise, benevolent humanist. 'Hopeless passions are part of a liberal education. That's the way adolescents learn how to sublimate sex.'

'Do they?' said Mrs. Thwale with a seriousness so absolute that a more perspicacious man would have divined the underlying irony.

But Paul De Vries only nodded emphatically.

'By discovering the values of romantic love,' he said. 'That's how they achieve sublimation. Havelock Ellis has some beautiful things to say about it in one of his . . .'

Becoming suddenly aware that this wasn't at all what he really wanted to talk to her about, he broke off.

'Damn Havelock Ellis!' he said; and there was a long silence.

Mrs. Thwale sat quite still, waiting for what she knew was going to happen next. And, sure enough, he suddenly sat down on the sofa beside her, took her hand and squeezed it between both of his.

She raised her eyes, and Paul De Vries gazed back at her with a tremulous little smile of the most intense yearning. But Mrs. Thwale's face remained unalterably grave, as though love were too serious a thing to be smiled over. With those nostrils of his, she was thinking, he looked like one of those abjectly sentimental dogs. Ludicrous, but at the same time a bit distasteful. But then it was always a question of choosing between two evils. She looked down again.

The young man raised her unresponsive fingers to his lips and kissed them with a kind of religious reverence. But her perfume had a kind of sultry and oppressive sweetness; her neck was flawlessly round and smooth and white; under the stretched black silk he could imagine the firmness of the small breasts. Yearning came sharply into focus as desire. He whispered her name and, abruptly, rather clumsily, put one arm round her shoulders and with the other hand raised her face towards his own. But before he could kiss her Mrs. Thwale had drawn away from him.

'No, Paul. Please.'

'But, my darling . . .'

He caught hold of her hand and tried once again to draw her towards him. She stiffened and shook her head.

'I said no, Paul.'

Her tone was peremptory: he desisted.

'Don't you care for me at all, Veronica?' he said plaintively.

Mrs. Thwale looked at him in silence, and for a moment she was tempted to answer the fool as he deserved. But that would be silly. Gravely, she nodded.

'I'm very fond of you, Paul. But you seem to forget,' she added with a sudden smile and change of tone, 'that I'm what's known as a respectable woman. Sometimes I wish I weren't. But there it is!'

Yes, there it was—an insurmountable obstacle in the way of modified celibacy. And meanwhile he loved her as he had never loved anyone before. Loved uncontrollably, beyond reason, to the verge of insanity. Loved to the point of being haunted by the thought of her, of being possessed by the lovely demon of her desirableness.

The small inert hand which he had been holding came suddenly to life and was withdrawn.

'Besides,' she went on gravely, 'we're forgetting poor Mr. Barnack.'

'Damn Mr. Barnack!' he couldn't help snapping.

'Paul!' she protested, and her face took on an expression of distress. 'Really . . .'

'I'm sorry,' he said, between his teeth.

Elbows on knees, head between hands, he stared unseeingly at the patch of Chinese carpet between his feet. He was thinking, resentfully, how the demon would break in upon him while he was reading. There was no preservative or exorcism; even the most excitingly new and important books were powerless against the obsession. Instead of quantum mechanics, instead of the individuation field, it would suddenly be the pale oval of her face that filled his mind, it would be her voice, and the way she looked at you, and her perfume, and the white roundness of her neck and arms. And yet he had always sworn to himself that he would never get married, that he'd give all his time and thought and energies to this great work of his, to the bridge-building which was so obviously and providentially his vocation.

All at once he felt the touch of her hand on his hair and, looking up, found her smiling at him, almost tenderly.

'You mustn't be sad, Paul.'

He shook his head.

'Sad, and mad, and probably bad as well.'

'No, don't say that,' she said, and with a quick movement she laid her fingers lightly over his mouth. 'Not bad, Paul; never bad.'

He caught her hand and covered it with kisses. Unprotestingly, she abandoned it for a few seconds to his passion, then gently took it back.

'And now,' she said, 'I want to hear all about your visit to that man you were telling me about yesterday.'

His face brightened.

'You mean Loria?'

She nodded.

'Oh, that was really exciting,' said Paul De Vries. 'He's the man who's been carrying on Peano's work in mathematical logic.'

'Is he as good as Russell?' asked Mrs. Thwale, who recalled an earlier conversation on the same subject.

'That's just the question *I've* been asking myself,' the young man cried delightedly.

'Great minds think alike,' said Mrs. Thwale.

Smiling an enchantingly playful smile, she rapped with her knuckles first on her own forehead, then on his.

'And now I want to hear about your exciting Professor Loria.'

CHAPTER SEVENTEEN

TO the tune of 'Under the Bamboo Tree,' to the accompaniment of Timmy Williams's knowing laughter, again, again:

> *Probably constip,*
> *Probably constip,*
> *Probably constipaysh . . .*

But of course it wasn't true. He had always known that it wasn't true.

There was an awareness once more of an all-pervading silence that shone and was alive. Beautiful with more than the beauty of even Mozart's music, more than the beauty of the sky after sunset, of the evening star emerging into visibility between the cypresses.

And from those cypresses he found himself moving across the lattice to the discovery of himself at Paestum in the dusk of a windy autumn twilight, to a memory of the Vale of the White Horse as the July sunshine poured down with a kind of desperate intensity out of a blue gulf between mountainous continents of thunder-cloud. And here was the Maize God from Copan, and the 'Last Communion of St. Jerome.' And that thing of Constable's at the Victoria and Albert, and—yes!—'Susanna and the Elders.'

But this wasn't Tintoret's pale silhouette of a marbly and majestic nakedness. This was Mimi. Mimi as she squatted on the divan, short-legged, opaquely white against the garish cushions.

And suddenly he was participating once more in that relentless knowledge of an absence so hideous that there could be nothing but self-abhorrence, nothing but shame, judgment, condemnation.

To escape from the pain he turned once more towards the parting of the dressing-gown, towards the fondlings and the dandlings, the cigar and the laughter. But this time the light refused to be eclipsed. Instead, it grew brighter, impossibly; grew unendurably more beautiful.

Terror modulated into resentment, into a passion of rage and hatred. And as though by magic he had, at one stroke, repossessed himself of all his four vocabularies of obscenity—the native English, the painstakingly acquired German and French and Italian.

The uprush of his anger, the torrent of those words, brought him immediate relief. The urgency of the light diminished, and there was no more participation in the knowledge, by which he was compelled to judge himself shameful. Nothing remained but that beauty, far off in the background, like the sky after sunset. But now he had seen through its loveliness, knew it was only a bait to lure one on into some horrible kind of suicide.

Suicide, suicide—they were all trying to persuade one to commit suicide. And here was the fragment of himself represented by Bruno in the bookshop, Bruno on the way to the station. Looking at one with those eyes of his, talking so gently about the need of allowing oneself to be forgiven, even trying to hypnotize one. To hypnotize one into self-destruction.

Slipping sideways, as it were, on to another plane of the lattice, he found himself all of a sudden in contact with a knowledge which he knew immediately as Bruno's. The knowledge, dim and irrelevant, of a bare hotel bedroom and, at the same time, overpoweringly, of the light. Tenderly blue, this time. Blue and somehow musical. A systole and diastole of radiance, singing voicelessly within the whorls of an unseen shell.

Beauty and peace and tenderness—immediately recognized and immediately rejected. Known, only to be hated, only to be defiled, idiomatically, in four languages.

St. Willibald saying his prayers in the bedroom of a fourth-rate hotel. St. Wunnibald staring at his navel. It was asinine. It was contemptible. And if the fool imagined that, by playing these tricks, he could shame one into wanting to commit suicide, he was entirely mistaken. Who did he think he was, fooling about with that damned light? But whatever he might think, the fact remained that he was just old man Bruno, just a scrubby little bookseller with a half-baked intelligence and a gift of the gab.

And then he was aware that Bruno was not alone, that Bruno's knowledge of the light was not the only knowledge. There was a whole galaxy of awarenesses. Bright by participation, made one with the light that gave them their being. Made one and yet recognizable, within the Universal Possibility, as possibilities that had actually been realized.

In the hotel bedroom the knowledge of that tender and musical radiance was growing more complete. And as it did so, the blueness brightened up towards a purer incandescence, the music modulated from significance through heightened significance into the ultimate perfection of silence.

'Willibald, Wunnibald. In a fourth-rate hotel. And let's hope there's a couple of German honeymooners in the next room.' Showing off what he could do with the light! But that didn't prevent him from being a silly little rag-and-bone merchant, a pedlar of mouldy rubbish. 'And if he seriously imagines he can browbeat one into feeling ashamed . . .'

Abruptly, Eustace was aware of what the other knew. Was aware by acquaintance, not from the outside only, but in an act of identification. And in the same instant he became aware again of the unutterable ugliness of his own opaque and fragmentary being.

Shameful, shameful. . . . But he refused to feel ashamed. He'd be damned if he'd let himself be dragooned into suicide. Yes, he'd be damned, he'd be damned! . . .

In the brightness and the silence his thoughts were like lumps of excrement, like the noise of vomiting. And the more repulsive they seemed, the more frantic became his anger and hatred.

Damned light! Bloody little rag-and-bone man! But now there was no longer any rest or respite to be found in being angry. His hatred blazed, but blazed in the face of an unobscured radiance. The four vocabularies of obscenity vomited themselves out in a silence with which in some sort he was identified, a silence that merely emphasized the hideousness of that which interrupted it.

All the elation of anger and hatred, all the distracting excitement, died away, and he was left with nothing but the naked, negative experience of revulsion. Painful intrinsically and at the same time a cause of further pain. For the unobscured light and the uninterruptible silence, which were the objects of his loathing, compelled him once again to know himself to sit in judgment, to condemn.

Other fragments of himself made their appearance. Ten pages of Proust, and a trot round the Bargello; St. Sebastian among the Victorian ornaments, and the Young Man of Peoria. *Fascinatio nugacitatis.* But all the trifling which had once enchanted him was now not only profoundly wearisome, but also, in some negative way, profoundly evil. And yet it had to be persisted in; for the alternative was a total self-knowledge and self-abandonment, a total attention and exposure to the light.

So now it was Mimi again. And in the brightness, with which he was now unescapably identified, those too had to be persisted in—those long afternoons in the little flat behind Santa Croce. Interminable cold frictions; the strigil rasping and rasping, but without titillation. *Adesso comincia la tortura.* And it never stopped, because he couldn't allow it to stop, for fear of what might happen if he did. There was no escape, except along this path which led him yet further into captivity.

Suddenly Bruno Rontini stirred a little and coughed. Eustace was aware, at one remove, of a heightened awareness of the bleak little bedroom and the noise of the traffic climbing in low gear up the steep approaches to Perugia. Then this irrelevant knowledge was quietly put aside, and there was only silence again and brightness.

Or was there perhaps another path? A way that would lead one around these excremental clots of old experience and the condemnation they imposed? The silence and the brightness were pregnant with the unequivocal answer: there was no way round, there was only the way through. And of course he knew all about it, he knew exactly where it led.

But if that way were followed, what would happen to Eustace Barnack? Eustace Barnack would be dead. Stone dead, extinct, annihilated. There'd be nothing but this damned light, this fiendish brightness in the silence. His hatred flared up again;

and then, almost instantly, the delightful and exhilarating heat was quenched. Nothing was left him but a frigid and frightened revulsion and, along with the revulsion, the excruciating knowledge that his hatred and his revulsion were equally disgusting.

But better this pain than its alternative; better this knowledge of his own hatefulness than the extinction of all knowledge whatsoever. Anything rather than that! Even these eternities of empty foolery, these eternities of a lust devoid of all pleasure. Ten pages of Proust, and the juxtaposition of wax flowers and St. Sebastian. Again and again. And after that the repetitions of those corpse-cold sensualities, the fondlings, the dandlings, the endless obligatory fumblings, to the accompaniment of 'Probably Constip' and 'The Young Man of Peoria.' Thousands of times, hundreds of thousands of times. And the little joke about St. Willibald, the little joke about St. Wunnibald. And Mr. Cheeryble with his thurible, Mr. Chatterjee with his Mr. Chatterjee with his Mr. Chatterjee with . . . And again the same ten pages of Proust, the same wax flowers and St. Sebastian, the same blind brown breast-eyes and the torture of compulsory lust, while the Young Man of Peoria kept on murmuring the Credo, murmuring the Sanctus, murmuring a string of flawlessly idiomatic obscenities in a luminous silence which made each one of their million repetitions seem yet more senseless than the last, yet more drearily disgusting.

But there was no alternative, no alternative except giving in to the light, except dying out into the silence. But anything rather than that, anything, anything. . . .

And then suddenly there was salvation. A knowledge, first of all, that there were other knowledges. Not like Bruno's beastly conspiracy with the light. Not like that galaxy of awarenesses within the knowledge of all possibility. No, no. These other awarenesses were cosily similar to his own. And all of them were concerned with himself, with his own beloved and opaque identity. And their concern was like the fluttering shadow of a host of wings, like the cry and chatter of innumerable agitated little birds, shutting out that insupportable light, shattering that accursed silence, bringing respite and relief, bringing the blessed right to be himself and not ashamed of the fact.

He rested there in the delicious, twittering confusion, of which he had become the centre, and would have been happy so to rest for ever. But better things were reserved for him. Suddenly and without warning there dawned a new, more blissful phase of his salvation. He was in possession of something infinitely precious, something of which, as he now realized, he had been deprived throughout the whole duration of these horrible eternities—a set of bodily sensations. There was an experience, thrillingly direct and immediate, of the warm, living darkness behind closed eyelids; of faint voices, not remembered, but actually heard out there in front; of a touch of lumbago in the small of the back; of a thousand obscure little aches and pressures and tensions from within and from without. And what an odd kind of heaviness in the lower inwards! What curiously unfamiliar sensations of weight and constriction out there in front of the chest!

'I think she's gone under,' said the Queen Mother in a harsh stage whisper.

'She certainly seems to be breathing very stertorously,' Paul De Vries agreed. 'Snoring is always indicative of relaxation,' he added instructively. 'That's why thin nervous people so seldom . . .'

Mrs. Gamble cut him short.

'Kindly let go of my hand,' she said. 'I want to blow my nose.'

Her bracelets tinkled in the darkness. There was a rustling and a snort.

'Now, where are you?' she asked, clawing for his hand. 'Ah, here! I hope everybody's holding tight.'

'*I* certainly am,' said the young man.

He spoke gaily; but the squeeze he administered to the soft hand on his right was lingeringly tender. To his delight the pressure was faintly, but quite perceptibly, returned.

Ambushed in the darkness, Mrs. Thwale was thinking of the shameless essence of love.

'And what about you, Sebastian?' she asked, turning her head.

'I'm all right,' he answered with a nervous giggle. 'I'm still holding on.'

But so was that stinking De Vries! Holding on and being held on to. Whereas if *he* were to squeeze her hand, she'd probably announce the fact to the rest of the company, and they'd all simply howl with laughter. All the same, he had a good mind to do it in spite of everything. As an outrage—just as she had said. De Vries was in love with her and, for all he knew, she was in love with De Vries. Very well, then; the biggest *non sequitur* possible in the circumstances would be for him to say or do something to show that *he* was in love with her. But when it came to actually committing the outrage of squeezing her hand, Sebastian found himself hesitant. Did he have the nerve or didn't he? Was it really worth it, or wasn't it?

'They say that holding hands does something to the vibrations,' announced the Queen Mother from her end of the row.

'Well, it's not impossible,' said Paul De Vries judicially. 'In the light of the most recent researches into the electric potentials of the various muscle groups . . .'

In five seconds, Sebastian was saying to himself, with the imaginary pistol barrel pressed once again to his temple, in five seconds the world would have come to an end. Nothing mattered any more. But still he didn't act. Nothing mattered, nothing mattered, he was still despairingly repeating, when all at once he felt her hand coming to life within his own. Then, startlingly, her finger-tips began to trace little circles on his palm. Again, again, deliciously, electrically. Then without warning she dug her pointed nails into his flesh. For a second only, after which the fingers straightened out and relaxed, and he found himself holding a hand as limp and passive and inert as it had been before.

'And then,' Paul De Vries was saying, 'one has to consider the possibility of mitotic radiations as a factor in the phenom . . .'

'Sh-sh! She's saying something.'

Out of the darkness in front of them came a squeaky childish voice.

'This is Bettina,' it said. 'This is Bettina.'

'Good-evening, Bettina,' cried the Queen Mother, in a tone that was intended to be gay and ingratiating. 'How are things over on the other side?'

'Fine!' said the squeak, which belonged, as Mrs. Byfleet had explained before the lights were turned out, to a little girl who had passed on in the San Francisco earthquake. 'Everything's fine. Everyone's feeling good. But poor old Gladys here— she's quite sick.'

'Yes, we're all *so* sorry that Mrs. Byfleet shouldn't be feeling well.'

'Not feeling good at all.'

'Most unfortunate!' replied the Queen Mother with hardly disguised impatience. It was she who had insisted on Mrs. Byfleet's giving the séance in spite of her indisposition. 'But I hope it won't interfere with the communications.'

The squeak said something about 'doing our best,' and tailed off into incoherence. Then the medium sighed profoundly and snored a little. There was a silence.

What did it mean, Sebastian was wondering. What on earth could it mean? His heart was beating like a sledge-hammer. Once again the barrel of the revolver was pressed against his forehead. In five seconds the world would come to an end. One, two, three . . . He squeezed her hand. Waited a second. Squeezed it again. But there was no responsive pressure, no indication of any kind that she had even noticed what he had done. Sebastian felt himself overcome by the most excruciating embarrassment.

'I always like to have my first séance as soon after the funeral as possible,' the Queen Mother remarked. 'Even before it, if the thing can be arranged. Nothing like striking the iron while it's hot.'

There was a pause. Then, eager but monotonously flat, Paul De Vries's voice broke in.

'I keep thinking,' he said, 'of Mr. Pewsey's address at the graveside this afternoon. Most touching, didn't you think? And so felicitously worded. "Friend of the arts and artist in friendship." He couldn't have phrased it better.'

'Which doesn't prevent him,' rasped the Queen Mother, 'from having the most disgusting habits. If it weren't for Veronica and that boy, I'd tell you a few of the things I happen to know about Tom Pewsey.'

'There's somebody here,' the squeak startlingly announced. 'He's very anxious to get in touch with you folks.'

'Tell him we're waiting,' said the Queen Mother in the tone of one who gives orders to the footman.

'Only just come over,' the squeak went on. 'Seems he doesn't rightly know he's passed on.'

For Paul De Vries the words were like the fresh scent of a rabbit to a nosing dog; he was off in a flash.

'Isn't that interesting!' he exclaimed. 'He doesn't know he's passed on. But they all say that, from the Mahayana Buddhists down to . . .'

But the squeak had begun to mutter something.

'Can't you stop interrupting?' said the Queen Mother.

'I'm sorry,' he murmured.

In the darkness Mrs. Thwale sympathetically pressed his right hand and, in the same instant, disinterested and platonic, crooked a delicate forefinger and across the centre of Sebastian's left palm traced out the four letters, L, O, V, E, and then another, unavowable combination, and another. An effervescence of soundless laughter bubbled up within her.

'He's so glad you folks are all here,' said the squeak, becoming suddenly articulate. 'He can't say how happy it makes him.'

'Not that one would have expressed it with quite so much pathetic emphasis,' Eustace was thinking. 'But substantially it's the truth.'

That damned light was now definitively out; and with these newly recovered sensations hopping and twittering like twenty thousand sparrows, there was no question any more of silence. And how delightful even lumbago could be, even this obscure and unfamiliar belly-ache! And the Queen Mother's nutmeg-grater voice—no Mozart had ever sounded sweeter! Of course, it was unfortunate that, for some reason, everything had to pass through the filter of this intermediate knowledge. Or rather this intermediate ignorance; for it was just a lump of organized imbecility, that was all. You gave it the choicest of your little jokes, and four times out of five it came out with unadulterated nonsense. What a hash, for example, it made of the things he said when that American fellow started talking about psychic factors, or whatever it was! And when he wanted to quote Sebastian's line about two buttocks and a pendulous bub, it kept on talking in a bewildered way about pendulums—bucks and pendulums. Too idiotic! However, he did at least manage to get in one good dig at the Queen Mother, to get it in almost verbatim; for even a half-wit couldn't make a mistake about the word 'claws.'

And then something very curious happened.

'Is it true,' Mrs. Thwale suddenly enquired in a tone of excessive and altogether improbable innocence, 'is it true that, where you are, there isn't any marrying or giving in marriage?'

The words seemed to touch a trigger; there was a kind of mental jerk, an almost violent displacement of consciousness—and Eustace found himself aware, as though in vivid memory, of events which had not happened to himself, events which, he somehow knew, had not as yet happened at all. Wearing a broad-shouldered fur coat and a preposterous hat like something out of a Winterhalter portrait of the Empress Eugénie, Mrs. Thwale was sitting on a platform with a lot of naval officers, while a man with tousled hair and a Middle Western accent bellowed into a microphone. 'Liberty Ship,' he kept saying, 'four hundred and fifty-ninth Liberty Ship.' And, sure enough, that enormous precipice of iron out there to the left was a ship's prow. And now Mrs. Thwale was on her feet swinging a champagne bottle on the end of a string. And then the precipice began to move away, and there was a lot of cheering. And while she was smiling up at an Admiral and some Captains, De Vries came running up and began to talk to them about the exciting new developments in ballistics . . .

'I'm not the one who's thinking about marriage,' he said jocularly.

But what the imbecile actually uttered was, 'We don't think about marriage over here.'

Eustace began to protest, but was distracted from his irritation by the emergence of another of those clear memories of what had not yet happened. Little Thwale on a sofa with a very young officer, like those beardless children one used to see during the war. And really, really, the things she permitted herself! And always with that faintly ironical smile, that expression of detached curiosity in the bright dark eyes, which always remained wide open and observant, whatever might be happening. Whereas the boy, in his effort to hold the pleasure in, to shut the shame and the embarrassment out, kept *his* eyes tightly closed.

The moving images faded into nothingness and, at the thought of De Vries's horns and the inevitable connection between war and lust, between the holiest crusades and the most promiscuous copulations, Eustace started to laugh. 'Backwards and downwards, Christian soldiers,' he said in the interval between two paroxysms of amusement.

'He says we're all Christian soldiers,' pronounced the squeak;

and then, almost immediately, 'Good-bye, folks,' it called, 'good-bye, good-bye.'

Laughter, a crescendo of laughter. Then, all of a sudden, Eustace realized that the blissful experience of sensation was beginning to ebb away from him. The voices from outside grew dimmer and more confused; the small obscure awarenesses of pressure, touch and tension faded away. And at last there was nothing left, not even the lumbago, not even the idiot inter-preter. Nothing but the hunger for what he had lost and, emerging again from its long eclipse behind the opacity and the delicious noise, that pure, shining silence of the light. Brighter, ever more urgently, ever more austerely and menacingly beauti-ful. Perceiving his danger, Eustace directed all his attention to little Thwale and her uniformed adolescent, to the enormous, cosmic joke of crusades and copulation. 'Downwards and back-wards, Christian soldiers,' he repeated. Making a deliberate effort, he laughed more heartily than ever.

CHAPTER EIGHTEEN

IT was only a little after seven when Sebastian came down next morning for another solitary stroll in the garden—another wandering through *Lycidas* in the direction of his own as yet unnamed and unwritten poem. It would begin, he had decided, with the Venus of the balustrade—shaped by a mind out of the shapelessness of stone. Order born of a chaos that itself was composed of innumerable lesser orders. And the statue would be the emblem of an individual life in its possible and ideal excellence, just as the garden as a whole would stand for the ideally excellent life of a society. From the ideally excellent he would pass to the actualities of ugliness, cruelty, ineptitude, death. After which, in a third part, ecstasy and intelligence would build the bridges leading from the actual to the ideal—from the blue tart and his father's severities to Mrs. Thwale and Mary Esdaile, from the corpse in the lavatory to Theocritus and Marvell.

Precisely how all this would be put across without becoming a bore he wouldn't know until he had actually got to work among the words in which it was to be expressed. Hitherto the only words that had come to him were connected with poor old Uncle Eustace and last night's séance, and would take their place somewhere in the second part.

'This Thing was once a man,' he repeated to himself, as he walked up and down the terrace in the early sunshine.

> *This Thing was once a man—*
> *Take it for all in all,*
> *Like the old piano . . .*

No, no, that was wrong: make it 'old Bechstein.'

> *Like the old Bechstein, auctioned off for nothing;*
> *And men in aprons come for it with a van,*
> *Shuffling across the hall.*

Of the lines that followed, he still felt a bit uncertain.

> *But somebody in the empty drawing-room,*
> *Strumming the non-existent keys . . .*

He shook his head. 'Non-existent' was journalistic. The word to aim at was 'absence.' 'Strumming the absence of its keys.' Or, better perhaps, 'strumming an absence of departed keys.'

> *But somebody in the empty drawing-room,*
> *Strumming an absence of departed keys,*
> *Still plays the old Chaconne and Für Elise*
> *And Yes, sir, she's my baby, yes, sir, she's*
> *My baby, yes, sir, till the crack of doom.*

Which was certainly what it had seemed like at the séance, with that idiotic squeak quoting Uncle Eustace's smallest jokes, and even misquoting, as Sebastian had finally realized, his own little effort about Degas. But meanwhile there was that 'crack of doom' to be considered. Did circumstances justify the cliché? Or mightn't it be better to protract the sentence a little to lead it on, winding and serpentine, through 'tomb,' perhaps, or alternatively through an interrogatory 'whom?' into further recesses of the subject?

Sebastian was still debating the question, when something happened to interrupt the flow of his thoughts. The small girl he had seen that dreadful morning in the hall suddenly appeared at the top of the steps carrying, not a baby this time or a chicken, but a large basket. Startled by his unexpected presence, she halted and looked at him for a few seconds with an expression of uncertainty, almost of fear. Sebastian gave her a smile. Reassured by this display of benevolence on the part of one of the terrifying *signori*, the little girl smiled back and, walking in an excess of deference on the very tips of her clumsy boots, crossed the terrace and began to weed the flower-bed which ran in a narrow strip of colour and perfume at the foot of the villa's long façade.

Sebastian continued his promenading. But the presence of the child was an insurmountable obstacle to further composition. It was not that she made any noise, or indulged in any violence of movement. No, the trouble lay deeper. What distracted him was the fact that she was working messily in the earth, while he strolled up and down with his hands in his pockets. The proximity of the poor always made him feel uncomfortable, and to discomfort was added, when they worked and he apparently did nothing, a sense of shame. These were feelings which ought, he supposed, to have made him want to follow in his father's footsteps. But politics always seemed so futile and unimportant. His ordinary reaction from the shame and discomfort was a flight from the situation which had occasioned them. And today the situation was even worse than usual. For the worker was a child, who ought to have been playing; and the poverty, contrasted with this surrounding magnificence, seemed peculiarly outrageous. Sebastian glanced at his watch and, in case she might be looking at him (which she wasn't), overacted the part of one who suddenly realizes that he is late for an important business appointment and hurried away. Half-way to the front door he suddenly remembered that he actually had a reason to hurry. He was going down into the town after lunch. Nominally to do some sight-seeing. But really, he had already decided, to get himself measured for his evening clothes—that was to say, if he could first sell the Degas.

He ran up to his room and came down again with his dispatch-case. The drawing-room was empty, and the old persistent whiff of Uncle Eustace's cigars had so far faded that it smelt only of potpourri. A long pencil of sunlight crossed the room and, as though with some mysterious purpose, lit up the three pelicans in the background of Piero's picture.

The drawings were lying on the marble-topped table that stood in the embrasure of the central window. Sebastian walked over, unfolded the brown paper, and from between the two protecting sheets of cardboard withdrew his legacy. Two buttocks and a pendulous bub. He placed the drawing in his dispatch-case and closed the lid. Then, very carefully, he folded the paper as it had been before. Degas and dinner jacket—now that poor old Uncle Eustace was dead, they were nobody's business but his own.

A thin little noise of treble singing made him start. He looked out through the open window. There, almost immediately below him, squatted the child from whom he had just fled. Her small grubby hands moved delicately among the hyacinths, pulling up here a groundsel, there a couple of blades of grass, so that all might be perfect and in order for the *signori*.

'*Gobbo rotondo*,' she sang to herself, '*che fai in questo mondo?*'

Then, becoming somehow aware of the alien presence above

her, she looked up and saw Sebastian. An expression of guilt and terror came into her eyes; the almost colourless cheeks flushed crimson.

'*Scusi, signore,*' she muttered in a trembling voice. '*Scusi.*'

Sebastian, who was almost as much embarrassed as the little girl, withdrew his head abruptly and, moving away from the window, bent down to pick up his dispatch-case.

'What *are* you doing?' a low clear voice enquired behind him.

He started and turned. But without waiting for his answer, Mrs. Thwale had gone over to the window and was looking out.

'*Cosa fai?*' she asked.

From the terrace outside, the frightened voice made some incomprehensible answer.

Mrs. Thwale shrugged her shoulders and came back into the room.

'What were you talking to the child about?'

'I wasn't,' Sebastian stammered. 'I was just . . . well, she was singing.'

'So you listened, and now you're going to sit down and do a slight Wordsworth about it?'

He laughed uncomfortably.

'And those are your manuscripts, I suppose?'

She indicated the dispatch-case.

Only too grateful for the suggestion, Sebastian nodded.

'Well, put them down and come out into the garden.'

Obediently he followed her across the hall and through the front door.

'And how did you enjoy the séance?' she asked, as he came up with her on the terrace.

'Oh, it was interesting,' he answered non-committally.

'Interesting?' she repeated. 'Only that?'

Sebastian blushed and averted his eyes. She was giving him an opportunity to say something about what had happened last night—to ask her what it had meant, to tell her about Mary

Esdaile. But the words wouldn't come. They simply wouldn't come.

Mrs. Thwale glanced at the red, agonized face beside her, and almost laughed aloud. What exquisitely comic situations could arise with a person too timid to speak! The most outrageous actions, and not a word uttered, no reference ever made to them. Officially nothing would have happened; for there wouldn't be any communiqué. But actually, actually . . .

'What a Punch and Judy show!' she said at last, breaking the long silence.

'You mean the séance?'

Mrs. Thwale nodded.

'All the same, it seemed genuine, didn't it? I mean, sometimes,' Sebastian added, hedging a little for fear of finding himself compelled to defend a too explicit opinion.

But the precaution was unnecessary.

'Perfectly genuine,' she agreed. 'Death cocking snooks at reverence and piety in exactly the same way as life does.'

They had reached the head of the steps, and she halted to look down, between the cypresses, at the roofs of Florence. Shamelessness at the core; but on the surface Brunelleschi and Michelangelo, good manners and Lanvin clothes, art and science and religion. And the charm of life consisted precisely in the inconsistency between essence and appearance, and the art of living in a delicate acrobacy of *sauts périlleux* from one world to the other, in a prestidigitation that could always discover the obscenity of rabbits at the bottom of even the glossiest high hat and, conversely, the elegant decency of a hat to conceal even the most pregnant and lascivious of rodents.

'Well, we can't stand here for ever,' Mrs. Thwale said at last. They moved on. As though casually and unreflectingly, she laid a hand on Sebastian's shoulder.

CHAPTER NINETEEN

' A DRAWING to sell?'

A M. Weyl put on the bored, contemptuous expression he always assumed on these occasions. But when the boy opened his case and revealed the Degas that had been sold to *ce pauvre Monsieur Eustache* only four days before, he could not restrain a start of surprise.

'From where have you got this drawing?' he asked.

'It was given to me,' Sebastian answered.

'Given?'

'*Tout est possible*,' M. Weyl said to himself. But there had never been any suggestion that the old man was a homosexual.

Conscious that he had become an object of suspicion, Sebastian blushed.

'By my uncle,' he said. 'You probably knew him. Mr. Barnack.'

'Your uncle?'

M. Weyl's expression changed. He smiled; he seized Sebastian's hand in both of his and shook it.

One of his most valued clients. One of his truest friends, he ventured to say. He had been *bouleversé* by the tragic news. An irreparable loss to art. He could only offer his sincerest condolences.

Sebastian stammered his thanks.

'And the good uncle, he gave you this drawing?'

The other nodded.

'Just a few hours before . . .'

'Before the supreme adieu,' said Gabriel Weyl poetically. 'What a sentimental value it must possess for you!'

Sebastian blushed a deeper crimson. To justify himself, he mumbled something about his having no place to hang the drawing. Besides, there was a sum of money which had to be paid out immediately—almost a debt of honour, he added as a picturesque afterthought. Otherwise he wouldn't have dreamt of parting with his uncle's present.

M. Weyl nodded sympathetically; but his eyes were bright with calculation.

'Tell me,' he asked, 'for what reason did you address yourself to me in this affair?'

'For no reason,' Sebastian answered. M. Weyl's happened to be the first art dealer's shop he had seen as he walked up the Via Tornabuoni.

That meant that he didn't know where the drawing had been bought. M. Weyl laughed gaily and patted Sebastian on the shoulder.

'The hazard,' he said sententiously, 'is often our surest guide.'

He looked down at the drawing, screwed up his eyelids and critically cocked his head.

'Pretty,' he said, 'pretty. Though hardly the master's best work.' He laid his finger on the buttocks. 'One remarks the effects of failing sight, *hein*?'

'Well, I didn't think so,' said Sebastian, in a manful effort to defend his property from disparagement.

There was a little pause.

'If your good uncle gave you other things,' said M. Weyl in a casual tone, without looking up, 'I would be more than happy to make an offer. Last time I had the honour of visiting his collection, I recall that I was struck by some of the Chinese bronzes.' His thick, agile hands came together at the level of his face, as though he were clasping and cherishing some almost sacred object. 'What volumes!' he cried enthusiastically. 'What rhythmic sensuality! But small, quite small. One could almost carry them in the pockets.'

Turning to Sebastian, he smiled ingratiatingly.

'I could make you a very good offer for the bronzes,' he said.

'But they're not mine. I mean . . . he only gave me this.'

'Only this?' the other repeated in a tone of incredulity.

Sebastian dropped his eyes. That smile, that insistent bright regard, made him feel uncomfortable. What was the fellow trying to suggest?

'Nothing except this,' he insisted, wishing to God that he had picked on another dealer. 'But of course, if you're not interested . . .'

He started to put the drawing away again.

'But no, but no!' cried M. Weyl, laying a restraining hand on his sleeve. 'On the contrary. I interest myself in everything that Degas ever did—even in the smallest things, the most unimportant.'

Ten minutes later it was all over.

'. . . Nineteen, twenty, twenty-one and twenty-two. Correct, *hein*?'

'Thank you,' said Sebastian. He took the thick wad of hundred-lire notes and crammed them into his wallet. His face was flushed; his eyes shone with excitement and irrepressible triumph. The man had begun by offering only a thousand. Greatly daring, he had demanded three. They had compromised at last on two thousand two hundred. Ten per cent. above the figure that would have split the difference between demand and offer. Feeling that he had a right to be proud of himself, Sebastian put the wallet back into his pocket and looked up, to find the dealer smiling at him with almost paternal benevolence.

'A young man who knows how to sell his article of commerce,' said M. Weyl, patting him once more. 'In business you will have the most brilliant career.'

'No business for me,' Sebastian said. And when the other questioningly raised his eyebrows, 'You see,' he added, 'I'm a poet.'

A poet? But that had been M. Weyl's own youthful ambition. To express the lyricism of a heart which suffers . . .

Les chants désespérés sont les chants les plus beaux,
Et j'en sais d'immortels qui sont de purs sanglots.

'*De purs sanglots,*' he repeated. '*Mais, hélas,* the duty led me otherwise.'

He sighed, and went on to question Sebastian about his family. Doubtless, in so cultivated a milieu, there was a tradition of poetry and the fine arts? And when the boy answered that his father was a barrister, he insisted on Mr. Barnack's being one of those legal luminaries who devote their leisures to the Muses.

The idea of his father ever having any leisures or, if he had, devoting them to anything but Blue books, was so funny that Sebastian laughed aloud. But M. Weyl looked offended; and he hastily broke off in order to offer an explanation for his merriment.

'You see,' he said, 'my father's rather peculiar.'

'Peculiar?'

Sebastian nodded, and in his broken incoherent style embarked upon an account of John Barnack's career. And somehow, in his present mood, it seemed the most natural thing in the world to make the picture heroic—to harp on his father's successes as an advocate, to magnify his political importance, to stress the greatness of his self-sacrifice.

'But what generosity!' cried M. Weyl.

Sebastian responded to the words as if they had been a compliment addressed to himself. A tingling warmth ran up his spine.

'He has lots of money,' he went on. 'But he gives it all away. To political refugees and that kind of thing.'

The pleasure of vicariously boasting had made him momentarily forget his hatred of those bloodsuckers who took what rightfully should have been his and left him without even a dinner jacket.

'There's a chap called Cacciaguida, for example . . .'

'You mean the Professor?'

Sebastian nodded. M. Weyl cast a quick glance round the shop and, though it was empty, resumed the conversation in a lower tone.

'Is *he* a friend of your father's?'

'He came to dinner with us,' Sebastian answered importantly, 'just before we started for Florence.'

'Personally,' M. Weyl whispered, after taking another look round the shop, 'I find him a great man. But permit me to give you a good advice.'

He winked expressively, raised a forefinger to his floridly sculptured lips, and shook his head. 'The silence is of gold,' he pronounced oracularly.

The sudden jangling of the door-bell made them turn with a start, like a pair of conspirators. Two ladies in the early forties, one rather plump and dark, the other fair, sunburnt and athletic, were entering the shop. An expression of rapturous delight appeared on M. Weyl's face.

'*Gnädige Baronin!*' he cried, '*y la reina de Buenos Aires!*'

Pushing Sebastian aside, he jumped over a *cassettone*, ducked under the right arm of a life-sized crucified Christ and, rushing up to the two ladies, ecstatically kissed their hands.

Unobtrusively, Sebastian slipped out of the shop and, whistling, walked jauntily up the Via Tornabuoni in the direction of the cathedral and Uncle Eustace's tailor.

CHAPTER TWENTY

CHRISTIAN soldiers, copulating soldiers; and all those wars, those holy wars, while echo answers, 'Whores, whores, whores!' The God of Battles is always the God of Brothels, always and inevitably the God of Brothels. . . .

For Eustace Barnack, there was no longer any need to force the laughter. It pealed now of its own accord, shattering what remained of that detestable silence, darkening and dissipating the last far gleams of the light.

The whole universe quivered with amusement, rumbled with enormous hilarities. And through the laughter echo kept answering, 'Whores and Brothels, Whores and Brothels.'

A whole section of his intellectual being was suddenly restored to him. He remembered his collection of Historical Jokes. A million casualties and the Gettysburg Address, and then those abject, frightened negroes one sees in the little towns of Georgia and Louisiana. The crusade for liberty, quality, fraternity, and then the rise of Napoleon; the crusade against Napoleon, and then the rise of German nationalism; the crusade against German nationalism, and now those unemployed men, standing, like half-animated corpses, at the corners of mean streets in the rain.

And this was John's voice that he now remembered—vibrant with repressed enthusiasm, talking about the end of *laissez-faire* and production for use and the Russian Revolution. In other words, two and a half times the population of London exterminated, in order that political power might be taken from one set of ruffians and given to another set; in order that a process of industrialization might be made a little more rapid and a great deal more ruthless than it otherwise would have been. 'Downwards and backwards, Anti-Christian soldiers!' Laughter swelled to a crescendo. He was filled with an enormous elation, with the glory of universal derision, the ecstasy of contempt for everyone.

Silliness and murder, stupidity and destruction! He found the phrases waiting for him. And the motive was always idealism, the instruments were always courage and loyalty— the heroic courage and loyalty without which men and women would never be able to persevere in their long-drawn suicides and assassinations.

And all those treasures of knowledge placed so unhesitatingly at the service of passion! All the genius and intelligence dedicated to the attempt to achieve ends either impossible or diabolic! All the problems inherited from the last crusade and solved by methods that automatically created a hundred new problems. And each new problem would require a new crusade, and each new crusade would leave fresh problems for yet further crusades to solve and multiply in the good old way.

And then there were the Triumphs of Religion and Science. Reforming Protestantism—sponsor of capitalistic exploitation. Francis of Assisi miraculously upholding a Mystical Body that was also a political machine and a business concern. Faraday and Clerk Maxwell working indefatigably that the ether might at last become a vehicle for lies and imbecility.

And then the Triumph of Education—that deity to which his poor father had offered fifty thousand pounds and a Polytechnic Institute in yellow brick. Education, compulsory and gratuitous. Everybody had been taught to read, and the result was Northcliffe and advertisements for cigarettes and laxatives and whisky. Everybody went to school, and everywhere the years of schooling had been made a prelude to military conscription. And what fine courses in false history and self-congratulation! What a thorough grounding in the religions of nationalism! No God any more; but forty-odd infallible Foreign Offices.

Once again, the whole universe shook with laughter.

CHAPTER TWENTY-ONE

IT was to be a small, informal dinner; and Eustace, after all, was only a relation by marriage, not blood. The Queen Mother had therefore seen no reason for cancelling her acceptance of Lady Worplesden's invitation. And as for staying at home to be with Daisy when she arrived that evening—why, the idea simply didn't occur to her.

'You'll have to entertain my granddaughter single-handed,' she announced to Sebastian at tea-time.

'Single-handed? But I thought Mrs. Thwale . . .?'

'I'm taking Veronica with me, of course.'

Mrs. Thwale put in a word of reassurance.

'You won't find her in the least formidable.'

'Formidable!' The Queen Mother's tone was contemptuous. 'She's like blancmange.'

'So there'll be no excuse for mumbling. Or for not saying anything at all,' Mrs. Thwale added casually, reaching out for a lump of sugar as she spoke. 'Which is a slight defect of yours that I seem to have noticed.'

'That reminds me,' said the Queen Mother. 'How's he getting on with his mumbling lessons?'

'I'm hoping he'll give you a demonstration one of these days,' Mrs. Thwale answered gravely.

'A demonstration? What demonstration?'

There was no immediate answer. Sebastian raised his eyes and gave Mrs. Thwale a look of agonized entreaty. But the smile she returned was one of bright, impersonal amusement— as if she were looking on at some delicate comedy of manners.

'How do you write a poem?' she murmured under her breath.

'What's that you're saying?' asked the Queen Mother sharply.

On its withered tortoise's neck the old head turned questingly from side to side in a succession of quick blind movements.

'What's that?'

'Please.' Sebastian implored, framing the word voicelessly with lips that trembled in distress. 'Please!'

For an awful second he was left in uncertainty of what she was going to do next. Then she turned to Mrs. Gamble.

'It's nothing,' she said. 'Just a silly little joke we have together at our mumbling lessons.'

'I don't like people having jokes together,' the old woman rasped in a harsh resentful tone. With unseeing eyes she glared ferociously at Mrs. Thwale across the tea-table. 'I don't like it,' she repeated: 'I don't like it at all.'

In silence Mrs. Thwale examined the fossil scorpion from the Carboniferous.

'It shan't happen again, Mrs. Gamble,' she said at last.

But as she thought of what the submissive words really signified, her eyes brightened and her lips twitched into a little smile of secret triumph. That morning a special messenger had brought her a letter from Paul De Vries—six pages, typewritten, of frenzy and long words. Not yet specifically a proposal of marriage. But it was pretty obvious that Mrs. Gamble would soon have to find herself a new companion.

She got up, stepped softly over to the back of Sebastian's chair and, singling out one of those scandalously charming curls of his, gave it a short but very painful tug. Then, without even glancing at him, she moved on to where the Queen Mother was sitting and took the cup from between her claw-like hands.

'Let me give you some fresh tea,' she said in her low musical voice.

Another woman might have been vexed to find herself treated in this off-hand and discourteous fashion. But Daisy Ockham was so singularly lacking in a sense of her own importance that she was hardly even surprised when the butler gave her Mrs. Gamble's message.

'My grandmother's gone out to dinner,' she explained to her companion. 'So we shall be alone this evening.'

The other inclined his head and, in an accent which betrayed that he had not been educated at one of the more ancient and expensive seats of learning, said that it was a pleasure he looked forward to.

Thin, sharp-featured and middle-aged, with brown, damp hair brushed back over a bald spot on the top of his head, Mr. Tendring was dressed for the part of an eminent barrister or Harley Street specialist, but unfortunately without much verisimilitude; for the dark striped trousers had been shoddy even in their palmiest days, the black jacket was manifestly ready-made. Only the collar came up to professional standards—high, with flaring wings and an inordinately wide opening through which Mr. Tendring's neck, with its protuberant Adam's apple, looked pathetically stringy and at the same time rather un-pleasantly naked, almost indecent. A black leather brief-case, too important to be handed over to the footman, who had relieved him of his overcoat, was carried under the right arm.

'Well, I expect you'd like to go up to your room before dinner,' said Mrs. Ockham.

Again he inclined his head, this time without speaking.

As they followed the butler towards the staircase, Mr. Tendring looked about him with small appraising eyes—took in the pillars and barrel vaulting of the hall, darted, through the tall double doors, a glance down the long rich vista of the drawing-room, observed the pictures on the walls, the porcelain, the carpets. The thought of all the money that must have been spent to make the house what it was gave him an almost sensual pleasure. He had a deep, disinterested respect for wealth, a tender and admiring love of money for its own sake and without any reference to himself or his immediate needs. Surrounded by these exotic and unfamiliar splendours, he felt no envy, only veneration tinged with a secret satisfaction at the thought that here he was, the greengrocer's son, the ex-office boy, enjoying the splendours from the inside, as a guest, as the indispensable financial adviser, tax expert and accountant of their new owner. Suddenly, the grey sharp-featured face relaxed and, like a schoolboy who has succeeded in scoring off his companions, Mr. Tendring positively grinned.

'Quite a mansion,' he said to Mrs. Ockham, showing a set of teeth which the suburban dentist had made so brilliantly pearly that they would have seemed improbable in the mouth even of a chorus girl.

'Quite,' said Mrs. Ockham vaguely. 'Quite.'

She was thinking how poignantly familiar it all seemed. As though it were only yesterday that she had been a schoolgirl, coming out to Florence every Christmas and Easter to spend the holidays. And now all the rest were dead. Her father first of all. So old and awe-inspiring, so tall and bushy-eyebrowed and aloof, that his going had really made no difference. But then had come her mother's turn; and, for Daisy Ockham, her mother had died twice over—once when she married Eustace, and again, for ever, five years later. And when that anguish had been lived down, there had come her marriage and those years of happiness with Francis and little Frankie. Nearly fourteen years of the richest, the intensest living. And then one brilliant holiday morning, with the sea-gulls screaming, and the air full of blown spray, and the great green glassy waves exploding into foam along the beaches, they had gone down for a bathe. Father and son, the man's hand on the boy's shoulder, laughing together as they walked. Half an hour later, when she followed them down to the beach with the thermos of hot milk and the biscuits, she met the fishermen carrying the two bodies up from the water. . . . And now it was poor Eustace, whom her mother had loved and whom, for that reason, she herself had passionately hated. But then her mother had died, and Eustace had fallen out of her life, had become a casual acquaintance, encountered occasionally in other people's houses—and once every year or so, when there was business to discuss, they would meet by appointment at the solicitor's and, from Lincoln's Inn, when everything had been settled, he would take her to lunch at the Savoy, and she would listen to his odd, disconcerting talk, so utterly unlike anything she heard at home, and laugh and reflect that, after all, he was really very nice in his funny way. Very nice indeed and very clever, and it was a shame he didn't do anything with his gifts and all that money.

Well, now he was dead, and all that money was hers—all that money and, along with it, all the responsibility for using it as it ought to be used, as God would want it to be used. At the mere thought of the future burden, Mrs. Ockham sighed profoundly. This house, for example—what on earth should she do with it? And all the servants? There must be a dozen of them.

'It was terribly sudden,' she said in Italian to the butler as they started to climb the stairs.

The man shook his head and an expression of genuine sadness appeared on his face. The *signore* had been so kind. *Tanto buono, tanto buono*. Tears came into his eyes.

Mrs. Ockham was touched. And yet she simply couldn't keep all these servants. Perhaps if she offered them a year's wages when she gave them notice—or, better, a year's board wages. . . . But Mr. Tendring would never allow that. She shot an apprehensive glance at that grey face with its sharp nose and tight-shut, almost lipless mouth. Never, she repeated to herself, never. And after all, that was what he was there for—to keep her in order, to prevent her from doing anything too silly. She remembered what Canon Cresswell was always dinning into her. 'It takes two people to make a swindle—the swindler and the swindlee. If you let yourself be a swindlee, you're an accessory before the fact—you're leading an innocent person into temptation. So don't do it. Don't!' Golden advice—but how difficult it had been for her to follow it! And now that, instead of her all too comfortable twelve hundred a year, she was to have six thousand and a whole fortune in buildings, furniture and works of art, it would be even harder, because there would be so many more outstretched hands. She had hired Mr. Tendring, among other reasons, to protect her from her own sentimentality. And yet she couldn't help feeling that those poor servants ought to have a year's board wages. After all, it was no fault of theirs that Eustace had died so suddenly; and some of them had been with him for years and years. . . . She sighed again. How hard it was to know what was right! And then, when one knew, the knowledge had to be acted upon. That was fairly easy if there were nobody but oneself involved. But mostly one couldn't do what was right without upsetting almost as many people as one satisfied. And then their disappointment and their bitterness made one wonder whether, after all, one had been doing right. And then the whole debate had to begin again. ....

Half an hour later, refreshed by a hot bath and a change of clothes, Mrs. Ockham entered the drawing-room. She had expected to find herself alone; and when, from the depths of one of the enormous chintz-covered chairs, a small figure suddenly uncurled its legs and jumped respectfully to its feet, she uttered a startled exclamation of surprise. Diffidently, the figure advanced, and as it came within range of her rather short-sighted eyes Mrs. Ockham recognized it as the boy she had talked to in the Hampstead public library. The boy who had reminded her of Frankie; had actually *been* Frankie, so it excruciatingly seemed; had been her little precious one as he would have become if she had been allowed to keep him another year or two. How often, since that chance meeting of a couple of weeks before, she had reproached herself for having lacked the presence of mind to ask his name and where he lived! And now, impossibly, he was here in Eustace's drawing-room.

'You?' she whispered incredulously. 'But . . . but who are you?' The living ghost of Frankie smiled at her shyly.

'I'm Sebastian,' he answered. 'Uncle Eustace was . . . well, he was my uncle,' he concluded lamely.

Suddenly and rather heavily—for she was feeling strangely weak about the knees—Mrs. Ockham sat down on the nearest chair. Another moment, and she might have fainted. She shut her eyes and took three or four deep breaths. There was a long silence.

Standing in front of her, Sebastian fidgeted uneasily and wondered whether he oughtn't to say something—'What a funny coincidence!' or 'That was awfully good chocolate you gave me.' But after all, she had lost her son. He ought to say something about that. 'I didn't have time to say how sorry I was.' But somehow even that sounded pretty bad. Seeing how upset she obviously was, poor old thing!

Mrs. Ockham looked up.

'It's the hand of Providence,' she said in a low voice.

There were tears in her eyes, but she was also smiling—a smile that transfigured the soft and snubby face, making it seem almost beautiful.

'God wants to give him back to me.'

Sebastian writhed. This was really awful!

God wanted to give her Frankie back to her, Mrs. Ockham was thinking; yes, and perhaps to give Himself back. For Frankie had been the living sacrament, the revelation, the immediate experience of divinity.

'God is love,' she said aloud. 'But what's love? I never knew until after my little boy was born. Then I began to learn. And every day I learned a little more. Different forms of love, deeper intensities—every day for nearly fourteen years.'

She was silent again, thinking of that windy summer's morning, and the fishermen toiling slowly up the beach; remembering those first weeks of almost insane, rebellious despair, and then the months of emptiness, of being numb and hopeless and half dead. It was Canon Cresswell who had brought her back to life. After the disaster she had refused to go near him. Perversely—because she knew in her heart that he could help her, and she didn't want to be helped; she wanted to suffer in solitude, for ever. Then, somehow, Mrs. Cresswell had discovered where she was; and one wet November afternoon there they were on the doorstep of the dismal little cottage she had chosen as her hiding-place. And instead of condoling with her on the tragedy, instead of telling her sympathetically how ill she looked, Canon Cresswell made her sit down and listen, while he called her a cowardly, self-indulgent emotionalist, a mutineer against God's Providence, a self-willed sinner guilty of the most inexcusable despair.

An hour later, Mrs. Cresswell was helping her to clean up the cottage and pack her bags. That evening she was back at the Girls' Club, and the next day, which was Sunday, she went to early Communion. She had come back to life again—but it was a diminished life. In the past God had been with her almost every day. For example, when she came and said good-night to Frankie, and he got out of bed and knelt there in his pink pyjamas and they repeated the Lord's Prayer together—there He was, Our Father in the heaven of her love. But now even Communion failed to bring Him close to her. And though she loved the poor children at the Club, though she was ready to do much more for them now than she had done when her work there was only a thank-offering for so much happiness, it was all a second best; there was nobody to take the place of Frankie. She had learnt to accept God's will; but it was the will of somebody at a distance—withdrawn and unrevealed.

Mrs. Ockham took a handkerchief out of her bag and wiped her eyes.

'I know you think I'm a dreadful old sentimentalist,' she said with a little laugh.

'Not a bit,' Sebastian protested politely.

But for once the Queen Mother had been quite right: blanc-mange was the word for her.

'You're John Barnack's son, I suppose?'

He nodded.

'Then your mother . . .?'

Mrs. Ockham left the sentence unfinished. But her tone, and the expression of distress which appeared in her grey eyes, sufficiently indicated what she meant to say.

'Yes, she's dead,' said Sebastian.

'Your mother's dead,' she repeated slowly.

But imagine poor little Frankie, all alone in a harsh, indifferent world, with nobody to love him as she alone was capable of loving him! To the love in her heart there was added an over-powering compassion.

Blancmange, Sebastian was thinking. Blancmange with Jesus sauce. Then, to his great relief, the butler entered and announced that dinner was served.

With a sigh Mrs. Ockham put away her handkerchief, then asked the man to go and tell the *signore*. Turning to Sebastian, she began to explain Mr. Tendring.

'You'll find him a bit . . . well, you know, not quite . . .' The deprecating gesture sufficiently indicated what he quite wasn't. 'But a good soul underneath,' she hastened to add. 'He's a Unitarian, and he's got two children, and he grows tomatoes in the sweetest little greenhouse in his back garden. And as for business—well, I don't know what I'd have done without him these last five years. That's why I asked him to come along with me now—to deal with all this.'

In a limp gesture of all-embracing ineptitude she waved her hand at Eustace's treasures.

'I wouldn't even know where to begin,' she concluded hopelessly.

The sound of footsteps made her turn.

'Ah, I was just talking about you, Mr. Tendring. Telling Sebastian here—he's Mr. Barnack's nephew, by the way—how utterly lost I'd be without you.'

Mr. Tendring acknowledged the compliment with a slight bow, silently shook hands with Sebastian, then turned and apologized to Mrs. Ockham for having kept her waiting.

'I was compiling a catalogue of the furnishings in my bedroom,' he explained; and in confirmation of his words he pulled a small black notebook out of the side pocket of his jacket and held it up for her inspection.

'A catalogue?' Mrs. Ockham repeated in some astonishment, as she got up from her chair.

Mr. Tendring further compressed his tight-shut mouth, and nodded importantly. In the wide, barristerial opening of his stiff collar, the Adam's apple stirred like a thing endowed with a small spasmodic life of its own. Deliberately, in phrases modelled on those of the business letter and the legal document, he began to speak.

'You have informed me, Mrs. Ockham, that the late owner carried no insurance against fire or theft.'

Surprisingly, Mrs. Ockham uttered a little peal of rich, bubbly laughter.

'He used to say he couldn't afford it. Because of the duty on Havana cigars.'

Sebastian smiled; but Mr. Tendring contracted his brows, and his Adam's apple sharply rose and fell, as though it too were shocked by such a blasphemy against Prudence.

'Personally,' he said with severity, 'I don't hold with joking about serious matters.'

Mrs. Ockham hastened to placate him.

'Quite right,' she said, 'quite right. But I don't see what *his* having no insurance has to do with *your* making a catalogue.'

Mr. Tendring permitted himself a smile. The Gaiety-Girl teeth flashed triumphantly.

'The fact,' he said, 'constitutes presumptive evidence that the late owner caused no list of his personal property ever to be drawn up.'

He smiled again, evidently delighted with the beauty of his language.

'So that's what you're writing in your little black book,' said Mrs. Ockham. 'Is it really necessary?'

'Necessary?' Mr. Tendring repeated almost indignantly. 'It's a *sine qua non.*'

It was final and crushing. After a little silence Mrs. Ockham suggested that they should go in to dinner.

'Will you take me in, Sebastian?' she asked.

Sebastian began by offering her the wrong arm, and was horribly embarrassed and ashamed when Mrs. Ockham smiled and told him to go round to the other side. Making a fool of himself in front of this awful little bounder. . . .

'Too stupid,' he muttered. 'I know perfectly well, really.'

But Mrs. Ockham was enchanted by his mistake.

'Just like Frankie!' she cried delightedly. 'Frankie could *never* remember which arm to give.'

Sebastian said nothing; but he was beginning to have enough of Frankie.

Intimately, as they walked towards the dining-room, Mrs. Ockham squeezed his arm.

'What luck that the others should have been out for our first evening!' she said; but added quickly, 'Not but what I'm very fond of poor dear Granny. And Veronica's so . . .'

She hesitated, remembering the Cresswells' concern over the disquieting spirit that had started, before she was even out of pigtails, to peep through their daughter's calm, bright eyes.

'So pretty and clever,' she concluded. 'But all the same, I'm awfully glad they're not here. I hope you are too,' she added, smiling at him almost archly.

'Oh, very,' Sebastian answered without much conviction.

CHAPTER TWENTY-TWO

BUT after all, he had to admit long before the evening was over, she wasn't a bad old thing by any manner of means. A bit blancmangeish, of course; but really very decent. She was going to give him all the volumes of the Loeb Classics that had been in her husband's library. And the Oxford Press edition of Donne. And Saintsbury's two volumes of *Minor Caroline Poets*. And on top of being kind, she wasn't even such a fool. True, she had confessed to being unable to sing 'Abide with me' without crying; but she also liked George Herbert. And though she had an exasperating habit of referring to everyone she knew as 'dear So-and-so,' or at the very worst and most uncharitable as 'poor dear,' she had quite a sense of humour, and some of the stories she told were really very funny.

But her most precious gift was that she never made you feel shy. In that respect she was like Uncle Eustace; and in both of them, it seemed to Sebastian, the secret consisted in a certain absence of pretentiousness, a refraining from standing on rights or privileges or dignity. Whereas that fiendish old Queen Mother didn't merely stand on her own dignity; she went out and deliberately trampled on yours. And more subtly, for all her desirableness, Mrs. Thwale did the same thing. It was as though she were always using you, in some way or other, as a means to further her own private ends—and the ends were disquietingly mysterious and unpredictable. Whereas with Mrs. Ockham it was you who were the end, and all she asked was to be allowed to be the adoring means of your glorification. Which was really rather pleasant. So pleasant, indeed, that Sebastian soon did more than merely cease to be shy with her; he began to show off and lay down the law. Except for Susan—and Susan didn't really count—he had never known anyone who was ready to listen so respectfully to what he had to say. Stimulated by her admiration, and quite unhindered by Mr. Tendring, who never put in a word and allowed his presence to be completely ignored, he became, especially after his second glass of wine, extraordinarily loquacious. And when his own ideas failed him, he did not hesitate to fall back on Uncle Eustace's. His remarks about the affinity between Mid-Victorian English and Italian Primitive were thought to be very startling and brilliant. Still, even with the wine to give him courage and take away discretion, he didn't venture to repeat what Uncle Eustace had said in connection with Piero's Venus and her Adonis. It was Mrs. Ockham who finally broke the silence that had settled down on them as they stood looking at the picture after dinner.

'Art's a funny thing,' she said, pensively shaking her head. 'Very funny indeed, sometimes.'

Sebastian gave her an amused and pitying smile. Her remark had made him feel delightfully superior.

'Works of art aren't moral tracts,' he said sententiously.

'Oh, I know, I know,' Mrs. Ockham agreed. 'But all the same . . .'

'All the same what?'

'Well, why bother about that sort of thing so much?'

She hadn't bothered—except, of course, negatively, inasmuch as she'd always felt that the whole business was profoundly unpleasant. And, in spite of her mother's vague but fearful warnings about the male sex, her darling Francis had really bothered very little. So why did other people find it necessary to think and talk so much about it, to write all those books and poems, to paint such pictures as this thing they were now looking at? Pictures which, if they weren't Great Art, one would never dream of tolerating in a decent house, where innocent boys like Frankie, like Sebastian here . . .

'Sometimes,' she went on, 'I just cannot understand . . .'

'Excuse me,' Mr. Tendring broke in, suddenly pushing his way between them and the mythological nudities.

Horizontally first, then vertically, he applied a tape-measure to the painting. Then, taking the pencil from between his pearly teeth, he made an entry in his notebook: *Oil Painting : Antony and Cleopatra. Antique. 41 ins.× 20½ ins. Framed.*

'Thanks,' he said, and passed on to the Seurat. Twenty-six by sixteen; and the frame, instead of being gilded and genuine hand-carved, was the cheapest-looking thing, painted in different colours, like one of those camouflaged ships during the war.

Mrs. Ockham led Sebastian away to the sofa and, while they sipped their coffee, began to ask him about his father.

'He didn't get on too well with poor dear Eustace, did he?'

'He hated Uncle Eustace.'

Mrs. Ockham was shocked.

'You mustn't say that, Sebastian.'

'But it's true,' he insisted.

And when she started trying to smother the whole thing in that soft sentimental blancmange of hers— mooing away about brothers not seeing eye to eye perhaps, but never hating one another, never really forgetting that they were brothers—he became annoyed.

'You don't know my father,' he snapped.

And forgetting all about the heroic portrait he had painted for the benefit of Gabriel Weyl, Sebastian launched out into an embittered account of John Barnack's character and behaviour. Greatly distressed, Mrs. Ockham tried to persuade him that it was all just a case of misunderstanding. When he was older he would realize that his father had always acted with the best intentions. But the only effect of these well-meaning interventions was to stimulate Sebastian to a greater intemperance of language. Then, by a natural transition, his resentment modulated into complaint. He felt all at once extraordinarily sorry for himself, and began to say so.

Mrs. Ockham was touched. Even if Mr. Barnack wasn't as bad as he had been painted, even if he were nothing worse than a busy man with harsh manners and no time for affection, that would be quite enough to make a sensitive child unhappy. More than ever, as she listened to Sebastian, she felt convinced that it was God who had brought them together—the poor motherless boy, the poor mother who had lost her child—brought them together that they might help one another and, helping one another, might be strengthened to do God's work in the world.

Meanwhile, Sebastian had begun to tell the story of the evening clothes.

Mrs. Ockham remembered how adorable Frankie had looked in the dinner jacket she had bought him for his thirteenth birthday. So grown-up, so touchingly childish. Her eyes filled with tears. But in the meantime it really did seem hard on poor Sebastian that his father should sacrifice him to a mere political prejudice.

'Oh, how sweet of dear old Eustace to give it you!' she cried, when he reached that point in his story.

Sebastian was offended by her cheerful all's-well-that-ends-well tone.

'Uncle Eustace only promised,' he said gloomily. 'Then . . . well, this thing happened.'

'So you never got it after all?'

He shook his head.

'Poor darling, you *do* have bad luck!'

To Sebastian, in his mood of self-pity, her commiseration was as balm. To be told, in that tone, that he had had bad luck was so delightful that it would be almost sacrilegious to mention the drawing, the two thousand two hundred lire, the visit to the tailor's. Indeed, it never even occurred to him that they ought to be mentioned. In the present circumstances of mood and feeling these things were irrelevant to the point of being practically non-existent. Then, suddenly, they jumped out into the foreground of immediate reality. Mrs. Ockham leaned forward and laid her hand on his knee; her soft snubby face was transfigured by a smile of intense yearning tenderness.

'Sebastian, I've got a favour to ask of you.'

He smiled charmingly and raised a questioning eyebrow.

'Eustace made you a promise,' she explained. 'A promise he wasn't able to keep. But I *can* keep it. Will you allow me, Sebastian?'

He looked at her for a moment, uncertain whether he had understood her aright. Then, as it became clear that her words could have only one meaning, the blood rushed up into his cheeks.

'You mean . . . about the evening clothes?'

He averted his eyes in confusion.

'I'd so love to do it,' she said.

'It's awfully decent of you,' he muttered. 'But really . . .'

'After all, it was one of poor Eustace's last wishes.'

'I know; but . . .'

He hesitated, wondering whether to tell her about the drawing.

But she might think, as that Weyl fellow had obviously thought, that he oughtn't to have sold it—not so quickly, not immediately after the funeral. And to her he couldn't say it was for a debt of honour. Besides, if he were going to mention the drawing at all, he ought to have done it long ago. To mention it now would be to admit that he had been enjoying her sympathy and inviting her generosity on false pretences. And what a fool he would seem, as well as a humbug!

'After all,' said Mrs. Ockham, who had attributed his hesitation to a quite understandable reluctance to accept a present from a stranger, 'after all, I'm really part of the family. A step-first cousin, to be precise.'

What delicate feelings he had! More tenderly than ever, she smiled at him again.

From the depths of his discomfort Sebastian tried to smile back. It was too late to explain now. There was nothing for it but to go ahead.

'Well, if you really think it's all right,' he said.

'Oh, good, good!' cried Mrs. Ockham. 'Then we'll go to the tailor's together. That *will* be fun, won't it?'

He nodded and said it would be great fun.

'It must be the best tailor in town.'

'I noticed one in the Via Tornabuoni,' he said, determined at any cost to head her off from the place near the cathedral.

But what a fool he had been to get rid of the drawing in such a hurry! Instead of waiting to see what might turn up. And now he'd be landed with two evening suits. And it wasn't as though he could save up one of them for use later on. In a couple of years he'd have grown out of both. Well, after all, it didn't really matter.

'When we're back in London,' said Mrs. Ockham, 'I hope you'll come and dine with me sometimes in your evening clothes.'

'I'd love to,' he said politely.

'You'll be my excuse for going to all the plays and concerts I never have the heart or the energy to go to by myself.'

Plays and concerts. . . . His eyes brightened at the prospect.

They began talking about music. Mrs. Ockham, it seemed, had been a great concert-goer when her husband was alive, had travelled to Salzburg for Mozart and the moderns, to Bayreuth for Wagner, to Milan for *Otello* and *Falstaff*. Against these achievements Sebastian could only set a few poor evenings at the Queen's Hall. In mere self-defence he found himself compelled to expatiate, with a kind of boastful possessiveness, on the wonderful playing of an old pianist friend of his own, retired now from the concert stage, but as brilliant as ever—Dr. Pfeiffer by name; she had probably heard of him. No? But in his day he had enjoyed a European reputation.

In the background, meanwhile, Mr. Tendring had measured all the paintings and was now working his way through the porcelain, jade and ivory. Thousands of pounds, he said to himself from time to time, lingering voluptuously over the Cockney diphthongs, thousands of pounds. . . . He felt extraordinarily happy.

At a quarter past ten there was a sudden commotion in the hall, and a moment later, as from a ghostly parade ground, the Queen Mother's voice came to their ears.

'There's poor dear Granny,' said Mrs. Ockham, interrupting Sebastian in the middle of a sentence.

She rose and hurried towards the door. In the hall, Mrs. Gamble's maid had just divested the old lady of her wrap and was in process of handing over the Pomeranian.

'Little Foxy-woxy,' cried the Queen Mother. 'Did he miss his old granny-wanny? Did he, then?'

Foxy VIII licked her chin, then turned to bark at the new-comer.

'Granny dear!'

Scintillating like a whole chandelier of diamonds, Mrs. Gamble wheeled in the direction of the voice.

'Is that Daisy?' she rasped enquiringly.

And when Mrs. Ockham had said yes, she presented her with

a withered brick-red cheek, lowering Foxy, as she did so, out of range, so that her granddaughter might not be bitten as she paid her respects.

Mrs. Ockham kissed her safely.

'How nice to see you!' she said through the yapping.

'Why is your nose so cold?' the Queen Mother asked sharply. 'You haven't got a chill, I hope?'

Mrs. Ockham assured her that she had never felt better, then turned to Mrs. Thwale, who had remained standing a little to one side, a silent, bright-eyed, faintly smiling spectator.

'And here's dear little Veronica,' she said, holding out both her hands.

Mrs. Thwale took the cue and offered both of hers.

'Looking more beautiful than ever,' exclaimed Mrs. Ockham in a tone of whole-hearted admiration.

'Now, Daisy,' rasped the Queen Mother, 'for goodness' sake, stop gushing like a schoolgirl.'

To hear other people complimented in her presence was distasteful to her. But instead of taking the hint, Mrs. Ockham proceeded to deepen her original offence.

'I'm not gushing,' she protested, as she took her grandmother's arm and started with her towards the drawing-room. 'It's the simple truth.'

The Queen Mother snorted angrily.

'I've never seen Veronica look so radiant as she does tonight.'

Well, if that was true, Mrs. Thwale was thinking, as she followed them, it meant that she had been living in a fool's paradise. Flattering herself with the conviction that she had built up an ironclad facial alibi, when in fact she could still be read like an open book.

She frowned to herself. It was bad enough to have a hypothetical God, unto whom all hearts were open, all desires known. But to be known and open to Daisy Ockham, of all people—that was the ultimate humiliation.

True, there were excuses. It wasn't every evening that one

was proposed to by Paul De Vries. But, on the other hand, it was precisely on the exceptional and important occasions that it was most necessary to keep other people in ignorance of what one was really feeling. And she had permitted the symptoms of her elation to appear so clearly that even a fat old goose like Daisy could detect them. Not that much harm had been done this time. But it just showed how careful one had to be, how sleeplessly vigilant.

Mrs. Thwale frowned once more; then, as she relaxed her facial muscles, made a conscious effort to assume an expression of detached indifference. No more of that tell-tale radiance. For the outside world, nothing but the opaque symbol of a rather distant and amused politeness. But behind it, for herself, what gay bright secrets, what an effervescence of unuttered laughter and private triumph!

It had happened after dinner, when old Lord Worplesden, who was an amateur astronomer, insisted on taking Mrs. Thwale and the little Contessina up to the top of the tower on which he had installed his six-inch refracting telescope. A first-rate instrument, he boasted. By Zeiss of Jena. But among the young ladies of the neighbourhood it was celebrated for other reasons. The star-gazer would take you in, under the dome of his baby observatory, and then, under the pretext of getting you and the telescope into the right position for seeing the satellites of Jupiter, would paw you about, booming away all the time about Galileo. Then, if you hadn't objected too much, he'd show you the rings of Saturn. And finally there were the spiral nebulae. These required at least ten minutes of the most laborious adjustment. Girls who had seen a spiral nebula got a big bottle of scent the next day, with a playful invitation, embossed with a coronet and signed, 'Yours very affectionately, W.,' to come again another time and really explore the Moon.

The Contessina's stock of scent had evidently run low; for it was nearly half an hour before she and the old gentleman emerged again from the observatory. Time enough for Paul, who had followed them uninvited up the tower, to look at the night sky and talk a little about Eddington; to look down at the lights of Florence and reflect aloud that they were beautiful, that earth had its constellations too; to be silent for a little, and then say something about Dante and the *Vita Nuova*; and again be silent and hold her hand; and at last, rather breathlessly and, for once, inarticulately, to ask her to marry him.

The intrinsic ludicrousness of what had happened, and the sudden glory of her own elation, had almost caused her to laugh aloud.

At last! The magnet had done its work; the philosophic Eye had finally succumbed to life's essential shamelessness. In the tug-of-war between appearance and reality, reality had won, as it always must, it always must.

Ludicrous spectacle! But for her, at least, the joke would have important and serious consequences. It meant freedom; it meant power over her surroundings; it meant a little cushioned world of privacy outside herself as well as merely within—a house of her own as well as an attitude, a suite at the Ritz as well as a state of mind and a luxuriant fancy.

'Will you, Veronica?' he had repeated anxiously, as her averted silence persisted through the seconds. 'Oh, my darling, say you will!'

Confident at last of being able to speak without betraying herself, she had turned back to him.

Dear Paul . . . touched inexpressibly . . . taken so utterly by surprise . . . would like to wait a day or two before giving her final answer. . . .

The door of the little observatory had opened and Lord Worplesden could be heard loudly recommending the Contessina to read the more popular writings of Sir James Jeans, F.R.S. In his case, she reflected, the Eye was astronomical and proconsular; but it was the same old magnet, the identical shamelessness. And in a few more years there would be the final shamelessness of dying.

Meanwhile, in the drawing-room, the Queen Mother had responded to Mr. Tendring's accent exactly as her granddaughter had feared and expected. To his polite enquiries after her health she responded merely by asking him to spell his name; and when he had done so, she said, 'How very odd!' and repeated the word 'Tendring' two or three times in a tone of extreme distaste, as though she were being forced against her will to speak of skunks or excrement. Then she turned to Daisy and, in a harsh stage-whisper, asked her why on earth she had brought such a dreadfully common little man with her. Fortunately, Mrs. Ockham was able to cover up the old lady's words by the first sentence of her own loud and enthusiastic account of her previous meeting with Sebastian.

'Oh, he's like Frankie, is he?' said the Queen Mother, after listening for a little while in silence. 'Then he must look very young for his age, very babyish.'

'He looks sweet!' cried Mrs. Ockham, with a sentimental unction which Sebastian found almost as humiliating as her grandmother's offensive.

'I don't like it when boys look sweet,' Mrs. Gamble went on. 'Not with men like Tom Pewsey prowling around.' She lowered her voice. 'What about that little man of yours, Daisy—is *he* all right?'

'Granny!' Mrs. Ockham exclaimed in horror.

She looked round apprehensively, and was relieved to see that Mr. Tendring had gone over to the other side of the room and was cataloguing the Capo di Monte figures in the cabinet between the windows.

'Thank goodness,' she breathed, 'he didn't hear you.'

'I wouldn't mind if he had,' said the Queen Mother emphatically. 'Penal servitude — that's what *those* people deserve.'

'But he isn't one of those people,' Mrs. Ockham protested in an agitated and indignant whisper.

'That's what *you* think,' the Queen Mother retorted. 'But

if you imagine you know anything about the subject, you're very much mistaken.'

'I don't want to know anything,' said Mrs. Ockham with a shudder. 'It's a horrible subject!'

'Then why bring it up? Particularly in front of Veronica. Veronica!' she called. 'Have you been listening?'

'In snatches,' Mrs. Thwale demurely admitted.

'You see!' said the Queen Mother in a tone of reproachful triumph to Mrs. Ockham. 'But luckily she's a married woman. Which is more than can be said of that boy. Boy,' she went on, speaking imperiously into the darkness, 'tell me what you think of all this.'

Sebastian blushed. 'You mean, the . . . penal servitude?'

'Penal servitude?' repeated the Queen Mother irritably. 'I'm asking you what you think of meeting my granddaughter again.'

'Oh, that! Well, of course, it's most extraordinary. I mean, it's a funny coincidence, isn't it?'

Impulsively, Mrs. Ockham put an arm round Sebastian's shoulders and drew him towards her.

'Not exactly funny,' she said. 'Joyful, if you like—the happiest kind of Godsend. Yes, a real Godsend,' she repeated, and her eyes filled with the tears that came to her so easily, her voice took on a vibrancy of emotion.

'God here, God there,' rasped the Queen Mother. 'You talk too much about God.'

'But how can one talk and think enough?'

'It's blasphemous.'

'But God *did* send him to me.'

And to lend emphasis to what she had said, Mrs. Ockham tightened her embrace. Inertly, Sebastian suffered himself to be hugged. He felt horribly embarrassed. She was making a fool of him in public—just how much of a fool he divined from the expression on Mrs. Thwale's face. It was the same expression as he had seen on it that afternoon when she tormented him with her talk of giving Mrs. Gamble a demonstration of outrage—the amused, impersonal expression of the spectator who looks on at a delightfully heartless little comedy of manners.

'And not only blasphemous,' the Queen Mother continued. 'It's bad taste to be always talking about God. Like wearing all one's pearls all day long, instead of only in the evening when one's dressed for dinner.'

'Apropos of dressing for dinner,' said Mrs. Ockham, trying to shift the conversation on to safer ground. 'Sebastian and I have agreed that we're going to a lot of plays and concerts together when we get back to London. Haven't we, Sebastian?'

He nodded his head and smiled uncomfortably. Then, to his vast relief, Mrs. Ockham dropped her hand from his shoulder, and he was able to move away.

From between the curtains of her spiritual private box, Mrs. Thwale observed it all and was delighted with the play. The Holy Woman was fairly itching with unsatisfied motherhood. But the boy, not unnaturally, didn't much relish being made the victim of that particular brand of concupiscence. So poor old Holy-Poly had to offer bribes. Theatres and concerts to induce him to become her gigolo-baby, to submit to being the instrument of her maternal lust. But, after all, there were other forms of the essential shamelessness—forms that an adolescent would find more attractive than mother-craving; there were magnets, she flattered herself, considerably more powerful than Daisy's pug-like face, Daisy's chaste but abundant bosom. It might be amusing perhaps, it might be an interesting scientific experiment. . . . She smiled to herself. Yes, doubly amusing just because of what had happened this evening on Lord Worplesden's tower, scientific to the point of outrage and enormity.

At the mention of concerts, the Queen Mother, who could never bear to feel that she was being left out of anything, had insisted that she should also be of the party whenever they went to one. But, of course, she drew the line at modern music. And Bach always made her go to sleep. And as for string quartets— she couldn't abide that tiresome scraping and squeaking. . . .

Suddenly Mr. Tendring reappeared upon the scene.

'Pardon me,' he said, when the Queen Mother had come to the end of her musical dislikes; and he handed Mrs. Ockham a slip of paper.

'What's this?' she asked.

'A discrepancy,' Mr. Tendring answered, with all the gravity due to a four-syllabled word used by chartered accountants.

Foxy, who had the rich dog's infallible ear and eye and nose for members of the lower orders, started to growl.

'There, there,' said the Queen Mother soothingly. Then, turning to Mrs. Ockham, 'What's the man talking about?' she barked.

'A discrepancy,' Mr. Tendring explained, 'between this receipt, delivered to the late owner on the day of his . . . ah . . . demise, and the number of articles actually contained in the package. He bought two: but now there's only one.'

'One what?' asked Mrs. Ockham.

Mr. Tendring smiled almost archly.

'Well, I suppose you'd say it was a work of art,' he said.

Sebastian suddenly felt rather sick.

'If you'll step over here,' Mr. Tendring went on.

They all followed him to the table by the window. Mrs. Ockham examined the one remaining Degas and then the slip of paper upon which M. Weyl had acknowledged payment for two.

'Let me have them,' said the Queen Mother, when the situation had been explained to her.

In silence she fingered the drawing's cardboard mount and the flimsy receipt, then handed them back to Mrs. Ockham. The old face lit up.

'The other one must have been stolen,' she said with relish.

Stolen! Sebastian repeated to himself. That was it; they'd think he'd stolen it. And of course, it now occurred to him for the first time, he had no way of *proving* that Uncle Eustace had given him the drawing. Even that little joke between them at the séance wasn't really evidence. 'Bucks and pendulums'—it had been obvious to him. But would it be obvious if he tried to explain it to anyone else?

Meanwhile Mrs. Ockham had protested against her grandmother's uncharitable suggestion. But the old lady was not to be put off.

'It's one of the servants, of course,' she insisted almost gleefully.

And she went on to tell them about that butler of hers who had drunk at least three dozen bottles of her best brandy, about the housemaid who had been caught with Amy's ruby brooch, about the chauffeur who used to cheat on the petrol and repairs, about the under-gardener who . . .

And the fact that he had immediately gone and sold the thing —that would look bad, of course. If only he'd mentioned the matter the very day they found the body! Or else at the séance; that would have been a golden opportunity. Or this morning to Mrs. Thwale. Or even this evening, when Mrs. Ockham had offered to give him the dinner jacket—even then, at the risk of looking as if he'd been asking for sympathy on false pretences. If only, if only . . . Because now it was too late. If he told them now, it would look as though he were doing it because he'd been caught. And the story of Uncle Eustace's generosity would sound like something invented on the spur of the moment to cover up his guilt—a particularly stupid and unconvincing lie. And yet, if he didn't tell them, goodness only knew what mightn't happen.

'But we have no right even to think that it's been stolen,' said Mrs. Ockham, as the Queen Mother's recollections of dishonest menials temporarily ran dry. 'Poor Eustace probably took it out of the package and put it somewhere.'

'He couldn't have put it somewhere,' the Queen Mother retorted, 'because he didn't go anywhere. Eustace was in this room with the boy until he went to the w.c. and passed on. All the time—isn't that so, boy?'

Sebastian nodded without speaking.

'Can't you answer?' the ghostly sergeant-major exploded.

'Oh, I'm sorry. I forgot. . . . I mean, yes, he was here. All the time.'

'Listen to that, Veronica,' said the Queen Mother. 'He mumbles worse than ever.'

Mrs. Ockham turned to Sebastian.

'Did you see him doing anything with the drawing that evening?' she asked.

For a second, Sebastian hesitated; then, in a kind of unreasoning panic, he shook his head.

'No, Mrs. Ockham.'

Feeling that he was violently blushing, he turned away and, to hide his tell-tale face, bent down to look more closely at the drawing on the table.

'I told you it was stolen,' he heard the Queen Mother saying triumphantly.

'Oh, Mr. Tendring, why *did* you have to find it out?' Mrs. Ockham wailed.

He began to say something dignified about his professional duty, when the Queen Mother interrupted him.

'Now listen, Daisy,' she said. 'I won't have you behaving like a sentimental imbecile, slobbering over a pack of good-for-nothing servants! Why, they're probably robbing you right and left at this very moment.'

'No, they aren't,' cried Mrs. Ockham. 'I simply refuse to believe it. And anyhow, why should we bother about this wretched drawing? If it's as ugly as the other one . . .'

'Why should we bother?' Mr. Tendring repeated in the tone of one whose most sacred feelings have been outraged. 'But do you realize what the late owner paid for this object?' He picked up the receipt and handed it again to Mrs. Ockham. 'Seven thousand lire, madam. Seven thousand lire.'

Sebastian started and looked up at him; his eyes widened, his mouth fell open. Seven thousand lire? And that stinker had offered him a thousand and congratulated him on his business ability for having screwed the price up to two thousand two hundred. Anger and humiliation brought the blood rushing up into his face. What a fool he'd been, what an unutterable idiot!

'You see, Daisy, you see?' The Queen Mother's expression was gleeful. 'They could sell the thing for the equivalent of a year's wages.'

There was a little silence; and then, from behind him, Sebastian heard Mrs. Thwale's low musical voice.

'I don't think it was one of the s-servants,' she said, lingering with delicate affectation over the sibilant. 'I think it was somebody els-se.'

Sebastian's heart started to beat very fast and hard, as though he had been playing football. Yes, she must have seen him through the door, while he was putting the drawing into his dispatch-case. And when, an instant later, she spoke his name, he felt absolutely certain of it.

'Sebastian,' Mrs. Thwale repeated softly, when he failed to answer.

Reluctantly he straightened himself up and looked at her. Mrs. Thwale was smiling again as she might smile if she were watching a comedy.

'I expect you know as well as I do,' she said.

He swallowed hard and looked away.

'Don't you?' Mrs. Thwale insisted softly.

'Well,' he began almost inaudibly, 'I suppose you mean . . .'

'Of course,' she broke in. 'Of course! That little girl who was out there on the terrace.' And she pointed at the darkness beyond the window.

Startled, Sebastian looked up at her again. The dark eyes were dancing with a kind of exultant light; the smiling lips looked as though they might part at any moment to give passage to a peal of laughter.

'Little girl?' echoed the Queen Mother. 'What little girl?'

Mrs. Thwale started to explain. And suddenly, with an over-powering sense of relief, Sebastian realized that he had been reprieved.

CHAPTER TWENTY-THREE

SEBASTIAN'S sense of relief gave place very soon to be-wilderment and uneasiness. Alone in his room, as he undressed and brushed his teeth, he kept wondering why the reprieve had come. Did she *really* think that the child had done it? Obviously, he tried to assure himself, she must have thought so. But there was a part of his mind which obstinately refused to accept that simple explanation. If it were true, then why should she have looked at him like that? What was it she had found so exquisitely amusing? And if she hadn't thought that it was the little girl, what on earth had induced her to say so? The obvious answer was that she had seen him take the drawing, believed he had no right to it, and tried to shield him. But again, in the light of that queer smile of hers, that almost irrepressible amusement, the obvious answer made no sense. Nothing she had done made any sense. And meanwhile there was that wretched little girl to think of. The child would be questioned and bullied; and then the parents would come under suspicion; and finally, of course, Mrs. Gamble would insist on sending for the police. . . .

He turned out all the lights but the reading-lamp on the night table, and climbed into the enormous bed. Lying there, open-eyed, he fabricated for the thousandth time a series of scenes in which he casually mentioned Uncle Eustace's bequest to Mrs. Thwale and the Queen Mother, told Mrs. Ockham that he had already bought an evening suit with the money he had got for the drawing, smilingly scotched Mr. Tendring's suspicions before they were well hatched. How simple it all was, and how credit-ably he emerged from the proceedings! But the reality was as painfully and humiliatingly different from these consoling fancies as the blue tart had been from Mary Esdaile. And now it was too late to tell them what had really happened. He imagined the Queen Mother's comments on his behaviour—like sandpaper for uncharitableness. And Mrs. Thwale's faint smile and ironic silence. And the excuses which Mrs. Ockham would make for him with such an effusive sentimentality that her grandmother would become doubly censorious. No, it was impossible to tell them now. There was only one thing to do—buy the drawing back from M. Weyl and then 'find' it somewhere in the house. But the tailor had insisted upon being paid in advance; that meant that ten out of his twenty-two precious banknotes had gone within an hour of his receiving them. And he had spent another hundred lire on books, and sixty for a tortoise-shell cigarette-case. So now he had little more than a thousand in hand. Would Weyl give him credit for the balance? Despondently Sebastian shook his head. He'd have to borrow the money. But from whom? And with what excuse?

Suddenly there was a little tap at the door.

'Come in,' he called.

Mrs. Ockham walked into the room.

'It's me,' she said; and crossing over to the bed, she laid a hand on his shoulder. 'It's rather late, I'm afraid,' she went on apologetically. 'Granny kept me up interminably. But I just couldn't resist coming to say good-night to you.'

Politely, Sebastian propped himself up on one elbow. But she shook her head and, without speaking, gently pushed him back on to the pillow.

There was a long silence while she looked down at him—looked down at little Frankie and her murdered happiness, looked down at the living present, at this other curly-headed incarnation of divine reality. Rosy and golden, a childish head upon a pillow. As she looked, love mounted within her, overwhelming, like a tide rushing up from the depths of that great ocean from which for so long she had been cut off by the siltings of a hopeless aridity.

'Frankie used to wear pink pyjamas too,' she said in a voice which, in spite of her effort to speak lightly, trembled with the intensity of her emotion.

'Did he?'

Sebastian gave her one of those enchanting smiles of his—not consciously this time, or deliberately, but because he felt himself touched into an answering affection for this absurd woman. And suddenly he knew that this was the moment to tell her about the drawing.

'Mrs. Ockham . . .' he began.

But at the same instant, and moved by a yearning so intense as to make her unaware that he was trying to say something, Mrs. Ockham also spoke.

'Would you mind very much,' she whispered, 'if I gave you a kiss?'

And before he could answer, she had bent down and touched his forehead with her lips. Drawing back a little, she ran her fingers through his hair—and it was Frankie's hair. Her eyes filled with tears. Once more she bent down and kissed him.

Suddenly, startlingly, there was an interruption.

'Oh, excuse me . . .'

Mrs. Ockham straightened herself up and they both turned in the direction from which the voice had come. In the open doorway stood Veronica Thwale. Her dark hair hung down in two plaits over her shoulders, and she was buttoned up in a long white satin dressing-gown that made her look like a nun.

'I'm so sorry to interrupt you,' she said to Mrs. Ockham. 'But your grandmother . . .'

She left the sentence unfinished, and smiled.

'Does Granny want me again?'

'She has something more to say about that lost drawing.'

'Oh dear!' Mrs. Ockham sighed profoundly. 'Well, I'd

better go, I suppose. Would you like me to turn the light out?' she added, addressing herself again to Sebastian.

He nodded. Mrs. Ockham turned the switch, then laid her hand for a moment against his cheek, whispered 'Good-night,' and hurried out into the corridor. Mrs. Thwale closed the door.

Alone in the darkness, Sebastian wondered uneasily what it was that the Queen Mother wanted so urgently to say about the drawing. Of course, if he'd had time to tell Mrs. Ockham about it, it wouldn't matter what she said. But as it was . . . He shook his head. As it was, whatever the old she-devil said or did was sure to complicate matters, was bound to make it more difficult for himself. Meanwhile such an opportunity as he had had just now might not come again; and to go and tell Mrs. Ockham in cold blood would be the most horrible ordeal. So horrible that he began to wonder whether it mightn't be better, after all, to try to get the drawing back from Weyl. He was in the middle of an imaginary interview with the dealer, when he heard behind him the sound of the door being quietly opened. On the wall at which he was looking a bar of light widened, then grew narrower and, as the latch clicked, there was darkness again. Sebastian turned in his bed towards the unseen rustle of silk. She'd come back, and now he could tell her everything. He felt enormously relieved.

'Mrs. Ockham!' he said. 'Oh, I'm so glad . . .'

Through the covers a hand touched his knee, travelled up to his shoulder, and with a sharp movement pulled back the bed-clothes and threw them aside. The silk rustled again in the darkness, and a wave of perfume came to his nostrils—that sweet hot scent that was a mingling of flowers and sweat, spring freshness and a musky animality.

'Oh, it's you,' Sebastian began in a startled whisper.

But even as he spoke an unseen face bent over him; a mouth touched his chin, then found his lips; and fingers on his throat moved down and began to undo the buttons of his pyjama jacket.

CHAPTER TWENTY-FOUR

DIVINELY innocent, a sensuality panting up through incandescence into pure ecstasy; in the intervals, the tender and yet wittily cultured lasciviousness of Mary Esdaile—that was what Sebastian had imagined it would be, what he had looked forward to. Certainly not those hands, deliberate in the darkness, that almost surgical research of the essential shamelessness. Nor yet the delicate gluttony of those soft lips that would suddenly give place to teeth and pointed nails. And not those imperiously whispered commands; not those spells of silent, introverted frenzy, those long-drawn agonies, under his timid and almost horrified caresses, of a despairing insatiability.

In his fancy, love had been a kind of gay, ethereal intoxication; but last night's reality was more like madness. Yes, sheer madness; a maniac struggling in the musky darkness with another maniac.

'Twin cannibals in bedlam . . .' The phrase came to him as he was examining the red and livid mark of teeth on his arm. Twin cannibals, devouring their own identity and one another's; ravening up reason and decency; obliterating the most rudimentary conventions of civilization. And yet it was precisely there, in that frenzy of the cannibals, that the real attraction had lain. Beyond the physical pleasure lay the yet more rapturous experience of being totally out of bounds, the ecstasy of an absolute alienation.

Mrs. Thwale had put on her dove-grey dress and was wearing round her neck the little gold and ruby cross which her mother had given her on the day she was confirmed.

'Good-morning, Sebastian,' she said, as he came into the dining-room. 'We seem to have the breakfast table to ourselves.'

Sebastian looked with panic at the empty chairs and the unfolded napkins. For some reason he had taken it for granted that Mrs. Ockham would be there to chaperone this dreadfully embarrassing encounter.

'Yes, I thought . . . I mean, the journey . . . They must have been pretty tired. . . .'

From her private box at the comedy Mrs. Thwale looked at him with bright ironic eyes.

'Mumbling again!' she said. 'I shall really have to buy that birch!'

To cover his confusion, Sebastian went over to the sideboard and started to look at what was under the lids of the silver dishes on the hot-plate. Of course, what he ought to have done, he realized as he was helping himself to porridge, what he ought to have done, when he saw that she was alone, was to go and kiss her on the nape of the neck and whisper something about last night. And perhaps it wasn't too late even now. Press the muzzle of the revolver against the right temple, count ten, and then rush in and do it. One, two, three, four . . . Porridge plate in hand, he advanced towards the table. Four, five, six . . .

'I hope you slept well,' said Mrs. Thwale in her low clear voice.

He looked at her in dismay, then dropped his eyes.

'Oh, yes,' he muttered, 'yes . . . very well, thanks.'

There was no question any more of that kiss.

'You did?' Mrs. Thwale insisted with an air of astonishment. 'In spite of the owls?'

'The owls?'

'You don't mean to say,' she cried, 'that you didn't hear the owls? Lucky boy! I wish I slept as soundly as you do. I was awake half the night!'

She took a sip of coffee, delicately wiped her mouth, bit off a morsel of her toast and butter and, when she had swallowed it, wiped her mouth again.

'If I were you,' she said, 'I'd make it a point today to go to San Marco and look at the Fra Angelicos.'

The door opened and Mr. Tendring entered and, a moment later, Mrs. Ockham. They too had failed to hear the owls—even though Mrs. Ockham hadn't been able to go to sleep for hours, because of worrying about that wretched drawing.

Yes, that wretched drawing, that stinking drawing. In his impotence, Sebastian indulged in a childish outburst of bad language as he ate his buttered eggs. But calling names brought him no nearer to the resolution of his difficulties, and instead of clearing the mental atmosphere, blasphemy and obscenity merely intensified his mood of oppression by making him feel ashamed of himself.

'Are you going to send for the police?' Mrs. Thwale enquired.

Sebastian's heart seemed to miss a beat. Keeping his eyes fixed upon his plate, he stopped chewing so as to be able to listen with undivided attention.

'That's what Granny wants to do,' said Mrs. Ockham. 'But I won't have it yet. Not till we've made a really thorough search.'

Sebastian renewed his mastication—too soon, as it turned out; for Mrs. Thwale was all for having the little girl brought up to the house for cross-questioning.

'No, I'll go and talk to the parents first,' said Mrs. Ockham.

'Thank God!' Sebastian said to himself.

That meant that he probably had the whole of the day before him. Which was something. But how on earth was he going to set to work?

A touch on the elbow startled him out of his abstraction; the footman was bending over him, and on the proffered salver were two letters. Sebastian took them. The first was from Susan. Impatiently he put it in his pocket, unopened, and looked at the second. The envelope was addressed in an unfamiliar hand, and the stamp was Italian. Who on earth . . . ? And then a hope was born, grew and, in an instant of time, was transformed into a conviction, a positive certainty that the letter was from that man at the art gallery; explaining that it had all been a mistake;

apologizing profusely; enclosing a cheque. . . . Eagerly he tore open the envelope, unfolded the single sheet of cheap commercial paper and looked for the signature. 'Bruno Rontini,' he read. His disappointment found vent in sudden anger. That fool who believed in Gaseous Vertebrates, that creeping Jesus who tried to convert people to his own idiocies! Sebastian started to put the letter away in his pocket, then decided after all to see what the man had to say.

'Dear Sebastian,' he read, 'Returning yesterday, I heard the news, distressing on more than one account, of poor Eustace's death. I don't know if your plans have been modified by what has happened; but if you are staying on in Florence, remember that I am one of the oldest inhabitants as well as some sort of a cousin, and that I shall be very happy to help you find your way about. You will generally find me at my apartment in the mornings, in the afternoon at the shop.'

'At the shop,' Sebastian repeated to himself ironically. 'And he can damned well stay there.' And then all at once it occurred to him that, after all, this fool might be of some use to him. A dealer in books, a dealer in pictures—the chances were that they knew one another. Weyl might be ready to do the other fellow a favour; and Uncle Eustace had said that old man Bruno was pretty decent in spite of his silliness. Pensively Sebastian folded up the letter and put it in his pocket.

CHAPTER TWENTY-FIVE

YES, the whole universe was laughing with him. Laughing cosmically at the cosmic joke of its own self-frustration, guffawing from pole to pole at the world-wide, age-old slapstick of disaster following on the heels of good intention. A counterpoint of innumerable hilarities—Voltairean voices, yelping in sharp shrill triumph over the bewildered agonies of stupidity and silliness; vast Rabelaisian voices, like bassoons and double basses, rejoicing in guts and excrement and copulation, rumbling delightedly at the spectacle of grossness, of inescapable animality.

Shaking in unison with the universal merriment, he laughed through long durations of increasing pleasure, durations of mounting exhilaration and glory. And meanwhile here was that light again, here was that crystal of luminous silence—still and shining in all the interstices of the jagged laughter. Not at all formidable, this time, but softly, tenderly blue, as it had been when he caught old Bruno at his tricks with it. A blue caressing silence, ubiquitously present, in spite of the yelping and the bassoons, but present without urgency; beautiful, not with that austere, unbearable intensity, but imploringly, as though it were humbly begging to be taken notice of. And there was no participation in its knowledge, no self-compulsion to shame and condemnation. Only this tenderness. But Eustace was not to be caught so easily, Eustace was forearmed against all its little stratagems. To the entreaty of that blue crystal of silence he returned only the explosions of his derision, more and more strident as the light became more tenderly beautiful, as the silence ever more humbly, ever more gently and caressingly solicited his attention. No, no, none of that! He thought again of the Triumphs of Education, the Triumphs of Science, Religion, Politics, and his merriment mounted to a kind of frenzy. Paroxysm after cosmic paroxysm. What pleasure, what power and glory! But suddenly he was aware that the laughter had passed beyond his control, had become a huge, autonomous hysteria, persisting against his will and in spite of the pain it was causing him, persisting with a life of its own that was alien to his life, with a purpose of its own that was entirely incompatible with his well-being.

Out there, in here, the silence shone with a blue, imploring tenderness. But none of that, none of that! The light was always his enemy. Always, whether it was blue or white, pink or pea-green. He was shaken by another long, harrowing convulsion of derision.

Then, abruptly, there was a displacement of awareness. Once again he was remembering something that had not yet happened to somebody else.

Shuddering in the universal epilepsy, an open window presented itself; and there was poor old John, standing beside it, looking down into the street. And what confusion down there, what a yelling in that golden haze of dust! Dark faces, open-mouthed and distorted, dark hands, clenched or clawing. Thousands and thousands of them. And from the bright sunlit square on the right, from the narrow side-street immediately opposite the window, squads of turbaned and black-bearded policemen were shoving their way into the crowd, swinging their long bamboo staves. On heads and shoulders, on the bone of thin wrists upraised to protect the frightened, screaming faces —blow after blow, methodically. There was another convulsion. The figures wavered and broke, like images in a ruffled pool, then came together again as the laughing frenzy died down. Overhead, the blue tenderness was not mere sky, but the bright crystal of living silence. Methodically, the policemen hammered on. The thought of those sharp or cushioned impacts was nauseatingly distinct.

'Horrible!' John was saying between his teeth. 'Horrible!'

'It would be a damned sight worse if the Japs were to get to Calcutta,' another voice remarked.

Slowly, reluctantly, John nodded his head.

The professional Liberal condoning a *lathi* charge! There was another convulsive seizure, and another. Derision kept on tearing at him, like the gusts of a hurricane among tattered sails; kept on carding the very substance of his being, as though with combs and iron claws. But through the torment Eustace was unsteadily aware that, immediately below the window, a boy had dropped unconscious, felled by a blow on the temple. Two other young men were bending over him. Suddenly, through the yelping and the bassoons, there was as it were a memory of wild shrill cries and the frightened repetition of one incomprehensible phrase. A line of steel helmets was moving forward across the square. There was a panic movement of the crowd, away from the approaching danger. Jostled and staggering, the two young men succeeded none the less in raising their companion from the ground. As though in some mysterious rite, the boy's limp body was lifted shoulder-high towards the blue, imploring tenderness of the silence. For a few seconds only. Then the rush of the frightened mob toppled them down. Rescuers and rescued, they were gone, engulfed in the trampling and the suffocation. Blindly, in terror, the crowd moved on. A gale of mirthless lacerating laughter blew them into oblivion. Only the luminous silence remained, tender, beseeching. But Eustace was up to all its tricks.

And suddenly there was another bleeding face. Not the face of the nameless Indian boy; but, of all people, Jim Poulshot's face. Yes, Jim Poulshot! That vacant pigeon-hole which was so obviously destined to contain the moderately successful stockbroker of 1949. But Jim was in uniform and lying at the foot of a clump of bamboos, and three or four little yellow men with guns in their hands were standing over him.

'Wounded,' Jim kept saying in a thin cracked voice. 'Bring doctor quick! Wounded, wounded . . .'

The three little yellow men broke out simultaneously into loud, almost good-humoured guffaws. And as though moved by a kind of secret sympathy, the whole universe shook and howled in chorus.

Then suddenly one of the men raised his foot and stamped on Jim's face. There was a scream. The heel of the heavy rubber-soled boot came down again and, with yet more force, a third time. Blood was streaming from the mangled mouth and nose. The face was hardly recognizable.

Horror, pity, indignation—but in the same instant a blast of frantic laughter clawed at his being. 'The empty pigeon-hole,' his memories kept howling, and then, with irrepressible glee: 'The stockbroker of 1949, the moderately successful stockbroker.'

Under the bamboos the stockbroker of 1949 lay still, moaning.

> *Under the bamboo,*
> *Under the bamboo,*
> *Probably constipaysh . . .*

The barrel-organ outside the Kensington Registry Office, and Timmy's explanation of what had happened on the cricket field.

> *Probably constip,*
> *Probably constip . . .*

Among the little yellow men there had been a short, gloating silence. Then one of them said something and, as though to illustrate his meaning, drove his long bayonet into Jim Poulshot's chest. Grinning, the others followed suit—in the face, in the belly, in the throat and the genitals—again and again, until at last the screaming stopped.

The screaming stopped. But the laughter persisted—the howling, the epilepsy, the uncontrollable lacerating derision.

And meanwhile the scene had repeated itself. The bleeding face, the horror of the bayonets, but all somehow mixed up with Mimi in her claret-coloured dressing-gown. *Adesso comincia la tortura*—and then the dandling, the fumbling, the fondling. And at the same time the stamping, the stabbing. With St. Sebastian among the Victorian flowers, and poor dear Amy, tremulous before the Kensington Registrar, and Laurina at Monte Carlo. *Ave verum corpus*, the true body, the prim Victorian mouth, the brown, blind breast-eyes. And while the bayonets stabbed and stabbed, there was the shameful irrelevance of a pleasure that died at last into a cold reiterated friction, automatic and compulsory. And all the time the yelping and the bassoons, the iron teeth, combing and carding the very substance of his being. For ever and ever, excruciatingly. But he knew what the light was up to. He knew what that blue tenderness of silence was beseeching him to do. No, no, none of that! Deliberately he turned yet again towards the parting of the dressing-gown, towards the mangled and unrecognizable face, towards the intolerable pain of derision and lust, compulsorily, self-imposed, for ever and ever.

CHAPTER TWENTY-SIX

THERE were almost as many stairs as at Glanvil Terrace, but the fifth-floor landing was reached at last. Sebastian paused before ringing the bell, to recover his breath and to remind himself that, on this occasion, the nausea on the threshold was entirely unjustified. Who was Bruno Rontini anyhow? Just an amiable old ass, too decent, by all accounts, to be sarcastic or censorious, and too completely a stranger, for all his vague cousinship, to have the right to say unpleasant things, even if he wanted to. Besides, it wasn't as if he, Sebastian, were going to confess his sins, or anything like that. No, no, he wouldn't ask for help on that basis. It would be a matter of just casually introducing the subject, as though it weren't really so very important after all. 'By the way, do you happen to know a fellow called Weyl?' And so on, lightly, airily; and as Bruno wasn't his father, there wouldn't be any unpleasant interruptions, everything would go through according to plan. So that there was really no possible excuse for feeling sick like this. Sebastian drew three deep breaths, then pushed the button.

The door was opened almost immediately, and there stood old man Bruno, strangely cadaverous and beaky, in a grey sweater, with crimson carpet slippers on his feet.

His face lit up with a smile of welcome.

'Good,' he said, 'good!'

Sebastian took the extended hand, mumbled something about its being so awfully kind of him to write, and then averted his face in an excess of that paralysing embarrassment which always assailed him when he spoke to strangers. But meanwhile, inside his skull, the observer and the phrase-maker were busily at work. By daylight, he had noticed, the eyes were blue and very bright. Blue fires in bone-cups, vivid not simply with awareness and certainly not with the detached, inhuman curiosity which had shone in Mrs. Thwale's dark eyes when, last night, she had suddenly turned on the light and he had found her, on hands and knees, spanning him like an arch of white flesh. For a long half-minute she had looked at him, wordlessly smiling. Microscopic, in the black bright pupils, he could see his own pale reflection. '"Nature's lay idiot, I taught thee to love,"' she said at last. Then the pure mask crumpled into a grimace, she uttered her tiny stertorous grunt of laughter, reached out a slender arm towards the lamp and once more plunged the room into darkness. With an effort, Sebastian exorcized his memories. He looked up again into those bright, serene and extraordinarily friendly eyes.

'You know,' said Bruno, 'I was almost expecting you.'

'Expecting me?'

Bruno nodded, then turned and led the way across an obscure cupboard of a hall into a small bed-sitting-room, in which the only articles of luxury were the view of far-away mountains across the house-tops and a square of sunlight, glowing like a huge ruby, on the tiled floor.

'Sit down.' Bruno indicated the more comfortable of the two chairs, and when they were settled, 'Poor Eustace!' he went on reflectively, after a pause. He had a way, Sebastian noticed, of leaving spaces between his sentences, so that everything he said was framed, as it were, in a setting of silence. 'Tell me how it happened.'

Breathless and somewhat incoherent with shyness, Sebastian began to tell the story.

An expression of distress appeared on Bruno's face.

'So suddenly!' he said, when Sebastian had finished. 'So utterly without preparation!'

The words caused Sebastian to feel delightfully superior. Inwardly he smiled an ironic smile. It was almost incredible, but the old idiot seemed actually to believe in hell-fire and Holy Dying. With a studiously straight face, but still chuckling to himself, he looked up, to find the blue eyes fixed upon his face.

'You think it sounds pretty funny?' Bruno said, after the usual second of deliberate silence.

Startled, Sebastian blushed and stammered.

'But I never ... I mean, really ...'

'You mean what everybody means nowadays,' the other interposed in his quiet voice. 'Ignore death up to the last moment; then, when it can't be ignored any longer, have yourself squirted full of morphia and shuffle off in a coma. Thoroughly sensible, humane and scientific, eh?'

Sebastian hesitated. He didn't want to be rude, because, after all, he wanted the old ass to help him. Besides, he shrank from embarking on a controversy in which he was foredoomed by his shyness to make a fool of himself. At the same time, nonsense was nonsense.

'I don't see what's wrong with it,' he said cautiously, but with a faint undertone almost of truculence.

He sat there, sullenly averted, waiting for the other's argumentative retort. But it never came. Prepared for attack, his resistance found itself confronted by a friendly silence and became somehow absurd and irrelevant.

Bruno spoke at last.

'I suppose Mrs. Gamble will be holding one of her séances pretty soon.'

'She has already,' said Sebastian.

'Poor old thing! What a greed for reassurance!'

'But I must say . . . well, it's pretty convincing, don't you think?'

'Oh, something happens all right, if that's what you mean.'

Remembering Mrs. Thwale's comment, Sebastian giggled knowingly.

'Something pretty shameless,' he said.

'Shameless?' Bruno repeated, looking up at him in surprise. 'That's an odd word. What makes you use it?'

Sebastian smiled uncomfortably and dropped his eyes.

'Oh, I don't know,' he said. 'It just seemed the right word, that's all.'

There was another silence. Through the sleeve of his jacket Sebastian felt for the place where she had left the mark of her teeth. It was still painful to the touch. Twin cannibals in bedlam. . . . And then he remembered that damned drawing, and that time was passing, passing. How the devil was he to broach the subject?

'Shameless,' Bruno said again pensively. 'Shameless. . . . And yet you can't see why there should be any preparation for dying?'

'Well, he seemed perfectly happy,' Sebastian answered defensively. 'You know—jolly and amusing, like when he was alive. That is, if it really *was* Uncle Eustace.'

'*If*,' Bruno repeated. '*If*.'

'You don't believe . . .?' Sebastian questioned in some surprise.

Bruno leaned forward and laid his hand on the boy's knee.

'Let's try to get this business quite clear in our minds,' he said. 'Eustace's body plus some unknown, non-bodily x equals Eustace. And for the sake of argument let's admit that poor Eustace was as happy and jolly as you seem to think he was. All right. A moment comes when Eustace's body is abolished; but in view of what happens at old Mrs. Gamble's séance we're forced to believe that x persists. But before we go any further, let's ask ourselves what it really was that we learned at the séance.

We learned that x plus the medium's body equals a temporary pseudo-Eustace. That's an empirical fact. But meanwhile what exactly is x? And what's happening to x when it isn't connected with the medium's body? What happens to it?' he insisted.

'Goodness knows.'

'Precisely. So don't let's pretend that *we* know. And don't let's commit the fallacy of thinking that, because x plus the medium's body is happy and jolly, x by itself must also be happy and jolly.' He withdrew his hand from Sebastian's knee and leaned back in his chair. 'Most of the consolations of spiritualism,' he went on after a little pause, 'seem to depend on bad logic—on drawing faulty inferences from the facts observed at séances. When old Mrs. Gamble hears about Summerland and reads Sir Oliver Lodge, she feels reassured; she's convinced that the next world will be just like this one. But actually Summerland and Lodge are perfectly compatible with Catherine of Genoa and . . .' he hesitated, 'yes, even the *Inferno.*'

'The *Inferno?*' Sebastian repeated. 'But surely you don't imagine . . .?' And making a last desperate effort to assure himself that Bruno was just an old ass, he laughed aloud.

His sniggering dropped into a gulf of benevolent silence.

'No,' said Bruno at last, 'I don't believe in eternal damnation. But not for any reasons that I can discover from going to séances. And still less for any reasons that I can discover from living in the world. For other reasons. Reasons connected with what I know about the nature . . .'

He paused, and with an anticipatory smile Sebastian waited for him to trot out the word 'God.'

'. . . of the Gaseous Vertebrate,' Bruno concluded. He smiled sadly. 'Poor Eustace! It made him feel so much safer to call it that. As though the fact were modified by the name. And yet he was always laughing at other people for using intemperate language.'

'Now he's going to start on his conversion campaign,' Sebastian said to himself.

But, instead, Bruno got up, crossed over to the window and, without a word, deftly caught the big blue-bottle fly that was buzzing against the glass and tossed it out into freedom. Still standing by the window, he turned and spoke.

'You've got something on your mind, Sebastian,' he said. 'What is it?'

Startled into a kind of panic suspicion, Sebastian shook his head.

'Nothing,' he insisted; but an instant later he was cursing himself for having missed his opportunity.

'And yet that's what you came here to talk about.'

The smile with which the words were accompanied was without a trace of irony or patronage. Sebastian was reassured.

'Well, as a matter of fact . . .' He hesitated for a second or two, then forced a rather theatrical little laugh. 'You see,' he said with an attempt at gaiety, 'I've been swindled. Swindled,' he repeated emphatically; for all at once he had seen how the story could be told without any reference to Mr. Tendring's discovery or his own humiliating failures to tell the truth— simply as the story of trustful inexperience and (yes, he'd admit it) childish silliness shamefully victimized and now appealing for help. Gathering confidence as he proceeded, he told his revised version of what had happened.

'Offering me a thousand, when he'd sold it to Uncle Eustace for seven!' he concluded indignantly. 'It's just plain swindling.'

'Well,' said Bruno slowly, 'they have peculiar standards, these dealers.' None more so, he might have added, on the strength of an earlier encounter with the man, than Gabriel Weyl. But nothing would be gained, and perhaps some positive harm might be done, if he were to tell Sebastian what he knew. 'But meanwhile,' he went on, 'what do your people up at the villa think about it all? Surely they must be wondering.'

Sebastian felt himself blushing.

'Wondering?' he questioned, hoping and pretending that he didn't understand what was being implied.

'Wondering how the drawing disappeared like that. And you must be pretty worried about it, aren't you?'

There was a pause. Then, without speaking, the boy nodded his head.

'It's difficult to come to any decision,' said Bruno mildly, 'unless one knows all the relevant facts.'

Sebastian felt profoundly ashamed of himself.

'I'm sorry,' he whispered. 'I ought to have explained. . . .'

Sheepishly, he began to supply the details he had previously omitted.

Bruno listened without comment until the end.

'And you were really intending to tell Mrs. Ockham all about it?' he questioned.

'I was just beginning,' Sebastian insisted. 'And then she was sent for.'

'You didn't think of telling Mrs. Thwale instead?'

'Mrs. Thwale? Oh, goodness, no!'

'Why *goodness*, no?'

'Well . . .' Embarrassed, Sebastian groped for an avowable answer. 'I don't know. I mean, the drawing didn't belong to her. She had nothing to do with it.'

'And yet you say it was she who suspected the little girl.'

'I know, but . . .' Twin cannibals in bedlam—and when the light went on, the eyes were bright with the look of one who enjoys a comedy from between the curtains of the most private of boxes.

'Well, somehow it never occurred to me.'

'I see,' said Bruno, and was silent for a few seconds. 'If I can get the drawing back for you,' he went on at last, 'will you promise to take it straight to Mrs. Ockham and tell her the whole story?'

'Oh, I promise,' Sebastian cried eagerly.

The other held up a bony hand.

'Not so quick, not so quick! Promises are serious. Are you sure you'll be able to keep this one, if you make it?'

'Certain!'

'So was Simon Peter. But cocks have a habit of crowing at the most inconvenient moments. . . .'

Bruno smiled, humorously, but at the same time with a kind of compassionate tenderness.

'As though I were ill,' Sebastian thought, as he looked into the other's face, and was simultaneously touched and annoyed—touched by so much solicitude on his behalf, but annoyed by what it implied: namely, that he was sick (mortally sick, to judge by the look in those bright blue eyes), of the inability to keep a promise. But really that was a bit thick. . . .

'Well,' Bruno went on, 'the quicker we get to work the better, eh?'

He peeled off his sweater and, opening the wardrobe, took out an old brown jacket. Then he sat down to change his shoes. Bending over the laces, he began to talk again.

'When I do something wrong,' he said, 'or merely stupid, I find it very useful to draw up—not exactly a balance sheet; no, it's more like a genealogy, if you see what I mean, a family tree of the offence. Who or what were its parents, ancestors, collaterals? What are likely to be its descendants—in my own life and other people's? It's surprising how far a little honest research will take one. Down into the rat-holes of one's own character. Back into past history. Out into the world around one. Forward into possible consequences. It makes one realize that nothing one does is unimportant and nothing wholly private.' The last knot was tied; Bruno got up. 'Well, I think that's everything,' he said, as he put on his jacket.

'There's the money,' Sebastian mumbled uncomfortably. He pulled out his wallet. 'I've only got about a thousand lire left. If you could lend me the rest . . . I'll return it as soon as I possibly . . .'

Bruno took the wad of notes and handed one of them back to the boy.

'You're not a Franciscan,' he said. 'At any rate, not yet—

though one day, perhaps, in mere self-defence against your-self . . .' He smiled almost mischievously and, cramming the rest of the money in a trouser pocket, picked up his hat.

'I don't suppose I shall be very long,' he said, looking back from the door. 'You'll find plenty of books to amuse you—that is, if you want an opiate, which I hope you don't. Yes, I hope you don't,' he repeated with a sudden, insistent earnestness; then he turned and went out.

Left to himself, Sebastian sat down again.

It had gone off quite differently, of course, from what he had imagined, but very well. Better, in fact, than he had ever dared to hope—except that he *did* wish he hadn't started by telling that revised version of what had happened. Hoping to cut a better figure, and then having to admit, abjectly, humiliatingly, that it wasn't true. Anyone else would have seized the opportunity to deliver the most frightful pi-jaw. Not Bruno, however. He felt profoundly grateful for the man's forbearance. To have had the decency to help without first taking it out of him in a sermon—that was really extraordinary. And he wasn't a fool either. What he had said about the genealogy of an offence, for example . . .

'The genealogy of an offence,' he whispered in the silence, 'the family tree. . . .'

He began to think of the lies he had told and of all their ramifying antecedents and accompaniments and consequences. He oughtn't to have told them, of course; but, on the other hand, if it hadn't been for his father's idiotic principles he wouldn't have had to tell them. And if it hadn't been for the slums and rich men with cigars, like poor Uncle Eustace, his father wouldn't have had those idiotic principles. And yet Uncle Eustace had been thoroughly kind and decent. Whereas that anti-fascist professor—one wouldn't trust him an inch. And how boring most of his father's left-wing, lower-class friends were! How unutterably dreary! But dreary and boring, he remembered, to *him*; and that was probably his fault. Just as it was his fault that those evening clothes should have seemed so indispensable—because other boys had them, because there would be those girls at Tom Boveney's party. But one oughtn't to consider what other people did or thought; and the girls would turn out to be just another excuse for sensual day-dreamings that were destined henceforward to be haunted by memories of last night's reality of unimaginable shamelessness and alienation. Cannibals in bedlam—and the door of the mad-house had been locked against the last chance of telling the truth. Meanwhile, in some crowded peasant's cottage at the remote, unvisited end of the garden, a child in tears was perhaps even now protesting her innocence under an angry cross-examination. And when blows and threats had failed to elicit the information she didn't possess, that old she-devil of a Mrs. Gamble would insist on sending for the police; and then everybody would be questioned, everybody—himself included. But would he be able to stick to his story? And if they took it into their heads to go and talk to Weyl, what reason would *he* have for withholding the truth? And then . . . Sebastian shuddered. But now, thank God, old man Bruno had come to the rescue. The drawing would be bought back; he'd make a clean breast of the whole business to Mrs. Ockham—irresistibly, so that she'd start crying and say he was just like Frankie—and everything would be all right. The children of his lie would either remain unborn or else be smothered in their cradles, and the lie itself would be as though it had never been uttered. Indeed, for all practical purposes, one could now say that it never *had* been uttered.

'Never,' Sebastian said to himself emphatically, 'never.'

His spirits rose, he began to whistle, and suddenly, in a flash of intensely pleasurable illumination, he perceived how well this notion of the genealogy of offences would fit into the scheme of his new poem. Patterns of atoms; but chaos of the molecules assembled in the stone. Patterns of living cells and organs and physiological functioning, but chaos of men's behaviour in time. And yet even in that chaos there was law and logic; there was a geometry even of disintegration. The square on lust is equal, so to speak, to the sum of the squares on vanity and idleness. The shortest distance between two cravings is violence. And what about the lies he had been telling? What about broken promises and betrayals? Phrases began to form themselves in his mind.

> *Belial his blubber lips and Avarice*
> *Pouting a trap-tight sphincter, voluptuously*
> *Administer the lingering Judas kiss . . .*

He pulled out his pencil and scribbling-pad, and started to write. '. . . the lingering Judas kiss.' And, after Judas, the crucifixion. But death had many ancestors besides greed and falsehood, many other forms than voluntary martyrdom. He recalled an article he had read somewhere about the character of the next war. 'And the dead children,' he wrote,

> *And the dead children lying about the streets*
> *Like garbage, when the bombardiers have done—*
> *These the mild sluggard murders while he snores,*
> *And Calvin, father of a thousand whores,*
> *Murders in pulpits, logically, for a syllogism. . . .*

An hour later a key turned in the lock. Startled, and at the same time annoyed, by the unwelcome interruption, Sebastian came to the surface from the depths of his absorbed abstraction and looked towards the door.

Bruno met his eye and smiled.

'*Eccolo!*' he said, holding up a thin rectangular package wrapped in brown paper.

Sebastian looked at it, and for a second couldn't think what it was. Then recognition came; but so completely had he convinced himself that Bruno would succeed, and that all his troubles were already over, that the actual sight of the drawing left him almost indifferent.

'Oh, the thing,' he said, 'the Degas.' Then, realizing that mere politeness demanded a display of gratitude and delight, he raised his voice and cried, 'Oh, thank you, thank you! I can never ... I mean, you've been so extraordinarily decent. ...'

Bruno looked at him without speaking. 'A small cherub in grey flannel trousers,' he said to himself, remembering the phrase that Eustace had used at the station. And it was true: that smile was angelical, in spite of its calculatedness. There was a kind of lovely and supernatural innocence about the boy, even when, as now, he was so obviously acting a part. And, incidentally, why should he be acting a part? And considering the panic he had been in an hour ago, why was it that he didn't now feel genuinely glad and grateful? Scrutinizing the delicately beautiful face before him, Bruno sought in vain for an answer to his questions. All he could find in it was the brute fact of that seraphic naïveté shining enchantingly through childish hypocrisy, that guilelessness even in deliberate cunning. And because of that guilelessness people would always love him—always, whatever he might be betrayed into doing or leaving undone. But that wasn't by any means the most dangerous consequence of being a seraph— but a seraph out of heaven, deprived of the beatific vision, unaware, indeed, of the very existence of God. No, the most dangerous consequence was that, whatever he might do or leave undone, he himself would tend, because of the beauty of his own intrinsic innocence, to spare himself the salutary agonies of contrition. Being angelical, he would be loved, not only by other people, but also by himself—through thick and thin, with a love inexpugnable by any force less violent than a major disaster. Once again, Bruno felt himself moved by a profound compassion. Sebastian, the predestined target, the delicate and radiant butt of God alone knew what ulterior flights of arrows—piercing enjoyments, successes poisoned with praise and barbed to stick; and then, if Providence was merciful enough to send an antidote, pains and humiliations and defeats. ...

'Been writing?' he asked at last, noticing the pad and pencil, and making them the excuse for breaking the long silence.

Sebastian blushed and stowed them away in his pocket.

'I'd been thinking of what you were saying just before you went out,' he answered. 'You know, about things having genealogies. . . .'

'And you've been working out the genealogy of your own mistakes?' Bruno asked with a glad hopefulness.

'Well, not exactly. I was . . . Well, you see, I'm working on a new poem, and this seemed to fit in so well. . . .'

Bruno thought of the interview from which he had just come, and smiled with a touch of rather rueful amusement. Gabriel Weyl had ended by yielding; but the surrender had been anything but graceful. Against his will—for he had done his best to put them out of mind—Bruno found himself remembering the ugly words that had been spoken, the passionate gestures of those hirsute and beautifully manicured hands, that face distorted and pale with fury. He sighed, laid his hat and the drawing on the book-case, and sat down.

'The Gospel of Poetry,' he said slowly. 'In the beginning were the words, and the words were with God, and the words *were* God. Here endeth the first, last and only lesson.'

There was a silence. Sebastian sat quite still, with averted face, staring at the floor. He was feeling ashamed of himself and at the same time resentful of the fact that he had been made to feel ashamed. After all, there was nothing wrong about poetry; so why on earth shouldn't he write, if he felt like it?

'Can I see what you've done?' Bruno asked at last.

Sebastian blushed again and mumbled something about its being no good; but finally handed over the scribbling-pad.

'"Belial his blubber lips,"' Bruno began aloud, then continued his reading in silence. 'Good!' he said, when he had finished. 'I wish *I* could say the thing as powerfully as that. If I'd been able to,' he added with a little smile, 'perhaps you'd have spent your time making out your own genealogy, instead of writing something that may move other people to make out theirs. But then, of course, you have the luck to have been born a poet. Or is it the misfortune?'

'The misfortune?' Sebastian repeated.

'Every Fairy Godmother is also potentially the Wicked Fairy.'

'Why?'

'Because it's easier for a camel to pass through the eye of a needle than for a rich man . . .' He left the sentence unfinished.

'But I'm not rich,' Sebastian protested, thinking resentfully of what his father's stinginess had forced him to do.

'Not rich? Read your own verses!' Bruno handed back the scribbling-pad. 'And when you've done that, look at your image in a mirror.'

'Oh, I see. . . .'

'And women's eyes—those are mirrors when they come close enough,' Bruno added.

When they come close enough—looking down at the comedy, with the microscopic image of nature's lay idiot reflected in their ironic brightness. Feeling extremely uneasy, Sebastian wondered what the man would say next. But to his great relief the talk took a less personal turn.

'And yet,' Bruno went on reflectively, 'a certain number of the intrinsically rich *do* succeed in getting through the needle's eye. Bernard, for example. And perhaps Augustine, though I always wonder if he wasn't the victim of his own incomparable style. And Thomas Aquinas. And obviously François de Sales. But they're few, they're few. The great majority of the rich get stuck, or never even attempt the passage. Did you ever read a life of Kant?' he asked parenthetically. 'Or of Nietzsche?'

Sebastian shook his head.

'Well, perhaps you'd better not,' said Bruno. 'It's difficult, if one does, to avoid uncharitableness. And then Dante. . . .' He shook his head, and there was a silence.

'Uncle Eustace talked about Dante,' Sebastian volunteered. 'That last evening it was—just before . . .'

'What did he say?'

Sebastian did his best to reproduce the substance of the conversation.

'And he was perfectly right,' said Bruno, when he had finished. 'Except, of course, that Chaucer isn't any solution to the problem. Being worldly in one way and writing consummately well about this world is no better than being worldly in another way and writing consummately well about the next world. No better for oneself, that's to say. When it comes to the effect on other people . . .' He smiled and shrugged his shoulders. '"Let Austin have his swink to him reserved." Or

> *e la sua volontate è nostra pace;*
> *ell'è quel mare al qual tutto si move,*
> *ciò ch'ella crea e che natura face.*

I know which of them *I'd* choose. Can you understand Dante, by the way?'

Sebastian shook his head, but immediately made up for this admission of ignorance by showing off a little.

'If it were Greek,' he said, 'or Latin, or French . . .'

'But unfortunately it's Italian,' Bruno interposed matter-of-factly. 'But Italian's worth learning, if only for the sake of what those lines can do for you. And yet,' he added, 'how little they did for the man who actually wrote them! Poor Dante—the way he pats himself on the back for belonging to such a distinguished family! Not to mention the fact that he's the only man who was ever allowed to visit heaven before he died. And even in Paradise he can't stop raging and railing about contemporary politics. And when he gets to the sphere of the Contemplatives, what does he make Benedict and Peter Damian talk about? Not love or liberation, nor the practice of the presence of God. No, no; they spend all their time, as Dante liked to spend his—denouncing other people's bad behaviour and threatening them with hell-fire.' Sadly, Bruno shook his head. 'Such a waste of such enormous gifts—it makes one feel inclined to weep.'

'Why do you suppose he wasted himself like that?'

'Because he wanted to. And if you ask *why* he went on

wanting to after he'd written about God's will being our peace, the answer is that that's how genius works. It has insights into the nature of ultimate reality and it gives expression to the knowledge so obtained. Gives expression to it either explicitly in things like "*e la sua volontate è nostra pace*," or implicitly, in the white spaces between the lines, so to speak—by writing beautifully. And of course you can write beautifully about anything, from the Wife of Bath to Baudelaire's *affreuse juive* and Gray's pensive Selima. And incidentally the explicit statements about reality don't convey very much unless they too are written poetically. Beauty is truth; truth, beauty. The truth about the beauty is given in the lines, and the beauty of the truth in the white spaces between them. If the white spaces are merely blank, the lines are just . . . just Hymns Ancient and Modern.'

'Or late Wordsworth,' put in Sebastian.

'Yes, and don't forget the very early Shelley,' said Bruno. 'The adolescent can be quite as inept as the old.' He smiled at Sebastian. 'Well, as I was saying,' he continued in another tone, 'explicitly or implicitly, men of genius express their knowledge of reality. But they themselves very rarely act on their knowledge. Why not? Because all their energy and attention are absorbed by the work of composition. They're concerned with writing, not with acting or being. But because they're only concerned with writing about their knowledge, they prevent themselves from knowing more.'

'What do you mean?' Sebastian asked.

'Knowledge is proportionate to being,' Bruno answered. 'You know in virtue of what you are; and what you are depends on three factors: what you've inherited, what your surroundings have done to you, and what you've chosen to do with your surroundings and your inheritance. A man of genius inherits an unusual capacity to see into ultimate reality and to express what he sees. If his surroundings are reasonably good, he'll be able to exercise his powers. But if he spends all his energies on writing and doesn't attempt to modify his inherited and acquired being in the light of what he knows, then he can never get to increase his knowledge. On the contrary, he'll know progressively less instead of more.'

'Less instead of more?' Sebastian repeated questioningly.

'Less instead of more,' the other insisted. 'He that is not getting better is getting worse, and he that is getting worse is in a position to know less and less about the nature of ultimate reality. Conversely, of course, if one gets better and knows more, one will be tempted to stop writing, because the all-absorbing labour of composition is an obstacle in the way of further knowledge. And that, maybe, is one of the reasons why most men of genius take such infinite pains not to become saints —out of mere self-preservation. So you get Dante writing angelic lines about the will of God and in the next breath giving vent to his rancours and vanities. You get Wordsworth worshipping God in nature and preaching admiration, hope and love, while all the time he cultivates an egotism that absolutely flabbergasts the people who know him. You get Milton devoting a whole epic to man's first disobedience and consistently exhibiting a pride worthy of his own Lucifer. And finally,' he added, with a little laugh, 'you get young Sebastian perceiving the truth of an important general principle—the inter-relationship of evil—and using all his energy, not to act on it, which would be a bore, but to turn it into verse, which he thoroughly enjoys. "Calvin, father of a thousand whores" is pretty good, I grant you; but something personal and practical might have been still better. Mightn't it? However, as I said before, In the beginning were the words, and the words were with God, and the words *were* God.' He got up and crossed over to the door of the kitchen. 'And now let's see what we can scrape together for lunch,' he said.

CHAPTER TWENTY-SEVEN

AFTER luncheon they did some sight-seeing, and it was with an imagination haunted by the frescoes of San Marco and the Medicean tombs that Sebastian finally made his way home. The sun was already low as he walked up the steep and dusty road to the villa; there were treasures of blue shadow, expanses not of stone or stucco, but of amber, trees and grass glowing with supernatural significance. Blissfully, in a mood of effortless alertness and passivity, like a wide-eyed somnambulist, who sees, but with senses somehow not his own, who feels and thinks, but with emotions that no longer have a personal reference, a mind entirely free and unconditioned, he moved through the actual radiance around him, through the memories of what he had so lately seen and heard—the huge, smooth marbles, the saints diaphanous in the whitewashed monastery cells, the words that Bruno had spoken as they came out of the Medici chapel.

'Michelangelo and Fra Angelico—apotheosis and deification.'

Apotheosis—the personality exalted and intensified to the point where the person ceases to be mere man or woman and becomes god-like, one of the Olympians, like that passionately pensive warrior, like those great titanesses brooding, naked, above the sarcophagi. And over against apotheosis, deification—personality annihilated in charity, in union, so that at last the man or woman can say, 'Not I, but God in me.'

But meanwhile here was the goat again, the one that had been eating wistaria buds under the head-lamps that first evening with Uncle Eustace. But this time it had a half-ruminated rose sticking out of the corner of its mouth—like Carmen in the opera, so that it was to the imagined strains of 'Toreador, toreador' that the creature advanced to the gate of its garden and, slowly chewing on the rose, looked out at him through the bars.

In the yellow eyes the pupils were two narrow slots of the purest, blackest mindlessness. Sebastian reached out and caressed the long curve of a nobly semitic nose, fondled six warm and muscular inches of drooping ear, then took hold of one of the diabolic horns. Carmen began to back away impatiently. He tightened his grip and tried to pull her forward. With a sudden, forceful jerk of the head, the creature broke away from him and went bounding up the steps. A large black udder wobbled wildly as she ran. Pausing at the top of the steps, she let fall half a dozen pills of excrement, then reached up and plucked another rose for her appearance in the Second Act. Sebastian turned and walked on, through the late afternoon sunshine and his memories. Somnambulistically happy. But uneasily, at the back of his mind, he was aware of the other, disregarded realities—the lies he had told, the interview with Mrs. Ockham that still lay ahead of him. And perhaps that wretched child had already been questioned, whipped, deprived of food. But no, he refused to give up his happiness before it was absolutely necessary. Carmen with her rose and her white beard; marble and fresco; apotheosis and deification. But why not apotragosis and caprification? He laughed aloud. And yet what Bruno had said, as they stood there in the Piazza del Duomo, waiting for the tram, had impressed him profoundly. Apotheosis and deification— the only roads of escape from the unutterable wearisomeness, the silly and degrading horror, of being merely yourself, of being only human. Two roads; but in reality only the second led out into open country. So much more promising, apparently, so vastly more attractive, the first invariably turned out to be only a glorious blind alley. Under triumphal arches, along an avenue of statuary and fountains, you marched in pomp towards an ultimate frustration—solemnly and heroically, full tilt into the insurmountable dead end of your own selfhood. And the dead end was solid marble, of course, and adorned with the colossal monuments of your power, magnanimity and wisdom, but no less a wall than the most grotesquely hideous of the vices down there in your old, all too human prison. Whereas the other road . . . But then the tram had come.

'You've been incredibly kind,' he had stammered as they shook hands, and then, suddenly carried away by his feelings: 'You've made me see such a lot of things. . . . I'll really try. Really. . . .'

The brown beaked skull had smiled, and in their deep sockets the eyes had brightened with tenderness and, once again, compassion.

Yes, Sebastian had repeated to himself, as the tram crawled along the narrow streets towards the river, he'd really try. Try to be more honest, to think less of himself. To live with people and real events and not so exclusively with words. How awful he was! Self-hatred and remorse blended harmoniously with the feelings evoked by the afternoon sunlight and the fascinating foreignness of what it illuminated, by San Marco and the Medici chapel, by Bruno's kindness and what the man had said. And gradually his mood had modulated out of its original ethical urgency into another key—out of the exaltation of repentance and good resolutions into the bliss of detached poetical contemplation, into this heavenly condition of somnambulism, in which he still found himself as he rounded the last hairpin of the road and saw the wrought-iron gates between their tall pillars of stone, the solemn succession of the cypress trees winding away towards the villa, out of sight, round the contour of the hill.

He slipped through the pedestrians' wicket. The fine gravel of the drive made a delicious crunching noise under his feet, like Grape Nuts.

> *Walking on Grape Nuts and imagination,*
> *Among recollected crucifixions and these jewels*
> *Of horizontal sunlight . . .*

Suddenly, from between two cypresses, twenty or thirty yards ahead of him, a small black figure came running out into the drive. With a start and a horrible sinking of the stomach,

Sebastian recognized the little girl with the weeding basket, recognized the incarnation of his own disregarded guilty conscience, the harbinger of that reality which, in his somnambulistic detachment, he had forgotten. Catching sight of him, the child halted and stood there staring with round black eyes. Her face, Sebastian noticed, was paler than usual, and she had evidently been crying. Oh, God. . . . He smiled at her, called 'Hullo' and waved a friendly hand. But before he had taken five more steps the child turned and, like a frightened animal, rushed away along the path by which she had come.

'Stop!' he shouted.

But of course she didn't stop; and when he came to the opening between the trees, the child was nowhere to be seen. And even if he were to follow and find her, he reflected, it wouldn't be any good. She understood no English, he spoke no Italian. Gloomily Sebastian turned and walked on towards the house.

No servants were about when he entered, and he could hear no sound from the drawing-room. Thank God, the coast was clear. He tiptoed across the hall and started to climb the stairs. On the last step he halted. A sound had caught his ear. Somewhere, behind one of those closed doors, people were talking. Should he run the invisible blockade and go on, or beat a retreat? Sebastian was still hesitating, when the door of what had been poor Uncle Eustace's room was thrown open and out walked old Mrs. Gamble, hugging that dog of hers in one arm while Mrs. Ockham held the other. They were followed by a pale, cow-like creature, whom Sebastian recognized as the medium. Then came Mrs. Thwale and, close behind Mrs. Thwale—of all horrors!—Gabriel Weyl and Mme Weyl.

'So different from the occidental art,' Weyl was saying. 'For example, you would not desire to *feel* a Gothic madonna—would you, madame?'

He dodged past Mrs. Thwale and the medium, and caught Mrs. Ockham by the sleeve.

'Would you?' he insisted, as she halted and turned towards him.

'Well, really . . .' said Mrs. Ockham uncertainly.

'What's that he's saying?' the Queen Mother questioned sharply. 'I can't understand a word of it.'

'Those folds of *trecento* drapery,' M. Weyl went on. 'So harsh, so emphatic!' He made a grimace of agony and with his left hand tenderly clasped the fingers of his right, as though they had just been caught in a mouse-trap. '*Qué barbaridad!*'

Still keeping his eyes fixed on the menace at the other end of the corridor, Sebastian stepped noiselessly down from the highest stair to the one below the highest.

'Whereas a Chinese object,' M. Weyl went on; and, from agonized, his large expressive face became suddenly rapturous. '*Un petit bodhisattva, par exemple. . . .*'

Another step down.

'. . . With his draperies in liquefaction. Like butter in the month of August. No violence, no Gothic folds—simply *quelques volutes savantes et peu profondes. . . .*'

Voluptuously the thick, white, hairy hands caressed the air.

'What deliciousness for the ends of the fingers! What sublime sensuality! What . . .'

Another step. But this time the movement was too abrupt. Foxy VIII turned a sharp nose towards the staircase and, wriggling frantically in Mrs. Gamble's clasp, began to bark.

'Why, it's Sebastian!' cried Mrs. Ockham delightedly. 'Come along and be introduced to Monsieur and Madame Weyl.'

Feeling like a criminal on his way to execution, Sebastian slowly mounted the last three stairs of the scaffold and walked towards the drop. The barking grew more hysterical.

'Be quiet, Foxy,' rasped the Queen Mother. Then, tempering command by argument, 'After all,' she added, 'he's a perfectly harmless boy. Perfectly harmless.'

'Sebastian Barnack, my stepfather's nephew,' Mrs. Ockham explained.

Sebastian looked up, expecting to meet a smile of ironic recognition, a voluble declaration that the Weyls had met him before. But, instead, the wife merely inclined her head politely, while the man held out a hand and said:

'Enchanted to make your acquaintance, sir.'

'Enchanted,' Sebastian mumbled back, trying to look and behave as though this were the usual kind of ordinary unimportant introduction.

'Without doubt,' said M. Weyl, 'you share your uncle's love of the arts?'

'Oh, rather . . . I mean, I . . .'

'The Chinese collection alone!' M. Weyl clasped his hands and looked up to heaven. 'And the fact that he kept most of it in his bedroom,' he went on, turning back to Mrs. Ockham, 'for no other eyes than his own! What delicacy, what sensibility!'

'I'd sell the whole lot if I were you, Daisy,' put in the Queen Mother. 'Sell 'em for cash and buy yourself a Rolls. It's an economy in the end.'

'How true!' breathed M. Weyl in the tone of one who comments reverently on an utterance by Rabindranath Tagore.

'Well, I don't know about the Rolls,' said Mrs. Ockham, who had been thinking of how she could use the money to help her poor girls. Then, to avoid further discussion with her grandmother, she hastily changed the subject. 'I wanted to talk to Monsieur Weyl about the drawing,' she continued, turning to Sebastian. 'So Veronica rang him up after luncheon, and he very kindly offered to come up here immediately.'

'No kindness at all,' protested M. Weyl. 'A pleasure and at the same time a sacred duty to the memory of our dear defunct.' He laid his hand on his heart.

'Monsieur Weyl is very optimistic,' Mrs. Ockham went on. 'He doesn't think it was stolen. In fact, he's absolutely certain we shall find it again.'

'Daisy, you're talking nonsense,' barked the Queen Mother. 'Nobody can be certain about that drawing except Eustace.

That's why I sent for Mrs. Byfleet again—and the quicker we get to our séance, the better.'

There was a silence, and Sebastian knew that the moment had come for him to keep his promise. If he failed to act now, if he didn't immediately hand over the drawing and explain what had happened, it might be too late. But to confess in public, before that awful man and the Queen Mother and Mrs. Thwale—the prospect was appalling. And yet he had promised, he had promised. Sebastian swallowed hard and passed the tip of his tongue over his dry lips. But it was Mrs. Gamble who broke the silence.

'Nothing will convince *me* that it wasn't stolen,' she went on emphatically. 'Nothing except an assurance from Eustace's own lips.'

'Not even the fact that it has been already found?' said M. Weyl.

His eyes twinkled, his tone and expression were those of a man on the verge of delighted laughter.

'Already found?' Mrs. Ockham repeated questioningly.

Like a conjurer materializing rabbits, M. Weyl reached out and twitched the thin, flat parcel from under Sebastian's left arm.

'In its original wrapping,' he said, as he broke the string. 'I recognize my paper of *emballage*.' And with a flourish, as though it were not rabbits this time, but infant unicorns, he pulled out the drawing and handed it to Mrs. Ockham. 'And as for our *jeune farceur*,' he went on, 'who holds himself there saying nothing with a funebrial face as if he was at an interment . . .' He exploded in a great guffaw and clapped Sebastian on the shoulder.

'What's that, what's that?' cried the Queen Mother, darting blind glances from one face to another. 'The boy's found it, has he?'

'"*Elle est retrouvée*,"' M. Weyl declaimed,

> '*Elle est retrouvée.*
> *Quoi? L'éternite.*

CHAPTER TWENTY-EIGHT

C'est la mer allée
Avec le soleil.

But seriously, my friend, seriously ... Where? Not by chance in the place where I always said it must be? Not in ...?' He paused, then leaned forward and whispered in Sebastian's ear, '... In the place where even the king goes on foot—*enfin*, the toilet cabinet?'

Sebastian hesitated for a moment, then nodded his head.

'There's a little space between the medicine cupboard and the wall,' he whispered.

CHAPTER TWENTY-EIGHT

PAIN and the howling of laughter. Nightmares of cruelty and cold lust, and this irrepressible derision tearing relentlessly at the very substance of his being. Without end; and the durations grew longer and progressively longer with each repetition of the ever-increasing agony.

After an eternity deliverance came with a kind of jerk, as though by miracle. Came with the sudden lapse out of mere incoherent succession into the familiar orderliness of time. Came with the multitudinous twittering of sensation, the fluttering consciousness of having a body. And out there lay space; and in the space there were bodies—the sensed evidence of other kindred minds.

'We have two old friends of yours with us this evening,' he heard the Queen Mother saying in her ghostly petty officer's voice. 'Monsieur and Madame—what's the name, by the way?'

'Weyl,' and 'Gabriel Weyl,' a masculine and a feminine voice answered simultaneously.

And sure enough, it was the Flemish Venus and her preposterous Vulcan.

'"Where every prospect pleases,"' he chanted, '"and only man is WEYL FRÈRES, Bruxelles, Paris, Florence...."'

But, as usual, the imbecile interpreter got it all wrong. Meanwhile the dealer had begun to talk to him about the Chinese bronzes. What taste in the collector of such treasures, what connoisseurship, what sensibility! Then, with a solemn earnestness that was in ludicrous contrast with her naughty-naughty French accent, Mme Weyl brought out something about their calligraphic polyphony.

Delicious absurdity!

'He thinks you're funny,' the interpreter squeaked, and broke into a shrill giggle.

But these Weyls, Eustace suddenly perceived, were much more than funny. In some way or other they were enormously significant and important. In some way and for some mysterious reason they were epoch-making—yes, there was no other word for it. They were absolutely epoch-making.

He seemed on the verge of discovering just how and why they were epoch-making, when the Queen Mother suddenly broke in.

'I suppose you're beginning to feel quite at home now, on the other side,' she rasped.

'At home!' he repeated with sarcastic emphasis.

But it was as a rather gushing statement of fact that the imbecile brought out the words.

'Sure, he feels quite at home,' she squeaked.

Then the Queen Mother suggested that it might be nice for those who had never attended a séance before if he gave them something evidential; and she began to fire off a string of the most idiotic questions. How much had he paid for those drawings he had bought from M. Weyl? What was the name of the hotel he had stayed at in Paris? What books had he been reading the day he passed on? And then Mrs. Thwale piped up, and both the Weyls; and the conversation became so incoherent, so senselessly trivial, that he grew confused, found it difficult to think straight or even remember the most familiar facts. In self-protection he turned his attention away from the significance of what was being said to him, concentrating instead on the mere sound of the words, on the pitch and timbre and volume of the different voices. And contrapuntal to these noises from without there were the muffled rhythms of blood and breathing, the uninterrupted stream of messages from this temporary body of his. Warmths and pressures, moistures and titillations, a score of little aches and stiffnesses, of obscure visceral discontents and satisfactions. Treasures of physiological reality, directly experienced and so intrinsically fascinating that there was no need to bother about other people, no point in thinking or trying to communicate. It was enough just to have this feeling of space and time and the processes of life. Nothing else was required. This alone was paradise.

And then, through the dark twittering aviary of his sensations, Eustace was aware, once again, of that blue shining stillness. Delicate, unutterably beautiful, like the essence of all skies and flowers, like the silent principle and potentiality of all music. And tender, yearning, supplicatory.

But meanwhile the air slowly came and went in the nostrils, cool on the intake, warm to the point of being all but imperceptible as it was breathed out; and as the chest expanded and contracted, effort was succeeded by a delicious effortlessness, tension by relaxation, again and again. And what pleasure to listen to the waves of blood as they beat against the ear-drums, to feel them throbbing under the skin of the temples! How fascinating to analyse the mingled savours of garlic and chocolate, red wine and—yes—kidneys, haunting the tongue and palate! And then, all at once, by a kind of exquisitely harmonious and co-ordinated earthquake of all the muscles of the mouth and gullet, the accumulations of saliva were swallowed; and a moment later a faint bubbling trill from below the diaphragm announced that the processes of digestion were sleeplessly going forward. That seemed to bring the ultimate reassurance, to perfect and consummate his sense of paradisal cosiness. And suddenly he found himself remembering St. Sebastian and the stuffed humming-birds, remembering the taste of cigar smoke on a palate warmed by old brandy, remembering Mimi and the Young Man of Peoria and his collection of facts about the ludicrous or disastrous consequences of idealism—remembering them not with shame or self-condemnation but with downright relish or, at the very worst, an amused indulgence. The light persisted, ubiquitously present; but this feeling of being in a body was an effective barrier against its encroachments. Behind his sensations he was safe from any compulsion to know himself as he was known. And these Weyls, he now perceived, this Venus with her swarthy Vulcan, could become the instruments of his permanent deliverance from that atrocious knowledge. There was a living uterine darkness awaiting him there, a vegetative heaven. Providence was ready for him, a providence of living flesh, hungry to engulf him into itself, yearning to hold and cradle him, to nourish with the very substance of its deliciously carnal and sanguine being.

Imploringly, the light intensified its shining silence. But he knew what it was up to, he was forearmed against its tricks. And besides, it was possible to make the best of Mozart *and* the Casino, of Mimi *and* the evening star between cypresses. Perfectly possible, provided always one owned a physiology to protect one against the stratagems of the light. And that protection could be had for the asking; or rather was being offered, greedily, with a kind of mindless frenzy. . . .

Suddenly the squeaking of the imbecile ceased to be nothing but a sensation, and modulated into significance.

'Good-bye, folks, good-bye.'

And from out there in the darkness came an answering chorus of farewells that grew momently dimmer, vaguer, more confused. And all the delicious messages from this body of his—they too were fading. The aviary fell silent and motionless.

And suddenly there was a kind of wrench, and once again he was out of the comfortable world where time is a regular succession and place is fixed and solid—out in the chaos and delirium of unfettered mind. In the vague flux of masterless images, of thoughts and words and memories all but autonomous and independent, two things preserved their stability, the tender ubiquity of the light and the knowledge that there was a fostering darkness of flesh and blood in which, if he chose, he could find deliverance from the light.

But here once more was the lattice of relationships, and he was in the midst of it, moving from node to node, from one patterned figure to its strangely distorted projection in another pattern. Moving, moving, until all of a sudden there he was, carefully putting down his cigar on the onyx ashtray and turning to open the medicine cupboard.

There was a kind of side-slip, a falling, as it were, through the intricacies of the lattice—and he knew himself remembering events that had not yet taken place. Remembering a day towards the end of summer, hot and cloudless, with aeroplanes roaring across the sky—across the luminous silence. For the silence was still there, shining, ubiquitously tender; still there in spite of what was happening on this long straight road between its poplar trees. Thousands of people, all moving one way, all haunted by the same fear. People on foot, carrying bundles on their backs, carrying children; or perched high on overloaded carts; or wheeling bicycles with suitcases strapped to the handle-bars.

And here was Weyl, paunchy and bald-headed, pushing a green perambulator packed full of unframed canvases and Dutch silver and Chinese jade, with a painted madonna standing drunkenly at an angle where the baby should have been. Heavy now with the approach of middle age, the Flemish Venus limped after him under the burden of a blue morocco dressing-case and her sealskin coat. '*Je n'en peux plus,*' she kept whispering, '*je n'en peux plus.*' And sometimes, despairingly, '*Suicidons-nous,*

Gabriel.' Bent over the perambulator, Weyl did not answer or even look round, but the little spindly boy who walked beside her, preposterous in baggy plus-fours, would squeeze his mother's hand, and when she turned her tear-stained face towards him would smile up at her encouragingly.

To the left, across a tawny expanse of stubble and some market gardens, a whole town was burning, and the smoke of it, billowing up from behind the towers of that sunlit church in the suburbs, spread out as it mounted through the luminous silence into a huge inverted cone of brown darkness. A noise of distant gunfire bumped against the summer air. Near by, from an abandoned farm, came the frantic lowing of unmilked cows and, overhead, suddenly there were the planes again. The planes— and almost in the same instant another roaring made itself heard on the road behind them. Dimly at first. But the convoy was travelling at full speed and, second by second, the noise swelled up, terrifyingly. There were shouts and screaming and a panic rush towards the ditch—the frenzy and blind violence of fear. And suddenly here was Weyl howling like a madman beside his overturned perambulator. A horse took fright, whinnied, reared up in the shafts; the cart moved back with a sudden jerk, striking Mme Weyl a glancing blow on the shoulder. She staggered forward a step or two, trying to recover her balance, then caught one of her high heels against a stone and fell face downwards into the roadway. '*Maman!*' screamed the little boy. But before he could pull her back the first of the huge lorries had rolled across the struggling body. For a second there was a gap in the nightmare, a glimpse between the trees of that distant church, bright against the billowing smoke, like a carved jewel in the sunshine. Then, identical with the first, the second lorry passed. The body was quite still.

But Eustace was alone again with the light and the silence. Alone with the principle of all skies and music and tenderness, with the potentialities of all that skies and music and even tenderness were incapable of manifesting. For an instant, for an eternity, there was a total and absolute participation. Then, excruciatingly, the knowledge of being separate returned, the shamed perception of his own hideous and obscene opacity.

But in the same instant there was the memory of those epoch-making Weyls, the knowledge that if he chose to accept it, they could bring him deliverance from the excess of light.

The lorries rolled on, identically grey-green, full of men and clanking metal. In the gap of time between the fourth and fifth, they managed to pull the body out from under the wheels. A coat was thrown over it.

Still crying, Weyl went back, after a little, to see if he could find any more fragments of the madonna's broken crown and fingers. A big red-cheeked woman laid her arm round the child's shoulders and, leading him away, made him sit down at the foot of one of the poplar trees. The little boy crouched there, his face in his hands, his body trembling and shaken by sobs. And suddenly it was no longer from outside that he was thought about. The agony of that grief and terror were known directly, by an identifying experience of them—not as his, but mine. Eustace Barnack's awareness of the child had become one with the child's awareness of himself; it *was* that awareness.

Then there was another displacement, and again the image of the little boy was only a memory of someone else. Horrible, horrible! And yet, in spite of the horror, what blessedness it was to feel the waves of blood beating and beating within the ears! He remembered the warm delicious sense of being full of food and drink, and the feel of flesh, the aromatic smell of cigar smoke . . . But here was the light again, the shining of the silence. None of that, none of that. Firmly and with decision, he averted his attention.

CHAPTER TWENTY-NINE

AS soon as breakfast was over, Sebastian slipped out of the house and almost ran down the hill to where the tram-cars stopped. He had to see Bruno, to see him as soon as possible and tell him what had happened.

His mind, as he stood there waiting for the tram, wavered back and forth between an overpowering sense of guilt and the aggrieved and plaintive feeling that he had been exposed to moral pressures which it was beyond the power of any ordinary human being to withstand. He'd broken his promise—the promise that (to crown wrongdoing with humiliation) he'd been so boastfully confident of being able to keep. But then who could have imagined that Weyl would be there? Who could possibly have anticipated that the fellow would behave in that extraordinary way? Inventing a story for him to tell, and fairly forcing it upon him! Yes, forcing him to lie, he kept repeating in self-justification. Forcing him against his better judgment, against his will; for hadn't he really been on the point of coming out with the truth, there in the corridor, in front of everybody? By the time the tram arrived, Sebastian had half persuaded himself that that was how it had been. He had just been opening his mouth to tell Mrs. Ockham everything, when, for some unknown and sinister reason, that beast of a man barged in and forced him to break his promise. But the trouble with that story, he reflected as they rattled along the Lungarno, was that Bruno would listen to it and then, after a little silence, very quietly ask some question that would make it collapse like a pricked balloon. And there he'd be, clutching the shameful vestiges of yet another lie and still under the necessity of confessing the previous falsehood. No, it would be better to start by telling Bruno the miserable truth—that he'd started by trying to run away and then, when he'd been cornered, had felt only too grateful to Weyl for showing him the way to break his promise and save his precious skin.

But here was Bruno's corner. The tram stopped; he got off and started to walk along the narrow street. Yes, at bottom he'd actually been grateful to the man for having made the lie so easy.

'God, I'm awful,' he whispered to himself, 'I'm awful!'

The tarry smell of Bologna sausages came to his nostrils. He looked up. Yes, this was it—the little *pizzicheria* next to Bruno's house. He turned in under a tall doorway and began to climb the stairs. On the second landing he became aware that there were people coming down from one of the higher floors; and suddenly some sort of soldier or policeman came into sight. With a fatuous assumption of majesty, he strutted along the landing. Sebastian squeezed against the wall to let him pass. A second later three more men turned the corner of the stairs. A man in uniform led the way, a man in uniform brought up the rear, and between them, carrying his ancient Gladstone bag, walked Bruno. Catching sight of Sebastian, Bruno immediately frowned, pursed his lips to indicate the need of silence and almost imperceptibly shook his head. Taking the hint, the boy closed his parted lips and tried to look blank and unconcerned. In silence the three men passed him, then one after another turned and disappeared down the stairs.

Sebastian stood there, listening to the sound of the receding footsteps. Where his stomach should have been, there was an awful void of apprehension. What did it mean? What on earth could it mean?

They were at the bottom of the stairs now, they were crossing the hall. Then abruptly there was no more sound; they had walked out into the street. Sebastian hurried down after them and, looking out, was in time to see the last of the policemen stepping into a waiting car. The door was slammed, the old black Fiat started to move, turned left just beyond the sausage shop and was gone. For a long time Sebastian stared unseeingly at the place where it had been, then started to walk slowly back by the way he had come.

A touch on the elbow made him start and turn his head. A tall bony young man was walking beside him.

'You came to see Bruno?' he said in bad English.

Remembering his father's stories of police spies and *agents provocateurs*, Sebastian did not immediately answer. His apprehension was evidently reflected on his face; for the young man frowned and shook his head.

'Not have fear,' he said almost angrily. 'I am Bruno's friend. Malpighi—Carlo Malpighi.' He raised his hand and pointed. 'Let us go in here.'

Four broad steps led up to the entrance of a church. They mounted and pushed aside the heavy leather curtain that hung across the open door. At the end of the high vaulted tunnel a few candles burned yellow in a twilight thick with the smell of stale incense. Except for a woman in black, praying at the altar rails, the building was empty.

'What happened?' Sebastian whispered when they were inside.

Struggling with his broken English and incoherent with emotional distress, the young man tried to answer. A friend of Bruno's—a man employed at police headquarters—had come last night to warn him of what they were going to do. In a fast car he could easily have got to the frontier. There were lots of people who would have taken almost any risk to help him. But Bruno had refused: he wouldn't do it, he simply wouldn't do it.

The young man's voice broke, and in the half-darkness the other could see that big tears were running down his cheeks.

'But what did they have against him?' Sebastian asked.

'He'd been denounced for being in touch with some of Cacciaguida's agents.'

'Cacciaguida?' Sebastian repeated; and with a renewal of that horrible sense of inner emptiness he remembered the elation he had felt as he stuffed the twenty-two bank-notes into his wallet, his stupid boasting about all that his father had done to help the anti-fascists. 'Was it—was it that man Weyl?' he whispered.

For what seemed an enormously long time the young man looked at him without speaking. Wet with tears and strangely distorted, the narrow elongated face twitched uncontrollably. He stood quite still, his arms hanging loosely by his sides; but the big hands kept clenching and unclenching, as though animated by a tortured life of their own. And at last the silence was broken.

'It was all because of you,' he said, speaking very slowly and in a tone of such concentrated hatred that Sebastian shrank away from him in fear. 'All because of *you.*'

And advancing a step, he gave the boy a back-handed blow in the face. Sebastian uttered a cry of pain and staggered back against a pillar. His teeth bared, his fists raised, the other stood over him menacingly; then, as Sebastian pulled out a handkerchief to stanch the blood that was streaming from his nostrils, he suddenly dropped his hands.

'Excuse,' he muttered brokenly, 'excuse!'

And quickly turning, he hurried out of the church.

By a quarter to one Sebastian was back again at the villa, with nothing worse than a slightly swollen lip to bear witness to his morning's adventures. In the church he had lain down across two chairs until his nose stopped bleeding, then had given his face a preliminary washing in holy water and gone out to buy himself a clean handkerchief and finish off his ablutions in the lavatory of the British Institute.

The goat was there again as he climbed the hill; but Sebastian felt obscurely that he had no right to stop and look at it, felt at the same time too horribly guilty even to wish to indulge in poetical fancies. Up the road, through the gate and between the stately cypresses he walked on, miserably, wishing he were dead.

On the low wall of the terrace in front of the villa, at the foot of the pedestal on which a moss-grown Pomona held up her cornucopia of fruits, the Queen Mother was sitting all alone, stroking the little dog on her knees. Catching sight of her, Sebastian halted. Would it be possible, he wondered, to tiptoe past her into the house without being heard? The old woman suddenly raised her head and looked sightlessly up into the sky. To his astonishment and dismay, Sebastian saw that she was crying. What could be the matter? And then he noticed the way Foxy was lying across her lap—limply, like one of those brown furs that women wrap round their necks, the paws dangling, the head lower than the body. It was obvious: the dog was dead. Feeling now that it would be wrong to sneak past unobserved, Sebastian started to walk across the crunching gravel with steps as heavy as he could make them.

The Queen Mother turned her head.

'Is that you, Daisy?' And when Sebastian gave his name, 'Oh, it's you, boy,' she said in a tone of almost resentful disappointment. 'Come and sit here.' She patted the sun-warmed stucco of the wall, then pulled out an embroidered handkerchief and wiped her eyes and her wet rouged cheeks.

Sebastian sat down beside her.

'Poor little Foxy. . . . What happened?'

The old woman put away her handkerchief and turned blindly towards him.

'Didn't you know?'

Sebastian explained that he had spent the whole morning in town.

'That fool, Daisy, thinks it was an accident,' said the Queen Mother. 'But it wasn't. I know it wasn't. They killed him.' Her thin, rasping voice trembled with a ferocious hatred.

'Killed him?'

She nodded emphatically.

'To revenge themselves. Because we thought it was that child who had stolen the drawing.'

'Do you think so?' Sebastian whispered in a tone of dismay. Bruno arrested, and now the little dog killed—and all because of what he had done or left undone. 'Do you really think so?'

'I tell you, I know it,' rasped the Queen Mother impatiently. 'They gave him rat poison—that's what it was. Rat poison. Veronica found him after breakfast, lying dead on the terrace.'

Suddenly she gave vent to a loud and horribly inhuman cry. Picking up the small limp body on her knees she held it close, pressing her face against the soft fur.

'Little Foxy,' she said brokenly. 'Little Foxy-woxy. . . .' And then the puckered grimace of despair gave place once again to an expression of intense hatred. 'The beasts!' she cried. 'The devils!'

Sebastian looked at her in horror. This was his fault, this was all his fault.

The hum of an approaching car made him turn his head.

'It's the Isotta,' he said, thankful to have an excuse to change the subject.

The car swung round past the front steps and came to a halt immediately in front of them. The door swung open and Mrs. Ockham jumped out.

'Granny,' she called excitedly, 'we've found one.' And from under her coat she brought out a little round handful of orange fur with two bright black eyes and a black pointed muzzle. 'His father's won three First Prizes. Here! Hold out your hands.'

Mrs. Gamble stretched out a pair of jewelled claws into the darkness, and the tiny puppy was placed between them.

'How small!' she exclaimed.

'Four months old,' said Mrs. Ockham. 'Wasn't that what the woman told us?' she added, turning to Mrs. Thwale, who had followed her out of the car.

'Four months last Tuesday,' said Mrs. Thwale.

'He's not black, is he?' questioned the old woman.

'Oh, no! The real fox-colour.'

'So he's Foxy too,' said the Queen Mother. 'Foxy the Ninth.' She lifted the little creature to her face. 'Such soft fur!' Foxy IX turned his head and gave her a lick on the chin.

The Queen Mother uttered a gleeful cackle. 'Does he love me then? Does he love his old granny?' Then she looked up in the direction of Mrs. Ockham. 'Five Georges,' she said, 'seven Edwards, eight Henries. But there's never been anybody the ninth.'

'What about Louis XIV?' suggested Mrs. Ockham.

'I was talking about England,' said the Queen Mother severely. 'In England they've never got further than an eighth. Little Foxy here is the first one to be a ninth.' She lowered her hands. Foxy IX leaned out from between the imprisoning fingers and sniffed inquisitively at the corpse of Foxy VIII.

'I bought my first Pomeranian in 'seventy-six,' said the Queen Mother. 'Or was it 'seventy-four? Anyhow, it was the year that Gladstone said he was going to abolish the income tax—but he didn't, the old rascal! We used to have pugs before that. But Ned didn't like the way they snored. He snored himself—that was why. But little Foxy-woxy,' she added in another tone, '*he* doesn't snore, does he?' And she raised the tiny dog again to her face.

Noiselessly, like a ghost, the butler appeared and announced that luncheon was served.

'Did he say lunch?' said the Queen Mother; and without waiting for anyone to help her, she almost sprang to her feet. With a little thud the body of Foxy VIII fell to the ground. 'Oh dear, I'd quite forgotten he was on my lap. Pick him up, boy, will you? Hortense is making a little coffin for him. She's got a bit of an old pink satin dress of mine to line it with. Give me your arm, Veronica.'

Mrs. Thwale stepped forward and they started to walk towards the house.

Sebastian bent down and, with a qualm of repulsion, picked up the dead dog.

'Poor little beast!' said Mrs. Ockham; and as they followed the others, she laid a hand affectionately on Sebastian's shoulder. 'Did you have a nice morning in town?' she asked.

CHAPTER TWENTY-NINE

'Quite nice, thanks,' he answered vaguely.

'Sight-seeing, I suppose,' she began, and then broke off. 'But I'd quite forgotten. There was a wire from your father after you'd gone.' She opened her bag, unfolded the telegraph form and read aloud: '"ACCEPTED CANDIDACY FORTHCOMING BY-ELECTION RETURNING IMMEDIATELY ARRANGE SEBASTIAN MEET ME FOUR PM WEDNESDAY NEXT THOMAS COOK AND SON GENOA." It's a shame,' she said, shaking her head. 'I thought we'd keep you here till the end of the holidays. And, oh dear! there won't be any time to get your evening clothes.'

'No, I'm afraid not,' said Sebastian.

No time, he was thinking, to get either suit; for the dinner jacket he had ordered at Uncle Eustace's tailor—ordered, yes, and paid for—was to have been tried on for a first fitting the very day he had to be in Genoa. It had all been for nothing—all these miseries he had gone through, all this guilt, and Bruno's arrest, and this wretched little dog. And meanwhile there was the problem of Tom Boveney's party, still unsolved and growing more agonizingly urgent with every passing day.

'It's a shame!' Mrs. Ockham repeated.

'What is?' asked the Queen Mother over her shoulder.

'Sebastian's having to leave so soon.'

'No more mum-mbling lessons,' said Mrs. Thwale, lingering a little over the word. 'But perhaps he'll be relieved.'

'You'll have to make the best of such time as is left you,' said the Queen Mother.

'Oh, we will, we will,' Mrs. Thwale assured her, and uttered her delicate little grunt of laughter. 'Here we are at the steps,' she went on gravely. 'Five of them, if you remember. Low risers and very broad treads.'

CHAPTER THIRTY

Epilogue

THE guns on Primrose Hill were banging away with a kind of frenzy; and though the desert was far away, though the nightmare under those swooping planes was long past, Sebastian felt some of the old quivering tension—as if he were a violin with knotted strings in the process of being tuned up, excruciatingly sharp and sharper, towards the final snapping point. Movement might bring relief, he thought. He jumped up—too abruptly. The papers lying on the arm of his chair scattered to the floor. He bent down and grabbed for them as they were falling—grabbed with the nearer of his hands; but the nearer of his hands wasn't there. Fool! he said to himself. It was a long time since he had done a thing like that. Forcing himself to be methodical, he picked them up with the hand that still remained to him. While he was doing this, the noise outside subsided; and suddenly there was the blessing of silence. He sat down again.

Hateful experience! But it had at least one good point; it made it impossible for one to cherish the illusion that one was identical with a body that behaved in direct opposition to all one's wishes and resolutions. *Neti, neti*—not this, not this. There could be no possible doubt about it. And, of course, he reflected, there hadn't been any doubt in the old days, when he wanted to say no to his sensuality and couldn't. The only difference was that, in those circumstances, it had been fun to surrender to one's alien body, whereas, in these, it was atrocious.

The telephone bell rang; he picked up the receiver and said, 'Hullo.'

'Sebastian darling!'

For a second he thought it was Cynthia Poyns and immediately started to think of excuses for refusing the impending invitation.

'Sebastian?' the voice questioned, when he didn't reply; and to his enormous relief he realized that he had made a mistake.

'Oh, it's *you*, Susan!' he said. 'Thank goodness!'

'Who did you think it was?'

'Oh, somebody else. . . .'

'One of the ex-girl friends, I suppose. Ringing up to make a scene of jealousy.' Susan's tone was playfully, but still reproachfully sarcastic. 'She wasn't pretty enough for you—was that it?'

'That was it,' Sebastian agreed. But Cynthia Poyns wasn't only passively good-looking; she was also actively a sentimentalist and literary snob, with a notorious weakness, in spite of her being such an exemplary young mother, for men. 'Oughtn't we to be wishing one another a Happy New Year?' he asked, in another tone.

'That's what I rang up for,' said Susan.

And she went on to hope that he'd started the year auspiciously, to wish and pray that 1944 might finally bring peace. But meanwhile, all three children had colds and Robin was even running a temperature. Nothing to worry about, of course—but all the same one couldn't help worrying. But her mother, happily, was much better, and she had just heard from Kenneth that there was a chance of his being transferred to a job in England—and what a marvellous New Year's present that would be!

Then Aunt Alice took over the instrument and opened with her favourite gambit: 'How's literature?'

'Still conscious,' Sebastian answered. 'But sinking fast.'

Jocularity, whenever one talked to Aunt Alice about art or philosophy or religion, was always *de rigueur*.

'I hope you've got another play on the way,' came the bright, perky voice.

'Luckily,' he said, 'I've still got something left of what I earned with the last one, five years ago.'

'Well, take my advice; don't invest it in the Far East.'

Gallantly making a joke of financial ruin, Aunt Alice uttered a little peal of laughter; then asked him if he had heard the story about the American corporal and the Archbishop of Canterbury.

He had, several times; but not wishing to deprive her of a pleasure, Sebastian begged to hear it. And when she duly told it, he made all the appropriate noises.

'But here's that Susan again,' she concluded.

And Susan had forgotten to ask him if he remembered Pamela, the girl with a snub nose who was at that progressive school. Lost sight of her for years till just a few weeks ago. A really wonderful girl! So intelligent and well-informed! Working on statistics for the Government, and really very attractive in that *piquant*, original kind of way—you know.

Sebastian smiled to himself. Another of those prospective wives that Susan was always indefatigably digging up for him. Well, one day she might dig up the right one—and of course he'd be very grateful. But meanwhile . . .

Meanwhile, Susan was saying, Pamela would be in London again next week. They'd all have to get together.

She was finished at last, and he hung up, feeling that curious mixture of humorous tenderness and complete despair which conversations like these always seemed to evoke in him. It was the problem, not of evil, but of goodness—the excruciating problem of sound, honest, better-than-average goodness.

He thought of dear Aunt Alice, indefatigably full of good works in spite of the never-ending discomfort of her rheumatism. Carrying on undramatically, without ever trying to play the part (and what a juicy part!) of one who carries on. Bearing her misfortunes with the same unaffected simplicity. Poor Jim killed in Malaya; her house burnt by an incendiary with all her possessions in it; nine-tenths of their savings wiped out by the fall of Singapore and Java; Uncle Fred breaking down under the shock and strain, and escaping at last into insanity. She didn't talk too much about these things, and she didn't talk too little, too repressedly. And meanwhile the old, rather metallic brightness of manner was still maintained, the little jokes and the pert answers were still uttered. As though she had resolved to go down with her sense of humour still flying and nailed to the mast.

And then there was Susan, there were the three admirably brought up babies, there were the all too priceless letters from Kenneth, somewhere in the Middle East, and Susan's own comments on war and peace, life and death, good and evil, bubbling up from the depths of a still almost untroubled upper-middle-class *Weltanschauung*.

Mother, daughter, son-in-law—looking at them with a playwright's eyes, he could see them as three deliciously comic characters. But in the other sense of that word and from the moralist's viewpoint, they were three characters of the most solid worth. Courageous and reliable and self-sacrificing as he himself had never been and could only humbly hope he might become. An absolutely sterling goodness, but limited by an impenetrable ignorance of the end and purpose of existence.

Without Susan and Kenneth and Aunt Alice and all their kind, society would fall to pieces. With them, it was perpetually attempting suicide. They were the pillars, but they were also the dynamite; simultaneously the beams and the dry-rot. It was thanks to their goodness that the system worked as smoothly as it did; and thanks to their limitations that the system was fundamentally insane—so insane that Susan's three charming babies would almost certainly grow up to become cannon fodder, plane fodder, tank fodder, fodder for any one of the thousand bigger and better military gadgets with which bright young engineers like Kenneth would by that time have enriched the world.

Sebastian sighed and shook his head. There was only one remedy, of course; but that they didn't want to try.

He picked up the loose-leaf book lying on the floor beside his chair. Fifty or sixty pages of random notes, jotted down at intervals during the last few months. This first day of the year was a good time to take stock. He started to read:

There is a higher utilitarianism as well as the ordinary, common or garden utilitarianism.

'Seek ye first the kingdom of God, and all the rest shall be added.' That is the classic expression of the higher utilitarianism—together with: 'I show you sorrow' (the world of ordinary, nice, unregenerate people) 'and the ending of sorrow' (the world of people who have achieved unitive knowledge of the divine Ground).

Set against these the slogans implicit in the lower, popular utilitarianism. 'I show you sorrow' (the world as it is now) 'and the ending of sorrow' (the world as it will be when Progress and a few more indispensable wars, revolutions and liquidations have done their work). And then, 'Seek ye first all the rest—creditable virtues, social reform, instructive chats on the radio and the latest in scientific gadgets—and some time in the twenty-first or twenty-second century the kingdom of God will be added.'

All men are born with an equal and inalienable right to disillusionment. So, until they choose to waive that right, it's three cheers for Technological Progress and a College Education for Everybody.

Read Aeschylus on the subject of Nemesis. His Xerxes comes to a bad end for two reasons. First, because he is an aggressive imperialist. Second, because he tries to get too much control over nature—specifically by bridging the Hellespont. We understand the devilishness of the political manifestations of the lust for power; but have so completely ignored the evils and dangers inherent in the technological manifestations that, in the teeth of the most obvious facts, we continue to teach our children that there is no debit side to applied science, only a continuing and ever-expanding credit. The idea of Progress is based on the belief that one can be overweening with impunity.

The difference between metaphysics now and metaphysics in the past is the difference between word-spinning which makes no difference to anybody and a system of thought associated with a transforming discipline. 'Short of the Absolute, God cannot rest, and having reached that goal He is lost and religion with Him.' That is Bradley's view, the modern view. Sankara was as strenuously an Absolutionist as Bradley—but with what an enormous difference! For him, there is not only discursive knowledge about the Absolute, but the possibility (and the final necessity) of a direct intellectual intuition, leading the liberated spirit to identification with the object of its knowledge. 'Among all means of liberation, Bhakti or devotion is supreme. To seek earnestly to know one's real nature—this is said to be devotion. In other words, devotion can be defined as the search for the reality of one's own Atman.' And the Atman, of course, is the spiritual principle in us, which is identical with the Absolute. The older metaphysicians did not lose religion; they found it in the highest and purest of all possible forms.

The fallacy of most philosophies is the philosopher. Enjoying as we do the privilege of Professor X's acquaintance, we know that whatever he personally may think up about the nature and value of existence cannot possibly be true. And what (God help us!) about *our* great thoughts? But fortunately there have been saints who could write. We and the Professor are free to crib from our betters.

It is wonderfully easy to escape the vices towards which one doesn't happen to be drawn. I hate sitting long over meals, am indifferent to 'good food' and have a stomach that is turned by more than an ounce or two of alcohol; no wonder, then, that I am temperate. And what about the love of money? Too squeamish and retiring to want to show off, too exclusively concerned with words and notions to care about real estate or first editions or 'nice things,' too improvident and too sceptical to be bothered about investments, I have always (except during a year or two of undergraduate idiocy) had more than enough for my needs. And for someone with my musculature, my kind of gift and my disastrous capacity for getting away with murder, the lust for power is even less of a problem than the lust for money. But when it comes to the subtler forms of vanity and pride, when it comes to indifference, negative cruelty and the lack of charity, when it comes to being afraid and telling lies, when it comes to sensuality . . .

I remember, I remember the house where *j'ai plus de souvenirs que si j'avais mille ans*, where emotion is recollected in tranquillity and there is *nessun maggior dolore che* death in life, the days that are no more. And all the rest, all the rest. For the nine Muses are the daughters of Mnemosyne; memory is of the very stuff and substance of poetry. And poetry, of course, is the best that human life can offer. But there is also the life of the spirit, and the life of the spirit is the analogue, on a higher turn of the spiral, of the animal's life. The progression is from animal eternity into time, into the strictly human world of memory and anticipation; and from time, if one chooses to go on, into the world of spiritual eternity, into the divine Ground. The life of the spirit is life exclusively in the present, never in the past or future; life here, now, not life looked forward to or recollected. There is absolutely no room in it for pathos, or remorse, or a voluptuous rumination of the delicious cuds of thirty years ago. Its Intelligible Light has nothing whatever to do either with the sunset radiance of those heart-rendingly good old days before the last war but three, or with the neon glow from those technological New Jerusalems beyond the horizons of the next revolution. No, the life of the spirit is life out of time, life in its essence and eternal principle. Which is why they all insist—all the people best qualified to know—that memory must be lived down and finally died to. When one has succeeded in mortifying the memory, says John of the Cross, one is in a state that is only a degree less perfect and profitable than the state of union with God. It is an assertion that, at a first reading, I found incomprehensible. But that was because at that time, my first concern was with the life of poetry, not of the spirit. Now I know, by humiliating experience, all that memory can do to darken and obstruct the knowledge of the eternal Ground. Mortification is always the condition of proficiency.

'Mortification'—the word had sent his mind flying off on a tangent. Instead of thinking about the dangers of memory, he was remembering. Remembering Paul De Vries in 1939—poor old Paul, as he had sat, so monotonously eager, so intelligently absurd, leaning across the table in the little café at Villefranche and talking, talking. The subject, of course, was one of those famous 'bridge-ideas,' with which he loved to link the island universes of discourse. A particularly 'exciting' idea, he insisted, harping on the word that had always irritated Sebastian so much—a generalization that spanned, a little precariously perhaps, the gulfs separating art, science, religion and ethics. The bridge, surprisingly enough, was mortification. Mortification of prejudice, cocksureness and even common sense, for the sake of objectivity in science; mortification of the desire to own or exploit, for the sake of contemplating an existing beauty or creating a new one; mortification of the passions, for the sake of an ideal of rationality and virtue; mortification of the self in all its aspects, for the sake of liberation, of union with God. He had listened, Sebastian remembered, with a good deal of interest —but patronizingly, as one listens to a very clever man who is also a fool, and with whose wife, moreover, one happens, the previous evening, to have committed adultery. It was the evening, incidentally, that Veronica had copied out for him that sonnet of Verlaine's:

> Ah! les oaristys! les premières maîtresses!
> L'or des cheveux, l'azur des yeux, la fleur des chairs,
> Et puis, parmi l'odeur des corps jeunes et chers
> La spontanéité craintive des caresses. . . .

Only in Veronica's case there was nothing timid about that surgical spontaneity and, in spite of Elizabeth Arden, the body was now thirty-five years old; while as for 'dear'—that it had never been, never. It had been only irresistible, the dreaded and fascinating vehicle of an alienation more total than that which he had known with anyone else of all the women he had loved or allowed himself to be loved by. And in the same instant he remembered his wife, unutterably weary under the burden of a pregnancy that seemed so strangely irrelevant to a being so small, bird-quick and fragile as Rachel had been. Remembered the promises he had made her, when he left Le Lavandou to go and stay with the De Vrieses, the vows of fidelity which he knew, even as he made them, that he wasn't going to keep—even though she was certain to find out. And of course she had found out, much sooner than he had expected. Sebastian remembered her as she lay in the hospital a month later, after the miscarriage, when the blood-poisoning had set in. 'It's all your fault,' she whispered reproachfully; and when he knelt beside her, in tears, she had turned her face away from him. When he came the next morning, Dr. Buloz waylaid him on the stairs. 'Some courage, my friend! We 'ave some bad newses about your wife.'

Bad newses, and it was all his fault, his fault *parmi l'odeur des corps*, amid the smell of iodoform and the memory of tuberoses on the coffin. Rachel's coffin, Uncle Eustace's coffin. And beside both the graves had stood Veronica, monastically elegant in mourning, with only the extremities of that warm white instrument of alienation projecting from under her disguise. And within two weeks of Rachel's funeral, once again the cannibals in bedlam. . . . 'It's all your fault.' The phrase had gone on repeating itself even in the extremities of an experience of otherness almost as absolute, on its own level, as the otherness of God. But he had gone on, just because it was such a vileness and for the express purpose of enjoying yet another repulsive taste of that mixture of sensuality, abhorrence and self-hatred which had become for him the all too fascinating theme of what turned out to be a whole volume of verses.

It was with one of those poems that he had been deliciously struggling when somebody sat down beside him on his favourite bench on the Promenade des Anglais. He turned irritably to see who had trespassed on his sacred privacy. It was Bruno Rontini—but Bruno ten years after, Bruno the ex-prisoner, now in exile and far gone in his last illness. An old man, bent and horribly emaciated. But in the beaked skull the blue bright eyes were full of joy, alive with an intense and yet somehow disinterested tenderness.

Speechless with a kind of terror, he took the dry skeleton hand that was held out to him. This was *his* doing! And what made it worse was the fact that, all these years, he had done everything he could to obliterate the consciousness of his offence. It had begun with excuses and alibis. He had been a child; and after all, who was there who didn't tell an occasional fib? And his fib, remember, had been told out of mere weakness, not from interest or malice. Nobody would have dreamed of making a fuss about it, if it hadn't been for that unfortunate accident. And, obviously, Bruno had it coming to him; Bruno had been on their bad books for years. That wretched little business of the drawing happened to have been made the pretext of an action which would have been taken anyhow, sooner or later. By no stretch of the imagination could he, Sebastian, be held responsible. And a couple of days after the arrest he was on his way home; and his father had taken him electioneering—which had been the greatest fun. And the next term he had worked tremendously hard for a scholarship which, to his own and everyone else's surprise, he had won. And when he went up to Oxford that autumn, Daisy Ockham secretly gave him a cheque for three hundred pounds, to supplement his allowance; and what with the intoxicating excitement of spending it, what with the new freedom, the new succession of amorous adventures, it ceased to be necessary to find excuses or establish alibis: he just forgot. The incident slipped away into insignificance. And now suddenly, out of the grave of his oblivion, this old dying man with the blue eyes had risen like some irrepressible Lazarus—for what purpose? To reproach, to judge, to condemn?

'Those arrows!' Bruno said at last. 'All those arrows!'

But what had happened to his voice? Why did he speak in that almost inaudible whisper? Terror deepened into sheer panic.

Bruno's smile had expressed a kind of humorous compassion. 'They seem to have started flying all right,' he whispered. 'The predestined target. . . .'

Sebastian shut his eyes, the better to recall that little house at Vence which he had taken for the dying man. Furnished and decorated with an unfailing bad taste. But Bruno's bedroom had windows on three sides, and there was a wide veranda, windless and warm with spring sunshine, from which one could look out over the terraced fields of young wheat, the groves of orange trees and the olive orchards, down to the Mediterranean.

'*Il tremolar della marina*,' Bruno would whisper when the reflected sunlight lay in a huge splendour across the sea. And sometimes it was Leopardi that he liked to quote:

> *e sovrumani*
> *Silenzi, e profondissima quiete.*

And then, again and again, voicelessly, so that it was only by the movements of the lips that Sebastian had been able to divine the words:

> *E'l naufragar m'è dolce in questo mare.*

Little old Mme Louise had done the cooking and the house-work; but except for the last few days, when Dr. Borély insisted on a professional nurse, the care of the sick man had been exclusively Sebastian's business. Those fifteen weeks between the meeting on the Promenade des Anglais and that almost comically unimpressive funeral (which Bruno had made him promise was not to cost more than twenty pounds) had been the most memorable period of his life. The most memorable and, in a certain sense, the happiest. There had been sadness, of course, and the pain of having to watch the endurance of a suffering which he was powerless to alleviate. And along with that pain and sadness had gone the gnawing sense of guilt, the dread and the anticipation of an irreparable loss. But there had also been the spectacle of Bruno's joyful serenity, and even, at one remove, a kind of participation in the knowledge of which that joy was the natural and inevitable expression—the knowledge of a timeless and infinite presence; the intuition, direct and infallible, that apart from the desire to be separate there was no separation, but an essential identity.

With the progress of the cancer in his throat, speech, for the sick man, became more and more difficult. But those long silences on the veranda, or in the bedroom, were eloquent precisely about the things which words were unfitted to convey —affirmed realities which a vocabulary invented to describe appearances in time could only indirectly indicate by means of negations. 'Not this, not this' was all that speech could have made clear. But Bruno's silence had become what it knew and could cry, 'This!' triumphantly and joyfully, 'this, this this!'

There were circumstances, of course, in which words were indispensable; and then he had resorted to writing. Sebastian got up, and from one of the drawers of his desk took the envelope in which he kept all the little squares of paper on which Bruno had pencilled his rare requests, his answers to questions, his comments and advice. He sat down again and, selecting at random, began to read.

'Would it be very extravagant to get a bunch of freesias?'

Sebastian smiled, remembering the pleasure the flowers had brought. 'Like angels,' Bruno had whispered. 'They smell like angels.'

'Don't worry,' the next scribbled message began. 'Having intense emotions is just a matter of temperament. God can be loved without any *feelings*—by the will alone. So can your neighbour.'

And to this Sebastian had clipped another jotting on the same theme. 'There isn't any secret formula or method. You learn to love by loving—by paying attention and doing what one thereby discovers has to be done.'

He picked up another of the squares of paper. 'Remorse is pride's *ersatz* for repentance, the ego's excuse for not accepting God's forgiveness. The condition of being forgiven is self-abandonment. The proud man prefers self-reproach, however painful—because the reproached self isn't abandoned; it remains intact.'

Sebastian thought of the context in which the words had been written—his passion for self-loathing, his almost hysterical desire to make some kind of dramatic expiation for what he had done, to pay off his debt of guilt towards Bruno, who was dying, towards the despairing and embittered Rachel, who had died. If he could submit to some great pain or humiliation, if he could undertake some heroic course of action! He had expected an unqualified approval. But Bruno had looked at him for a few seconds in appraising silence; then, with a gleam of sudden mischief in his eyes, had whispered, 'You're not Joan of Arc, you know. Not even Florence Nightingale.' And then, reaching for the pencil and the scribbling-pad, he had started to write. At the time, Sebastian remembered, the note had shocked him by its calm and, he had felt, positively cynical realism. 'You'd be inefficient, you'd be wasting your talents, and your heroic altruism would do a great deal of harm, because you'd be so bored and resentful that you'd come to loathe the very thought of God. Besides, you'd seem so noble and pathetic, on top of your good looks, that all the women within range would be after you. Not fifty per cent. of them, as now, but *all*. As mothers, as mistresses, as disciples—every one. And of course you wouldn't resist—would you?' Sebastian had protested, had said something about the necessity of sacrifice. 'There's only one effectively redemptive sacrifice,' came the answer, 'the sacrifice of self-will to make room for the knowledge of God.' And a little later, on another scrap of paper: 'Don't try to act somebody else's part. Find out how to become your inner not-self in God while remaining your outer self in the world.'

Bewildered and a little disappointed, Sebastian looked up and found Bruno smiling at him.

'You think it's too easy?' came the whisper. Then the pencil went to work again.

Sebastian rustled through the scattered leaves of paper. Here was what the pencil had written:

'Performing miracles in a crisis—so much easier than loving God selflessly every moment of every day! Which is why most crises arise—because people find it so hard to behave properly at ordinary times.'

Reading the scribbled lines, Sebastian had felt himself all of a sudden appalled by the magnitude of the task that had been set for him. And soon, very soon, there would be no Bruno to help him.

'I shall never be able to do it alone,' he cried.

But the sick man was inexorable.

'It can't be done by anyone else,' the pencil wrote. 'Other people can't make you see with their eyes. At the best they can only encourage you to use your own.'

Then, as an afterthought, he had added on another sheet of the scribbling-pad: 'And, of course, once you've started using your own eyes, you'll see that there's no question of being alone. Nobody's alone unless he wishes to be.'

And as though to illustrate his point, he put down his pencil and looked away towards the sunlit landscape and the sea. His lips moved. '"The corn was orient and immortal wheat"... *Ell'è quel mare al qual tutto si move . . . E'l naufragar m'è dolce* ... the shipwreck in that sea. . . .' He shut his eyes. After a minute or two he opened them again, looked at Sebastian with a smile of extraordinary tenderness and held out his thin bony hand. Sebastian took and pressed it. The sick man looked at him for a little longer with the same smile, then shut his eyes again. There was a long silence. Suddenly, from the kitchen, came the thin, piping voice of Mme Louise, singing her favourite waltz of forty years ago. '*Lorsque tout est fini. . . .*' Bruno's emaciated face puckered itself into an expression of amusement.

'Finished,' he whispered, 'finished?' And his eyes as he opened them were bright with inner laughter. 'But it's only just begun!'

For a long time Sebastian sat quite still. But, alas, the memory of the knowledge that had come to him that day was very different from the knowledge. And, in the end, perhaps even this memory would have to be mortified. He sighed profoundly, then turned back to his note-book.

War guilt—the guilt of London and Hamburg, of Coventry, Rotterdam, Berlin. True, one wasn't in politics or finance, one was lucky enough not to have been born in Germany. But in a less obvious, more fundamental way, one was guilty by just being imperviously oneself, by being content to remain a spiritual embryo, undeveloped, undelivered, unillumined. In part, at least, I am responsible for my own maiming, and on the hand that is left me there is blood and the black oily smear of charred flesh.

Look at any picture paper or magazine. News (and only evil is news, never good) alternates with fiction, photographs of weapons, corpses, ruins, with photographs of half-naked women. Pharisaically, I used to think there was no causal connection between these things, that, as a strict sensualist and aesthete, I was without responsibility for what was happening in the world. But the habit of sensuality and pure aestheticism is a process of God-proofing. To indulge in it is to become a spiritual mackintosh, shielding the little corner of time, of which one is the centre, from the least drop of eternal reality. But the only hope for the world of time lies in being constantly drenched by that which lies beyond time. Guaranteed God-proof, we exclude from our surroundings the only influence that is able to neutralize the destructive energies of ambition, covetousness and the love of power. Our responsibility may be less spectacularly obvious than theirs; but it is no less real.

The rain is over. On the spider-webs the beads of water hang unshaken. Above the tree-tops the sky is like a closed lid, and these fields are the flat bare symbols of a total resignation.

Invisible in the hedge, a wren periodically releases the ratchet of its tiny whirring clockwork. From the wet branches overhead the drops fall and fall in the unpredictable rhythm of an absolutely alien music. But the autumnal silence remains unflawed and even the rumble of a passing lorry, even the long crescendo and the fading roar of a flight of aeroplanes, even my memories of those explosions and all the long nights of pain, are somehow irrelevant and can be ignored. On the sphere's surface what a clatter of ironmongery! But here, at its glassy centre, the three old hornbeams and the grass, the brambles and the holly tree stand waiting. And between the repetitions of his mindless little declaration of personal independence, even the wren occasionally stops, down there at the bottom of the hedge, to listen for a moment to the silence within the silence; cocks his head and, for a second or two, is aware of himself, waiting, in the twiggy labyrinthine darkness, waiting for a deliverance of which he can have no inkling. But we, who can come, if we choose, to the full knowledge of that deliverance, have quite forgotten that there is anything to wait for.

Something of the happiness he had felt in the course of that long-drawn solitude under the dripping trees came back to him. Not, of course, that it was anything like enough to sense the significances of landscapes and living things. Wordsworth had to be supplemented by Dante, and Dante by . . . well, by somebody like Bruno. But if you didn't idolatrously take the manifestation for the principle, if you avoided spiritual gluttony and realized that these country ecstasies were only an invitation to move on to something else, then of course it was perfectly all right to wander lonely as a cloud and even to confide the fact to paper. He started to read again.

To the surprise of Humanists and Liberal Churchmen, the abolition of God left a perceptible void. But Nature abhors vacuums. Nation, Class and Party, Culture and Art have rushed in to fill the empty niche. For politicians and for those of us who happen to have been born with a talent, the new pseudo-religions have been, still are and (until they destroy the entire social structure) will continue to be extremely profitable superstitions. But regard them dispassionately, *sub specie aeternitatis*. How unutterably odd, silly and satanic!

Gossip, day-dreaming, preoccupation with one's own moods and feelings—fatal, all of them, to the spiritual life. But among other things even the best play or narrative is merely glorified gossip and artistically disciplined day-dreaming. And lyric poetry? Just 'Ow!' or 'Oo-ooh!' or 'Nyum-nyum!' or 'Damn!' or 'Darling!' or 'I'm a pig!'—suitably transliterated, of course, and developed.

Which is why some God-centred saints have condemned art, root and branch. And not only art—science, scholarship, speculation. Or remember Aquinas: the consummate philosophical virtuoso—but after achieving the unitive knowledge of that Primordial Fact, about which he had so long been spinning theories, he refused to write another word of theology. But what if he had come to union twenty years earlier? Would there have been no *Summa*? And, if so, would that have been a matter for regret? No, we should have answered a few years ago. But now some physicists are beginning to wonder if scholastic Aristotelianism may not be the best philosophy in terms of which to organize the findings of contemporary science. (But meanwhile, of course, contemporary science in the hands of contemporary men and women is engaged in destroying, not only things and lives, but entire patterns of civilization. So we find ourselves faced with yet another set of question marks.)

For the artist or intellectual, who happens also to be

interested in reality and desirous of liberation, the way out would seem to lie, as usual, along a knife-edge.

He has to remember, first, that what he does as an artist or intellectual won't bring him to knowledge of the divine Ground, even though his work may be directly concerned with this knowledge. On the contrary, in itself the work is a distraction. Second, that talents are analogous to the gifts of healing or miracle-working. But 'one ounce of sanctifying grace is worth a hundredweight of those graces which theologians call "gratuitous," among which is the gift of miracles. It is possible to receive such gifts and be in a state of mortal sin; nor are they necessary to salvation. As a rule, gratuitous graces are given to men less for their own benefit than for the edification of their neighbours.' But François de Sales might have added that miracles don't *necessarily* edify. Nor does even the best art. In both cases, edification is merely a possibility.

The third thing that has to be remembered is that beauty is intrinsically edifying; gossip, day-dreaming and mere self-expression, intrinsically unedifying. In most works of art, these positive and negative elements cancel out. But occasionally the anecdotes and the day-dreams are thought of in relation to first principles and set forth in such a way that the intervals between their component elements create some new unprecedented kind of beauty. When this happens, the possibilities of edification are fully realized, and the gratuitous grace of a talent finds its justification. True, the composition of such consummate works of art may be no less of a distraction than the composition of swing music or advertising copy. It is possible to write about God and, in the effort to write well, close one's mind completely to God's presence. There is only one antidote to such forgetting—constant recollection.

Well, he couldn't say that he hadn't given himself due warning, Sebastian reflected with a smile, as he turned the page. 'Minimum Working Hypothesis' was the heading to the next note.

Research by means of controlled sense-intuitions into material reality—research motivated and guided by a working hypothesis, leading up through logical inference to the formulation of a rational theory, and resulting in appropriate technological action. That is natural science.

No working hypothesis means no motive for starting the research, no reason for making one experiment rather than another, no rational theory for bringing sense or order to the observed facts.

Contrariwise, too much working hypothesis means finding only what you *know*, dogmatically, to be there and ignoring all the rest.

Among other things, religion is also research. Research by means of pure intellectual intuition into non-sensuous, non-psychic, purely spiritual reality, descending to rational theories about its results and to appropriate moral action in the light of such theories.

To motivate and (in its preliminary stages) guide this research, what sort and how much of a working hypothesis do we need?

None, say the sentimental humanists; just a little bit of Wordsworth, say the blue-dome-of-nature boys. Result: they have no motive impelling them to make the more strenuous investigations; they are unable to explain such non-sensuous facts as come their way; they make very little progress in Charity.

At the other end of the scale are the Papists, the Jews, the Moslems, all with historical, one-hundred-per-cent. revealed religions. These people have a working hypothesis about non-sensuous reality—which means that they have a motive for doing something to get to know about it. But because their working hypotheses are too elaborately dogmatic, most of them discover only what they were taught to believe. But what they believe is a hotch-potch of good, less good and even bad. Records of the infallible intuitions of great saints into the highest spiritual reality are mixed up with records of the less reliable and infinitely less valuable intuitions of psychics into lower levels of non-sensuous existence; and to

these are added mere fancies, discursive reasonings and senti-
mentalisms, projected into a kind of secondary objectivity and
worshipped as though they were divine facts. But at all times
and in spite of the handicap imposed by these excessive working hypotheses, a passionately persistent few continue the
research to the point where they become aware of the Intelligible Light and are united with the divine Ground.

For those of us who are not congenitally the members of
any organized church, who have found that humanism and
blue-domeism are not enough, who are not content to remain
in the darkness of spiritual ignorance, the squalor of vice
or that other squalor of mere respectability, the minimum
working hypothesis would seem to be about as follows:

That there is a Godhead or Ground, which is the unmanifested principle of all manifestation.

That the Ground is transcendent and immanent.

That it is possible for human beings to love, know and,
from virtually, to become actually identified with the Ground.

That to achieve this unitive knowledge, to realize this
supreme identity, is the final end and purpose of human
existence.

That there is a Law or Dharma, which must be obeyed, a
Tao or Way, which must be followed, if men are to achieve
their final end.

That the more there is of I, me, mine, the less there is of
the Ground; and that consequently the Tao is a Way of
humility and compassion, the Dharma a Law of mortification
and self-transcending awareness. Which accounts, of course,
for the facts of human history. People love their egos and
don't wish to mortify them, don't wish to see why they
shouldn't 'express their personalities' and 'have a good time.'
They get their good times; but also and inevitably they get
wars and syphilis and revolution and alcoholism, tyranny and,
in default of an adequate religious hypothesis, the choice
between some lunatic idolatry, like nationalism, and a sense
of complete futility and despair. Unutterable miseries! But
throughout recorded history most men and women have
preferred the risks, the positive certainty, of such disasters to

the laborious whole-time job of trying to get to know the divine Ground of all being. In the long run we get exactly what we ask for.

Which was all right so far as it went, Sebastian reflected. But it would be one of the tasks of the coming year to add the necessary developments and qualifications. To discuss the relationships, for example, between the Ground and its higher manifestations—between the Godhead and the personal God and the human Avatar and the liberated saint. And then there were the two methods of religious approach to be considered: the direct approach, aiming at an identifying knowledge of the Ground, and the indirect, ascending through the hierarchy of material and spiritual manifestations—at the risk, always, of getting stuck somewhere on the way. But meanwhile, where was the note he had made by way of commentary on those lines in Hotspur's final speech? He flicked through the pages. Here it was.

If you say absolutely everything, it all tends to cancel out into nothing. Which is why no explicit philosophy can be dug out of Shakespeare. But as a metaphysic by implication, as a system of beauty-truths, constituted by the poetical relationships of scenes and lines, and inhering in the blank spaces between even such words as 'told by an idiot, signifying nothing,' the plays are the equivalent of a great theological *Summa*. And, of course, if you choose to ignore the negatives that cancel them out, what extraordinary isolated utterances of a perfectly explicit wisdom! I keep thinking, for example, of those two and a half lines in which the dying Hotspur casually summarizes an epistemology, an ethic and a metaphysic.

> *But thought's the slave of life, and life's time's fool,*
> *And time, that takes survey of all the world,*
> *Must have a stop.*

Three clauses, of which the twentieth century has paid attention only to the first. Thought's enslavement to life is one of our favourite themes. Bergson and the Pragmatists, Adler and Freud, the Dialectical Materialism boys and the Behaviourists—all tootle their variations on it. Mind is nothing but a tool for making tools; controlled by unconscious forces, either sexual or aggressive; the product of social and economic pressures; a bundle of conditioned reflexes.

All quite true, so far as it goes; but false if it goes no further. For, obviously, if mind is only some kind of nothing-but, none of its affirmations can make any claim to general validity. But all nothing-but philosophies make such claims. Therefore they can't be true; for if they were true, that would be the proof that they were false. Thought's the slave of life—undoubtedly. But if it weren't also something else, we couldn't make even this partially valid generalization.

The significance of the second clause is mainly practical. Life's time's fool. By merely elapsing time makes nonsense of all life's conscious planning and scheming. No considerable action has ever had all or nothing but the results expected of it. Except under controlled conditions, or in circumstances where it is possible to ignore individuals and consider only large numbers and the law of averages, any kind of accurate foresight is impossible. In all actual human situations more variables are involved than the human mind can take account of; and with the passage of time the variables tend to increase in number and change their character. These facts are perfectly familiar and obvious. And yet the only faith of a majority of twentieth-century Europeans and Americans is faith in the Future—the bigger and better Future, which they *know* that Progress is going to produce for them, like rabbits out of a hat. For the sake of what their faith tells them about a Future time, which their reason assures them to be completely unknowable, they are prepared to sacrifice their only tangible possession, the Present.

Since I was born, thirty-two years ago, about fifty millions of Europeans and God knows how many Asiatics have been liquidated in wars and revolutions. Why? In order that the great-great-grandchildren of those who are now being butchered or starved to death may have an absolutely wonderful time in A.D. 2043. And (choosing, according to taste or political opinion, from among the Wellsian, Marxian, Capitalistic or Fascist blueprints) we solemnly proceed to visualize the sort of wonderful time these lucky beggars are going to have. Just as our early Victorian great-great-grandfathers visualized the sort of wonderful time *we* were going to have in the middle years of the twentieth century.

True religion concerns itself with the givenness of the timeless. An idolatrous religion is one in which time is substituted for eternity—either past time, in the form of a rigid tradition, or future time, in the form of Progress towards Utopia. And both are Molochs, both demand human sacrifice on an enormous scale. Spanish Catholicism was a typical idolatry of past time. Nationalism, Communism, Fascism, all the social pseudo-religions of the twentieth century, are idolatries of future time.

What have been the consequences of our recent shift of attention from Past to Future? An intellectual progress from the Garden of Eden to Utopia; a moral and political advance from compulsory orthodoxy and the divine right of kings to conscription for everybody, the infallibility of the local boss and the apotheosis of the State. Before or behind, time can never be worshipped with impunity.

But Hotspur's summary has a final clause: time must have a stop. And not only *must*, as an ethical imperative and an eschatological hope, but also *does* have a stop, in the indicative tense, as a matter of brute experience. It is only by taking the fact of eternity into account that we can deliver thought from its slavery to life. And it is only by deliberately paying our attention and our primary allegiance to eternity that we can prevent time from turning our lives into a pointless or diabolic foolery. The divine Ground is a timeless reality. Seek it first, and all the rest—everything from an adequate interpretation of life to a release from compulsory self-destruction —will be added. Or, transposing the theme out of the evangelical into a Shakespearean key, you can say: 'Cease being ignorant of what you are most assured, your glassy essence, and you will cease to be an angry ape, playing such fantastic tricks before high heaven as make the angels weep.'

A postscript to what I wrote yesterday. In politics we have so firm a faith in the manifestly unknowable future that we are prepared to sacrifice millions of lives to an opium smoker's dream of Utopia or world dominion or perpetual security. But where natural resources are concerned, we sacrifice a pretty accurately predictable future to present greed. We know, for example, that if we abuse the soil it will lose its fertility; that if we massacre the forests our children will lack timber and see their uplands eroded, their valleys swept by floods. Nevertheless, we continue to abuse the soil and massacre the forests. In a word, we immolate the present to the future in those complex human affairs where foresight is impossible; but in the relatively simple affairs of nature, where we know quite well what is likely to happen, we immolate the future to the present. 'Those whom the gods would destroy they first make mad.'

For four and a half centuries white Europeans have been busily engaged in attacking, oppressing and exploiting the coloured peoples inhabiting the rest of the world. The Catholic Spaniards and Portuguese began it; then came Protestant Dutch and Englishmen, Catholic French, Greek Orthodox Russians, Lutheran Germans, Catholic Belgians. Trade and the Flag, exploitation and oppression, have always and everywhere followed or accompanied the proselytizing Cross.

Victims have long memories—a fact which oppressors can never understand. In their magnanimity they forget the ankle they twisted while stamping on the other fellow's face, and are genuinely astonished when he refuses to shake the hand that flogged him and manifests no eagerness to go and get baptized.

But the fact remains that a shared theology is one of the indispensable conditions of peace. For obvious and odious historical reasons, the Asiatic majority will not accept Christianity. Nor can it be expected that Europeans and Americans will swallow the whole of Brahmanism, say, or Buddhism. But the Minimum Working Hypothesis is also the Highest Common Factor.

Three prostrate telegraph poles lying in the patch of long grass below my window at the inn—lying at a slight angle one to another, but all foreshortened, all insisting, passionately, on the fact (now all of a sudden unspeakably mysterious) of the third dimension. To the left the sun is in the act of rising. Each pole has its attendant shadow, four or five feet wide, and the old wheel tracks in the grass, almost invisible at midday, are like canyons full of blue darkness. As a 'view,' nothing could be more perfectly pointless; and yet, for some reason, it contains all beauty, all significance, the subject-matter of all poetry.

Industrial man—a sentient reciprocating engine having a fluctuating output, coupled to an iron wheel revolving with uniform velocity. And then we wonder why this should be the golden age of revolution and mental derangement.

Democracy is being able to say no to the boss, and you can't say no to the boss unless you have enough property to enable you to eat when you have lost the boss's patronage. There can be no democracy where . . .

Sebastian turned over a page or two. Then his eye was caught by the opening words of a note that was dated, 'Christmas Eve.'

Today there was an almost effortless achievement of silence —silence of intellect, silence of will, silence even of secret and subconscious cravings. Then a passage through these silences into the intensely active tranquillity of the living and eternal Silence.

Or else I could use another set of inadequate verbal signs and say that it was a kind of fusion with the harmonizing interval that creates and constitutes beauty. But whereas any particular manifestation of beauty—in art, in thought, in action, in nature—is always a relationship between existences not in themselves intrinsically beautiful, this was a perception of, an actual participation in, the paradox of Relationship as such, apart from anything related; the direct experience of pure interval and the principle of harmony, apart from the things which, in this or that concrete instance, are separated and harmonized. And somewhere, somehow, the participation and the experience persist even now as I write. Persist in spite of the infernal racket of the guns, in spite of my memories and fears and preoccupations. If they could persist always . . .

But the grace had been withdrawn again, and in recent days . . . Sebastian sadly shook his head. Dust and cinders, the monkey devils, the imbecile unholinesses of distraction. And because knowledge, the genuine knowledge beyond mere theory and book learning, was always a transforming participation in that which was known, it could never be communicated—not even to one's own self when in a state of ignorance. The best one could hope to do by means of words was to remind oneself of what one once had unitively understood and, in others, to evoke the wish and create some of the conditions for a similar understanding. He reopened the book.

Spent the evening listening to people talking about the future organization of the world—God help us all! Do they forget what Acton said about power? 'Power always corrupts. Absolute power corrupts absolutely. All great men are bad.' And he might have added that all great nations, all great classes, all great religious or professional groups are bad—bad in exact proportion as they exploit their power.

In the past there was an age of Shakespeare, of Voltaire, of Dickens. Ours is the age, not of any poet or thinker or novelist, but of the Document. Our Representative Man is the travelling newspaper correspondent, who dashes off a best seller between two assignments. 'Facts speak for themselves.' Illusion! Facts are ventriloquists' dummies. Sitting on a wise man's knee they may be made to utter words of wisdom; elsewhere, they say nothing, or talk nonsense, or indulge in sheer diabolism.

Must look up what Spinoza says about pity. As I remember, he considers it intrinsically undesirable, in so far as it is a passion, but relatively desirable, in so far as it does more good than harm. I kept thinking of this yesterday, all the time I was with Daisy Ockham. Dear Daisy! Her passionate pity moves her to do all sorts of good and beautiful things; but because it is just a passion, it also warps her judgment, causes her to make all kinds of ludicrous and harmful mistakes, and translates itself into the most absurdly sentimental and radically false view of life. She loves to talk, for example, about people being transformed and ameliorated by suffering. But it's perfectly obvious, if one isn't blinded by the passion of pity, that this isn't true. Suffering may and often does produce a kind of emotional uplift and a temporary increase in courage, tolerance, patience and altruism. But if the pressure of suffering is too much prolonged, there comes a breakdown into apathy, despair or violent selfishness. And if the pressure is removed, there's an immediate return to normal conditions of unregeneracy. For a short time, a blitz engenders sentiments of universal brotherliness; but as for permanent transformation and improvement—that occurs only exceptionally. Most of the people I know have come back from battle unchanged; a fair number are worse than they were; and a few—men with an adequate philosophy and a desire to act upon it—are better. Daisy is so sorry for them that she insists that they are all better. I talked to her a little about poor Dennis C., and what suffering has done for him—drink, recklessness, indifference to simple honesty, a total cynicism.

Buddhist writers distinguish between compassion and Great Compassion—pity in the raw, as a mere visceral and emotional disturbance, and pity informed by principle, enlightened by insight into the nature of the world, aware of the causes of suffering and the only remedy. Action depends on thought, and thought, to a large extent, depends on vocabulary. Based on the jargons of economics, psychology, and sentimental religiosity, the vocabulary in terms of which we think nowadays about man's nature and destiny is about the worst. . . .

Suddenly the door-bell rang. Sebastian looked up with a start. At this hour, who could it be? Dennis Camlin probably. And probably rather drunk again. What if he didn't open the door? But, no, that would be uncharitable. The poor boy seemed to find some sort of comfort in his presence. 'It's all true,' he used to say. 'I've always known it was true. But if one *wants* to destroy oneself—well, why not?' And the tone would become truculent, the words violently obscene and blasphemous. But a few days later he'd be back again.

Sebastian got up, walked into the hall and opened the door. A man was standing there in the darkness—his father. He cried out in astonishment.

'But why aren't you on the other side of the Atlantic?'

'That's the charm of war-time travel,' said John Barnack, in the studiedly unexcited tone which he reserved for partings and reunions. 'No nonsense about sailing lists or premonitory cables. Can you put me up, by the way?'

'Of course,' Sebastian answered.

'Not if it's the least trouble,' his father continued as he put down his suitcase and began to unbutton his overcoat. 'I just thought it would be easier for me to open up my own place by daylight.'

He walked briskly into the sitting-room, sat down and, without even asking Sebastian how he was or volunteering the slightest personal information, began to talk about his tour through Canada and the States. The remarkable swing to the left in the Dominion—so strikingly different from what was going on across the border. But whether the Republicans would actually win the presidential election was another matter. And anyhow it wasn't by any party or president that the country's future policy would be dictated—it was by brute circumstance. Whoever got in, there'd be more government control, more centralization to cope with the post-war mess, continuing high taxes. . . .

Sebastian made the gestures and noises of intelligent attention;

but his real concern was with the speaker, not with what was being said. How tired his father looked, how old! Four years of war-time overwork, at home, in India, back again in England, had left him worn and diminished; and now these two months of winter travel, of daily lectures and conferences, had consummated the process. Almost suddenly, John Barnack had passed from powerful maturity to the beginnings of old age. But, of course, Sebastian reflected, his father would be much too proud to acknowledge the fact, much too strong-willed and stubborn to make any concessions to his tired and shrunken body. Ascetical for asceticism's sake, he would continue to drive himself on, pointlessly, until the final collapse.

'. . . The most consummate imbecile,' John Barnack was saying in a voice that contempt had made more ringingly articulated. 'And of course, if he hadn't been Jim Tooley's brother-in-law, nobody would ever have dreamed of giving him the job. But naturally, when one's wife is the sister of the world's champion lick-spittle, one can aspire to the highest official positions.'

He uttered a loud metallic bray of laughter; then launched out into an animated digression on nepotism in high places.

Sebastian listened—not to the words, but to what they concealed and yet so plainly expressed: his father's bitter sense of grievance against a party and a government that had left him all these years in the ranks, without office or any position of authority. Pride did not permit him to complain; he had to be content with these ferociously sardonic references to the stupidity or the turpitude of the men for whom he had been passed over. But, after all, if one couldn't refrain from talking to one's colleagues as though they were subnormal and probably delinquent children, one really ought not to be surprised if they handed out the sugar plums to somebody else.

Old, tired, bitter. But that wasn't all, Sebastian said to himself, as he watched the deeply furrowed, leathery face and listened to the now incongruously loud and commanding voice. That wasn't all. In some subtle and hardly explicable way his father gave an impression of deformity—as though he had suddenly turned into a kind of dwarf or hunchback. 'He that is not getting better is getting worse.' But that was too sweeping and summary. 'He that isn't growing up is growing down.' That was more like it. Such a man might end his life, not as a ripened human being, but as an aged foetus. Adult in worldly wisdom and professional skill; embryonic in spirit and even (in spite of all the stoical and civic virtues he might have acquired) in character. At sixty-five his father was still trying to be what he had been at fifty-five, forty-five, thirty-five. But this attempt to be the same made him essentially different. For then he had been what a busy young or middle-aged politician ought to be. Now he was what an old man ought not to be; and so, by straining to remain unmodified, had transformed himself into a gruesome anomaly. And, of course, in an age that had invented Peter Pan and raised the monstrosity of arrested development to the rank of an ideal, he wasn't in any way exceptional. The world was full of septuagenarians playing at being in their thirties or even in their teens, when they ought to have been preparing for death, ought to have been trying to unearth the spiritual reality which they had spent a lifetime burying under a mountain of garbage. In his father's case, of course, the garbage had been of the very highest quality—personal austerity, public service, general knowledge, political idealism. But the spiritual reality was no less effectually buried than it would have been under a passion for gambling, for example, or an obsession with sexual pleasure. Perhaps, indeed, it was buried even more effectually. For the card-player and the whoremonger didn't imagine that their activities were creditable, and therefore stood a chance of being shamed into giving them up; whereas the well-informed good citizen was so certain of being morally and intellectually right that he seldom so much as envisaged the possibility of changing his way of life. It had been the publicans who came to salvation, not the Pharisees.

Meanwhile, the talk had veered away from nepotism, to settle, inevitably, on what might be expected to happen after the war. . . . Up till quite recently, Sebastian was thinking as he listened, this staunch idolater of future time had been rewarded by his god with the grace of an inexhaustible energy in the service of his favourite social reforms. Now, instead of the beneficiary, he was the victim of what he worshipped. The future and its problems had come to haunt him like a guilty conscience or a consuming passion.

There was first the immediate future. On the continent a chaos so frightful that, to millions of people, the war years would seem in retrospect a time positively of prosperity. And even in England, along with the enormous relief, there would be a certain nostalgia for the simplicities of war economy and war organization. And meanwhile, in Asia, what political confusion, what hunger and disease, what abysses of inter-racial hatred, what preparations, conscious and unconscious, for the coming war of colour! John Barnack raised his hands and let them fall again in a gesture of utter hopelessness. But of course, that wasn't all. As though spurred on by avenging Furies, he proceeded to explore the further distances of time. And here there loomed for him, like the menace of an inescapable fate, the quasi-certainties of future population trends. An England, a Western Europe, an America, hardly more populous thirty years hence than at the present time, and with a fifth of their inhabitants drawing old-age pensions. And contemporary with this decrepitude, a Russia of more than two hundred millions, preponderantly youthful, and as bumptious, confident and imperialistically minded as England had been at a corresponding point in her own long-past phase of economic and demographic expansion. And east of Russia would be a China of perhaps five hundred millions, in the first flush of nationalism and indus-trialization. And, south of the Himalayas, four or five hundred millions of starving Indians, desperately trying to exchange the products of their sweated factory labour for the wherewithal to survive just long enough to add an additional fifty millions to the population and subtract yet another year or two from the average expectation of life.

The main result of the war, he went on gloomily, would be the acceleration of processes which otherwise would have taken place more gradually and therefore less catastrophically. The process of Russia's advance towards the domination of Europe and the Near East; of China's advance towards the domination of the rest of Asia; and of all Asia's advance towards industrialism. Torrents of cheap manufactures flooding the white men's markets. And the white men's reaction to those torrents would be the *casus belli* of the impending war of colour.

'And what *that* war will be like . . .'

John Barnack left the sentence unfinished and began to talk instead about the present miseries of India—the Bengal famine, the pandemic of malaria, the prisons crowded with the men and women at whose side, a few years before, he himself had fought for *swaraj*. A note of despairing bitterness came into his voice. It was not only that he had had to sacrifice his political sympathies. No, the roots of his despair struck deeper—down into the conviction that political principles, however excellent, were almost irrelevant to the real problem, which was merely arithmetical, a matter of the relationship between acreage and population. Too many people, too little arable land. Thanks to technology and the Pax Britannica, Malthus's nightmare had become, for a sixth of the human race, their everyday reality.

Sebastian went out to the kitchen to brew some tea. Through the open door he heard a momentary blast of trumpets and saxophones, then the distressing noise of actresses being emotional, then the quieter intonations of a masculine voice that talked and talked. His father was evidently listening to the news.

When he came back into the living-room, it was over. His eyes shut, John Barnack was lying back in his chair, half asleep. Taken off guard, the face and the limp body betrayed an unutterable fatigue. A cup clinked as Sebastian set down the tray. His father started and sat up. The worn face took on its familiar look of rather formidable determination, the body was taut again and alert.

'Did you hear that about the Russians and the Czechs?' he asked.

Sebastian shook his head. His father enlightened him. More details about the twenty-year pact were coming out.

'You see,' he concluded almost triumphantly, 'it's beginning already—the Russian hegemony of Europe.'

Cautiously, Sebastian handed him an overflowing cup of tea. Not so long ago, he was thinking, it wouldn't have been 'Russian hegemony,' but 'Soviet influence.' But that was before his father had begun to take an interest in population problems. And now, of course, Stalin had reversed the old revolutionary policy towards religion. The Greek Orthodox Church was being used again as an instrument of nationalism. There were seminaries now, and a patriarch like Father Christmas, and millions of people crossing themselves in front of ikons.

'A year ago,' John Barnack went on, 'we would never have allowed the Czechs to do this. Never! Now we have no choice.'

'In that case,' Sebastian suggested after a brief silence, 'it might be as well to think occasionally about matters where we *do* have a choice.'

'What do you mean?' his father asked, looking up at him suspiciously.

'Russians or no Russians, one's always at liberty to pay attention to the Nature of Things.'

John Barnack assumed an expression of pitying contempt, then burst into a peal of laughter that sounded like a carload of scrap iron being tipped on to a dump.

'Four hundred divisions,' he said, when the paroxysm was over, 'against some high-class thoughts about the Gaseous Vertebrates!'

It was a remark in the good old style—but with this difference, that the good old style was now the new style of a self-stunted dwarf who had succeeded in consummating his own spiritual abortion.

'And yet,' said Sebastian, 'if one thought about it to the point of . . .' he hesitated, 'well, to the point of actually becoming one of *its* thoughts, one would obviously be very different from what one is now.'

'Not a doubt of it!' said John Barnack sarcastically.

'And that sort of difference is infectious,' Sebastian went on. 'And in time the infection might spread so far that the people with the big battalions would actually not wish to use them.'

Another load of scrap iron was tipped down the chute. This time Sebastian joined in the laughter.

'Yes,' he admitted, 'it *is* pretty funny. But, after all, a chance of one in a million is better than no chance at all, which is what *you* look forward to.'

'No, I didn't say that,' his father protested. 'There'll be a truce, of course—quite a long one.'

'But not peace?'

The other shook his head.

'No, I'm afraid not. No real peace.'

'Because peace doesn't come to those who merely work for peace—only as the by-product of something else.'

'Of an interest in Gaseous Vertebrates, eh?'

'Exactly,' said Sebastian. 'Peace can't exist except where there's a metaphysic which all accept and a few actually succeed in realizing.' And when his father looked at him questioningly, 'By direct intuition,' he went on; 'the way you realize the beauty of a poem—or a woman, for that matter.'

There was a long silence.

'I suppose you don't remember your mother very well, do you?' John Barnack suddenly asked.

Sebastian shook his head.

'You were very like her when you were a boy,' the other went on. 'It was strange . . . almost frightening.' He shook his head, then added, after a little pause: 'I never imagined you'd do this.'

'Do what?'

'You know—what we've been talking about. Of course, I think it's all nonsense,' he added quickly. 'But I must say . . .' A look of unwonted embarrassment appeared on his face. Then, shying away from the too emphatic expression of affection, 'It certainly hasn't done you any harm,' he concluded judicially.

'Thank you,' said Sebastian.

'I remember him as a young man,' his father went on over the top of his teacup.

'Remember whom?'

'Old Rontini's son. Bruno—wasn't that his name?'

'That was it,' said Sebastian.

'He didn't make much impression on me then.'

Sebastian wondered whether anybody had ever made much impression on him. His father had always been too busy, too completely identified with his work and his ideas, to be very much aware of other people. He knew them as the embodiments of legal problems, as particular examples of political or economic types, not as individual men and women.

'And yet I suppose he must have been remarkable in some way,' John Barnack went on. 'After all, *you* thought so.'

Sebastian was touched. It was the first time that his father had paid him the compliment of admitting that perhaps he wasn't an absolute fool.

'I knew him so much better than you did,' he said.

With what was obviously a rather painful effort, John Barnack hoisted himself out of the depths of the armchair. 'Time to go to bed,' he said, as though he were enunciating a general truth, not expressing his own fatigue. He turned back to Sebastian. 'What was it you found in him?' he asked.

'What was it?' Sebastian repeated slowly. He hesitated, uncertain what to answer. There were so many things one could mention. That candour, for example, that extraordinary truthfulness. Or his simplicity, the absence in him of all pretensions. Or that tenderness of his, so intense and yet so completely unsentimental and even impersonal—but impersonal, in some sort, above the level of personality, not below it, as his own sensuality had been impersonal. Or else there was the fact that, at the end, Bruno had been no more than a kind of thin transparent shell, enclosing something incommensurably other than himself—an unearthly beauty of peace and power and knowledge. But that, Sebastian said to himself, was something his father wouldn't even wish to understand. He looked up at last. 'One of the things that struck me most,' he said, 'was that Bruno could somehow convince you that it all made sense. Not by talking, of course; by just being.'

Instead of laughing again, as Sebastian had expected him to do, John Barnack stood there, silently rubbing his chin.

'If one's wise,' he said at last, 'one doesn't ask whether it makes any sense. One does one's work and leaves the problem of evil to one's metabolism. *That* makes sense all right.'

'Because it's not oneself,' said Sebastian. 'Not human, but a part of the cosmic order. That's why animals have no metaphysical worries. Being identical with their physiology, they *know* there's a cosmic order. Whereas human beings identify themselves with money-making, say, or drink, or politics, or literature. None of which has anything to do with the cosmic order. So naturally they find that nothing makes sense.'

'And what's to be done about it?'

Sebastian smiled and, standing up, ran a finger-nail across the grille of the loud-speaker.

'One can either go on listening to the news—and of course the news is always bad, even when it sounds good. Or alternatively one can make up one's mind to listen to something else.'

Affectionately, he took his father's arm. 'What about going to see if everything's all right in the spare room?'

THE HISTORY OF VINTAGE

The famous American publisher Alfred A. Knopf (1892–1984) founded Vintage Books in the United States in 1954 as a paperback home for the authors published by his company. Vintage was launched in the United Kingdom in 1990 and works independently from the American imprint although both are part of the international publishing group, Random House.

Vintage in the United Kingdom was initially created to publish paperback editions of books bought by the prestigious literary hardback imprints in the Random House Group such as Jonathan Cape, Chatto & Windus, Hutchinson and later William Heinemann, Secker & Warburg and The Harvill Press. There are many Booker and Nobel Prize-winning authors on the Vintage list and the imprint publishes a huge variety of fiction and non-fiction. Over the years Vintage has expanded and the list now includes great authors of the past – who are published under the Vintage Classics imprint – as well as many of the most influential authors of the present. In 2012 Vintage Children's Classics was launched to include the much-loved authors of our youth.

For a full list of the books Vintage publishes,
please visit our website
www.vintage-books.co.uk

For book details and other information about the classic authors we publish, please visit the Vintage Classics website
www.vintage-classics.info

www.vintage-classics.info

Visit www.worldofstories.co.uk for all your
favourite children's classics